NIGHTMARES

VAMPIRE TWINS

A TRILOGY

THREE BOOKS IN ONE

Lions

More heart-stopping Nightmares
three books in one...

Tales from Nightmare Inn
T.S. Rue
Three Books of Blood
M.C. Sumner
Three Tales of Terror
Bebe Faas Rice/Nicholas Adams
Three Times the Fear
Nicholas Adams/Bebe Faas Rice/M.C. Sumner

NIGHTMARES

VAMPIRE

1 BLOODLINES

2 BLOODLUST

3 BLOODCHOICE

TWINS

Janice Harrell

Lions
An Imprint of HarperCollins Publishers

First published in the USA in 1994
by HarperCollins Publishers Inc.
First published in Great Britain in Lions 1995
1 3 5 7 9 8 6 4 2

Lions is an imprint of CollinsChildren'sBooks,
a division of HarperCollins*Publishers* Ltd,
77-85 Fulham Palace Road,
Hammersmith, London W6 8JB

Text Copyright © 1994 Daniel Weiss Associates Inc.
and Janice Harrell

ISBN 0 00 675111 3

The author asserts the moral right to be
identified as the author of the work.

Printed and bound in Great Britain
by HarperCollins Manufacturing Ltd, Glasgow

NIGHTMARES

Vampire Twins 1

BLOODLINES

Janice Harrell

CHAPTER
ONE

MRS. MONTCLAIR PALED AND CLOSED THE NEWSPAPER hastily. Paul took the paper from her hands and scanned the headline. "Jeez," he said, "the serial killer is at it again."

"Creepy!" said Anne-Marie. She dipped a scoop of mashed potatoes, dented it with her spoon, and neatly dribbled gravy into the dent.

Paul frowned at the newspaper story. "It's kind of weird. All of them have bled to death, but the cops don't find the bodies in a puddle of blood or anything. The guy must kidnap them, take them somewhere else to slit their throats, then dump the bodies on the street."

Mrs. Montclair took a long shuddering breath. "Paul, do you have to talk about this now? Why can't you read the comics like other kids?"

Paul tossed the paper aside. "I don't know what you're worried about, Mom. It's always drunks he

1

goes after. I mean, half the time they find the bodies right outside a bar. That tells you something, doesn't it?"

"Nope," said his sister. "You just said they couldn't have been killed near the bar—else there would have been lots of blood around. So he could have kidnapped them somewhere else."

"Yeah, right," said Paul. "For your info, Ari, they always print the alcohol content of the corpse, and lots of times these guys were drunk."

Anne-Marie's name was always shortened to Ari because that was as much as she could manage when she was small. At sixteen, the nickname still stuck. She rested her chin on her hand. "It's funny the way he kills them. Why not just shoot them? Maybe he's got a sick thing about liking the blood."

The saucepan slipped from Mrs. Montclair's fingers with a clatter and gravy spattered the floor. "That's enough!" she cried, stooping to wipe it up with a paper towel. "I don't want to hear another word about this deranged killer." Her voice shook. "Not a word, do you hear me?"

Ari and Paul glanced at each other and shrugged. They knew from the tone of their mother's voice that she meant business. Paul flipped to the comics and did not glance out the kitchen window that gave onto the dark backyard.

Outside, a shadowy cloaked figure darted with swift, fluid movement up onto the Montclairs' back porch, then tiptoed up to the open kitchen window. He gripped the window frame tightly

2

with his pale hands and peered hungrily in at the twins and their mother.

"What's that?" he heard Ari cry.

"Nothing," Paul said, glancing at her. "Calm down."

The vampire drew back at the sound of the twins' voices. Then silently he stepped down off the porch. The print of his hand glowed phosphorescent on the window frame for some seconds. The garden gate creaked as he let himself out of the yard. In the next garden, a dog yipped. The vampire cringed and thrust his hands deeply into his pants pockets. Moving slowly, he made his way out to the sidewalk.

On either side of the old street in New Orleans's French Quarter, town houses rose tall and gray in the semidarkness; scaffolding and ladders threw spidery shadows onto the broken concrete. The vampire whistled a monotonous tune under his breath. Suddenly, a man in a raincoat stumbled into the lamplight. He smelled of liquor and his grin was vacant. The man grabbed at the lamppost to steady himself. "Oops!" he mumbled to himself. "Steady now. Take it easy, Cholly-boy. Let's get home in one piece, hey?"

"Excuse me," said the vampire courteously. "Can you tell me the time?"

The drunk fell into peals of laughter and slapped his thigh. "Man, I thought you were going to ask for a light. That's what you're s'posed to ask for. A light. Like they do in the movies. Don't you ever go to the movies?"

3

The vampire recoiled for a moment. The street-lamp showed the glossy white of his handsome face, its aquiline nose with the flesh drawn tightly over the bone. "No," he answered softly. "I don't need a light. Only the time, if you please."

"Sure," said the drunk. "Jusht a minute, man. Hang on." He shot his cuff to expose his watch, but he had no chance to speak. In a movement almost too fast to see, the vampire buried his face against the man's soft neck. With an impatient toss of his head, the vampire tore the flesh. The carotid artery spurted violently, and dark blood spattered the vampire's face. The vampire pressed his lips tightly against the man's neck and sucked greedily. His victim slumped and the vampire made a quick gesture of impatience and let him fall to the cement. The man's head lolled to the side, and in the lamplight, his open eyes were lifeless. Glancing around first to be sure no one was watching, the vampire dragged the body between the houses and let it slip to the ground. Most of the corpse was hidden in shadows. He glanced down at the trousered legs and brown shoes that pressed against a clump of rank weeds. Fastidiously, he wiped the sticky blood off his lips and cheeks with a corner of his cape. Then he smiled. In the weak light of the nighttime street, his pale face appeared almost to have taken on the glow of life. He thrust his hands once more into his pockets and walked off whistling.

Moments later, a neighbor knocked at the Montclairs' front door, and Ari ran to open it. The

4

neighbor held out a folded newspaper. "Congratulations to your mom on her promotion, Ari. I saved this for you in case she wants to send a clipping to the kinfolk."

"We didn't even see the story, Mr. Wilson," cried Ari, taking the paper. "Thanks. I'll show Mom. Want to come in?"

"Nah, I've got to be getting back."

Ari smiled. "Well, thanks again."

In the Montclairs' kitchen, the twins and their mother pored over the section of paper the neighbor had brought. "It was nice of George to bring it over," said Mrs. Montclair.

Ari dimpled. "He said he thought we would want to send a clipping to the kinfolk. He doesn't know that we don't have any kinfolk."

"Unless you count Aunt Gabrielle," said Paul.

"I don't," said Ari promptly. "One Christmas card a year? That's not real kinfolk."

Paul threw his arm around his sister, and they burst into song. "We are po-ooor little lambs," they crooned, "with no kinfolk."

Their mother covered her ears. "Stop! Stop!" She laughed.

Paul made a sad face. "Our own mother thinks we can't sing. We must be bad."

"Very bad," agreed Ari.

Their mother blushed. "I never said you couldn't sing," she said.

"It's okay, Mom. We know we can't carry a tune, don't we, Ari?" Paul looked down at his sister. He was taller, but except for height the twins were as alike as bookends, with dark hair curling slightly at the temples, fair skin, and dark, fringed brown eyes.

The phone on the wall rang and Ari grabbed for it. "Speak for yourself, Paul." She stuck out her tongue. "I'm planning a singing career." Then into the receiver she said, "Hullo? Oh, hi, Laurie. Wait a minute. I'm going to switch to the phone in my room."

Once Ari had gone to her bedroom, Paul picked up the receiver.

"Hang up, Paul!" his mother insisted.

Paul covered the receiver with his hand. "Heck, Mom, Ari knows I listen. She doesn't care."

"A young woman is entitled to some privacy," said his mother firmly. "You two are not children anymore. Now hang up."

Paul shrugged and strolled out of the kitchen. When he got to his room, he smiled to himself and quietly picked up the receiver on his bedside table. His mom didn't understand the first thing about being a twin, he thought. She couldn't seem to grasp that he and Ari shared everything.

"And take out the garbage!" his mother called after him. "Now!"

Paul put the phone down and groaned. Reluctantly, he went out to the back porch and lifted the black plastic liner out of the can. Outside, the cool night air was rich with the familiar scents of the neighborhood—fried fish, the fresh bread smell that came at night from the big ovens at the bakery. But also on the breeze was the scent of garbage and the vaguely ominous smell of the cold stale water in a nearby pond. Behind the lot, black leaves rotted, and pond beetles skimmed the water.

Paul twisted a tie around the top of the black plastic bag, hoisted it, and made his way down the wooden steps. In the next garden, a chain rattled and a dog whimpered. Paul kicked the garden gate open and backed out. The overstuffed plastic bag banged against his shins and caught on the gate latch. Paul heard it rip. "Damn," he said, wrenching the bag free. Once he had squeezed through, he kicked the gate shut behind him. He could smell the crushed ragweed under his sneakers as he backed toward the street. Tired of carrying it, he let the bag drag on the ground, hoping it wouldn't split. He hated taking the garbage down the narrow, weed-clogged passageway between the houses, but his mother wouldn't think of letting him take it through the living room.

Suddenly, Paul's foot struck something and he turned, startled. A chill slithered up his back when he saw the dark shape at his feet. Headlights from a passing car cast a sudden moving light on the gaping mouth and pale face of a man whose head was only inches from Paul's foot. For an instant, Paul was half-blinded by the sudden light. The next moment, the car disappeared down the street, and the dead man at his feet was again swallowed up by the shadows.

Paul gulped and tried to speak, but at first nothing would come out. "Are . . . are you all right?" he whispered, kneeling. He had only meant to touch the man's shoulder, but he lost his balance and fell against him. The stranger's head rolled to the side. When Paul pulled away from the man, he realized, horrified, that his hand was damp and sticky.

He backed away and fell against the garbage bag. Scrambling to his feet, he ran to the garden gate and raced up the porch steps. The dog next door howled mournfully, but Paul scarcely noticed. He was dizzy and a loud noise roared in his ears. Somehow he made it to the door and an instant later, stumbled into the brightly lit kitchen. He stood still a moment, breathing heavily. The kitchen clock hummed quietly. He reached out for the counter to steady himself, then turned on the tap and furiously began washing the blood off of his hands.

Ari stepped into the kitchen, twirling a strand of long dark hair around her finger. "Guess who Terry Hobbes has a crush on?" she sang. "Me, me, me, that's who. He asked Laurie if she thought I liked him. What do you think about that?"

Paul turned off the tap and stared at her in disbelief. She seemed to come from a different, more sunlit world. "Ari," he whispered, "there's a dead man outside. I touched him."

Her jaw dropped. "Are . . . are you sure?"

"I kicked him with my foot," said Paul. "I was carrying the garbage out, and I kicked him and he never moved, not even when I fell against him."

Mrs. Montclair appeared white-faced at the open kitchen door. "What are you saying, Paul?"

8

"We'd better call nine-one-one," said Paul. "There's a dead guy right at our gate."

"Maybe he's only passed out," said Mrs. Montclair. "I'll call an ambulance."

Paul exchanged a glance with Ari. He didn't have to say anything, because Ari could read the grim meaning in his eyes. The man was dead, all right. Paul reached into the kitchen drawer and pulled out a large flashlight. Behind him, he could hear the phone beeping one high note and two low as his mother dialed 911.

"Don't you dare go back outside, Paul Montclair!" his mother cried. "Don't you move!"

Paul stepped onto the porch and Ari followed him. He could hear his mother speaking excitedly to the 911 operator as Ari closed the door.

"You better go back in," Paul told his twin. "Mom's about to have a heart attack." He felt the familiar wooden steps under his sneakers as he played the beam of the flashlight nervously around the overgrown garden in their narrow, fenced backyard. Long shadows leapt to life, and scraggly bits of greenery were bleached by the flashlight's beam.

"You're not going by yourself," said Ari, clutching his arm. "What if the murderer is still out there?"

Paul licked his dry lips. "Who said the guy was murdered?"

"You know I can read your mind, Paul." Ari tightened her grip. "Don't try to pull anything over on me." It was a long-standing joke between

9

them that they could read each other's minds. Sometimes, they actually could.

Paul played the flashlight once more over the yard. No one seemed to be hiding in their garden. But in all the darkness and shadows, who could be sure?

His stomach squeezed painfully when he thought of the corpse, but he made himself push the garden gate open.

Ari slipped through the gate after him. Paul aimed the flashlight at the ground, and the weeds became a nightmare of shadows. Suddenly the strong beam of light rested on the man's face. The corpse's blank eyes gleamed in the light, then the beam wobbled. The flashlight rattled to the ground and went dark.

"He looks dead to me," said Ari, shivering.

"He is dead," said Paul. "I shone the light right in his face, and his pupils didn't contract."

"Let's go inside, Paul. I feel sick."

Her twin picked up the flashlight and restlessly clicked its switch several times. "Damn. It's broken." Paul heard the distant sound of a siren. "Did you see whether there was any blood on the ground?" he asked.

"I don't think there's much blood," she said, clinging fearfully to her twin. "The weeds looked dry."

"There's blood on him, Ari," said Paul. "I got it on my hand."

"Paul? Ari?" Their mother called out the back door.

Ari jerked at Paul's arm. "Let's go inside," she

said. "We can't see anything out here now anyway."

Reluctantly, Paul followed Ari back through the garden gate. He wished he hadn't been so shaken as to drop his flashlight. Now that he could hear the siren growing closer, he wasn't nearly as afraid of what might have been lurking in the shadows. It would have been exciting to get a better look at the murder scene.

Their mother, her brow furrowed anxiously, stood at the back door. "The police are on their way. What are you two doing out there? Trying to scare me out of my wits?" She shooed the twins back into the kitchen and locked the door.

Paul walked into the living room. The siren was wailing close at hand now, and he could see a flashing blue light outside. "They're here. I'd better go show them where the body is," he said.

"Paul!" wailed Mrs. Montclair. "Why can't you stay put?"

"Don't you understand, Mom?" asked Paul. "It's as close as we'll ever get to a real murder investigation. If I hadn't broken the flashlight, Ari and me might even have found a clue."

Shadowy figures mounted the steps on the front porch. There was a rap on the door, and Paul opened it. Two uniformed policemen confronted him. "We got a call from this address," said an officer.

"I'm the one that found the body," Paul told them. "I was taking out the garbage, and I ran right into him. I'll show you."

Paul led the police officers to the side of the house. The rotating blue light cast an unearthly

11

glow on the shadowed corpse. A policeman switched on a flashlight and played its beam over the dead body.

A wave of nausea swept over Paul when he saw that the man's shirt was spattered with dark red blood. "I've never seen a dead person before," he whispered.

"You better go inside, son," said one of the officers. "Just give your name to the officer in the patrol car."

Paul went out to the street and gave his name and address to the officer in the patrol car. "Do you think it's the serial killer?" Paul asked the officer.

"Can't say at this point. But don't you worry. We'll take care of it."

Paul cast a regretful glance over his shoulder but reluctantly went up on the porch. The police didn't seem to be doing a very good job of tracking the serial killer. According to the newspaper, they didn't have any leads.

The shadowy figure of the police photographer knelt beside the body. A flash briefly whitened the murder victim's face.

One of the officers stepped up to the side of the porch and fixed a thin yellow tape to the bannister.

"Do you think it's the serial killer, Officer?" asked Paul.

The officer glanced up at him. "Hadn't you better go inside and do your homework?" The police officer strung the yellow tape alongside the porch. He pulled it out as far as the street and tied it to the lamppost. "POLICE LINE—DO NOT CROSS," it said.

Paul's mother plucked at him. "Let's go inside, Paul. You heard the man. They don't want us out here." An ambulance pulled up before the house, and the attendants slid out a stretcher.

Paul hesitated. "Heck, Mom."

"Inside," she commanded.

Reluctantly, Paul obeyed. Ari had pushed the curtains aside and was staring out at the shadowy uniformed figures of the police officers.

"Get away from that window, Anne-Marie Montclair," said her mother.

Paul's gaze met Ari's. They could see that their mother was upset. Paul realized that he didn't feel exactly calm himself.

"Well, it is creepy," Ari murmured as they followed their mother to the kitchen.

"Nah, it's like a movie," said Paul in a low voice. "The body didn't even look real. His face was dead-white, like plastic."

"You were pretty shaken up," argued Ari. "You dropped the flashlight, remember."

Paul recalled the bony slackness of the victim's jaw. "I guess it was kind of sickening," he admitted.

Mrs. Montclair poured herself a cup of coffee with a shaking hand. "Kids, we may have to move out of town."

Paul and Ari stared at her in amazement.

"But what about your promotion?" protested Ari.

"Mom, crime happens everywhere," said Paul. "Nobody picks up and moves these days just because one body is dumped in their neighborhood."

Mrs. Montclair ran her fingers frantically through her gray-streaked hair. "We'll talk about it later. I have to think about what's best for the entire family. We . . . we may have to go far away quite suddenly. I'd rather you didn't mention it to any of your friends. Or anyone else, for that matter."

The twins glanced at each other anxiously. What was she talking about? She sounded completely crazy—moving and not telling anyone? How could the dead body bother her that much? Paul had the sudden, awful sensation that their secure world had begun shifting under their feet.

Later that night when Ari had gone to bed, Paul crept into her room. "Ari?"

"I'm awake," she said. She scooted over in the bed to make room for him.

Paul slid in under the covers. "What do you think is going on with Mom? I know she's been jumpy lately, but tonight she's completely losing it."

"A dead body would upset anybody," said Ari.

"I know. That's what I figured at first, too. But think about it—she didn't even see the guy. And it's not like it has anything to do with us. If the serial killer did it, that means the guy probably wasn't even killed in our neighborhood."

"I wish you'd quit reading that stuff out of the paper about the serial killer, Paul. Mom hates hearing about it. And now look what's happened. He dumps a body on our street, and all of a sudden she's talking about moving."

Paul shivered. "Well, naturally, I never figured he was going to strike right in our own neighborhood."

"Maybe she'll calm down if we don't mention it anymore," suggested Ari.

"That's what I think," said Paul, relieved. "Boy, she scared the heck out of me. Moving! It's crazy!"

"We'll pretend she never mentioned it," repeated Ari. "Don't bring it up."

"Don't worry! Jeez, did you hear her? 'Someplace far away.' Sounded like she was talking about Oregon or San Diego. I'd hate those places."

"All our friends are right here in New Orleans," said Ari in a small voice.

"She can't be serious," said Paul. "She just got that big promotion." He hugged his twin. "We won't let her do it. It's two against one, remember? We'll make her see it our way."

"We stick together no matter what happens," said Ari, squeezing him tightly.

"We're not leaving New Orleans!"

"Never!" cried Ari.

"I feel a hundred percent better," said Paul. "I swear, it beats me why people who aren't twins don't go nuts." Smiling in the darkness, he slipped out of her bed and tiptoed back to his own room.

CHAPTER
TWO

THE NEXT MORNING IN THE TWILIGHT BETWEEN WAKING
and sleeping, Paul sensed the presence of his father. It was as if inexpressible warmth and bright
happiness were almost within his grasp. He felt his
father leaning over him, breathing on him. His
longing was so strong that he was sure he could he
reach out and touch him. But when he awoke, he
saw only the cold washstand beside his bed, the
first rays of light glittering on the white enamel
pitcher. He felt a thud of disappointment, coupled
with a nagging uncomfortable sensation that he
had misplaced something important. He did his
best to push the feeling away.

Paul went in the bathroom, splashed cold water
on his face, and got dressed. As he was buttoning
his shirt, he walked into the living room and
glanced out the window. A stiff breeze blew a cel-
lophane bag along the street, and the yellow plas-

tic tape the police had strung around the scene of the crime flapped in the wind. If it hadn't been for the tape marking off the space between the houses, Paul might almost have imagined the dead body was another of his strange dreams. Now that it was daylight, everything that had happened the night before seemed unreal.

When he had finished getting dressed, Paul went downstairs to the living room. He noticed something on the floor—an envelope that had fallen from the trash can by his mother's desk. He bent to pick it up. It was addressed to "Ms. Mary Ellen Montclair" on Rampart Street. The broad sweeping strokes of the handwriting, faintly reminiscent of his aunt Gabrielle's script, made Paul catch his breath sharply. The support checks from his father always came with no return address on the envelope. He squinted at the postmark but could not make it out. It was always the same. There was never any clue where the envelopes were mailed from. Paul dropped it back into the trash. Then he pushed back the curtains and gazed out the window. He knew he had to quit thinking about his father.

The body had been removed by the police, but the black plastic bag of garbage still lay in the weeds. Paul wondered how long the garbage would lie there rotting. He couldn't take it out to the curb now because the area between the houses was roped off by the yellow police tape, and no one was supposed to cross that line. The day was heavily overcast, and the scene outside looked somber and gray.

Ari came out of her bedroom and stretched. Paul's eyes softened as he looked at her. Her straight dark eyebrows matched his, but everything else about her was nicer. She was beautiful. Her face was flushed with sleep, and her cheek still bore the mark of a crease from her pillowcase.

"Mom not up yet?" Ari yawned.

"Nope."

The twins heard their mother's alarm go off. That meant their mother would be appearing soon. Paul plucked the envelope from the trash and showed it to Ari.

She looked frightened. "Paul, you're not going to talk about Dad, are you? Mom's already upset."

"No, I'm not going to talk about Dad. But don't you wonder where he is, Ari?"

She hesitated. "No."

"Liar," he said amiably.

"Okay, sometimes I do wonder. A little. But he's never going to come see us. Never. All these years and not a single birthday card, no Christmas present—I don't even remember what he looks like."

"I figure he must look sort of like you and me," said Paul. "Mom's not dark the way we are."

Ari cast an anxious glance over her shoulder. "If she hears us talking about him, you know it's going to make her sad."

Paul glanced down at the envelope. When he read it, the letters swirled and danced with color, but when he held it too far away to read, he

18

could tell the ink was black. He couldn't remember when he started seeing letters and numbers in color. Sometimes it slowed him down when he was doing math problems or reading. Sea green, baby blue, tangerine, he would think, dazzled by the color of the letters and numbers. No one else seemed to see them that way—not that he had asked. He hadn't even mentioned it to Ari. What if it meant he had some kind of slow-growing brain tumor? He quietly dropped the envelope back into the trash. "Okay," he said, his face expressionless. "Let's get breakfast."

The morning paper had a brief mention of the murder. "SERIAL KILLER STRIKES AGAIN." Paul and Ari usually divided the paper in the morning, Paul taking the front page and Ari the inside section and comics, but when they saw the ominous news on the front page, Ari silently folded the paper up and hid it under the telephone book.

In the weeks that followed, the police removed the yellow tape, the garbage was carried to the curb, and Paul was careful to avoid mentioning the serial killer. He was relieved that there had been no more discussion of moving, but he sensed that murder was never far from his mother's mind. She had floodlights installed on the back porch, and she began to insist that Paul take the garbage out to the curb before dark. He noticed that she made excuses to keep him and Ari from going out at night.

But Paul didn't argue with her. The truth was he wasn't that eager to go out after dark himself.

He couldn't shake the feeling that a killer might be waiting for him in the shadows.

"Mom is still really nervous," Ari murmured one evening. She glanced sideways toward the living room where their mother had gone to bolt the front door. "And it's been weeks now since you found that body." She got up and stared out the window in the back door. "Paul!" she said softly. "Someone's out there!"

He jumped up and ran to the door. Transparent figures moved beyond the windowpane, a blank-faced boy and someone shorter standing beside him. For a minute Paul's heart stopped, then suddenly he laughed. "It's our reflections, Ari!" His voice was shaky. Paul lifted his hand and the transparent ghostly hand on the window rose to meet it.

Ari clutched him. "Is that all? Are you sure there's no one outside?"

Paul flicked off the light in the kitchen. Standing in darkness, with no reflections on the glass, he could see outside. The porch floodlights threw a path of light onto the worn wooden porch and lit up the stepping-stones and, farther back, a forlorn cracked birdbath. Beyond that lay profound darkness. Paul knew that past their neglected garden lay the stagnant pond surrounded by a tangle of live oaks, vines, and undergrowth. How could he tell Ari that nothing was out there? Anything could be hiding in the dark mass of vegetation.

"Someone is out there," said Ari in a low voice. "I know it. And he's looking for us."

Paul felt the hair on the back of his neck prickle. He teased Ari about being overimaginative, but amazingly often her sixth sense turned out to be right. Maybe there *was* someone out there.

The wall switch clicked and the kitchen was flooded with light. "What are you two standing here in the dark for?" cried Mrs. Montclair shrilly.

Paul gulped. "We were only taking a look outside, Mom. The new floodlights work great. We can see halfway to the back fence."

Mrs. Montclair closed her eyes. "If we lit up this entire quarter like a football stadium, it still wouldn't be bright enough for me," she said. "All these dark old houses, the shadows under the balconies, the walled gardens. There are altogether too many places around here where someone can hide."

"You used to love the French Quarter," said Ari softly.

Her mother stared at her blankly as if she hadn't heard. "Don't you think it's time you kids got down to your homework?" she asked.

The twins looked at each other in dismay. Since they found the body, there'd been no sign that their mother was calming down.

The next day, Paul found a typed business envelope with an Oregon postmark in the mail. The postmark jolted him.

"Let's steam it open," he suggested to Ari.

"But that's so sneaky!" cried Ari. "We ought not to read Mom's private mail."

"It's our lives we're talking about," said Paul. "Mom won't be home for hours. Don't we want to know what's going on? Are you ready to move to Oregon?"

Reluctantly Ari put a pot on the stove and turned on the burner. When steam began to roll from the pot in puffy clouds, Paul held the envelope over it until the adhesive loosened. Then he carefully slipped his fingers under the envelope flap and lifted it open. The twins read it together. "Thank you for your inquiry about the position of station manager," it began.

They stared at each other. "She's already applying for jobs out of state," whispered Ari.

"We've got to glue this envelope shut," said Paul. He got some white glue from the desk and squeezed some on the flap.

"Don't put too much on it," warned Ari. "We don't want it to look gloopy."

By the time Mrs. Montclair got home from work, the glue on the envelope was dry. She ripped the envelope open and read the letter with excitement. Ari glanced at Paul. He looked so guilty that she was sure her mother would guess what they had been up to. She looked down and buttered her soft roll. "Ann Hendricks says she thinks I've got a good chance at being newspaper editor next year," she said.

Mrs. Montclair slid the letter back into its envelope. "Don't make too many plans for next year, Ari. You remember I told you we might have to move."

The twins gazed at each other in dismay. "But we love it here!" protested Ari. "We don't ever want to move, do we, Paul?"

Paul shook his head.

"Things don't always go the way we would like, sweetheart." Mrs. Montclair made a wry face. "I'm sure you'll both make friends wherever we go. And don't forget we've got each other." She avoided looking at them. Ari knew it was because she hated to see them unhappy.

Ari wanted to scream, "Look at me! See the tears streaming down my face. See what you're doing to me! I can't move in the middle of my junior year!"

Mrs. Montclair pushed her chair away from the table. "I'm going to have to be away for a few days to go to a job interview. Maybe you can stay with Laurie, Ari. And Paul might like to stay with one of his friends."

Ari and Paul exchanged a panicky look. "Laurie can put us both up, Mom," said Ari. "I can sleep with Laurie and Paul can sleep on the couch the Bergers have in the den." Ari couldn't be separated from her twin now when so much was going wrong.

"If it's okay with the Bergers, it's fine with me," said Mrs. Montclair. "But please don't let on that we might be leaving town."

"You mean not even tell Laurie?" asked Ari in amazement.

23

"Not even Laurie," said her mother. "We . . . we may need to make a clean break of it. Luckily, the post office has a new rule that they don't give out forwarding addresses. I want to keep this move a secret. I know I can count on you both." She hastily turned on her heel and left the room.

"Does she think I'm going to move and not even mention it to anyone?" asked Ari.

The twins sat in silence. A moment later their mother swept into the kitchen. "I have to run to the grocery store before it gets dark." She smiled at them tremulously. "Now, don't worry, kids. We're going to be fine. It will all work out." When she bent to kiss them, Ari smelled the faint scent of peppermint that clung to her.

A minute later, they heard the front door of the house close behind her.

"Maybe she won't get the job," said Paul.

Ari was too choked up to speak. Leave her friends? Her mother couldn't be serious!

The twins heard the crunch of metal on metal and ran to the living room window. Mrs. Montclair's blue Chevrolet had locked bumpers with the neighbor's car. Their mother stood in the street pantomiming dismay while Mr. Wilson, dressed in a business suit, stood on the locked bumpers. Flinging his arms in the air, he bounced. At last both cars rocked free. Ari and Paul could see their mother's lips moving, but they couldn't make out what she was saying.

"And she has the nerve to call me a bad driver," said Paul. "I bet she wasn't looking."

24

Ari let the curtain drop. "Anybody can see she's not herself, Paul. That's what we've just been saying."

"It's because of that dead body," said Paul promptly. "I have to admit I'm still kind of jumpy lately myself."

"If that's all it is, then what's the deal with the secrecy, the 'clean break'? Did you hear her say that stuff about the post office not giving out forwarding addresses? You'd think we were fugitives."

"What are you getting at?"

Ari fell into a chair. "I don't know. But something's wrong." She hesitated. "I wonder if it doesn't have something to do with our father."

Paul froze. "Why do you say that?"

"Because I feel as if he's close by." Ari's voice sank to a whisper. "Don't you?"

Paul glanced toward the door, as if he were afraid their mother might walk in and catch them talking. "What makes you think he's around here?"

Ari twirled a dark lock around her finger. "I don't know," she said. "It's a feeling I have. When I turn corners, I keep expecting him to be there. Does that make sense?"

"I bet it happens with lots of kids whose parents are divorced," said Paul. "It's maybe worse with us because Mom never talks about our dad. A kind of wish fulfillment, probably."

"Maybe you're right." It was hard for Ari to believe that Paul didn't share her feeling that their father was close by. "You honestly think it doesn't mean anything?" she asked.

Paul hesitated.

Ari stared at him a moment, then smiled. "You do have the same feeling, don't you? I knew it!"

"Maybe I do," he admitted. "But still it doesn't mean anything. Feelings aren't the same as facts."

"Yes," said Ari. "But if he were in town, it would explain why Mom was so nervous, wouldn't it?"

"I've got a lot of homework," Paul said, turning away from her abruptly. But Ari could see his pain.

CHAPTER
THREE

THE VAMPIRE STEPPED OUT OF THE RAIN INTO A DIM and dusty shop near the French Market. The man behind the shop counter was round-shouldered with faded, thinning hair and gold-rimmed glasses the shape of half-moons. The glass display cases on which he rested his hands contained packets of tarot cards in different designs. On the shelves behind him were boxes of incense, joss sticks, clove cigarettes, and small wax dolls.

"May I help you?" inquired the shopkeeper.

"I would like a reading," said the vampire. Rain dripping from his cape made small puddles on the dusty floor. Drops of the rain had beaded on his soft, wide-brimmed hat.

"Have you had a reading here before?" asked the man.

"Yes," said the vampire.

"I'm sure I would remember," said the man,

peering curiously at the vampire's leprous white skin. "You have such an unusual face."

"It's been a long time since my last reading," the vampire said. He pushed through the cloth curtains that marked the entrance to the dark back room. It was little more than a closet situated directly behind the main part of the tiny shop. The vampire perched on one of the stools in front of the inclined board that stood, easel-like, at shoulder height. On it lay packs of tarot cards wrapped in soft cloths.

The shopkeeper shrugged and stepped into the reading room with him. He climbed onto the other stool and unwrapped a pack of cards. "Don't you want me to take your hat and coat?" he asked. "I can hang them up for you."

"No," said the vampire quickly. "I'm a little chilly. I . . . I haven't been well."

The shopkeeper smiled. "Nothing catching, I hope."

The vampire shook his head. "No. Nothing like that."

"Shuffle the cards," commanded the shopkeeper, handing the pack to him. "As you know, you must touch the cards."

Reluctantly, the vampire peeled off his gloves. In the dim light of the back room, his hands were a flash of white. He took half the deck in each hand and fanned them together so swiftly the cards were a blurred whir.

The shopkeeper giggled nervously. "You shuffle like a riverboat gambler." He paused. "Now,

28

you must choose a card that can represent you."

The vampire chose a voluptuous woman in a gown spangled with stars.

The shopkeeper gazed at it a moment. "An unusual choice for a man," he commented.

"I'm an unusual man," said the vampire smoothly.

The shopkeeper laid the cards out on the board. For a moment he didn't speak. "Perhaps you'd like to reshuffle," he suggested, his voice expressionless. "There'll be no extra charge."

The vampire's cape rustled as he reached out to touch the shopkeeper's neck. His thin white hand rested there, and the man's glasses fell to the floor. Without them, his eyes looked watery and confused.

"Read the cards!" commanded the vampire.

"Someone whose life is closely entwined with yours will die today," said the shopkeeper.

The vampire embraced the man suddenly, and the stool he had been sitting on fell and tumbled against the cloth curtains, parting them slightly. He pressed his mouth against the man's neck and ripped the pulsing flesh with his teeth. The shopkeeper cried out, but the vampire covered his mouth until he was still. Then he sucked noisily, his face buried in the torn flesh until his nose and lips were smeared with blood. He let the body fall to the floor

"Fool!" he said contemptuously. He stepped over the man's body and carefully straightened the fallen stool so that the curtains hiding the back room swung closed once more. *Just in time,* he thought. A bell tinkled as the door to the shop opened.

"Anybody here?" called a voice.

"They've got tarot cards," said a different voice. "But I don't see anybody. The owner must be taking a coffee break."

He should have let the fool finish the reading, thought the vampire. But it was too late now for regrets. He pushed the back door of the shop open and slipped out to the alley behind the shop. Rain drummed noisily on the broken glass and pebbles that paved the alley. The vampire crouched on his haunches and peered into a muddy puddle at the rippled reflection of his face. *Handsome devil,* he thought, baring his white fangs in a smile. At least he had fed now, so he didn't look deathly pale. He scooped up the water in his cupped hands and splashed it on his face until the blood ran off his cheeks in pink rivulets.

His ears pricked at a thin shriek, and he lifted his head to glance at the back door of the shop. Someone had found the body already. He stood up abruptly, pulled his hat down over his eyes, and slipped away down the dark alley.

At school Ari stared out the tall window next to her desk. *This is what it must feel like to be lost at sea,* she told herself. *Lost and alone.* The glass was frosted with condensation inside, and rain ran in unending rivulets down the glass, melting the world outside into shapelessness. The teacher's voice droned on as Ari stared out the window. She wished she could tell Laurie that her mom was talking about moving out of town, but she was afraid to. What if her mother was in some kind of terrible trouble? She could have embezzled money or killed someone in a hit-and-run accident. Why else would she be so concerned about the post office giving out their new address? Ari gazed around the room. Half the class was asleep. She reminded herself that she mustn't let her imagination run away with her. Paul was always telling her that. It simply wasn't possible that their mother was on the run from the law—she was too honest. More likely she was trying to escape their father.

Ari knew that Paul longed to see their father, but even thinking about him frightened her. There must be some good reason their mother refused to talk about him, she figured. Perhaps he had made death threats against them all. Perhaps he was a drunk—or even an insane person. For all they knew, he was stalking them at this moment. Ari stared at the window, listening to her heart thump. She was definitely letting her imagination run away with her again.

Suddenly, a white face appeared at the rain-streaked window of the classroom. Dark eyes burned in the masklike face, blurred by the rain. Ari gasped and a whimper escaped her. The room around her grew dim.

Suddenly, a hand touched her shoulder. "Are you all right?" whispered Laurie.

Ari stared at her friend. "Look!" she cried. "The face at the window!" But when Laurie turned to look at the rain-streaked window, Ari noticed, the face was gone.

Mr. Burgess had given out graded tests, and kids were busy comparing answers.

"Someone was at the window," whispered Ari. "Look! His hand touched the glass."

The condensation on the window showed the clear print of a hand, as if something warm had touched the glass on the other side.

"An *A* for you as usual, Ari," said the teacher, tossing Ari's test on her desk.

But Ari continued to gaze at the handprint.

"No one is out there, Ari," Laurie told her. "You must have put your hand on the glass yourself."

"But I didn't," Ari whispered. She reached out to the cold glass and hesitantly fitted her hand into the handprint. The print was much larger than her hand. "Someone was out there," she said. "Someone is watching me."

"I think you've got this post-traumatic stress syndrome we studied in psychology," said Laurie. "Ever since Paul found that dead body, both of you have been on edge. That's the only reason you think somebody is watching you."

"No," said Ari. "Someone *is* watching me."

Laurie cleared her throat uncomfortably. Ari knew her friend didn't believe her.

When the twins got home from school, Ari could not shake a sense of uneasiness. She felt the stirring of old memories—of coming home from the playground at dusk and turning to see a dark figure standing in the shadows, his eyes glittering. "I'm sure someone was out there," she insisted to Paul. "Laurie didn't believe me, but someone was looking through the window."

"Maybe it was a janitor," suggested Paul.

"What would a janitor be doing outside in the pouring rain?"

Paul had no answer.

When darkness fell, the mist made a glowing halo around the streetlamp outside. The patter of the rain had stopped, but the cars outside made a noisy, whishing progress along the wet street.

"Mom's running late," said Paul. "Maybe we ought to go ahead and set the table and start dinner. She's going to be tired when she gets in."

Ari jumped up from her homework, thankful for the distraction of fixing dinner. But as soon as the twins got to the kitchen, the doorbell rang. "I'll get it," said Paul.

Ari was close behind him when he threw the door open. Two uniformed police officers were outside. One of them glanced at a card in his hand. "Is this Mary Ellen Montclair's house?" asked one of them.

"That's right," said Paul. "She's our mother. Can we help you?"

"Is your dad at home, kids?" asked the fat officer.

Ari glanced at Paul. "We don't have a dad. At least, he doesn't live here, and we don't even know where he is."

The older officer pushed his cap back on his head. "Maybe you should get your grandma to come over. Or your aunt or somebody."

"What is it?" asked Ari in a shrill birdlike voice she could hardly recognize as her own. "What's wrong?"

Paul put his arm around her. "We don't have any close relatives, Officer. Why don't you tell Ari and me what's going on?"

"I'm afraid your mother's been in an accident," said the fat officer.

"Is she in the hospital?" cried Ari. "We'd better go to her. Is she hurt? When did it happen?"

The officer shook his head. The pity in his eyes frightened Ari so much that she could not say any more.

"I'm sorry," he said. "They weren't able to save her."

"We have to go to her," sobbed Ari. "She'll be worried about us."

Paul squeezed her tight. "She's gone, Ari. That's what they're telling us. She's dead." He choked. "We have an aunt in Washington, D.C., Officer. I'll call her right away."

The two men looked relieved. "Do you have a friend you can stay with tonight?" the fat officer asked. "We can get a social worker to come pick you up, if you don't."

"I'll call the Bergers," said Paul. "They're friends of ours."

Paul was absolutely numb. It seemed that everything should stop in a freeze frame, yet cars

34

continued to whoosh by on the treacherously wet streets outside. Paul could hear the static of the cops' radio in their patrol car. The shock was simply too much to comprehend. He dialed Mrs. Berger and told her what had happened. Then he found his mother's address book and called his father's sister, Aunt Gabrielle.

"Hello?" a male voice answered.

"Is Gabrielle there, please?" Paul asked. "This is her nephew, Paul."

"Sorry," the stranger's voice said. "Gabri's out jogging. May I take a message?"

"Tell her our mother has been killed in a car wreck. The police are here now, and they said we should call our next of kin."

"I'm so sorry! Of course, I'll tell Gabri as soon as she gets back."

Paul gave Aunt Gabrielle's friend the Bergers' number and hung up. His insides were an empty ache.

The policemen sat in the living room, impassive and still, while Paul and Ari packed.

Paul was in a daze as he threw some things in a duffel bag. He kept having the awful feeling that he could hear his mother's key turning in the lock. She would walk in any minute, as she had so many times before. *Better to get out of the house,* he thought, choking on his tears.

It seemed an eternity until Laurie's mother arrived. "You poor, poor lambs," Mrs. Berger cried, embracing them. "Laurie's still at the school play, but I came right over. You poor, poor babies." The

35

police were obviously relieved to see an adult who could take charge of the twins.

Paul turned off the lights of the house as they left, then locked the door. When he glanced back at the dark, empty house, he felt a cold stab of pain. Nothing would ever be the same, he thought. All the life and warmth had bled from their house. It was an empty shell. Mrs. Berger shepherded them to her car. She blew her nose. "You poor, poor babies," she repeated brokenly.

"I've called our aunt," said Paul. "She wasn't in but I left a message for her. I gave her your phone number."

"I expect she'll take care of everything as soon as she gets here," said Mrs. Berger, looking relieved. "It's good you have a relative you can count on at a time like this."

Paul did not mention that he and Ari had never met their aunt. He already hated it that Mrs. Berger felt sorry for them. He dreaded seeing the pity in his friends' eyes even more. He glanced over at Ari. Her face was shiny and slick in the dim light of the car. As they sped through the quarter, her eyes brimmed, dark and gleaming with tears.

"Aunt Gabrielle will tell our father about what happened, Paul," Ari whispered to him. "He'll have to come for us now. He's all we've got."

Paul felt a sick clutch in his stomach. A horrible fear swept over him. Had he brought this disaster on them by wishing for his father to come?

*   *   *

36

The day of their mother's funeral was sunny. If only this bright interval had come a few days earlier, thought Ari bitterly, their mother would not have skidded on a rain-slicked street. The glare made her wince as she filed into the first row of folding chairs under a green canvas canopy. Their mother's shiny mahogany casket was before them, blanketed with fresh flowers. A crowd of friends filled the chairs under the canopy and spilled out onto the lawn of the cemetery. Ari recognized some of them—people from her mother's office, kids from school. They stood quietly on the dry, bleached grass, shifting their feet uncomfortably, looking stiff and formal in their best clothes.

Ari had cried most of the night, and her head ached. She knew she had to try not to think about her mother. She wished she could stop feeling altogether. If only she could blot everything out, she thought, and lose this pain! She was so desperate she might have stepped in front of a speeding car—but as soon as the thought formed in her mind, she knew that wouldn't be fair to Paul.

"Who's that?" Paul suddenly grabbed her arm.

Ari followed her twin's gaze and saw that he was looking at a tall, dark man who stood a bit apart from the crowd. The light glinted blankly on the man's sunglasses, robbing his face of expression.

"That's Mr. Cowgen, my calculus teacher," said Ari.

"Oh." Paul sighed his disappointment.

"Our father's not coming, Paul," said Ari harshly.

"He doesn't care about us. He never has." As soon as she said it, she felt better. It was as if her anger at her father burned away her grief. Ari watched the sick disappointment grow in Paul's eyes and knew that it mirrored the look on her own face.

Ari was sure Aunt Gabrielle had told their father about their mother's death—if anyone knew how to reach him, it would be his sister. At first, she and Paul had both felt certain they would hear from him, and for days they had jumped every time the Bergers' phone rang. They had stared at each other wide-eyed whenever the doorbell sounded. But there had been no word. No message. No phone call.

The twins had expected their aunt to come for the funeral, but a lawyer had contacted the Bergers instead and said that Aunt Gabrielle had been laid low by the flu. As her representative, he would take care of the funeral arrangements, he had said. Aunt Gabrielle planned to take the twins to live with her and she would come for them as soon as she was able to travel.

Paul looked over his shoulder at the crowd of well-wishers standing on the grass. He put his arm around Ari. "All we've got to do is get through this ceremony," he said softly. "Then it's got to get better."

Ari said nothing. Hot tears spilled out of her eyes. Paul pulled her close to him and they both sobbed.

* * *

The next day found the twins waiting for their aunt in the empty living room of the house on Rampart Street.

"I'm not sure I want to live in Washington, D.C.," said Ari nervously. "It's going to be awful going to a new school. I've seen the way people treat new kids."

"We have each other to talk to," Paul pointed out. "It could be worse."

"They'll probably make fun of our accents and our clothes. We won't have any friends at all."

"Trying to cheer us up?" said Paul with a crooked smile. "Look, it's going to be fine. We've got each other, don't we? We'll get along."

"I wish Aunt Gabrielle would show up." Ari shivered. Her voice echoed in the empty room. "She said she'd be here by eight. That was hours ago. And I wish the stupid lawyer hadn't had the electricity turned off so soon. And the phone. We're marooned here. We can't even call anybody."

She was glad Paul didn't point out that it had been her idea that they come back to Rampart Street to say good-bye to the old house. It had seemed like a good plan at the time, but Ari had not realized quite how unnerving it would be to wait in the empty place after dark. And she had not expected Aunt Gabrielle to be so late.

The streetlight outside cast an uncertain illumination through the bare front windows of the living room. It threw a glow on the uneasy faces of the twins, who sat on their suitcases. Shadows in the corners of the room seemed to move and grow.

A cloaked figure darted with swift, fluid movement up onto the porch, then tiptoed up to the door and peered through the window at the twins. Shadowed by a broad-brimmed hat, violet eyes glowed in the dark like radioactive jewels. An abundance of hair fell to the shoulders of the cape, which shimmered, intensely black, in the lamplight. A skeletally thin hand was lifted; its white fingers with pink oval nails nervously crept up the window frame, and tiny phosphorescent dots glowed where each fingertip touched.

CHAPTER
FOUR

ARI GLANCED AT THE WINDOW, TROUBLED BY THE
feeling she was being watched, but no one was
there. "What'll we do if she doesn't show up?" she
asked suddenly.

"We could probably stay with the Bergers for a
little while longer," said Paul. "I guess."

Ari did not see how Paul could sleep on the
Bergers' couch indefinitely. And it wasn't as if they
had been invited. "I wonder if orphanages still
exist," she said in a small voice.

"She's going to show up," said Paul. "She's late,
that's all."

"What's that?" Anne-Marie cried suddenly.

Paul glanced at the window. "Nothing," he said.
"Calm down."

Ari hugged herself and shivered. A signature
on a card, a disembodied flutey voice—Aunt
Gabrielle seemed so insubstantial. If only they

knew her, she thought, maybe they wouldn't feel so nervous.

Ari wished she had a flashlight, but the flashlight had been packed along with all the other household goods. Her flesh crawled with self-consciousness. She was sure she could feel a stranger's eyes on her. She stood up abruptly. "I can't stand this anymore. I think we ought to wait over at Mr. Wilson's house. We can leave a note for Aunt Gabrielle."

A rapid knock sounded on the door, and the twins started.

"Darlings! It's Auntie Gabrielle!" trilled a richly musical voice.

Paul jumped up and threw the door open. He was greeted by a cape swishing through the air and white extended arms. At first, crushed close to his aunt's breast, he had only an impression of a large hat, sparkling violet-colored eyes, and a stifling expensive scent. "Dearest, dearest," she murmured, her breath tickling his ear. He didn't know what to say to her and was relieved when she turned to Ari. "Ari, dearest!"

Paul's gaze fell to his aunt's small, tightly laced boots. They looked like the sort of shoes a witch might wear, he thought. But when Aunt Gabrielle turned toward him again, he could see that she was a fashionably dressed woman in a long camel-colored skirt and a cashmere sweater. She was so thin he could see the points of her hipbone under the soft material of the skirt. Her cheekbones were broad and in the uncertain light almost seemed to cast shadows. Gold bracelets glimmered at one bony wrist. Her eyes glowed at him—violet and hypnotic like a cat's. Meeting her gaze, Paul had the odd sensation that he was falling, tumbling into something deep. Her cheerful voice startled him back to consciousness. "Darlings, it's dreadful we have to rush like this, but we literally don't have a minute to waste. Our tickets are on the next flight out!" she cried. "If only my beastly plane hadn't been so late."

"No problem," said Paul. "Ari and I are all packed." He hoisted the suitcases.

After they stepped out, Paul carefully locked the door of the house even though there was nothing left inside. Then he tossed the suitcases into the trunk of Aunt Gabrielle's shiny rental car.

"Allons, mes enfants!" Aunt Gabrielle cried as she got in behind the wheel. "Let's get a move on!"

"I think she wears contact lenses," hissed Ari, "and they're tinted. That's what gives them that strange violet color."

The twins got into the backseat of the car. Aunt Gabrielle plucked a long hat pin from her crown and set her big hat on the seat beside her. "Gracious, it's warm down here," she said. "I hope you packed sweaters. It's cooler in Washington, and the movers won't be arriving with the rest of your things for a few days."

The twins assured her that they had packed warm clothes. The streets of the French Quarter whizzed by the car windows. Old-fashioned streetlamps cast a glow on gently decaying old town houses with lacy black balconies. Plastic garbage bags bulged by the curb. Perhaps this was the last time they would be gazing on the streets of their hometown and smelling the familiar smells of gumbo, filé, and garbage, thought Ari. The shiny car passed college kids in T-shirts, silver-haired tourists from the Midwest, thin punk couples with spiked hair. Ari could feel her throat filling up with tears. She realized she would miss the tourists. The house on Rampart Street was empty now and was to be sold. Would they ever come home again?

"Everywhere I look there are T-shirt shops," complained Aunt Gabrielle, peering ahead. "Can't something be done before they take over the entire Quarter?"

"I think somebody's formed an association," said Paul. "I saw a T-shirt about it the other day."

Ari laughed suddenly and covered her mouth, embarrassed by the explosive sound.

"Did you have any trouble finding our house?" asked Paul.

His aunt's smile flashed in the rearview mirror. "Not a bit. Your directions were wonderful, darling. And I do know my way around here a little. I spent a summer in New Orleans once many years ago."

The twins exchanged a look. Aunt Gabrielle had once lived in New Orleans? Had it been perhaps the summer their parents had met?

The rented car sped past the dark shores of Lake Pontchartrain with its silent fishermen standing

44

on the banks. They drove past dark bayous, the ancient riverbeds of the Mississippi. Overhead planes droned. Paul peered out the window and saw one coming in low, its red lights glowing.

The rented Lincoln pulled up at the brightly lit terminal, and Paul opened his door and got out. A luggage cart squeaked by, narrowly missing him. Aunt Gabrielle unlocked the trunk. "You go on in, darlings. There's no need for you to return the rental car with me. Go on to the gate and I'll catch up with you." She climbed back into the car.

As she drove off, the twins stood together on the sidewalk and silently watched the shiny Lincoln disappear. "She's very pretty." Ari turned to her twin. "Do you think she looks like our dad?"

Paul shrugged. "Maybe." The crushing disappointment of not having his father even show up for the funeral had left a painful emptiness aching inside of him. The twins moved toward the terminal and the automatic doors swung open.

The air-conditioning of the terminal hit them like a blast, and Ari tightened her grip on her suitcase. "It's very possible that after the split Mom didn't want to have anything to do with Dad's family. Maybe that's why Aunt Gabrielle never came to see us."

"You mean, just because she's Dad's sister?" asked Paul.

"Well, it's not like our parents had one of those friendly divorces," said Ari.

The terminal was packed with passengers carrying tote bags slung over one shoulder or pulling

45

suitcases behind them on wheels. Indian families in saris, college students in sweat suits, businesswomen in gray flannel moved purposefully down the broad corridor.

At gate ten, the first-class passengers were already lined up to board. Aunt Gabrielle swept up suddenly, her cape flying. "That's us, *mes cheris.* We'd better get in line."

"We're flying first class?" Ari stared in astonishment

Aunt Gabrielle nodded. She was groping in her pocketbook for the tickets. The twins got into line at once. "She must be rich if we're flying first class," said Ari in a low voice.

The twins had gone with their mother to California on vacation the year before, and Paul had learned then that he was too tall to fit comfortably into a regular coach seat. The seats in first class were much roomier, Paul discovered. Stretching out, he decided he could easily get used to being rich.

Aunt Gabrielle settled into the aisle seat and beamed at him. "There, isn't this nice? I was able to get us three seats together so we can chat."

Coach passengers were filing in now. Nearby two men talked rapidly in German. Somewhere a baby cried.

At last the "FASTEN SEAT BELT" sign flashed on, and the plane began to hum and vibrate.

Aunt Gabrielle leaned over Paul and said, "I'm so sorry I couldn't make it down for your mother's funeral." She smiled wryly. "That wretched flu.

And at the worst possible time." She patted Paul on the knee. "But now we're going to get to know each other and make up for all those lost years, aren't we?" Paul felt his ears pop and forced himself to yawn. The stewardess appeared with a beverage cart, and to his astonishment she offered them glasses of champagne. He supposed the laws on underage drinking didn't apply on planes.

"The bubbles tickle," complained Ari. She downed her glass at once. "I'll have another, please," she said to the stewardess. Smiling, the stewardess refilled her glass.

Paul had never tasted champagne. He didn't like it and decided to down it quickly as Ari had. The stewardess instantly refilled his glass.

"The second glass tastes better than the first," Ari confided, looking at him owlishly.

But after the second glass, Paul's head felt too large, and the seat in front of him seemed to swell and recede. The boundaries of the plane were vague, as if he were flying through the air in a phantom jet. The reflection of Ari's face in the dark oval of the window hinted at the presence of spirits outside in the blackness.

"Darlings, you're going to simply adore Washington!" Aunt Gabrielle's voice seemed to come from far away.

"I'm not so sure," said Paul. His voice sounded too loud to his ears. "My friend David used to live in Washington when his dad was an aide for Senator Nussbaum, and he hated it. He said the place is full of bloodsuckers."

Aunt Gabrielle's hand jerked suddenly, and her glass tipped over. A spray of droplets glimmered on the cashmere sweater like tiny jewels. Her smile was rigid as she righted the glass quickly, then grabbed a paper cocktail napkin and blotted her sweater. "Stupid of me," she said.

"Anyway," Paul went on, "David hated it."

Aunt Gabrielle gave a throaty laugh. "But of course, my dear, your life won't be like your friend's. You'll move in quite different circles." She squeezed his knee. "I know it's a wrench for you, dear, leaving your home, but I hope you'll learn to love your new home as much as you did your old one."

Paul must have fallen asleep after that, because all of a sudden he felt the plane touch down with a bump and his eyes flew open. The seat belt signs were on, but already he could hear shuffling in the aisles and the thud of carry-on luggage being pulled down from overhead compartments. His head ached.

Ari rubbed a circle on the frosted window. "It's raining outside." She sniffled. Her dark hair was tousled, and her cheeks were flushed from sleep.

Paul felt drugged as they made their way off the plane. He wasn't wearing a watch, but he knew it must be the small hours of the morning. Not that he could have guessed it by looking around the terminal. The fluorescent lights were harsh, and the uniformed airport employees hurried about with brisk energy. Only the waiting passengers slumped exhausted in their plastic seats, like bags of laundry.

48

Aunt Gabrielle pinned her hat to her hair. "There's no sense in all of us getting wet," she said. "I'll get the car and pick you up in front." Her dainty black boots clicked on the marble flooring as she walked away. The twins watched as the big glass doors swung open and their aunt's cloaked figure became vague and insubstantial in the gray half-light. Then she disappeared into blackness.

"Does it seem to you Aunt Gabrielle is kind of strange?" asked Ari.

"Everything seems strange to me all of a sudden," said Paul, shaking his head. "I wish I hadn't drunk that champagne."

"She must be a lot younger than our father," said Ari. "I mean, I figure Dad must be about forty, like Mom was. Aunt Gabrielle doesn't look forty."

"She doesn't look like a kid either, though," Paul suggested. His gaze rested on his twin with satisfaction. The gold hoops in Ari's ears made glimmers of light where they peeked through her dark hair.

"Aunt Gabrielle doesn't look any particular age at all," Ari said, puzzled. "Not old. Not young exactly, either."

"She looks good, though," suggested Paul. In fact, something about her reminded him of Ari.

A car horn blew outside the door. "That's her," cried Ari. "She's here."

"Ari." Paul gave his twin a stern look. "Listen, don't start imagining things. You know how you get carried away sometimes. Aunt Gabrielle's being really nice to us, and we don't want to do anything that might hurt her feelings."

Aunt Gabrielle's black Mercedes hummed at the curb. Paul heaved the suitcases in, the doors slammed, the car's big engine roared, and they were off. The wet roadway gleamed under their wheels, and the car's windshield wipers clacked monotonously.

Paul had the sense that vast black skies stretched overhead. Even in the dark, Washington seemed more open than New Orleans.

"Do you think you'll be up to going to school this first day?" Aunt Gabrielle smiled over her shoulder. "Or do you want to sleep in?"

"Might as well get started," said Ari.

Paul glanced at her in surprise. He knew that she was dreading going to the new school.

"Well, you probably should start as soon as possible," agreed Aunt Gabrielle, "if you think you're up to it. The course work moves very quickly, and you don't want to get behind. St. Anselm's is one of the best schools in Washington." She looked smug. "It has everything—a marvelous library, a theater, lovely playing fields. It's a favorite with the children of diplomats and high government officials."

Ari's heart sank. Already she could imagine the freezing looks she would get from the snobby kids at St. Anselm's. She longed for the familiar run-down brick school building in New Orleans.

"It's very tough to get in," said Aunt Gabrielle, "but I was able to pull a few strings for you.

50

Luckily, there are still some places in Washington where family connections count."

The car made a soft drumming noise as it crossed the seams in the cement bridge over the Potomac River. On either side of them stood rose-white government buildings. Looming ahead and then filling up the sky was the huge, floodlit Washington Monument. The circlet of American flags planted around it in the grass flapped in the rainy wind. Brightly lit streets, shiny in the rain, whizzed by Paul's window.

"My housekeeper, Carmel, is coming in the morning," Aunt Gabrielle went on, "so she can drive you to school. I still have some work to do tonight, so I'll be sleeping late."

The black car glided up in front of an elegant brick town house. Its shiny front door gleamed in the lamplight. "Home, sweet home!" Aunt Gabrielle cried.

Aunt Gabrielle pressed a black disk in her hand, and a green garage door to the left of the house slowly lifted. "Like magic, isn't it?" said Aunt Gabrielle with a strange little smile.

The garage was cold and dimly lit. Shivering, the twins unloaded their suitcases and followed their aunt out a side door and down a narrow path that ran between the house and the garage. Something scuttled in the dead leaves that littered the pathway, and Paul felt his flesh creep.

Aunt Gabrielle pushed open a tall gate and stepped out onto the sidewalk. Paul could see then that the entire street was lined with town houses.

51

To eyes accustomed to the funky charm of the French Quarter, the street looked too neat. Paul wasn't sure he liked the polished and citified look, all the glossy front doors and tidy brick. Nearby a tree's leaves shivered in the breeze.

"I feel like a zombie," Paul said thickly.

Aunt Gabrielle shot him a startled look as she pushed the front door open. "What did you say, dear?"

"I've got to get some sleep," said Paul. "Aren't you tired, Aunt Gabrielle? I'm dead on my feet."

She smiled at him. "I'm a night owl, I'm afraid." Paul heard a click and light flooded the long hallway. A black-and-white checkerboard floor stretched out before them. An umbrella stand was by the door next to a small table with an odd black statuette of a rooster. To their left, stairs rose into darkness.

"If you're tired," said Aunt Gabrielle, "we'll go right upstairs and get you to bed." She switched on the light on the staircase.

A step creaked under Paul's foot as they mounted the stairway.

A strip of blood-colored carpet ran the length of the windowless upstairs hall. Ari was vaguely conscious of mirrors, of odd pieces of tall black furniture and the stuffed body of a crow sitting on a small table, its black eyes glinting malignantly. When they were halfway down the hall, Ari turned back to give the bird a second look, halfway expecting to catch it moving. Its image was doubled by a narrow black mirror that hung behind it. Again she had that feeling that she was being watched. But the crow had not moved, and as Ari looked at it she realized that its feathers had been dulled by a film of dust.

Aunt Gabrielle stepped to the end of the hallway and pushed open a door. "Here is your room, Paul." She turned on the bedside lamp, and the room was flooded with spooky shadows. "I had Carmel make up the bed for you so you can turn right in. And look at this!" She flung open a door. It opened onto another bedroom. "Ari has the room right next to yours. This little door goes between them. Isn't that nice?"

Ari felt a thud of relief that Paul was going to be close at hand. They would be able to talk to each other privately without going out into the creepy hallway.

Aunt Gabrielle clasped her hands and regarded the twins, dewy-eyed. "I knew you'd want to be close," she cried. "I remember how close your dear father and I were at your age. We were absolutely inseparable!"

"Where is our father living these days?" asked Paul. Ari turned to him, her mouth open in shock.

Aunt Gabrielle had frozen a half-instant in midgesture. But like a film when the projector is turned on again, she quickly went on as if nothing had happened. "Oh, here, there, everywhere," she cried gaily. "Richard's quite the rolling stone. I never know where he's going to turn up next." She beamed at the twins. "Well, sleep tight, dear ones." She pecked Paul and Ari on their cheeks. Her lips were startlingly cold. "It's going to be simply delightful having you here. I'm so very happy!"

After the bedroom door closed, they heard her boot heels tap outside, then silence.

Ari felt miserable. The dark shadows of the old house were full of menace, and the thumping of her heart shook her. With all her heart she wished for their comfortable house in New Orleans. The loss of her mother was suddenly very real. Sobbing, she flung her arms around Paul. "Don't leave me!" she cried.

Paul stroked her hair. "I'm not going anyplace, Ari. I'll be right next door."

"Let's leave the connecting door open," said Ari.

"Hey, no problem," said Paul.

As he opened his suitcase and got ready for bed, Paul could hear Ari moving around in the next room. The sound was vaguely comforting. Even when Ari was getting all wrought up, her presence steadied him. It was as if she were being nervous for both of them. He could be calm while she was freaking out. It went the other way, too. He didn't fall apart as often as she did, but when he did—that time he had to get stitches at the hospital and there was blood all over the place, for instance—Ari was a rock. He wondered how people managed when they didn't have a twin.

He was exhausted but he had never felt less sleepy in his life. His jaw was clenched and he felt nerves jumping around under his skin.

"Paul?" came Ari's plaintive voice.

He sighed with relief and stepped into her room. A tree just outside her window cast a moving shadow on the wall, and crystal pendants hanging from the bedside lamp moved and glittered as if stirred by an unseen hand. Ari's face above the counterpane was a pale smudge in the darkness. "You're too far away!" she said in a small voice.

"Move over," he said. "I'll get in with you."

The bed was an old-fashioned three-quarter-sized bed, so it was a bit crowded with both of them. But that was okay. He needed the comfort of her warmth next to him and the sound of her breathing. It reminded him of when they were small and their mother used to put them down together to nap. Almost at once, he fell asleep.

CHAPTER
FIVE

THE NEXT MORNING, RAIN RATTLED AGAINST THE TALL panes of the window, and only a thin gray light leaked in. Ari could see the tall bureau and the fireplace, but brighter and more real than the furniture were the fanged creatures in the room. Their noses were blunt and their nostrils flared. Their ears were broad and pointed. They crouched beside the bed, domestic and unremarkable as cats, sitting on their hairy haunches, examining their front claws as if they were considering a manicure. A small one was peering in her suitcase. She could see his naked haunches, pink and sparsely haired. He tottered and almost lost his balance in his curiosity.

Don't touch my things! Ari wanted to scream. But she couldn't scream—the sound wouldn't come out. The creature by her bed smiled and she saw his fangs clearly. "No!" she cried aloud. At

56

once the creatures were gone, vanished like smoke in the wind. Ari propped herself up on her elbows and looked around. It had only been a dream. She was breathing hard. *They can't hurt me,* she assured herself. *They aren't real.* But she still felt strange, different somehow—as if something had changed. Then she remembered. Their mother was dead and they were living with Aunt Gabrielle.

Paul was breathing evenly, half-asleep. For an instant, Ari was tempted to wake him and tell him about the fanged creatures, but she was afraid to. What if they were a sign she was cracking up? She had never told Paul that she saw numbers and letters in color, either. She didn't like to think about it. It meant that she was seriously different. Different even from her twin.

"Ari?" Paul asked fuzzily. "You awake?"

"Yes, I'm awake," she said.

Paul swung his legs around over the side of the bed. "We'd better get moving. Look at the clock. It's already seven."

"I bet we don't have to be there on time the first day," said Ari, but she slid out of bed.

When the twins went downstairs, they found that a woman with her hair in a heavy dark braid was putting a silver-domed dish on the dining room table. The velvet curtains of the dining room were drawn tight against the gloom outside, and a large chandelier with hundreds of crystal prisms glittered over the table.

They heard Aunt Gabrielle's footsteps on the

marble floor of the hallway. Then she came in. Her face was deathly pale and her violet eyes were cast in shadow by the swirl of abundant black hair that fell partly over her face and rested on her shoulders. Her tight houndstooth jacket, cinched in to show her tiny waist, had double-breasted black buttons that matched her pencil-thin skirt.

"I don't want to trouble Carmel to drive you to school, after all," Aunt Gabrielle said. "I'll take you myself this morning. Of course, what we'll have to do as soon as possible is get you a car."

Paul wondered if Aunt Gabrielle had a spare Mercedes somewhere that she wasn't using. He certainly wouldn't mind driving one to school.

Carmel lifted the silver cover to reveal a steaming platter of eggs and bacon. "The usual school day starts at eight o'clock." Aunt Gabrielle tapped absentmindedly on the snowy tablecloth with a pink-enameled fingernail, then glanced at her watch. She smiled at the twins. "But don't rush with your breakfast."

Paul and Ari glanced at each other uneasily, then proceeded to bolt their food.

It was raining when the twins got to school. The windshield wipers swished with nerve-racking monotony as Aunt Gabrielle's Mercedes pulled up in the circular drive.

Misty rain swirled around the car when they got out. Ari and Paul were buffeted by the wind, and they struggled to keep a single umbrella over their heads. The wind lifted Aunt Gabrielle's plaid rain cape and forced her to keep one hand on top of her saucer-shaped hat. "Your father went to school here," said Aunt Gabrielle, raising her voice to be heard over the wind. "Of course, that was years ago, before the school went coed."

Ari stooped a bit to see out from under the umbrella. The foul weather made a kind of twilight into which the lighted windows of the school's buildings glowed, hinting at warmth and comfort within. The buildings, made of irregular stones and bricks, had windows like those in a church, pointed at the top and divided into many small glowing panes.

Looking around at the damp and plushy greenness of the gently rolling lawns and the splash of golden leaves overhead, Ari had a sudden strong sense that she belonged here—something inside her slid into place with an almost perceptible click. She had expected to feel overwhelmed; instead, she felt a pleasurable excitement, as if the curtain were about to go up and she was the star of the play.

Suddenly a boy rocketed around a corner and collided with them. The umbrella landed upside down in the muddy gutter. The boy bent over and hastily peeled his wet papers off of the sidewalk. When he straightened up, droplets of water glistened on his nose. He was almost eye to eye with Ari. "Wow!" he breathed. For a moment he stared at her in stunned silence.

"Nobody hurt?" cried Aunt Gabrielle. "I hope your papers didn't get too wet."

"I'm okay. No bones broken. I'd hang around a while and propose marriage," the boy said, looking at Ari, "but I think I'd better go get a towel or something first."

Ari laughed shyly.

"Try coming on strong," muttered Paul.

The boy was wearing a blazer and a tie that was half undone and dangled loosely around his neck. He might have conformed to the dress code, but he nevertheless managed to look disreputable. His wet hair was plastered onto his face and his smile was dazzling.

"Let's get out of this rain, children!" urged Aunt Gabrielle. "We're all getting soaked."

Paul retrieved the umbrella, shook it, then pulled Ari close next to him. He trudged after Aunt Gabrielle, who seemed at least to know where she was going. Rain leaked into his shoes and made his socks soggy. He saw Ari glance over her shoulder and he couldn't stop himself from looking back, too.

The boy they had run into was standing in the rain, watching them with a goofy smile on his face. "Jeez," muttered Paul. "Give me a break."

"I like this place," said Ari.

The Schuler Building—its name was cut into the stone archway over the entrance—had wide glass doors. They pushed the doors open and stepped in out of the rain. The headmaster's office, a corner room, was full of windows, but the day was so dark not even walls of windows could dispel the gloom. The bookshelves were tightly

60

packed with well-used books. Paul sank into a chair. He wished he could take off his wet socks and put his head under a dryer.

The headmaster wrung Aunt Gabrielle's hand. "So glad you could make it, after all, Gabri. And these are our new scholars, eh?"

The headmaster and Aunt Gabrielle were old pals, it turned out. They had served together on a panel discussion about Romania. They fell to talking about people they both knew. Someone named Taki had gotten in trouble with the government and some senator—Paul didn't catch the name—was threatening to publish his racy and revealing diaries. "Blackmail," said Aunt Gabrielle, shaking her head.

"He must be desperate," said the headmaster.

Paul sat, feeling a bit left out of things, wondering where he fit in. Aunt Gabrielle and the headmaster were obviously lost in mutual admiration.

Ari caught a glimpse of the expression on her twin's face and wanted to put her arms around him and reassure him, but she felt an unfamiliar sense of constraint. Hugging each other was okay back at their old school where everyone had known them since first grade. But here, among strangers, she was afraid people would think it was odd.

Ari was in a more advanced math class than Paul, so they had different class schedules. During first-period calculus, Ari sensed she was the center of attention and felt nervous and excited. It was turning out to be more interesting than she had thought to be the new girl. But she missed her twin, and to make it worse, when she caught a brief glimpse of Paul in the hall, he looked confused. His unhappiness tugged at her, spoiling her pleasure in the new school.

But her spirits lifted when she saw the boy she had run into that morning standing outside the library. Ari noticed that a petite, dark girl was looking up at him, her hand resting confidingly on his chest while he frowned down at her unhappily. Neither of them noticed Ari as she passed, but she was acutely conscious of their presence as if they'd been outlined in neon. *The pretty girl must be his girlfriend,* Ari figured. If that was the way it was, she hoped the relationship was on the skids. *Interesting possibilities there,* she thought, and as she moved to her next class, she smiled to herself. Maybe something good was going to happen with that boy who had smiled at her so dazzlingly that morning.

Later in the morning, she bumped into her twin on a staircase, and she caught her breath sharply in sudden relief. She hated knowing that she would be in different classes from Paul all day. It made her feel unplugged.

"Where are you going?" Paul asked.

"I don't know," Ari said. "I'm lost."

Paul laughed. "Me, too."

"Are you okay, Paul?" She searched his face anxiously.

He smiled. "Sure. You know it takes me longer to get to know people than it does you. I'm just feeling a little out of it. I'll get over it. Don't let me rain on your parade. I can tell you're feeling at home already."

"I like it here," she admitted. "It's funny. I was so worried about fitting in, but as soon as we got here I felt right away that I belonged." She glanced up at the narrow stained-glass window that gave the staircase its only light. "I don't know why exactly." She shot Paul an anxious look. She wanted him to like it, too.

"One thing's the same, anyway," Paul said. "We've still got each other."

At lunch, the students sat at round tables, each with an oversized bottle of apple juice—and a teacher. There was little noise and confusion. This, obviously, was not a school where food fights were routine. Ari's history teacher sat near her. He was a young-looking man with a beard who seemed more interested in the food than in conversation. Ari looked around the long, noisy dining room they called the refectory. Stained-glass panes were inset into the top of long, pointed windows, and the walls were wood paneled. The place had the look of a dining room in a medieval castle. Ari kept an eye out for the boy she had run into, but so far no luck. The girl next to her was a skinny girl with braces and high, arched eyebrows that gave her a perpetually surprised look. "I'm Sybil," she said. "You're new, huh? You're already in calculus? Is that a mix-up in your schedule or are you some kind of genius?"

63

Ari shrugged. "I like math."

"So who was that guy you checked in with this morning?"

"My brother, Paul."

"Are you French?" asked Sybil. Ari pronounced Paul's name in the French way, "pole" instead of "pawl."

Ari frowned. "No. Well, not exactly. A lot of people in our family have French names. I'm not sure why."

"Where are you from?"

"New Orleans."

"Oh, well, that explains it. Cajun."

The French names came from her father's side of the family, and as far as Ari could make out her father's family wasn't from New Orleans—but she didn't want to get into that.

Sybil lifted a forkful of turkey and dressing. "So your brother's in the fourth form?"

Ari looked blank.

"That's the tenth grade," the girl explained. "I'm sorry. I know it takes a while to catch on to the lingo around here."

"No, he's a junior." Ari smiled. "I mean he's in the fifth form, same as me. We're twins."

"Oh? Identical?" Sybil blushed. "Stupid of me. Of course, you can't be identical. You're a boy and he's a girl. I mean, he's a boy and you're a girl."

Ari grinned. "If you're being friendly just to get to know my brother, Sybil, I'm going to be *so* disappointed."

"I'm not." Sybil's face was pink. "I only happened to notice him, that's all. May I be brutally frank?"

Ari blinked. She hated it when people were brutally frank. They always seemed determined to tell you that your hairstyle didn't become you or that your character was full of flaws. "Sure," she said hesitantly. "Shoot."

"My best friend just moved away. Her dad got a posting in Japan. So I am now interviewing possible replacements."

"Fair enough," said Ari equably. "I myself am new in school and looking for transitional people that I can hang around with until I find some real friends."

"Jeez!" Sybil stared at her. "Talk about brutally frank!"

Suddenly both girls burst into laughter.

Paul heard Ari's laughter when he came into the refectory. He glanced over at her and brightened. She was sitting next to a skinny girl with a frizzy mane of red-gold hair. As soon as he got his food, he went over and squeezed a chair in between them. Ari introduced him to Sybil with a self-conscious glance and Sybil turned pink. It didn't take a mind reader to figure out that Sybil found Paul attractive.

"If you weren't some kind of math whiz, Ari," he mumbled, "we might have some classes together. You having calculus throws our schedules out of sync."

"Sorry about that." Ari smiled. "Sybil here says

she noticed us when we checked in this morning."

"Stands to reason that anybody would notice Aunt Gabrielle," said Paul.

"The lady in the cape?" Sybil straightened suddenly. "The one getting into the Mercedes?"

"That's her. That's our aunt," said Ari. "We're living with her now since our mother died."

Sybil paled. "Oh, I'm so sorry!"

An awkward silence fell.

"I think I'm going to like it here," said Ari, determinedly changing the subject. "This looks like a nice school. An interesting place."

Sybil glanced around the room. "It looks a lot more diverse than it is. If you struck out everybody whose parents didn't work with some government or another, the place would be practically empty. Maybe just me and Jack Montgomery."

"Seriously?" asked Ari.

"I may exaggerate some," admitted Sybil. "I usually do. I guess a lot of people's parents are doctors or lawyers or something. And some of them are from Pongo Pongo or someplace where the government isn't really a government. Not the way we think of it, anyway. What does your aunt do?"

"She teaches night classes at the foreign policy school of Johns Hopkins," said Paul.

"Spook!" Sybil whooped, then hastily covered her mouth with her hand. "Sorry."

"W-what do you mean?" asked Ari, darting an anxious glance at Paul.

Sybil blushed. "I mean that sounds like a CIA

front job. All the people who work for the CIA have jobs like that. Did I mention that we have some CIA kids and a kid whose dad was ex-KGB, too?" She glanced first at one twin and then the other. "Not that I mean your aunt is really CIA," she said hastily. "It stands to reason that some perfectly legitimate people must work at these jobs, right? I didn't mean anything."

"I don't think she's CIA," said Paul shortly.

The twins were silent for a moment, taken aback by Sybil's remark. "Spook" was slang for "spy," but it reminded them powerfully of Aunt Gabrielle. Something about her was uncomfortably spooky.

Paul glanced around the table at the other kids, all of whom were talking animatedly and ignoring him. He was going to have to join the track team or something, he thought. It would be a way to get to know people.

Just then Paul saw the boy who had run into Ari that morning. Paul hoped the guy would not notice them. No such luck. He came right over to their table.

"You're late for lunch, Cos," said Mr. Fleming. "A creative excuse, as usual? Come on, you must have one. Don't disappoint us."

"The cat ate my gym shoes," said Cos, glancing at Ari.

Mr. Fleming's beard twitched. "That one's been overused. Not one of your better efforts."

"Actually," Cos admitted, "I left my book bag at

the activities building and I had to go get it."

"Boring but probably true," said Mr. Fleming. "You'd better get something to eat before it's all gone. You may be irritating, but we don't want you to starve to death."

"Who's that?" Ari whispered to Sybil.

"Cos Cosgrove," Sybil whispered back. "But don't get your hopes up. He's already taken. He goes with Nadia Tanasescu."

"Nadia? Is she a tiny little girl, very pretty?" Ari remembered the girl she had seen Cos with that morning.

"That's her," said Sybil.

Suddenly Ari longed for the confusion of her old cafeteria. She had never realized before how its chaos had offered a certain privacy. At these circular tables with a teacher at each one, she felt she had to be careful what she said.

"Mr. Fleming," Sybil piped up, "Ari and I have already finished. May we go?"

Mr. Fleming eyed their plates dubiously, but he nodded.

"Let's go to the commons, where we can talk," hissed Sybil. The hallway outside the refectory was lined with book bags that students had tossed to the floor when they went in to eat. Stepping over them, Sybil led Ari to the commons room. A broad archway separated the commons room from the hallway. It was a brightly lit room with a grouping of comfortable chairs in front of a fireplace. The walls were decorated with photographs of long-ago sports teams. A brightly colored heraldic shield hung over the mantel. Sybil hurled herself into a leather chair. "So, do you like Cos?" she asked breathlessly.

Ari was a bit taken aback, but she laughed.

"He's absolutely Nadia's greatest coup," Sybil went on. "Nobody noticed her until Cos did."

"How long have they been going together?"

Sybil frowned. "I'm not sure. It must have happened over the summer, because I remember on the first day he was sort of hanging around her and she was looking really happy, like a lightbulb was turned on inside her. He used to say he didn't want to go with somebody who went to school here, but I guess that was before he fell for Nadia. He always used to go with somebody he met at camp or at a math competition or something. You know, somebody he didn't have to see every day."

"So, what's Nadia really like once you get to know her?"

"Who gets to know her?" Sybil shrugged. "I don't know. I guess she's very sweet. Her family's from Romania."

Aunt Gabrielle and the headmaster had been talking about Romania that morning, thought Ari. It seemed she was bumping into Romania everywhere. She would have to check it out on a map.

"Where is that?" she asked Sybil.

Sybil shrugged. "Central Europe somewhere. You've heard of it. The mountainous part of it used to be called Transylvania."

Ari had heard of Transylvania, all right. That

was where the vampires in movies came from.

"Look, Ari," said Sybil, "I'm not sure going after Cos is a good idea. Not that I want to discourage you or anything, but I think when you're new at school it's better to sort of ease in carefully."

Ari thought of Cos's dazzling smile. "Maybe Nadia and Cos aren't getting along very well. Maybe Cos is looking around for somebody else."

"Wishful thinking?" asked Sybil, raising her eyebrows. "If he breaks up with her, Nadia will crack up. She adores him. And Amanda will hate you for it." She cringed. "Jeez, speak of the devil. Here she comes."

A girl with a determined look suddenly walked by them. She was flushed with color, and her ruffled cap of hair brushed against a firm jaw.

"That's Amanda," whispered Sybil. "She's Nadia's best friend."

Ari gazed after the girl. "She sure looks different from Nadia. Nadia looks so meek."

"You're right," Sybil agreed at once. "They're completely different. Amanda tells dirty jokes, gets carried away when she dances, and doesn't ever get embarrassed. Honestly, Amanda might do *anything*. Kelly Griswold was in second grade with her at some Quaker school, and she said Amanda glued the class turtle to the turtle bowl." Sybil paused. "So anyway, tell me about Paul."

"Paul?" Ari looked blank.

"Your brother, remember? If you can make yourself stop thinking about Cos for just a minute, I'd like to hear what your brother is like."

"Paul?" Ari shrugged. "I don't know. I guess he's a lot like me."

"Does he have a girlfriend back in New Orleans?" Sybil asked.

Ari shook her head.

"What sort of girl does he like, do you think?"

"Empty-headed and sexy," said Ari promptly. No sense letting Sybil get her hopes up. "He hasn't actually had a serious girlfriend yet, but from what I've seen so far he has rotten taste."

"How can you say he's like you, then?" asked Sybil. "Well, I kind of like sexy types myself," Ari admitted.

"Sexy is a relative term," said Sybil stoutly. "Everybody is sexy to somebody. It's a personal and mysterious quality."

"Not true! What about Mr. Fleming, the history teacher? Beards are definitely not sexy," protested Ari.

"That's different," said Sybil.

Ari grinned. "Whenever people know you're right they always say, 'That's different.'"

"You may be a teensy bit right," admitted Sybil. "Some people do seem to have—objectively speaking—a low sexiness quotient. Like my dentist, for example. I mean, he is definitely not sexy."

"Or my aunt," said Ari suddenly.

Sybil nodded. "You're right. I got a good look at her when she was leaving. She's pretty and her clothes and her car are great, but—"

"But something about her makes my flesh creep," said Ari, thinking aloud.

71

Sybil was puzzled. "What do you mean?"

Ari thought of the touch of her aunt's cold lips and her white fingers. She felt herself shudder. "I don't know what I mean." She shook her head. "Forget it."

Kids began pouring out of the refectory. Sybil struggled to her feet. "We'd better get on to class. Here, let me give you my phone number."

Ari watched Sybil write her phone number. The marker she wrote with was black, but still Ari saw the numbers in color—blue, green, yellow. *Maybe I'm losing my mind,* she thought. With a cold feeling in her stomach, she remembered the fanged creatures that had haunted her consciousness only that morning. What made her think she could have a normal life? she wondered. "Give me a call," said Sybil, handing her the folded piece of paper with a smile.

"Sure," said Ari in a hollow voice. "I will."

CHAPTER
SIX

WHEN THE TWINS GOT BACK TO THE HOUSE, THEY learned that Carmel knew only one English phrase—"beauty sleep." She uttered it before disappearing into the kitchen to cook dinner. Aunt Gabrielle, it seemed, was not to be disturbed.

"Okay by me," muttered Paul. "It gives us a chance to poke around the house some by ourselves."

A large Oriental gong gleamed at the end of the hallway. Past the gong was the dining room where they had eaten breakfast. Only now the heavy velvet curtains had been pulled back, and they could see that a garden lay beyond the dining room.

Ari slid open a broad door to her right to reveal an elegant living room with a striped satin sofa and an elaborate white stone fireplace. A gilt clock under a glass dome stood on the mantel. It was decorated in blue and gold with the

73

signs of the zodiac. Paul whistled. "Fancy!"

Ari ran her fingers across the face of the fireplace mantel. "Look at this, Paul."

Paul stooped down to get at eye level with the mantel. "It looks old. Maybe Aunt Gabrielle bought it off some mansion they were tearing down or something."

"Something's carved into it," said Ari.

Paul sat down on the hearth. From that angle, he could see better. A woman's face encircled with acanthus leaves had been carved into the stone. He guessed, judging from the style of simpering prettiness, that it must date from the turn of the century. He had seen Victorian valentines with exactly that sort of cloyingly sweet face. He let his fingers slide across the face. "Wait a minute," he cried. "It moves." Paul nudged the face gently with the heel of his hand. He heard a click and the face pivoted easily in its stone socket to reveal its other side, the carving of a macabre skull, its jaw held on by shreds of rotting flesh. Empty eye sockets stared at Paul. The skull had the wide grin of death, but the most curious thing was that its teeth were bats' teeth, jagged and with two long fangs.

"Horrible!" Ari cried disgustedly. "Why would Aunt Gabrielle want such a thing? Turn it back around so we don't have to look at it."

Paul was in no hurry to turn the skull around. "It must have cost a fortune," he said, frowning at it. "An antique mantel with this sort of shock value would be worth a lot to a collector, wouldn't you think?" He had prowled around New Orleans antique shops with his mother and knew about the absurdly high prices of interesting bits of old mansions.

Ari stood up and dusted her hands. "It makes me wonder what other creepy things are hidden around here."

"I wonder where she gets her money," said Paul. "It's not like teaching night classes in college brings in big bucks."

"Well, don't ask her!"

"Like I'm really going to ask her a bunch of personal questions." Paul hesitated. "Well, don't you think we'd better look around some more while we've got the chance?"

Ari shook her head. "I think we ought to go upstairs and lock our doors."

"Oh, come on, Ari. We've got to look around sometime, don't we? I mean, we live here now."

Ari was silent for a moment. "Okay," she said at last.

The twins tiptoed out into the hallway. They heard pans clattering in the kitchen where Carmel was preparing dinner. Ari opened the door across from the living room and peeked in. "Powder room," she said shortly, closing the door. The next room turned out to be a handsome library, its walls lined with books to the ceiling. A ladder on rollers leaned against the shelves.

Ari checked out a few titles. "She's got an awful lot of stuff on Romania and Central Europe, plus a lot that's in French."

"Reference-book-type stuff," Paul concluded.

"Books for her teaching." He wasn't sure what led him to the darkest corner of the library. It was as if the brown, untitled book on the shelves there had a magnetic attraction to his fingers. His palms tingled, and for a moment he had the unnerving sensation that his hands were being moved by some unseen force. Jerkily, Paul pulled the book off the shelf.

"What have you got there?" Ari asked.

"I don't know," he said, gazing down at it. The wooden cover was hinged with a brown silk cord, and a woodcut bookplate had been glued on the inside cover. Its darkly inked design showed a globe, a quill pen, and a skull, but something brown had been splotched on it so Paul could not read the name of the book's owner. The pages were heavy, crisp, and smooth, and the writing was in an odd block script. His hands stopped tingling once the book was open. "It's in French," he said, glancing at her. "Can you read it?"

She peered over his shoulder. "It's old French," she said. "See here where it says *teste*? Nowadays they write *tête*."

"How long has it been since they replaced that *s* with the circumflex?"

"I don't know." Ari shrugged "A long time. I think I can make out the gist of it, though. Most of the French isn't all that different."

Paul handed the book to her. He wished he had always done his French homework the way Ari did; all the words they had learned in class swam in his brain. He was never sure whether *quel dommage* meant *too bad* or was a compliment meant for cheese.

Ari scanned the text. "A woman wrote it."

"How can you tell?" asked Paul, peering over her shoulder.

"She calls herself *'blonde,'* with the feminine ending. She's talking about the spring flowers," reported Ari, reading over it swiftly. "She says they smell sweet at night. For some reason she's crazy about night—says it's *plus noir qu'une meure,* blacker than a blackberry." Ari made a face. "Funny way of putting it. She's in love with the moon and she's had good hunting."

"Women don't hunt," protested Paul. "You must be reading it wrong."

"They did in the Middle Ages," retorted Ari. "On those old tapestries of the hunt, there are ladies on horseback with greyhounds and the whole bit." Ari frowned. "Here's another odd line. *'Je vive sans vie.'*" She glanced up at Paul.

"What does it mean?" he asked impatiently.

"I live without life. It doesn't make any sense, does it?" Ari glanced down again at the book and blanched suddenly. "Oh, no! She's hunting peasants, Paul."

"Are you sure you're getting this right?" asked Paul, making a move toward her.

"*Paysan* is peasant. They run from her, but she runs like the wind, she says. She catches them and sinks her teeth into them!"

"Are you sure you're getting this right?" asked Paul.

"Dents, that's teeth. She's sucking their blood! It's a vampire's diary, Paul! Put it back on the shelf!" Ari thrust the book at him.

Paul took it from her and held it open gingerly with his thumb.

"Aunt Gabrielle probably has it because she's an expert on Romania," said Ari, grimacing. "Vampires come from Romania. The mountainous part of it used to be called Transylvania. Sybil was telling me that. It's where that girl Nadia comes from."

"But did the nobility in Romania speak French?" asked Paul, puzzled.

"I wish you wouldn't hold your thumb there," said Ari, glancing at him. "That's probably the blood of some poor peasant splashed all over the bookplate."

Paul hastily moved his thumb off of the bookplate and closed the volume. Ari grabbed the book from him and shoved it back into the empty slot in the bookshelf.

"I want to wash my hands," said Ari in a small voice.

Paul froze. His tingling hands felt the wetness of blood, but he looked down at them and they were clean. "Our imaginations are too strong for our own good," he said shakily.

"Why does Aunt Gabrielle have such horrible things in her house?" asked Ari quietly. She shivered. "But it's none of our business. It doesn't have anything to do with us."

Paul wondered if there was any way he could

soak the blood off that bookplate and read the name underneath. Probably not. If it really went as far back as the Middle Ages, the blood might have mixed chemically with the fibers of the parchment. "Maybe we'd better get out of here," he said, glancing uneasily at the brown book.

The other door of the library opened onto the dining room. In the slanting afternoon sunlight, the prisms of the candelabra shot shards of light over the room. Glass-paned doors opened out onto the brick terrace, with its flower beds of roses, azaleas, and sodden petunias. They could hear Carmel humming to herself in the nearby kitchen. A small service hall connected the dining room to the kitchen. Ahead the twins saw a pantry, and just to their right rose a small, dark staircase. "I guess this is the staircase the servants used to use," Ari said.

Paul pushed open the door to a room opposite the narrow staircase.

Carmel stuck her head out of the kitchen. "No, no!" she admonished them, shaking her finger.

Paul quickly closed the door.

"What was in there?" whispered Ari as they left the narrow hallway.

Paul shrugged. "It was just a study. A desk, books, stuff like that. Tall glass doors out to the terrace, kind of like in the dining room."

"What this house needs is a den," Ari said. "With a big color television and some tacky souvenirs from vacations."

Paul grinned. "Yeah, Mickey Mouse dolls from

Disney World and flamingoes made out of sea-shells."

The twins' footsteps sounded on the marble floor as they ran down the hallway and up the dark staircase to their rooms. Together they fell onto Paul's bed.

Ari sat up. "You know something, Paul? I bet Aunt Gabrielle could get to her study using that back staircase. She could go out the French doors, and we wouldn't even see her leave."

"Why would she want to sneak out of her own house like that?"

"I don't know. It just hit me that this place would be perfect for anybody who had a secret life."

"Your imagination is working overtime again," said Paul.

"We find a skull on the mantel and a vampire's diary in the library and you have the nerve to tell me the trouble is with my imagination?"

"You're right," said Paul, avoiding her eyes. "This place is scary, Ari."

"There's just one other thing I want to check," she said.

She tiptoed out into the hall and Paul trailed after her. Tentatively, she approached the black crow that stood outside Aunt Gabrielle's bedroom. Paul expected her to pick it up; instead, she reached out and touched the obsidian mirror that hung on the wall behind it.

"What—?" Paul exclaimed.

Ari raised her finger to her lips, and he shut up

80

at once. Neither of them wanted to risk waking Aunt Gabrielle. Ari's hands felt the glassy surface of the black mirror, then groped along the edges of its frame. She gestured to Paul to look, but he couldn't see what she was getting at. The narrow black mirror was built into the woodwork—that was all he could see. Ari took a tissue from her pocket and polished her finger marks off the black surface. The tissue on glass gave a squeak that made them both jump. They tiptoed silently down the blood-red carpet and darted with relief back into Paul's room.

Paul wiped his brow. "What was all that about?" he asked, annoyed at himself for being afraid.

"Most mirrors are hung on the wall with a piece of wire, like a picture," said Ari.

"Some are installed with those little doohickeys," said Paul. "Screws and mirror hangers. So what?"

"Have you *ever* seen one that was built in?"

Paul thought about it. "No. But I'm not sure I've ever seen a black one either. Aunt Gabrielle has weird ideas about interior decoration."

Ari hesitated. "Now promise me you won't laugh at what I'm going to say."

"Ari, I don't think I have a laugh left in me."

"Last night when we came in, I had the sensation I was being watched. What I'm wondering is whether that's a two-way mirror. You know, on one side you get a reflection, but on the other side you see through it like a window."

81

Paul thought about the sinister crow and its reflection in the black glass. He, too, had had the feeling that the crow was looking at him. What if he had been right that something or *someone* was looking at them—someone at the window behind the crow? "Aunt Gabrielle was with us when we came in," he said, puzzled. "Who could have been watching us through that mirror?"

"I don't know," she said. "But I'm sure we were being watched. I felt it, didn't you?"

Paul didn't say anything. He *had* had the same uncomfortable feeling. "But why would anyone want to watch us?"

CHAPTER
SEVEN

THE SEMINAR ROOM USED FOR ARI'S AMERICAN LIT class was small and windowless and was completely filled by a round table and chairs. She took the seat next to Cos, who was sprawled over a chair in the corner. He straightened up and pursed his lips appreciatively. One of his legs dangled over the arm of the chair—his black-topped Reebok was within inches of her—and for a second she had trouble catching her breath. The room was so small she had an intoxicating feeling of intimacy, even though she avoided his eyes.

The teacher, Ms. Betancourt, was a slender woman with wispy long hair and bags under her eyes.

It wasn't hard for Ari to follow the class discussion, because she was pretty familiar with Poe's short stories, but she was distracted by Cos's closeness.

It looked as if all her ideas about this new school had been wrong. She had been here only a week but she was already starting to feel at home. With such small classes, it was going to be easier than she thought to get to know people. So far kids hadn't been snobby and standoffish at all—maybe they were glad to see a new face.

After class, Cos cornered her in the hall. "So where are you from?" he murmured, bracing one hand against the wall as he leaned over her. Ari noticed that several Band-Aids were wrapped around his knuckles.

"I'm from New Orleans," said Ari, smiling up at him. "But I'm starting to like it here."

Suddenly a boy came out of the classroom and stared at her for a moment. The blueness of his gaze was startling. Ari averted her eyes uncomfortably, remembering how the boy had introduced himself on her first day in class. *I'm Jessie Driscoll, and I collect guns.*

"Old Jess is the complete paranoid," Cos whispered in Ari's ear. "Don't let it get to you."

"I gotta go, Cos," said Jessie. "If I'm late to Michaels's class again, he's going to dock my grade."

"Go on without me," said Cos. "Come on, Ari. I'll walk you to chemistry."

Ari gave him a startled glance. "How did you know I had chemistry next?"

"Lifted your schedule off the computer," Cos said. "Hey, maybe I shouldn't have told you that. Better for you to think I've got ESP. That touch of mystery, huh?"

84

"I don't like mysteries," said Ari firmly. "Is Jessie a good friend of yours?" She couldn't help noticing that Jessie had been standing by even while Cos was handing her his line.

"Jessie? Yeah. I guess he is. We go way back. It's not really his fault he's so paranoid. He had a bad experience in South America. His dad is a high-up executive in a banana company that is like some capitalist octopus or something down there. Anyway, Jess was kidnapped by extremists. They thought that was the way to twist his dad's arm, I guess, and have him give away a lot of free bananas. Anyway, the military went house to house, shaking people down and shooting the ones who wouldn't talk, until they found Jess. The extremists didn't actually torture him or anything, but the whole experience made him slightly weird."

"I'm not sure I like people who are weird," said Ari, thinking of her aunt Gabrielle. "Normal is what I go for."

Cos put his arm around her. "Hey, nobody is normal, Ari. Welcome to the real world."

"You seem pretty normal." She gazed up at him.

"I fake it," he said promptly. "Inside I'm weird like everybody else. So, how'd you get to know Sybil?"

"We met at lunch on my first day here. I like her."

"Now, Sybil is weird."

"She's a little blunt, maybe, but I don't think she's weird," said Ari.

85

Cos laughed. "Nah, I'm kidding. She's great. I like her, too. Well, here's your chemistry class. Have fun." He stopped short of the classroom, pivoted, and abruptly took off running.

When Ari stepped in the classroom, she realized why Cos had lost no time leaving. His girlfriend, Nadia, was by the window. Her black hair was pulled back from her face and fell in a cascade down her back. A few curly wisps clung to her temples. Her teeth were startlingly white. Ari watched her closely, noting her tentative way of moving, her nervous smile. She was so delicate and shy looking, she was like a forest animal. Obviously, Cos wasn't ready to break up with her yet. Otherwise, why had he been so careful to get away before she spotted him?

Paul noticed Sandy MacAdams peering at his sketchbook. "What's that?" Sandy asked.

Paul glanced down at his charcoal drawing. He added fangs to the face in his drawing of a dark man in a cape. The drawing seemed to flow out of his pencil without his thinking about it. It was as if his brain were a transmitter picking up someone else's nightmare.

"Hey, it's a vampire! Not bad!" exclaimed Sandy. "The cape is really good."

The vampire's cape was like Aunt Gabrielle's, Paul thought. The only difference was a stiff collar that stood up behind the vampire's neck.

"Getting in the Halloween spirit, huh?" asked Sandy.

Paul scratched his head. "Guess it shows what kind of mood I'm in, huh?"

He put down his charcoal pencil and gazed at the girl perched on the broad windowsill. Susannah Rodgers. He had seen her name on her portfolio. He loved her little nose and the way she had drawn a line of charcoal makeup slightly upward at the corners of her eyes. Her blond hair was in an untidy knot on top of her head, and the light from the window picked out its silver threads. A gold bangle glimmered on her wrist as her pencil sped over the paper of her sketchbook.

Glancing down at his own drawing, he added a highlight to the vampire's eyes. He shivered. Ever since he had come to Washington, his mind had been flooded with vampires; he wished he could shake the macabre images, but they were vivid and insistent, like a horror film projected on the inside of his skull.

Sandy was peering at everyone else's sketches. He slid up to the window, craned his neck to look at Susannah's sketchpad, then glanced at Paul. He looked from the sketchpad back to Paul several times, then grinned.

Paul blushed. Was Susannah drawing a cartoon of him or something? He wanted to talk to her, but he'd like to make sure first that she wasn't going to blow him off. She was so serene, dreamy even, that it was hard to figure out how to make the first move.

"Take your sketchbooks home, people," said Mrs. Bromley, glancing at her watch. "The more you practice, the better you'll be. Sharpen your eyes. Look at what really is there, not what you think should be there. Expect the unexpected. The artist has a fresh eye."

Expect the unexpected. Mrs. Bromley's words rang in Paul's ears. He felt as if he expected a vampire to jump out at him. He wondered if finding that dead body had done something awful to his nervous system. Sometimes at night when he was falling asleep, he could feel damp blood on his hands. Horrible. He couldn't speak of it, even to Ari.

Chairs scraped against the linoleum floor as kids rose and gathered up their books. Sandy nudged Paul. "You know what Susannah was drawing? She was drawing you, man. You!"

Paul flushed. He would have noticed that Susannah was drawing him if he hadn't been so distracted, he thought.

Paul lingered outside the classroom, hoping Susannah would come out. Then he could at least smile at her and say hi. But she was showing Mrs. Bromley her portfolio. He gazed at a poster outside the classroom door. On it a ghost with cartoon-wide eyes held an orange pumpkin under one arm. "THE BOO BALL," it said. "ANNUAL COSTUME PARTY. COME AS YOUR FAVORITE MONSTER!"

Paul wondered if Susannah had a date for the Boo Ball. He glanced at his watch. He'd better shove off. His ride would be waiting out in front of the school. He hoisted his book bag. It would be good to see Ari, he thought. Without her at his side, he had been feeling oddly incomplete, as if he were listening expectantly for the next note in a song.

But he wasn't looking forward to going back to Aunt Gabrielle's creepy house. He hated the shadowy halls and that stuffed crow with the strangely glittering eyes that seemed to follow him as he walked to his room. *Home, sweet home,* he thought bitterly. No wonder he had been dreaming about vampires.

Ari stepped outside the Lane Building, relieved that the rain had let up. She was sick of trying to figure out the school's confusing maze of corridors. It would be easier to go around on the outside of the classroom buildings, she decided. That way she wouldn't risk getting lost again. The grass was wet and yellow leaves stuck to the cement walk that skirted the building. She shouldered her book bag and set off walking. The overcast skies were ominous. Someone was whistling tunelessly nearby—a gardener maybe? The sound was more like wheezing than like a melody, she thought irritably. She wished he would shut up. She couldn't see whoever it was. The trees and bushes in back were pretty thick. She could make out the shape of the old chapel beyond the thick stand of maples. *Forget going around the entire building,* she thought nervously. She would go in the first door she saw. She hurried, suddenly breathless. It had been a mistake to come outside. Being alone behind the school made her uneasy, almost frightened.

Suddenly there was a harsh cry and the bushes flailed wildly. Ari shied away from them. She backed off the path and onto the grass, then froze, staring at the moving branches. *A cat,* she told herself, trying to still the loud thumping of her heart. Biting her lip, she slowly inched back onto the sidewalk. A brown glimpse of fur caught her eye, and in spite of herself she stooped to look under the tangle of bushes. The dead animal's white teeth showed in a rigid snarl, and its blank eyes stared at her. The cat had been killed. Jumping up suddenly with a gasp, Ari stumbled up the steps of the back entrance to the building and struggled with the doorknob. After what seemed like an eternity, the heavy door swung open, and she slipped inside the building. She was standing near a dark stairwell, but at least she could hear voices. She rushed toward the sounds, past empty class-rooms until she turned the corner and saw people. Talking to some kids, a teacher in a vest leaned against a door. She was safe. But in an uncomfort-able corner of her mind, the cat's death cry echoed. *Some animal has killed it,* she told herself. *A weasel, maybe. Or another cat.*

Ahead of her, Sybil's red-gold hair shone in the gloom of the hallway.

"Sybil!" cried Ari.

Sybil turned around and grinned at her. "Hi! How's it going?"

"I guess I'm pretty tired." Ari ran her fingers through her hair.

"It'll get better when you learn your way

around," Sybil said. "It takes a while." Suddenly she leaned toward her confidentially. "Stephanie Bowers said she saw Cos hit his fist against a brick wall this morning."

"Cos?" exclaimed Ari. Then she remembered the Band-Aids on Cos's fist.

"It happened right outside the library. Nadia took off for class, and then Stephanie saw him turn around and slam his fist into the wall."

"Maybe he's thinking of breaking up with Nadia," Ari said hopefully.

Sybil glanced at her watch. "Maybe. Anyway, I better run. I don't want the car pool to leave me. Give me a call, okay?" She dashed off.

Ari stared at a nearby poster on the wall. "COME O THE BOO BALL! A COSTUME EXTRAVAGANZA. THRILLS. CHILLS. EXCITEMENT." On the sign, a jack-o'-lantern sneered at a black cat.

Ari shivered and hurried away down the corridor. She opened a door to the outside, but it led only to trees and a playing field. Kids dressed for track were converging there, and for a moment she thought she heard the whistling again. She hurried away down a confusing tangle of hallways and tried another door. To her relief, from this door she could see the circular drive that ran in front of the Schuler Building. Paul was there, standing by the car. Ari ran to him. The Mercedes's engine idled quietly at the curb, but Aunt Gabrielle wasn't inside. It was Carmel who was behind the wheel.

"Are you okay?" asked Paul. He looked into

Ari's eyes and saw the fear there. "What's wrong?" he demanded.

Ari had decided not to tell Paul about the dead cat. She already felt stupid that she had gotten so upset about it.

"I don't know my way around yet—I keep getting lost." She let her voice trail off.

They got in the car and slammed the car doors shut. Ari could feel herself relaxing. Now that she and Paul were together, her spinning wheels had wound down. "How did your day go?" she asked.

"Not bad," Paul said.

Ari leaned forward. "Is Aunt Gabrielle still sleeping?" she asked Carmel in a loud, slow voice.

"*Que?*" replied Carmel.

"Never mind." Ari sighed and fell back against the leather cushions. She did know a few words in Spanish—*feliz navidad, tortilla.* But they wouldn't get her far in an actual conversation.

Autumn leaves made a vivid splash of color against the gray sky. Around the circular drive, kids from St. Anselm's were piling into station wagons piloted by mothers in sweaters and tweed jackets.

The Mercedes pulled out onto busy Massachusetts Avenue. A Metro Bus pulled noisily ahead of them, spouting diesel fumes.

Paul said abruptly, "Do you have Susannah Rogers in any of your classes?"

"Blond hair, perfect nails? I know the one you mean. She's in my chemistry class. The complete bimbo."

Paul flushed. "Jeez, Ari, do you have to be so critical of every girl I even mention?"

"I'm not critical," said Ari promptly. "I'm observant. But don't stop—go on. I'm interested. Exactly what is it you like about her?"

"I'm not sure," Paul said. "But she's definitely got something."

"She's got perfect nails," said Ari.

"I'm not exactly crazy about what's-his-face, either," Paul pointed out.

Ari opened her mouth to protest, but suddenly the silliness of their sniping at each other struck her. She looked at Paul and they both laughed.

"Truce?" said Paul.

"Okay," agreed Ari. "I won't say anything about the bimbo if you won't say anything about Cos."

The bimbo crack was not in keeping with the spirit of a truce, but Paul decided to let it go by.

"Cos walked me to chemistry today," Ari said. Outside, behind a black iron fence, she saw thick trees and gently rolling green lawns. A white cement anchor marked the U.S. Naval Observatory.

"Honestly, that guy is so full of himself," muttered Paul. "He only just met you and already he's closing in for the kill."

"Self-confidence is a good thing," said Ari.

Paul knew he was being petty. He needed to get a life. He gazed out the window. A girl on a bicycle passed them. The traffic moved slowly. "You know, this guy, Sandy, told me that they hardly take any transfers into the fifth form." Paul glanced at his twin. "He wanted to know whether

I was some kind of genius or whether my family had pull."

"I guess you told him you were a genius, right?" said Ari.

"Very funny," said Paul.

"The trouble is," said Ari with a frown, "we don't know anything about what kind of pull Aunt Gabrielle has. We don't know anything at all about her. Nothing."

"It was pretty clear she was chummy with the headmaster," Paul pointed out. "And she did say our dad used to go to St. Anselm's."

"I guess that could be it," said Ari, shivering a little. "Some kind of old boy network."

The Mercedes passed the grand iron gates of the British Embassy where the statue of Churchill stood. "You know, I think this new town is going to work out for us," said Paul, smiling. "All these embassies and flags—it makes you feel like anything could happen, doesn't it? Like the city's probably full of spies and all." He glanced at his twin. "It's kind of exciting."

Ari had felt that way herself earlier in the day. But since she had encountered the dead cat, her mood had changed. "I've had about all the excitement I can take for a while," she said.

But Paul felt his spirits rising. He figured Aunt Gabrielle would let him borrow the car for the dance. Or better yet, maybe she would get him a car of his own. "Well, I think this is really a neat city," he said.

The streets were beginning to take on a recognizable Georgetown look. Brick sidewalks. Restaurants. Antique stores. Ari gazed doubtfully at the expensive shops. "I guess it's okay for people who've got money and influence," she said.

Paul laughed. "We've got both now, don't we?"

CHAPTER
EIGHT

THE NEXT MORNING WHEN PAUL'S ROOM WAS GRAY with the first morning light, he looked down at the foot of his bed and saw that a lady in a long green velvet dress was sitting at his desk, writing with a quill pen. Her eyes looked feverishly hot, and her forehead was unnaturally high, as if she had plucked out the first inch or so of her hair. Her odd headdress, a soft white cloth draped over a tall twin-peaked frame, moved softly as she wrote. Her skin was the same dead-white color as her headdress. Long blond hair streamed thinly to her waist.

The wardrobe opened and a muscular man stepped out, lifting his blue cape to keep the velvet from catching on the wood. The man wore a plate-sized fur hat, and Paul could see that either he had shaved his head or he was bald—the bulging bones of his skull showed under his shiny white skin. His cape's material puckered where it had been heavily embroidered with gold asterisks. A large hound leapt out of the wardrobe after him. The hound's heavy jowls and ears swung slightly as it lurched toward Paul's bed. Its flesh hung loosely on its bones, and he could see that its eyes were ruby-colored and bloodshot. It snuffled at him, and he could feel its breath on his toes.

The caped man pulled open Paul's dresser drawer and tossed Paul's underwear to the floor. The man and woman looked at him, as if daring him to protest, and grinned suddenly. He saw then that they had fangs. The woman's white, glistening fangs pressed against her thin lower lip, denting the flesh. Paul opened his mouth to scream, but no sound came out. He heard Ari's alarm go off, and as if they had been frightened by the sound, the figures grew thin and vanished.

Paul sat up in bed abruptly, his heart pounding in fear. It was a minute or two before he could force himself to get out of bed. When he did, the cold floor felt reassuringly real under his bare feet. He padded over to the dresser, bent down to pick up a pair of underwear, and tossed it back in the drawer. He must have dropped it last night without noticing, he told himself.

Paul wasn't sure what made him go over to his desk. The vampire's quill pen had disappeared, but something had been written on the paper blotter in odd block letters. *"Je m'appelle Blanche."*

He could feel a cold sweat breaking on his forehead. "My name is Blanche." He had enough

French to decipher the words, but the problem was those words shouldn't even have been there—the vampire lady had existed only in his imagination!

That line could have been there for months or even years, he told himself wildly. Some maid had been practicing her French lesson. Or a guest of Aunt Gabrielle's could have written it. There could be a hundred logical explanations. He tore the top sheet of paper off the blotter, crumpled it, and tossed it into the trash.

Days passed before Paul could think of his strange vision without shaking. He was tempted to tell Ari about it, but he couldn't bring himself to. He was weighed down by the memory of it and by the sensation of blood on his hands, which made it difficult for him to focus and concentrate at school. He kept seeing Ari in the hall with Cos, laughing, flirting, looking happy. He hated the idea that Ari might be mentally comparing him to Cos, who seemed to walk around in his own private beam of sunshine. Worse yet, Paul thought, if he told Ari about his visions, she might even confide in Cos about her troubled brother. The thought made him shudder.

Paul worked hard on his French lessons without quite acknowledging to himself that he'd like to have another go at deciphering the strange diary in Aunt Gabrielle's library. Things could have been worse, he told himself. He was getting to know some people at school—Sandy, Susannah.

He was pretty sure that Susannah liked him. He was finding his way around okay.

The following week when Paul's English class went to the library to do research, he found a dark corner and combed the card catalogue for everything it had to offer on visions and hallucinations. He came up with a stack of books and periodicals and began plowing through them. As he read, his mind cleared.

He regretted that he had pitched the crumpled paper in the trash. Carmel had presumably carried it out to the curb in the normal course of things, and it was buried in a landfill somewhere. He was feeling calmer now about his strange vision. But nagging at the back of his mind was the thought that he could have compared the writing with the writing in the vampire diary in Aunt Gabrielle's library.

The phone beside Paul's bed rang suddenly before dinner one night and he grabbed it.

"It's probably for me," said Ari. "Sybil wanted me to call her."

"Hullo?" said Paul. "Yeah, just a minute." He handed Ari the receiver. "It's not Sybil," he said flatly.

"I'll take it in my room," Ari said. She stepped into her bedroom and picked up the phone.

"Ari? It's Cos."

Ari waited until she heard Paul hang up before she spoke. "Just a minute, Cos. Let me close the door."

She used to let me listen to everything she said to boys, Paul thought, watching the connecting door swing closed. He heard the click as it snapped shut. It sounded in his heart like a bell of loneliness. He discovered that he hated Cos.

Ari snuggled her bare feet under the bed-spread. The prisms on her bedside lamp twinkled gaily.

"How did you get my number?" she asked Cos.

"It's on the computer," he said. "Piece of cake."

"Good grief! What else about me is on the computer?"

"I know your dearest, darkest secrets," Cos intoned. "I know your deepest secret fears."

Ari gulped, thinking suddenly of the fanged creatures of her dreams and the odd whiteness of Aunt Gabrielle's taut skin. "All of that is on the computer?" she said faintly.

"Nah. I'm just kidding. Have you read 'The Tell-Tale Heart' yet?"

"Not yet," said Ari, eyeing her book bag uneasily. Somehow, now that she was living in Aunt Gabrielle's dark house, the last thing in the world she wanted to do was to read a scary Poe story. She was afraid she would jump clear out of her skin. "What about you?" she asked. "Have you read it?"

"Yup, but don't tell anybody. I make out like I never study, because then when I get an *A* people think I'm smart. But why are we talking about schoolwork? Do you know what you were wearing

the first time I saw you?" Cos asked. He recited
every detail of Ari's outfit from her ribbed navy
tights to the black pearl buttons on her shirt.

"What a memory you've got!" She laughed.

"I'm obsessed."

Ari didn't reply. The line was silent for a few
seconds.

"What's wrong?" Cos asked at last.

"I'm thinking about Nadia," said Ari. "Aren't
you supposed to be going with her?"

Another long silence fell on the telephone line.

"I've got to let Nadia down easy," Cos said at
last.

Ari's heart squeezed in disappointment. Cos
should have broken up with Nadia by now. He had
been walking with Ari to class for weeks, but she
noticed that he always took care not to run into
Nadia. He must have been more deeply entangled
than she had guessed.

"You know what?" asked Cos, abruptly changing the subject. "My dad is already riding me
about colleges. Is that grim or what? Sometimes I
feel like throwing myself under a bus. Do you ever
get depressed, Ari? I mean black, black depressed."

"Yes," Ari said softly. "My mother was killed in
a car wreck. That's why we came here to live with
our aunt."

"I'm sorry," said Cos after a few seconds. "I
didn't know."

"Yes," said Ari in a small voice. "I wish she was
alive so much I can't stand it. It's so awful it seems

101

like it can't have happened to us. But it did."

"What about your dad? Where's he?"

"He's out of the picture," said Ari. "Paul and I don't even remember what he looks like."

"That's tough," said Cos.

"Well, Paul and I have got each other," said Ari, a lump growing in her throat. "And Aunt Gabrielle, of course," she added as an afterthought.

"I wish I could put my arms around you and kiss those tears away," said Cos.

Ari smiled sadly to herself. Cos didn't understand that some tears are too deep to kiss away.

"You still there?" asked Cos anxiously.

"Still here," she said.

"Jeez, that's my mom's calling me. Look, I better go. See you tomorrow."

Ari sat on her bed a minute, thinking. If she wanted Cos, it was going to take careful handling. She didn't want to scare him off by pushing him to break up with Nadia, but on the other hand, she had to make it clear at some point that Nadia was going to have to go. This was the modern world—boys didn't have harems.

Ari got up and knocked on the connecting door. Paul opened the door. "So, how's what's-his-face?" he asked sourly.

"I think he's in deep with that girlfriend of his," said Ari. "I don't know what's going to happen."

"Is he?" asked Paul, looking more cheerful. "Gee, that's too bad."

The gong sounded downstairs.

The twins filed down the sweeping staircase and

went into the dining room. Carmel brought steaming casseroles to the dining room table. Her face was pink from the heat of the kitchen. The twins sat down, uncertain whether to begin eating or not. Then Aunt Gabrielle appeared at the door. She was wearing a luminescent pink jacket, shiny tights, and a baseball cap that cast a mask of shadow over her eyes so that her strange half-smile looked even more enigmatic. "I've already had a bite to eat," she said. "You two go ahead. I'm off on my evening jog."

"Are you sure it's a good idea for you to keep jogging by yourself after dark?" Paul asked.

"I'm perfectly safe!" Aunt Gabrielle ran a few steps in place. "I have my pepper spray." She whipped a small metal canister out of her jacket pocket. "And I'm an a aikido master," she added. "So don't worry." She gave a low throaty chuckle. "Of course, if I catch either of you going out alone after dark you'll be grounded for the rest of your life. Ta, kids!" She jogged down the long hallway and disappeared out the front door.

"It's always the same," said Paul. "Have you noticed that? It's do as I say, not as I do. Remember how Mom used to sneak smokes in the backyard? And then she told us she'd kill us if she ever caught us with a cigarette."

"That was for our own good," said Ari. She wiped her eyes with the corner of a napkin.

"Ari, don't start," said Paul. "You'll have us both bawling."

Ari blew her nose. "I'm fine. Perfectly fine. Pass me the salad."

Paul passed her the salad, then dipped himself a serving of paella. "Did you hear Aunt Gabrielle say she had 'a bite to eat'? She probably ate a carrot. It's no wonder she's so skinny. I'm not sure I've ever actually seen her eat anything."

Ari thought about how diet checklists, scales, and pamphlets entitled "How to Lose Ten Pounds in Two Weeks" had littered their kitchen at home. Their mother had been trying to lose twenty pounds for what seemed like forever. But her lap was perfect for sitting on, and her bosom was perfect for snuggling. Ari couldn't imagine snuggling up against Aunt Gabrielle.

When Aunt Gabrielle got back, Paul was forced to admit that the exercise had done her good. Her corpse-pale skin always had a warm glow when she came back. But he still thought it was funny the way she went jogging at night. It was a part of her inflexible routine, like the way she slept nearly every day until sunset and stuck to it even on beautiful days. He kept having the feeling that something strange was behind it, the way the strange hidden skull was behind the simperingly pretty face on the mantel.

"You look great," said Ari. "Maybe I should take up jogging myself."

Aunt Gabrielle pinched Ari's cheek playfully, and Ari winced at her touch. "You don't need to jog, sweetest," she said. "You're perfect the way you are." She stripped off her cap and inhaled deeply.

"Aunt Gabrielle," said Ari, "we're going to have a party at school for Halloween. Do you think Paul and I could get some costumes?"

Aunt Gabrielle brightened. "What fun! I know the perfect little man—a real artist. He has a delightful shop down by the canal. You must go by and see him." She cocked her head at them. "Another thing. I almost forgot. Paul, Carmel's not going to come in early tomorrow, so if you'd like, you and Ari can drive the Mercedes to school. Do you think you can find your way?"

"Sure!" Paul said.

"This weekend, we'll have to get a car for you children to use. But I won't need mine tomorrow except to drive to my classes in the evening, so you might as well use it."

Imagining himself driving up to school in the black Mercedes, Paul felt his spirits lifting. Good food, the chance to drive a great car, and on top of that a pretty girl at school who seemed to like him—he could be in worse shape. But suddenly his gaze met Aunt Gabrielle's, and he was struck by the oddness of her lavender eyes. Was it only the way the light hit them, or had they actually begun to glow? Paul shivered and hastily looked away.

CHAPTER
NINE

THE FOLLOWING MORNING, HOWEVER, AS PAUL PULLED up to the gatehouse at the main entrance to the school, he was not quite so sure his luck was improving. It turned out that only seniors could park on campus. It took him a long time to find a parking place, and it was blocks away from the school. The twins hoisted their heavy book bags and trudged uphill to St. Anselm's. "I'm beginning to see why practically everyone belongs to car pools," said Paul.

"I can't imagine Aunt Gabrielle driving a car pool," said Ari.

"Then I guess we look for a parking place every morning and walk a mile uphill," said Paul.

Ahead of them stood the chapel and the thick trees that clustered in front of it. "Let's don't go across the back of the school," Ari said suddenly. "Let's go around the front way."

"Are you nuts?" Paul stared at her. "It's twice as far to go around that way."

Ari didn't argue with him. She set her jaw and struck off along the drive. Paul swore a second or two, then ran and caught up with her. "What's going on with you?" he asked.

"I saw a dead cat back there once," she said.

Paul laughed. "Good grief, Ari. Cats die all the time. Everything dies sooner or later. A dead cat's no big deal."

"Shut up!" she cried. "Stop it!"

"I'm sorry," Paul said, watching her face. "We'll go the long way around. No problem."

Someone had piled stacks of hay and pumpkins in front of the Schuler Building. A sign advertising the Boo Ball was propped up on the hay, wedged between two pumpkins.

"Let's coordinate our costumes for the Boo Ball, Paul," said Ari suddenly. "Remember when we were six, and we were Raggedy Ann and Andy?"

"Actually," Paul said. "I was thinking about asking Susannah to go with me."

"Oh. No problem," Ari said, looking let down. "I can probably go with Sibyl."

Later that morning, Ari was mounting the dark staircase in the Lane Building when she met Nadia coming down. Nadia backed against the wall and crossed herself, muttering something under her breath.

"Hello?" Ari said.

But Nadia only opened her mouth wide, like a

gaping goldfish, then closed it. Her teeth and the whites of her eyes were startlingly bright in the gloom of the staircase. She turned around suddenly and ran back up the stairs.

"Well," muttered Ari. "Good morning to you, too."

Ari felt strange, as if Nadia had somehow picked up on something that was wrong with her. She knew Nadia's snub was getting to her only because her nerves were rubbed raw, but she couldn't help herself. She stepped into the girls' room and checked herself in the mirror. A thin light filtered in the high frosted windows of the room, giving her a ghostly look. What was she expecting? she wondered. To find out that she had sprouted fangs?

At lunch Ari told Sybil about her strange encounter with Nadia on the dark staircase.

"She actually crossed herself?" asked Sybil incredulously. "Jeez, do you think she knows about you and Cos?"

Ari poured herself some apple juice. "How can she? Nothing much has happened between me and Cos. Not yet, anyway."

"Maybe she foresees that he's going to dump her for you," said Sybil. "Somebody told me she's got second sight. She's from Romania, you know."

"So you told me," said Ari irritably. "Romania's all I seem to hear about lately."

Sybil gave a sinister chuckle. "Dracula! Vampires! Maybe Nadia's related to Count Dracula or something." She grabbed a roll from the bread basket. "I think her family used to have a castle in the mountains over there or something."

Ari didn't respond. Sybil's remarks about vampires had given her an uneasy feeling in her stomach.

"Very Halloweenish, isn't it?" said Sybil. "Hey, you want to go to the Boo Ball?"

"I'd love to," said Ari, taking a deep breath. "This isn't one of those things where everybody's got a date, is it?"

"Oh, it won't be like that at all," Sybil assured her. "Half the fun is not knowing who anybody is. I mean, everybody's kissing everybody else and making out in the bushes. But since we're all in masks, it's all very confusing, and nobody gets committed to anything. It's great! And the costumes are *spectacular*. You've got to be careful what you decide to be, though. Last year somebody went as a pack of cards and they couldn't sit down all night."

"So everybody wears masks?" asked Ari.

"Yep. Of course, people still sort of guess who's who," admitted Sybil. "But really, the costumes are incredible. People go all out. I don't know where people get some of these things. Last year, Jessie came in a full suit of armor!"

"How did you know it was him?" asked Ari.

Sybil blushed. "Well, at one point, he, uh, did lift up his visor."

Ari wouldn't kiss Jessie if he were the last boy on earth. She'd always be wondering if he had a gun stashed on him somewhere.

"If Cos is going to dump Nadia," Ari said

under her breath, "I wish he'd go ahead and do it."

"Boys!" sighed Sybil.

That night at dinner, the candelabra on the buffet burned with steady electric light. Ari thought it was odd that Aunt Gabrielle used fake candles wired for little electric bulbs. It seemed so tacky, and everything else about the house looked expensive and elegant.

"Our family has always been liberal," said Aunt Gabrielle, pushing a tidbit of food around on her china plate. "I hate to say it, but some people of our sort," she made a face, "are almost fascist. Even positively predatory. When it comes right down to it, they want to decide things *for* other people. Our family has never believed in that."

Ari was a little unclear what Aunt Gabrielle was talking about. How could anyone decide something for someone else? It wasn't as if the U.S. was a dictatorship.

"What about our father?" said Paul. "Is he a liberal, too?"

Aunt Gabrielle winced. "Well, dear, Richard is so unconventional, it's hard to fit him into any pattern."

A drunk, Paul translated mentally. He had begun to suspect that his father might have a drinking problem. Aunt Gabrielle's evasiveness whenever his father's name came up seemed to confirm his suspicions.

"Aunt Gabrielle, I've been thinking I'd like to get my teeth capped," Ari said, eager to avoid the subject of their father.

110

"Your teeth?" Aunt Gabrielle looked surprised.

Ari bared her teeth. "The canines," she said. "Most people, in case you haven't noticed, have smooth ones. Mine are pointy."

Aunt Gabrielle folded her napkin. "Oh, really, Ari. I can't approve of filing down perfectly good teeth. At least not while you're so young. Who knows but in a few years you might regret it? Anyone for dessert? Carmel has fixed some lovely flan."

"I could eat dessert," said Paul.

Aunt Gabrielle smiled at him. Ari wondered if Aunt Gabrielle herself had pointed incisors and that was why she had that funny Mona Lisa smile that showed no teeth. Aunt Gabrielle got up to go into the kitchen to tell Carmel they were ready for dessert. As she pushed the door open, Spanish floated out of the kitchen.

"I bet she's had six kinds of plastic surgery," said Ari heatedly. "Face lifting, tummy tucking, liposuction, the works. I don't see what's the big deal about getting my teeth capped."

"What's wrong with your teeth?" asked Paul. "They're just like mine."

Ari cast a nervous glance toward the kitchen. "Paul, do you ever have . . . funny dreams?"

"Sometimes," he admitted cautiously.

Aunt Gabrielle returned smiling. "What a lovely, lovely flan Carmel has made for you two!" she said. "It's such a joy to see healthy young appetites."

"Aren't you going to have any, Aunt Gabrielle?"

Paul shot a glance at Ari. The way Aunt Gabrielle picked at her food was a joke between them.

"None for me tonight," said Aunt Gabrielle. "I'm saving my calories for tomorrow. The caterers and the florist's men will probably be here by the time you get in from school." She waved her thin hand, and her diamond rings glittered. "I'm having a little soiree."

Catered dinner parties with fresh flowers did not come cheap, Ari knew. "Aunt Gabrielle," she asked suddenly, "where does our family's money come from?"

Aunt Gabrielle looked at her blankly.

"You know," Ari continued stubbornly, "like at school Jessie's dad is a bigwig in the banana industry, and Nadia's family has a castle in Transylvania somewhere. I just wondered where our family's money comes from."

"Wise investments, my dear," said Aunt Gabrielle firmly. She glanced toward the kitchen. "Oh, look! Here comes Carmel with that lovely flan!"

112

CHAPTER
TEN

AFTER DINNER, ARI TOOK OFF FOR SYBIL'S. PAUL WAS sure she and Sybil planned to hash out the entire business with Cos word by word. It used to be that Ari talked to *him* about the boys who had crushes on her. But Cos was different. That was becoming pretty obvious.

But if she can have her secrets, so can I, thought Paul with satisfaction. He had his own plan for tonight, and it was something he had no intention of sharing with Ari. When Aunt Gabrielle went upstairs to put on her jogging clothes, Paul went upstairs directly after her and changed into black jeans, a turtleneck, and a black leather jacket. He peeked out his bedroom door and saw Aunt Gabrielle, all in pink, headed for the stairs. He waited until she had had time to get outside; then he pulled a dark knit cap low over his ears and took off after her. He reached the front door breathless with anxiety. But when he stepped outside, she was still in sight, hesitating at the corner traffic light.

He galloped down the steps and took off after her. He was careful to jog close to the buildings so he could take cover in a doorway or an alley if she looked back. But she didn't look back. His sneakers thudded softly on the brick sidewalks as he jogged at a safe distance behind her. He noticed that passersby avoided his path. His black clothes and dark knit cap made him look like a mugger.

The sidewalk grew crowded. People were getting out of their cars and going into restaurants. He passed a bunch of college students starting the weekend early, singing as they staggered along the sidewalk. Still it was easy to keep Aunt Gabrielle in sight. Her fluorescent jogging gear was like a pink beacon ahead of him.

Paul began to lose track of where he was as she zigzagged through the streets, but he had the vague sense they were heading down toward the desolate canal and harbor area. He was not enthusiastic about jogging in that neighborhood at night. It was deserted, Paul thought uneasily. But he was not about to give up at this point. He kept after her doggedly, then all of a sudden he lost her. He stopped dead in his tracks for an instant in sheer surprise. She had seemed to disappear into thin air. He took off running and skidded to a stop at the lamppost where he had lost sight of her.

Patrons were spilling out of a neon-lit bar onto the sidewalk in front of Paul. Just beyond the bar was a narrow alley. Paul peered down it, noting the glitter of broken glass on the ground. *She couldn't have gone down the alley,* he decided. There was barely space to squeeze through, much less to run. He glanced dubiously into the teeming bar. Perhaps she had nipped into the bar for a drink, he thought. He could have used a glass of water himself, and he had done long-distance running for years and was presumably in a lot better shape than Aunt Gabrielle was. He hesitated for a moment. He was five years underage, but the bar did not look to him like the sort of place that would check I.D.'s. He squeezed through the crowd at the door and found himself suddenly engulfed in a bear hug.

"Rich!" cried a deep voice. "Where've you been?" Paul struggled free of the man's grasp and stared at the bearded face of a huge fellow draped in gold chains. "Excuse me!" the man said, startled. "I thought you were a friend of mine."

Paul felt trapped by the press of the crowd in the dark bar. Most of them were wearing thin, shiny clothes, and he kept getting pressed uncomfortably against bracelets and chains. Feeling hot and conspicuous, he tore off his knit cap. At once a woman sitting on a bar stool ruffled his hair.

"Where've you been, lover?" she asked. She had a foreign accent, maybe Dutch. Surprised, Paul wheeled around to face her and was embarrassed to see that her thin white blouse, unbuttoned to the waist, hardly covered her at all. He could see the ribs in her bony chest under the thin material.

She was very thin and pale, with straight blond hair that fell in bangs to her nose and splayed carelessly over her shoulders. "Why, you're a kid!" she said, laughing. She covered her mouth suddenly with a bony, jewel-encrusted hand. She reached out and touched his forehead with one finger, laughed again, and Paul saw a flash of fangs. He blinked and they were gone.

An optical illusion, he told himself, badly shaken.

He looked around, but did not see Aunt Gabrielle. It had been stupid to come in here, he thought. This wasn't her sort of place. He pushed his way to the less crowded back of the bar. There a rotating light made him dizzy. Suddenly he was jerked off his feet by powerful hands. "Caught up with you at last, Richard," a man growled. A sudden blow from nowhere sent a blinding pain through Paul's jaw. The rotating light doubled suddenly. Paul shook his head to clear it, and his knees buckled with the pain. He was dimly aware of the feel of a door against his back and of screams of protest.

"That's not Richard," cried a high voice in a Dutch accent. "You're beating up on some kid!"

Paul felt a doorknob under his fingers, twisted it, and fell outside into the darkness of a back alley. He lay propped on his elbows a moment, feeling sick. A shaft of light came out through the cracked door, and he could see that he was sitting on a handful of discarded newspaper. A rotting cabbage lay nearby. At least, he thought, he was

116

not still seeing double. Whoever hit him hadn't come after him. His head felt terrible and he wasn't sure he should stand up.

He rolled over and found himself nose to nose with a news story. "BODY FISHED OUT OF CANAL." The paper recounted that the murder victim had bled to death when his carotid artery had been severed by a jagged instrument. "The serial killer!" Paul said aloud, astonished.

He thought about taking the newspaper back to show Ari, but it was wet and smelled of cabbages. It was going to be hard enough, he thought, fingering his jaw, to get himself home.

As he limped back to N Street, moving slowly and carefully, Paul wondered if Aunt Gabrielle had somehow spotted him and had deliberately tried to lose him. That would explain her zigzag path through the streets. Was he wrong to think that it was odd for a woman to jog through dark city streets every night? Still, no matter how he tried to talk himself out of it, there *was* something peculiar about Aunt Gabrielle's appetite for nighttime jogging.

When Paul got back to the house, instead of going in the front door, he opened the garden gate and slipped around the back way. He went in the back door through the dining room, then after a moment's hesitation, began mounting the servants' dark staircase. Aunt Gabrielle might have made it back to the house before him, and he didn't want her to realize that he had been tailing her. He wanted to get out of his black clothes before she saw him.

The dark and narrow staircase made him nervous, but at least no stairs creaked under his feet. The trouble was, he wasn't sure where it ended up on the second floor. Remembering Ari's theory about their aunt's secret life, he was worried that it would end smack in Aunt Gabrielle's bedroom.

When he reached the second landing, he was confronted with two doors at right angles to each other. He stood there for a moment, wondering which one he should try. The landing was dark, and he could see only faint cracks of light under the doors. He heard the muffled sound of running water and a swishing sound, and he smiled. Aunt Gabrielle must be washing out her delicate things in her bathroom. He had heard those sounds often enough back in New Orleans when Ari was tying up the only bathroom in the house washing cotton sweaters. Relieved, he chose the other door and found that it opened onto the hallway. He was only a few steps from his own bedroom. Breathlessly, he slipped into his room and began stripping off his clothes.

"Paul?" Ari's voice sounded frightened.

He pulled on his blue jeans and peeked in her room. "Hi." He smiled, trying to clear his head. "What's up?"

"Where have you been?" she cried. "When I got back from Sybil's you weren't anywhere around. I was worried sick."

"You didn't tell Aunt Gabrielle, did you?" he asked quickly.

"Of course not," she said. "But where were you,

Paul? You look awful! Your hair is all messed up!"

Paul ran his fingers through it and watched a bit of cabbage leaf fall to the floor.

Ari touched his face and he winced. "What happened to you?" she asked incredulously.

"You think I'm going to get a bruise?" he asked. "Somebody hit me. I was trailing Aunt Gabrielle, but I lost her. I went into this bar, thinking she had gone in there, and the next thing I knew some guy was belting me." He gave a wry smile, then thought better of it. His head was still ringing with pain. "He mistook me for some guy named Richard."

Paul had intended to tell Ari then about the news item that reminded him of the serial killer, but what she said next knocked that thought clear out of his mind.

"You must have been right about us looking like our dad, Paul," said Ari, wide-eyed. "I'll bet that's who he got you mixed up with."

Paul blinked. He was used to hearing his father's name pronounced in the French way, "Ree-shar." That was the way Aunt Gabrielle said it. He felt so stupid. He hadn't even made the connection. The woman at the bar had seemed to be on intimate terms with this "Richard," yet she had mixed the two of them up. And so had the guy who hugged him at the door. "Rich," he had called him. "I thought you were a friend of mine," he had said. Then there was the guy who belted Paul.

"Maybe I found out something tonight after all," he said slowly.

119

CHAPTER
ELEVEN

WHEN ARI'S GAZE DARTED FEARFULLY AROUND THE dimly lit room the next morning, she saw no sign of the fanged creatures. She sighed in relief. But then the curtains stirred, and from behind them stepped a tabby-striped cat that seemed to grow larger as it approached, fluffing its fur. It hissed at her and drew up its snout to show two pointed teeth and a rough pink tongue. Its glowing green eyes rolled back in fear. Suddenly its back arched. It let out a human scream and leapt up onto Ari's knees. Its hair stood on end as if it had been electrified. Ari felt its claws and squirmed frantically to get away. With a thump she fell out of bed, entangled in her sheets.

The door flew open and Paul ran in. "Ari?" he cried. "Are you all right?"

Ari scrambled up. Her heart pounding, she patted the sheets and bedspread. The cat had vanished.

"I guess I had a nightmare," she said. "It was horrible." She got down on her knees and peered under her bed, holding her breath and half-expecting to see green cat's eyes glowing at her from the darkness. "I don't know what I'm looking for," she said.

"I heard this awful sound—" Paul began.

"You heard something?" asked Ari, looking up at him quickly.

"I heard a loud thump. It must have been you falling out of bed."

Ari stood up. She didn't know whether she was relieved or not that Paul hadn't heard the cat's strangely human scream.

"Hey," said Paul. "Come here." He held out his arms.

Ari leaned her head against his shoulder and let him stroke her hair. "You know how you can take an aspirin for a headache?" she whimpered. "I wish there were something you could take for . . . nightmares."

"Yeah. Me, too," he said softly.

When she looked up at him, she could see that a bruise was swelling on his jaw, making the skin there puffy and shiny.

"Does it hurt?" she asked.

"What? Oh, this." He touched his jaw gingerly. "Yeah. Especially when I think about it. That guy was pretty mad at Richard, whoever he was. Wouldn't you figure that meant he'd seen him pretty recently?"

Ari thought about it. "I don't know. Sometimes people hold grudges for a long time."

"Well, I think it means our dad is in town," said Paul.

"Why hasn't he come by to see us, then?" asked Ari.

Paul didn't respond.

"It doesn't matter to us whether he's here or in Timbuktu if he doesn't care about seeing us," Ari said quickly. "You know it's the truth, Paul."

Paul turned away. "I'd just like to see him and . . . tell him what I think of him," he said thickly.

In one of those flashes in which the twins read each other's mind, Ari heard in Paul the anger booming, and over it the thin violin strain of longing and hope. She wished she could tell their father what she thought of him, too. She herself had given up on him long ago, but she hated him for what he was doing to Paul.

Cos was waiting for Ari when she got to school. He put both hands on her shoulders and backed her up against a wall. "I broke up with Nadia," he said. "Will you go to the Boo Ball with me?"

"I'm going with Sybil," said Ari.

"She can come with us," said Cos unhesitatingly.

"I didn't think the Boo Ball was one of those things where people take dates," Ari said.

He looked stricken. "Are you telling me you don't want to go with me?"

"Sure, I'll go with you," she said. "But we have to take Sybil."

"I like Sybil. So that's fine. Besides, it's not the

kind of thing where everybody pairs off."

She hesitated and glanced up at him. "So why are you asking me, then?"

His eyes looked haunted. "I think I need to sort of solidify this breakup with Nadia," he said. "Like, you and me have to go somewhere public together so she gets the message that we really are finished."

"But we'll be in disguise. She won't even know we're together."

"Everybody will guess who we are." He put his hand under her chin, leaned close, and kissed her on the lips.

"More solidifying of the breakup with Nadia?" she asked sweetly.

"Is that a nice thing to say when a guy kisses you?" he asked.

Ari smiled warmly at him, and reassured, he drew her close to him until his breath tickled her ear. Then he pressed his lips against hers again in a long kiss that made her breath come fast. Her toes were warm and that morning's nightmare suddenly seemed far away. But Ari forced herself to pull away from him just the same. Cos had only recently broken up with Nadia. It didn't seem tactful for them to make out in public so soon. "What are you going as?" she asked.

"What?"

"The Boo Ball? What are you wearing?"

"I'm not telling." He grinned. "It ought to be a surprise."

"How will I know it's you? I could end up

going to the party with the wrong guy."

"Come on! Do you really think you could get me mixed up with somebody else?"

She shook her head, smiling. She knew she couldn't get him mixed up with anyone else in the world.

Ari couldn't wait to tell Sybil that Cos had finally broke up with Nadia. But at lunchtime when she slid her chair in next to Sybil's, it turned out Sybil already knew. "Nadia's suicidal," Sybil reported.

"How do you know, Sybil?" asked Ari, irritated.

"Oh, the usual way," said Sybil. "Tom-tom, grapevine, AT&T. Poor Nadia's prostrate—she's not even at school today. But if I were you, I'd be worried about Amanda." Sybil grinned. "Her position is that Cos is a criminal because he made Nadia cry. Melanie Russell saw Amanda in the hall, and she was muttering darkly about revenge."

"Well, I don't care what Amanda thinks." Ari stabbed her breaded veal cutlet. "But honestly! You'd think Nadia would have some pride. How can she let everybody know she's falling apart?"

"Cos is the only guy she ever loved. That's what she's telling everyone. She wants him back. Of course, Amanda keeps trying to persuade her that she doesn't want him back." Sybil shrugged. "She favors getting even."

Ari frowned. "Why doesn't Amanda mind her own business?"

"I don't know. But I'd watch my step, if I were you. Particularly at the Boo Ball. Amanda's a pretty average size and shape. She could be disguised as anybody!"

"The Boo Ball!" Ari exclaimed. "Oh, I forgot. Cos asked me to go with him."

"Oh," said Sybil.

"We can all three go together. It's all set," said Ari.

"Great," said Sybil sarcastically. "You and Cos making out in the front seat while I do my homework by flashlight in the back seat."

"We won't do that!"

"I think I know Cos a little better than you do," said Sybil. She cleared her throat. "Is Paul going?"

"Not with us," said Ari. "He can't stand Cos."

"Well—" began Sybil.

"He's got his eye on somebody to ask," said Ari quickly. "He told me so."

Sybil's face fell. "Not a red-haired girl with an interesting personality, huh?"

"A glamorous, empty-headed blonde with perfect fingernails," said Ari.

Sybil rested her chin on her fist. "Maybe I'll ask Nadia if she'd like to go with me. We could go as the public waterworks."

"Come with Cos and me," Ari urged her. "I promise it'll be fun."

When the twins got home that afternoon, a florist's black van was parked in front of the house. "Friendship Florist" was emblazoned in pink on its side. A man had the front door propped open with one foot while he slipped in the house with a vast arrangement of lilies and chrysanthemums. The twins followed him inside. The house dripped with flowers—the mantels and tables, even the table in the entry hall, were all banked with roses and lilies, and the faintly rotting scent of hothouse lilies filled the hallway.

A slender young man waltzed toward them and began talking very fast in Spanish to Carmel. Ari shrugged at Paul as streams of Spanish flowed over her head. To her relief, the young man switched to English. "You must be the niece and nephew," he said cheerfully. "I'm Ricardo, the caterer's man. You can go on with whatever it is that you do. We'll take care of absolutely everything." He smiled. "We are having a little problem obtaining fresh lobsters, but not to worry. We will cope. I have done Professor Montclair's parties before, and I absolutely understand that she must not be disturbed."

Ari exchanged a glance with Paul. Even the caterers knew about Aunt Gabrielle's beauty sleep, she thought. Didn't anybody else think it was weird for a grown woman to sleep all day and stay up all night?

As darkness fell, the twins heard car doors slamming, and the shrill hum of many voices downstairs. They went down at last to get something to eat and were astonished by the sheer crush of people. All the closely pressed bodies raised the temperature of the house by ten degrees. The white shirtfronts of the men and the

126

white, powdered shoulders of the women gleamed in the dim light, and there was a discreet glitter of jewels. Paul finally managed to make his way to the buffet spread in the dining room. Cold lobster and crab claws dredged through a mayonnaise dip wasn't his usual supper, but he figured he would manage. He piled his plate high with tiny, fancy meringues and cheese pastries. He didn't see anything to drink but champagne, so he poured himself a glass. After he drank it, he still felt thirsty, so he poured himself another.

"You must be Gabrielle's nephew," said a red-faced man with a walrus moustache. He extended his hand. "Joe Donovan. Hear you're at St. Anselm's. My boy was there, too. He's at Dartmouth now. So have you given any thought to college yet?"

"Not yet," mumbled Paul. He polished off the crab legs, then grabbed a hard roll from the basket while Mr. Donovan talked about Dartmouth's football team. "Excuse me," Paul said after a few minutes. "I need to find my sister." It was slow going through the crowd. Several white-shirted men waylaid him and asked him how he liked Washington so far and whether he had given any thought to college. Paul did his best to be polite, but he began to wonder if Aunt Gabrielle had ordered these guys by the dozen from Central Casting. As far as he could make out, they generally worked for government agencies that were identified only by their initials.

He finally found Ari in the living room. She was standing by the fireplace, talking to two women who looked like a matched pair. Both were equally thin and both were in black. One wore a short slip dress and had her hair slicked back so tightly it looked enameled to her skull. Her eyebrows were plucked to a thin line over deeply shadowed gray eyes. The other wore full black crepe pants and had a thick fringe of blunt-cut hair that fell over one eye. It must have been a problem when she was driving, Paul thought, if she wanted to see who was coming at her from the left. Ari introduced the women as Gwendolyn and Tippi.

"About fifty people have asked me about my college plans," said Paul. "Is this what I've got to look forward to for the next two years?"

Gwendolyn tossed her hair out of her eye and gave him a warm smile. "I'm afraid so, kiddo. They can't think of anything else to say to someone your age. Haven't you ever wondered why people are called 'stuffed shirts'?"

"Not after tonight," said Paul.

Tippi giggled.

"Gwendolyn's a graphic artist," explained Ari. "Don't you think that's cool?"

Gwendolyn made a face. "It has its good points and bad points, like any job. Maybe you've seen our shop down by the harbor? It's the one with the dead body."

Paul stared at her.

"Not a real body," Tippi said with a smile. "It's for Halloween. Gwendolyn made a wild window display with a mannequin. It's terrifically realistic,

128

with blood and guts spilling out all over the place. Very gruesome."

"I worked from some illustrations in *Gray's Anatomy*. I was pretty satisfied with it," admitted Gwendolyn. "It took me all night, but I think people expect something spectacular from a graphic arts firm, don't you?"

Aunt Gabrielle appeared suddenly and threw her arms around Paul and Tippi. "Tippi and Gwendolyn! Two of my favorite people! I'm so glad you've met, darlings. Tippi and Gwen and I are the oldest of friends." Aunt Gabrielle smiled. "And both of them are so talented! Tippi doesn't like to say it, but she's a gifted dancer."

"You know I don't perform these days, Gabri," said Tippi. "I'm retired. But I do keep my hand in by teaching some night classes." Tippi perked up. "Oh, look, it's Derek!"

A cave-cheeked, blond man made his way over to them. He was wearing a black turtleneck. Something about him was familiar, but Paul couldn't put his finger on it. "Derek is the lead singer of Screaming Parsnips," Tippi explained. Paul supposed he had seen him on a poster somewhere.

After a flurry of air-kissing, the adults settled down to a discussion of Derek's recent trip to England. "Rain and gloom the entire time," Derek announced. "I went around everywhere muffled up."

"Neat-o!" cried Tippi. "Absolutely perfect."

It didn't seem perfect to Paul, but he had given up trying to figure Aunt Gabrielle's friends. He gulped down the last of his champagne and let the noise of the party wash over him. He noticed that there were two completely different sorts of people at the party—the stuffed-shirt government types and the skinny, offbeat types. Strange.

Ari touched his hand. "Are you all right, Paul?"

"Sure. I'm fine," he said, conscious of a certain difficulty forming consonants.

"You're sort of swaying," whispered Ari. "I think you'd better go upstairs and lie down until that champagne wears off."

Paul looked at his empty glass. Maybe Ari was right. His knees felt wobbly.

"I'll go with you," Ari said.

Aunt Gabrielle was talking animatedly to her friends when they left.

"I wish you'd lay off the booze," Ari said as she tucked Paul into bed. "What will I do if you become an alcoholic?"

"I only had a few glasses, Ari."

"Are you sure?" she asked.

"Well, I may have kind of lost track. The caterer's guys kept refilling my glass while I was talking to the old geezers about my not having any college plans."

Ari pulled the bedspread up under his chin and smiled at him. "Sleep tight."

But when she closed the door behind her, Paul didn't go to sleep. Instead he picked up the slip of paper by the bed. Susannah's phone number. He stared at it intently. The three was a sea-green color. The six was a pale blue. *The heck with it,* thought Paul. So he saw colors and numbers in color. It might be a little distracting, but it hadn't killed him yet. He picked up the phone and dialed Susannah's number.

When he heard her voice, his heart flipped over. "Susannah? This is Paul," he choked out.

"Hi," she said in a sweet, breathy voice.

He had tried to make chitchat with Susannah in class, but this was different. The usual conversation ploys, such as "So how's your sketchbook coming along," weren't any good to him in this instance. There was a long silence. Susannah didn't say anything, and Paul certainly couldn't think of anything to say. "Look, I was wondering if you'd like to go to the Boo Ball with me?" he said at last. "I hope you don't think this is too short notice or something."

"I'd like to go with you," she said.

"You would?" he asked. "Oh, good. Well, uh . . . see you in class."

After he hung up, Paul lay staring at the ceiling for a long time, worrying about what on earth he was going to say to Susannah for a whole evening at the Boo Ball. *Art*, he thought suddenly. He could talk to her about Michelangelo and people like that. It would be all right once he was actually with her, he assured himself, because then he could look at her and kiss those soft lips of hers. That was more what he had in mind. If he wanted intelligent conversation, he had Ari. He dozed off.

When he woke up, he was conscious that the house was quiet. The moving shadows in his room

131

were so creepy he switched on the light.

"Paul?" Ari pushed open her door and came in. She was in her nightgown. "Are you awake?"

"Now I am," he said irritably.

"Come in my room," she whispered. "I want to show you something."

"What's the big secret?" He threw back the covers and followed her into her room. Only the light that came from the door gave form to the bed and the fireplace in the shadows.

She tiptoed over to the window. "Look down there," she whispered. "Aunt Gabrielle is out on the terrace with a man."

"You're kidding me!" cried Paul.

"No—shh!"

He crept over to Ari's window and looked down onto the terrace below. The lights from the French doors in the dining room cast a fan of light onto the terrace. The view from the second floor made the figures below so foreshortened that he wasn't sure he would have recognized Aunt Gabrielle, but Ari had thrown her window open, and he heard Aunt Gabrielle's distinctive, musical voice. He couldn't make out what she was saying.

"That must be her boyfriend," hissed Ari.

Paul looked down. He could see the gleam of the man's white shirtfront and the roundness of his fleshy bald head. Suddenly he looked up and Paul drew back, but not before he saw a familiar face, strongly lit from one side, with a white walrus moustache. It was Joe Donovan, the man whose son had gone to St. Anselm's.

"Don't worry—they can't see us. We're in the shadows up here," whispered Ari. "Look, she's kissing his neck!"

Paul knew they shouldn't be watching, but he couldn't seem to help himself. He stared down and suddenly, to his horror, Mr. Donovan's head rolled to one side, and he slumped to the pavement. He lay on the bricks, his legs bent, his arms thrown out spread-eagle. "He passed out!" whispered Paul.

Aunt Gabrielle knelt beside him, her full shimmering skirt spread out around her in a circle. The French doors flew open, and two men hurried out and pulled Mr. Donovan to his feet. Paul was relieved to see that he didn't seem to be completely unconscious. He was able to hold his head up, at least, as they helped him inside.

The twins sat cross-legged on Ari's bed and stared at each other in wonder. "Jeez, talk about a passion pit," said Paul. "The guy actually fainted. If you ask me, he's too old for that kind of thing. He told me he's got a kid in college."

"I guess he must be divorced," said Ari doubtfully.

"Or he could still be married," said Paul. "He could have had a heart attack. You know, from the guilt."

Ari's door was ajar and a while later they heard the sharp tapping of Aunt Gabrielle's high heels coming up the stairs. The twins peeked out. "Has everybody gone home?" Ari called out.

Aunt Gabrielle turned and smiled at them. "Yes. But I'm afraid Derek and Tippi had to drive Joe home. He had too much to drink." Her mouth screwed up in an expression of sudden distaste. "He smokes too much. He stinks of it and his circulation isn't what it ought to be." She pulled jeweled combs out of her upswept hair and shook her magnificent mane of black hair loose. Her face had a faint glow of warmth, as if she had just gotten back from jogging. "It was a lovely party, though, wasn't it?" she said with an absent smile. Her eyes were half-closed, as if she were dreaming. "I love the night when it's *plus noir qu'une mûre*," she said softly. She blew them a kiss and went into her room, closing the door behind her.

Paul looked at Ari dubiously. "She's in an awfully good mood, considering some poor guy just passed out when she was kissing him."

Ari stared at her twin in silence.

"What's the matter?" Paul reached out to touch his sister. "Ari, are you okay?"

"Didn't you hear what she said?" whispered Ari.

"You know I don't follow it when she starts talking French," said Paul irritably. "Between Carmel spouting Spanish and Aunt Gabrielle showing off in French, half the time I don't know what is going on."

"*Plus noir qu'une mûre*," repeated Ari. "That's what she said. She said she loved the night when it was blacker than a blackberry."

Paul shrugged. "So?"

"Paul, that's exactly what the vampire said in the vampire diary!"

134

CHAPTER
TWELVE

A GRAYNESS AT THE WINDOW SHOWED THAT THE SUN was hovering at the verge of the horizon. A white face materialized before Ari's eyes, its skin taut over a handsome aquiline nose. Its dark eyes were bright and seemed to burn with an unearthly glow. Ari's stomach contracted with fear, and a scream welled up in her throat—she choked on her breath. The man's white skin looked as hard and glossy as the skin of a reptile, and his ears had a soft, feline point. His lips curled into a smile, and Ari saw his white fangs gleaming close before her. She was racked suddenly with nausea, and a low moan escaped her. The face drew back. If only she could make her frozen limbs move, she knew the horrible vision would vanish. With a painful effort, she reached her trembling arm toward the bedside lamp and clicked the light on. The fanged man froze a moment, his hand on the doorknob, his black-caped figure casting a distorted shadow in the corner. Then he turned swiftly, opened the door, and was gone. Ari stared after him, her mouth dry and her heart pounding. There had been a shadow on the wall! she realized with horror. A cold chill crept up her spine. None of her visions ever had shadows!

Ari sat bolt upright in bed. Her skin felt as if it had shrunk and her fingers were icy. She slid her feet to the cold floor and stood up, then ran over to the bedroom door and touched the knob. It was cold. Ice-cold. She felt a thud of relief. No warm hand had grasped that knob. The fanged man *had* been one of her visions. She ran to the connecting door between the bedrooms and threw it open. "Paul!" she cried.

He sat up. "Good grief, Ari." He glanced at the clock. "It's six thirty! What are you doing up already?"

She pulled back the covers and slid into bed with him, shivering. "Paul, you have weird dreams, right?"

"Yeah," he said cautiously. "I told you I did. I expect everybody does, sometimes."

"But do you . . . ever have them when you're awake?"

Paul swallowed. "Sometimes."

"What do you see?"

He thought of the fanged creatures in medieval dress. Somehow he couldn't bring himself to tell Ari about them. "Sometimes I see our father," he said hesitantly. "It happens just when I'm waking up."

Ari gazed at him wide-eyed. "What does he look like in your dream?"

136

"Sort of like me," said Paul simply.

Ari shivered. "I dream of fanged things," she said in a small voice. "Awful fanged things. This morning was the worst. I dreamed a fanged man was in my room. He was so real!"

"I sometimes have those dreams, too," said Paul. "But it's normal."

"Normal?" Ari gave a harsh laugh. "How can it be normal?"

"I looked it up when I was in the school library. There are these things called hypnagogic and hypnopompic images. Some people have them when they're waking up or going to sleep. It doesn't mean you're going crazy or anything."

Ari was silent for a moment. "Why didn't you tell me?"

"It was only a few days ago that I looked it up. Anyway, now you know."

"Paul," Ari darted an anxious look at her twin. She licked her dry lips. "When you see numbers, are they in color?"

He sucked in his breath sharply. "You see numbers in color, too?"

"Three is pink." She glanced at him shyly under her lashes. "Isn't that weird?"

"Yes." He grinned. "For me three is always seagreen." He felt as if a heavy weight had been rolled off his chest.

Ari took a deep breath. "It must be something hereditary," she said. "Like being born with an extra toe."

Ari felt her twin's hand in hers, and a surge of

137

sympathy coursed through their linked fingers, as still and quiet as the line of blue and green where ocean meets sky. Her heart beat in tune with his, a slow, quiet rhythm.

A spray of rain rattled against the windowpane. Dawn had come but it was a gray, wet dawn.

Suddenly Paul put his hands under Ari's arms and tossed her up. She laughed as he caught her. "Put me down!" she protested.

"I feel sorry for people who don't have a twin," he said, letting her slip down. "Don't you?"

It was almost time for school to start. Rain dripped with depressing regularity from the eaves of the school buildings. The courtyard formed by the three main classroom buildings smelled of wet earth and was clogged with sodden leaves. Two girls sat huddled together on a bench, listening to the mournful drip. "I was such an idiot," Nadia sobbed.

Amanda clenched her fists. "You're better off without him. What a jerk!"

"No, I'm not!" cried Nadia. "I love him!" She wiped her eyes. "And he loves me. I know he does. It's only that Ari's put a spell on him. Can't you see the way she looks at him?" Nadia shuddered. "Her teeth are pointy, like an animal's. How can he think she's pretty? She must have used magic. She's hypnotized him—I'm sure of it!"

"Look, you'd better pull yourself together before we go inside."

"No! I can't! And I don't even care!" wailed

Nadia. "If he feels sorry for me, maybe he'll come back to me!"

"You don't want him to come back to you because he feels sorry for you," protested Amanda, horrified.

"Oh, yes, I do!" cried Nadia. "I want to get him back any way I can."

"Think of the way he's treated you!" urged Amanda. "You should be furious! You should want to show him you don't care."

"But I do care," sniffled Nadia.

Amanda held out another tissue. "He's slime, Nadia. He's scum."

"How can he treat me this way?" cried Nadia, tears streaming down her cheeks. "All I've ever done is love him!"

Amanda's eyes narrowed. "If you could just get back at him, you'd feel so much better."

Cos sat next to Ari at lunch. Under the table, he had one hand possessively on her knee.

"It's nice to see you're finally keeping your elbows off the table, Cos," commented Mr. Fleming.

Cos flashed Ari a wicked grin.

"I wish Amanda would quit looking at me like that," he said. "It kills my appetite." He thrust a forkful of noodles into his mouth.

Ari glanced across the room. Sure enough, Amanda's dark eyes directed a look of malevolent hatred in their direction.

"I wonder what she's thinking," said Ari uneasily.

"Don't ask," groaned Cos. "She's probably plotting

139

murder. Did you hear about the time in second grade that she glued some poor turtle to a rock?"

"Actually, Sybil did tell me about that."

"It just goes to show you. The girl is capable of anything," said Cos. "Nadia used to be completely under her thumb. It was pathetic. She didn't have a single opinion of her own. I tried to show her that there was another way of looking at things than the way Amanda looked at them."

"Have you got your costume for the Boo Ball yet?" asked Ari. She was remembering Sybil's warning about the Halloween party. It would be easy for Amanda and Nadia to pull a trick on them there, when everyone was in disguise.

"I have got my costume." Cos smiled. "But I'm still not telling what it is. What about you?"

"Paul and I are going after school to get ours," said Ari.

Aunt Gabrielle had left a note on the dining room table for them, giving the address of a costumer and suggesting that they take a cab to his shop after school. "I hope it won't be too late for us to get something good," said Ari. "This is pretty short notice to be digging up a costume. Maybe all the good ones will be gone."

"You'd look great in anything," said Cos. "Have you thought about going as a belly dancer?"

"I'd freeze to death!" protested Ari.

"Don't worry," Cos said, leaning toward her and smiling. "I'll keep you warm."

*　　　*　　　*

140

The art class was doing a life study, and Susannah had volunteered to pose wearing a leotard. She could hardly have had a more electrifying effect on Paul if she had stripped bare. He sketched the graceful curve of her hip and thigh, but when he thought about how they were going to be in a dark car together on Friday night he could feel himself going warm all over.

"Are Ari and Cos going together these days?" Sandy asked, elaborately casual. He had sketched in an outline of Susannah's body and was working on carefully positioning eyes and ears on her oval head. Paul was astonished at his friend's inhuman detachment. Sandy was acting as if Susannah were merely an interesting arrangement of lines.

"What did you say, Sandy?" asked Paul. "Would you run that by me one more time?"

"Your sister, Ari," repeated Sandy. "What's the story between her and Cos?"

"Oh, him. He's going with Ari and Sybil to the Boo Ball."

"You mean Ari and Cos are just friends?" Sandy looked surprised.

Paul hesitated. "Cos is chasing after her," he said. "But, heck, we practically just got here. Ari has hardly had a chance to get to know anybody yet. She's still looking around."

"What's she going to wear to the Boo Ball?" asked Sandy.

"I don't know what we're going as yet," said Paul.

"You'll let me know what you decide on, won't you?"

"Sure," said Paul. He glanced down at his paper in astonishment. He had been drawing while he talked, more or less on automatic pilot, and he had almost finished. But the sketch didn't look exactly like Susannah. To his horror, Paul had unconsciously sketched in fangs. Quickly, with the heel of his hand, he smeared the charcoal before anyone could see.

Sandy glanced at Paul's sketch. "Jeez!" he said. "What happened? You've ruined the face."

"My hand slipped," said Paul in a flat voice. He was having trouble catching his breath. Vampires were lurking around every corner—in his dreams and in his waking life. There was no escape from them.

Later that afternoon, the cab dropped Paul and Ari off at a path that ran along the old C and O Canal. They could hear the water rushing in the nearby lift lock. Rainwater dripped damply from the trees onto the dark bronze bust of Chief Justice Douglas that stood on a plinth nearby. Small row houses had signs announcing their business—take-out pizza, law offices. Ari spotted the place they were looking for almost at once— "WILEY HOBAN, COSTUMER AND DESIGNER," said a wooden sign. The door had a glass window, but it was curtained with thin white material so they couldn't see inside the shop. The twins pushed the door open and a bell tinkled. At first, they saw

142

only the bolts of material that stood tall against the walls. Strings of glittering beads hung in one corner, and on the walls were jeweled crowns, felt hats, and rubbery masks—their expressions comically distorted by their hanging sagging on long nails.

A little man stepped out from behind a curtain at the back of the shop. He was gray and balding, with glasses that had slipped down on his nose. He was wearing a long white apron with a bib that was skewered with pins. "May I help you?" he inquired.

"We need costumes," said Paul. "I think you know our aunt, Gabrielle Montclair."

Mr. Hoban rubbed his hands together. "Oh, yes, I know Gabri very well indeed. She has an account here. Now what do you need?"

"We need something for a party next Friday night," said Ari.

The man blinked. "Next Friday! Dear me. Well, there's no time to design something new, then. You're welcome to step into the back and see what you can find from the stock I've got on hand."

The twins stepped behind the muslin curtain, and Ari sneezed. The dark room in the back of the shop was quite dusty. It contained department-store clothing racks. Each rack was heavy with costumes. Ari pulled out a glittery mermaid costume and held it up. It had a trailing quilted fish tail that could be a problem if she were dancing. Not to mention that the mermaid's thin, glittery bodysuit did not look exactly warm. "I want something

143

warmer," said Ari, putting it back on the rack.

"Medieval is very warm," said Mr. Hoban promptly. "In those days, people lived in drafty castles." He began pulling out burgundy-colored velvet robes, wimples, and chains of jewels, but Ari didn't want to go to her first party with Cos dressed in the equivalent of a velvet bathrobe.

"I had in mind something more alluring," Ari said.

Mr. Hoban tossed the velvet robes aside and led her to a corner of the room where embroidered satin dresses hung in shiny plastic dry cleaner's bags. "Many of our ladies like a Marie Antoinette look. You're kind of small. Can you wear an eight or a ten? I don't carry anything smaller in this look."

Ari held the ball gown up to her and felt a flutter of excitement. An eight or a ten was what she usually wore. And unlike some of the women at Aunt Gabrielle's party, she had a figure. When she went in the dressing room and tried it on, the dress seemed to fit. It was obviously supposed to be snug. She stepped outside and pirouetted before her twin.

"Jeez," said Paul. "It's cut low enough! You'll probably bust out of it. If you cough, the sides will split."

"Oh, our seams are reinforced." Mr. Hoban smiled. "This is a very popular model. It comes with a powdered wig and a beauty patch complete with adhesive."

"I'll take it," said Ari.

144

"The jeweled mask is extra," he said.

"I'll take that, too," she said.

Paul settled on a bright-red demon outfit. He didn't want to risk some complicated costume falling in his eyes or tripping him up. The last thing he wanted was to look like an idiot in front of Susannah.

Mr. Hoban boxed up the costumes to go. The ball gown took a huge box, and Ari's wig was in its own very large hatbox. The demon costume slipped neatly into a Ziploc plastic bag. "I'll send the bill to the usual address on N Street," Mr. Hoban said, twirling his Rolodex.

Minutes later, the twins piled into a taxi. Ari couldn't see over the box in her lap. "This is going to be fun," she said.

A slow smile spread over Paul's face. "I hope so."

CHAPTER
THIRTEEN

WHEN PAUL AND ARI WALKED DOWNSTAIRS, ARI caught a glimpse of herself in the mirror over the mantel in the living room. She saw a beautiful eighteenth-century lady in a tall, white powdered wig. The dress was very low-cut, and her breasts swelled above the tight embroidered satin.

Aunt Gabrielle clapped her hands in delight. "Utterly splendid!" she cried. "I love that little beauty patch by your eye!" She gave a low, throaty laugh. "You know, normally no one believes in restraint and self-control more than I do—I'm an absolute bore on the subject. But I do think that on Halloween one should . . . uh . . . let 'er rip."

Paul glanced at Ari. "I just hope it doesn't," he said.

Ari glared at him.

"I better get going," he said. "Susannah lives halfway across town."

"Drive carefully," said Aunt Gabrielle, looking anxious. "The streets are wet."

"Don't worry," said Paul. "I'm not about to put a dent in the new car." Aunt Gabrielle had arranged to have a little red Mazda delivered to the house for the twins, and they still hadn't gotten over the thrill of inhaling its new car smell.

After Paul left, Ari went in the living room where she could get a better look at herself in the mirror. The foaming white hair was quite dramatic with her dark eyebrows and lashes.

"You look beautiful," cried Aunt Gabrielle.

Ari felt a sudden catch in her throat. She wished that her mother could see her.

The doorbell rang. "That's your beau now," said Aunt Gabrielle. She pressed her cold cheek to Ari's affectionately. "I hope you have a wonderful time!"

"I will," said Ari, drawing away. She wished her aunt didn't have such white, clawlike hands. She ran to the door and threw it open. The blood drained from her face. A vampire stood on the stoop in a full black satin cape, his fangs pressing against his bottom lip. A tiny cry escaped Ari.

"Wow!" said Cos's voice. Then Ari recognized Cos, his face covered with thick white makeup. He was wearing wax fanged teeth over his own teeth and was staring at her as if struck speechless.

Ari flushed. Her costume was obviously a success. She regained her composure and hastily introduced Cos to Aunt Gabrielle. Cos tucked his fangs away in his pocket and bowed.

"Nice costume," purred Aunt Gabrielle. "Quite authentic-looking, if I may say so."

"Thanks," said Cos. "I wish we could stay and chat, but I'm double-parked."

Ari grabbed her jeweled mask off the table in the hall.

"Go, go!" cried Aunt Gabrielle, shooing them out.

Ari lifted her skirts as she moved carefully down the brick steps and the damp brick sidewalk to Cos's car. "Uh-oh," she said. "I don't think this eighteenth-century hair is made to fit in twentieth-century cars."

Cos opened the door. "Maybe if you sort of tilt your head back it'll be okay," he suggested.

Ari was barely able to squeeze in by scrunching down in her seat. Much of her hooped skirt had to be lifted up behind her and stuffed into the back seat of the car in order to give Cos room to drive.

"I wish I had a horse and carriage," said Cos, slamming his doors shut. "That dress wasn't made for a compact car." He slid in behind the wheel and cast a quick glance at Ari. "Sensational!"

"It is pretty," said Ari, looking down complacently at the gleaming satin.

"I wasn't talking about the dress," said Cos, doing a U-turn.

Sybil lived only a few blocks away. She came running out, wearing a sequined halter top and a glittery skirt with a jeweled yoke that began just below her belly button. Her earrings jingled as she got in the car. "I'm a belly dancer," Sybil announced, her teeth chattering.

148

"Aren't you freezing?" asked Ari.

"To death," said Sybil, wiggling into a navy-blue cardigan. "That's why my mom made me bring this sweater."

"You look terrific, Syb," said Cos. "I tried to get Ari to go as a belly dancer, but she had her own idea. Not that it wasn't a great idea." His fangs flashed white in the darkness.

The gym was dark and throbbing with loud music. Colored lights had been strung across the ceiling, and a strobe light rotated somewhere. Someone in a white bunny suit passed Ari. Under the colored lights, its ears turned blue then green before it disappeared into the crowd. Ari was confused by the shifting light.

"Stay close to me," Cos said to Ari. "I don't want to lose you." Immediately a farmer in a straw hat, plaid shirt, and overalls asked her to dance.

"Hey, I get the first dance," protested Cos, but the farmer whirled her away.

"What a dress!" said the farmer admiringly.

Ari recognized the voice of Paul's friend Sandy. "Thank you," she said, dimpling at him.

"Are you supposed to be somebody in particular?" asked Sandy.

"Marie Antoinette," she said.

"I hope you lose your head," he said, guiding her into a turn. He was wearing a black domino mask, but she could see that his neck was turning crimson. "Figuratively, I mean," he added.

"I thought that was what you meant," she said.

149

"I don't know why I said that," Sandy said. "I never make smart remarks. That's because I'm not any good at it. I just fall all over myself afterwards and end up looking stupid."

"I think you're doing fine," said Ari, smiling at him.

The vampire stepped into the gym and glanced up at the colored lights. The strobe light threw a band of pink over his white face. No one could tell who was human and who wasn't with this lighting, he thought with satisfaction. He spotted a heavily padded Humpty Dumpty moving awkwardly toward the punch bowl, his little blue hat wobbling. A skinny, red-haired belly dancer was doing a comical undulating dance with a boy who was wearing tight britches and a sweeping plumed hat. The vampire smiled. He loved Halloween! A celebration of rich diversity. And a perfect night for vampires. Even if someone looked at him closely, they would only compliment him on the artfulness of his costume. The vampire chuckled to himself as he looked around.

Suddenly he spotted Ari. Her wig swayed as she danced with the boy whose straw hat was pushed back on his head. Her lovely face was first green then blue as they danced under the colored lights. The moving light of the strobe made her seem ghostly, spiritlike. He pressed through the crowd until he reached them and tapped the farm boy on the shoulder.

"May I cut in?" he asked.

The boy looked at him, confused. Then the music stopped momentarily, and the boy dropped his arms to his side. "Oh," he said, glancing around at the vampire. "I guess you want to dance with the guy that brought you." He backed away from Ari, looking embarrassed.

"May I have the next dance?" asked the vampire in a silky voice.

"You aren't Cos!" cried Ari.

"No," said the vampire. "I'm not."

Ari's eyes opened wide. In the shifting light, she thought she recognized the face from her vision—the tightly drawn white skin and aquiline nose, the dark, glittering eyes of her nightmare.

"But can't we dance anyway?" suggested the vampire, his voice sweet. He reached out and she felt his cool hand on the back of her neck. She tingled from head to toe and felt vaguely sick as he took her in his arms and guided her into a slow two-step. Her head felt fuzzy and she was having trouble thinking clearly. The figures around them seemed to fade and grow dim.

"Tell me about yourself," he said softly.

Ari squirmed and tried to wriggle free from his grasp. She hated his eyes, like cat's eyes, staring into hers. A chill shook her. The achingly familiar feeling of being watched by alien eyes swept over her. She wanted to scream and break away from him, but she felt powerless, as if she were trapped in a dream. Her feet moved mechanically.

"I said, 'Tell me about yourself,'" said the man. His voice had taken on an edge. "Your thoughts, your secrets. You heard me. Do as I say."

Ari's eyes widened and her mouth fell open. With a sickeningly painful effort of will, she froze. "N—no!" she exploded suddenly. A couple dancing nearby stared at her.

The man's eyes grew red with anger, and his grip on her loosened. Ari turned suddenly and stumbled through the crowd of dancers. She heard the vampire's muttered "Damn!" as she escaped.

Ari ran blindly toward the door. Suddenly she ran against a black-caped figure. He turned to face her, and his white face blurred as she gasped and recoiled from him.

"Ari? What's wrong?" Cos caught her under the arms as she sagged.

"Oh, Cos, it's you! I'm scared," she sobbed. She leaned her head on his chest. Her stomach heaved.

Cos's eyes darkened. "Did Sandy—?"

"No!" Ari choked out. "Sandy didn't scare me. It was this . . . this other vampire. I thought it was you, and then when I saw him up close I realized that he wasn't!" She thought with horror of her dance with the strange vampire. The will to resist had seemed to leak out of her fingertips; for a minute she had felt as if she had been a brainless mechanical doll. What had happened to her? She choked on a sob.

"Calm down," said Cos softly. "It's okay. I'm right here." He put his arm around her, and she felt herself grow calm. Cos's solidity and warmth were what she needed to steady her. The uncanny resemblance of the strange vampire to her vision had stunned her for a moment, that was all, she decided. She wouldn't think about it anymore.

"I won't let him scare you again," said Cos. "Come on, let's get some punch, huh?"

Paul had found a place a little set off from the party to talk to Susannah. In one corner of the gym, a long curtain of synthetic cobwebs had been tacked to the ceiling and pulled down to the floorboard in front of the bale of hay. Through the long strip of gauzy cobweb, the colored lights looked pastel and fuzzy. Susannah was leaning back against a bale of hay. Her blue pillbox hat trailed chiffon veils that caught a little on the straw, and her full-legged chiffon harem pants had a spray of hayseed stuck to them. Her midriff, Paul thought, looking down at her, was a work of art. He wanted to touch the faint tracery of her ribs and the shadowy indentation of her navel. He wanted to press her against the hay as he kissed her. But he sensed this was not the right time. She was talking about her second-grade teacher, giving him her life story.

"I was always the tallest one in the class," said Susannah earnestly. "They put me on the back row when they took the class picture. Pretty soon my mom couldn't even find Mary Jane shoes in my size, and I had to wear these awful grown-up shoes. I felt so tall I was afraid my head was going to break right through the roof one day. It was this morbid fear I had."

"I think you're a wonderful height," said Paul.

Susannah smiled. "Well, now I can appreciate

being tall," she said complacently. "I wouldn't want to be a little mouse of a thing like Nadia. But back then I was only seven and it was tough looking so grown-up. People expected more of me. They'd forget I was only seven. And then—"

Paul's mind wandered. He wondered if girls wore underwear under those skimpy costumes. Ari, he had noticed, always wore underwear, even if it was just a tiny scrap of filmy material not worth talking about. It must be some kind of superstition with girls.

"Wasn't that horrible of her?" Susannah looked at him expectantly, her eyes moist.

"Terrible," said Paul at once. "Very insensitive."

"It really traumatized me," said Susannah earnestly. "After that, I decided I wanted to be a teacher, because I would never, never make a crack like that to a sensitive little girl. I think teachers should always be careful of children's feelings, don't you?"

"Oh, definitely," said Paul, his eyes burning. "That's very, very important." And as he said it, suddenly he believed it. It seemed horrible to him that some teacher had hurt Susannah's feelings when she was in the second grade. He was inches from pressing Susannah against the hay to kiss her. The bristles of hay bit into his knee through the cloth of his costume and made his palm itch as he leaned over her.

Susannah smiled dreamily. "I knew you were different from the guys around here," she said, "the same old boring guys I grew up with. There was something about you."

His face drew close to hers. He could feel her warm breath.

"I love your teeth," Susannah said.

Paul blinked, thrown off his stride. "My teeth?"

She reached a forefinger into his open mouth and touched them. She giggled. "Your pointy teeth! They're sort of animal-like, you know? Dangerous."

Paul figured that was his cue. Supporting his weight on his hand, he pressed his lips to hers. He was so close to her that he could feel her warmth and the beating of her heart.

"Paul!" she cried, squirming under him.

He drew away and swallowed hard. He was having trouble thinking straight.

"There are chaperones all over the place!" cried Susannah.

Paul glanced over his shoulder and was relieved to see no teacher bearing down on them. "Let's go outside, then," he suggested.

Susannah hugged herself and shivered. "Outside! Are you kidding? I'd freeze."

Paul sighed. Susannah's skimpy costume, though pretty, was impractical.

Susannah struggled up from the stacked bales. Bits of hay clung to her chiffon scarf. "Let's dance," she said. "Come on." She tugged at him until he reluctantly trailed after her to the middle of the gym floor, and they joined the dancers.

Paul wondered how Ari was getting along. He had been concentrating so much on Susannah that he hadn't seen his twin all evening.

"It's hot enough in here, isn't it?" said Cos.

Ari was trying to push the horrible memory of her dance with the strange vampire out of her mind, and she scarcely heard him. Already her mind was foggy on the details of what he had said and what she had said. She didn't even care. It was bad enough to recall that feeling of being drained of her strength.

Cos unfastened his cape and draped it over one arm. "Has my makeup started to run?" He fingered his jaw uneasily. "I bet I'm melting."

She gulped down the last of her punch and shook her head. "You're fine. The makeup must be waterproof."

Cos put his arm around her. "Jeez, get a load of that costume," he said, and she felt him shiver. "Isn't that sick?"

Ari turned to see a girl in a black leotard carrying a tall aluminum ax. A loose black hood fell to her shoulders, concealing her head completely.

"Who's she supposed to be?" asked Ari, relieved that her voice sounded normal.

"The public executioner," said Cos. "Old-time executioners always wore hoods like that so nobody could see who they were. I'm surprised she didn't tuck a severed head under her arm for that authentic touch."

"It would be hard to dance with a head under one arm and the ax in the other," Ari pointed out.

The hooded head swiveled suddenly and looked straight at them. Ari could see the girl's gleaming eyes peeking out at them from two holes in the black hood.

Cos squeezed Ari. "Watch her walk," he said in a low voice. "It's Amanda."

Ari watched the girl dressed in black walk away from them. There was something familiar about her long-legged stride.

"I hope she's not trying to send me a message with that executioner's costume," said Cos.

"Lots of people wear gruesome costumes on Halloween," she said. "After all, you came as Dracula, didn't you?"

"That's different," said Cos. "Everybody knows vampires aren't for real."

Ari blinked. She wasn't so sure anymore. "Nobody gets executed with axes anymore, either," she said in a faint voice. "Not in this country, anyway."

"I just wish I knew what Amanda was up to," said Cos. "She's making me nervous."

Ari gazed at the costumed figures on the crowded dance floor. She wished she could see the unknown vampire. She wanted to prove to herself that he was only a student and not the vampire from her dreams. Maybe Cos would recognize him and tell her who he was. She caught a glimpse of Paul in the red devil's costume. He whirled by them with Susannah in his arms, and her chiffon scarves wafted behind her in fluid swirls. A boy in a zebra-striped leotard poured himself some punch. His hair was brushed up into a Mohawk-style imitation of a zebra's mane. But Ari saw no sign of the vampire who had frightened her. Since she'd come to St. Anselm's, she'd thought on several occasions that she recognized kids from her old school, only to realize the next moment that she was mistaken. Her mind insisted on trying to find familiar faces. Perhaps she only thought she recognized the vampire face from her dream, she told herself. The light had been confusing. It was another trick her mind was playing on her.

Cos handed her another glass of punch, and Ari smiled. As long as she was with Cos, she thought, the world was reliable and solid. But when she looked out at the dancers on the gym floor in the unearthly light, uncertainty swept over her, and the ground of reality seemed to shift under her feet. A Cyclops with a rubbery, wrinkled face moved by them, dancing with a dragonfly girl. The girl's shimmering gossamer wings were first pink then green, and her black antennae bobbed as she danced. The Cyclops's large bloodshot eye leered over her shoulder at Ari. She put down her punch, untouched. "Let's dance," she suggested abruptly. Somehow she had to shake the black mood that had fallen over her.

As Ari and Cos danced, the flashing light and the moving costumed figures around them jiggled and jerked like the reel of an old movie. The beat was fast and the heavy satin of Ari's skirt bounced. She grew hot and the colors she saw seemed blurred. Suddenly Cos's white face and fangs began to look like one of the creatures from her nightmare, and she gasped. She closed her eyes.

No! she reminded herself. It was Cos she was dancing with. She felt safe with him. He was nothing like the horrible vampire she had met moments before. But the strange vampire's face floated before her eyes and got confused in her mind with Cos's. Frantically, she danced faster until her chest was gleaming with sweat. The music changed suddenly, and Cos drew close to her, folding his arms around her.

"Mmmph," he said, smiling. "You are the greatest." He kissed the tiny black beauty spot glued at the corner of her eye, laughed, then kissed her again. Ari closed her eyes and sighed. With Cos's arms around her, she knew she was safe.

Loud music poured out of the doors as Paul and Susannah came out. Chiffon scarves floated behind Susannah as they moved down the hall. "We could go get something to eat," Paul suggested.

Susannah laughed. "Paul, I can't go anywhere dressed like this!"

"We could get take-out somewhere," said Paul urgently. "We could park outside the pizza place with the car heater on." Paul could hear his own and Susannah's footsteps echoing in the empty hallway. He had the uneasy feeling someone was watching them. It was as if he felt a gaze pressing against his shoulder blades. He was about to open the door and step outside, but he couldn't stop himself from turning suddenly and looking back. A blurry white shape moved over the open door.

159

Paul refocused his gaze and got a better look. The bunny rabbit he had seen earlier was standing behind one of the open gym doors. For some reason it looked oddly tall. Too tall. Paul blinked a second at the white shape behind the door, its ears bobbing slightly. What was that bunny rabbit doing hiding behind the door? he wondered. And why was it so tall?

"Oh, okay." Susannah's face turned up to his confidingly. "I guess we could park at the pizza place."

Paul wasn't listening. He suddenly had realized that the bunny must be Nadia. She was standing on a ladder. What on earth was she doing?

At that moment, a shadowy figure clad in black with a long satin cape emerged from the gym. For a second, Paul thought it was Cos. Then he realized the vampire was taller than Cos, and somehow he moved differently. Paul couldn't see very well and caught only a glimpse of a pale face and white hands.

Then a sudden movement out of the corner of his eye caught his attention, and he was startled to see a cloud of white envelop the vampire's head.

In slow motion as if it were a dream, Paul saw that Nadia, her white bunny ears bobbing, was leaning over the open door, holding an upturned plastic bucket. The vampire below her was white with flour, his cloak streaked and dripping with a flour-water paste. His white face turned up to look at Nadia, and Paul saw her wobble dangerously on her ladder.

A chill shot up Paul's spine, and he unconsciously gave Susannah a little push. "Let's get out of here," he said urgently. "Quick."

"I'm going as fast as I can!" she said. "What's the rush?" She turned as if to look, but Paul pushed open the door and hurried her outside. A blast of cold air hit him in the face. His blood was pulsing so hotly the night air could not chill him. It was none of his business what the rabbit was up to, he thought, and his instinct was to get away before all hell broke loose. He put his arm around Susannah and held her tightly as they ran.

A minute later Nadia ran sobbing out into the cold air. Her throat hurt and her ankle throbbed. She had to get away! Suddenly she collapsed on the sidewalk, scraping her palms.

"Nadia!" Amanda's face loomed over her, her eyes alarmed. "What's wrong? Are you all right? Can you get up?" Nadia felt her friend's strong hands lifting her as she struggled to her feet.

"I hurt my ankle," she sobbed.

"Can you put your weight on it?" asked Amanda.

Nadia tested it, wincing. "Yes, but it hurts a lot."

"It isn't broken, then. It's probably only sprained," said Amanda. "You shouldn't have taken off all of a sudden like that. What happened?"

"The vampire wasn't Cos, Amanda!" Nadia screamed. "Didn't you see? It wasn't him! It was a real vampire! A real one!"

Amanda took off her black hood and tucked it

161

into her waistband. Her sweaty hair clung to her scalp. "It was just some other guy in a vampire costume, Nadia," she said soothingly. "It's too bad we didn't realize there were two of them. We got flour and water all over some kid we don't even know."

"No!" Nadia shivered. "It wasn't a kid, Amanda. His face was so smooth, and he had eyes like coals. Burning eyes! You couldn't see him the way I could." She shuddered. "He was only pretending to be a kid! It was a real vampire!"

"We need to get you home," Amanda said, uncomfortably. "You've had a scare, but you'll feel better once you calm down."

"You don't believe me!" Nadia cried.

"We should get an Ace bandage on that ankle of yours," said Amanda.

"Do you think you're smarter than all the peasants in my grandmother's village?" cried Nadia. "They knew all about vampires. Vampires lie in wait for innocent people and suck their blood."

"Superstition," said Amanda shortly.

Testing her ankle, Nadia hobbled a few steps. "Maybe I used to think that, too," she admitted, shivering, "but now I see I was wrong. When that vampire looked at me, I was afraid he was going to pull me toward him with his eyes."

Amanda shrugged. "You got away from him, didn't you?"

"You don't believe me, do you?" cried Nadia.

Amanda put her hands on her friend's shoulders and studied her face closely. "You haven't

162

been doing drugs, have you, Nadia?"

"No!" cried Nadia, twisting away from her. "This is real! It's not all in my mind."

"I didn't say it was all in your mind," Amanda said. "You're just . . . the sensitive type."

A sigh escaped Nadia. There was no use arguing, she thought. Amanda was incapable of understanding anything more supernatural than a soccer match.

"Trying to dump that flour on Cos was a stupid idea," Amanda said guiltily. "If I'd known how upset you were going to get, I never would have suggested it."

Nadia got in her car.

"Are you okay to drive?" asked Amanda.

"I'm fine," said Nadia.

"I'll give you a call tomorrow and see how you're feeling," said Amanda.

"Okay," said Nadia listlessly. She put the car in reverse and stepped firmly on the accelerator. Maybe Amanda would believe her, she thought grimly, once kids began to die.

CHAPTER
FOURTEEN

WHEN ARI WOKE UP THE NEXT MORNING, SHE stretched luxuriously. She felt snug and content. No fanged creatures were rummaging in her clothes, and she had almost forgotten the strange vampire at the dance.

Her embroidered satin ball gown hung on a hanger hooked over the door of the tall wardrobe. Her powdered wig, a mountain of white curls, was on a chair beside it, and the petticoat with its hoops collapsed sat untidily in a corner. She remembered Cos's lingering goodnight kiss as they stood shivering on the front stoop and smiled. Then she slipped into jeans and a shirt and knocked on the connecting door.

When Paùl opened the door, to her surprise, he was already dressed. Usually she heard him moving around and showering in the morning. She must have slept very soundly.

"I thought you'd never wake up," he said. "Let's go down and get some breakfast."

It was understood that neither of them wanted to go downstairs alone in Aunt Gabrielle's gloomy house. Ari glanced uneasily at the crow and its black mirror as they passed Aunt Gabrielle's door. Breathing fast, the twins fled from the crow's glassy gaze and hurried down the dark staircase.

"Jeez," said Paul, feelingly, "if I owned this place, I'd slap some white paint over the paneling. It gives me the creeps."

It was brighter downstairs. Sunlight poured in the big French doors of the dining room and made the brass gong beside the door glow.

In the kitchen, there was no sign of Carmel since it was Saturday. Paul poured himself some cold milk, then rummaged around until he found coffee cake in the fridge. "You want yours heated up?" he asked, his mouth full.

"Wait a minute," said Ari. Frowning, she went back to the narrow hallway that served the kitchen and pantries. "Paul, come back here!"

He found her kneeling in the service hallway. Her fingers trailed across the white smear that lightened the floor just outside the kitchen. "I thought the floor looked funny." Ari frowned. "I figured I'd better come back and take a second look."

"Looks like something was spilled," said Paul, "and Carmel didn't do such a hot job of cleaning it up."

Ari glanced up at her twin. "It's flour. I can feel that it's powdery."

165

Paul stared uneasily at the stain. "Flour," he repeated dully.

Ari stood up and went back into the kitchen without saying a word and poured herself some milk. She stared absently at the glass. "Paul, what time did you leave the party last night?"

"Oh, I don't know. About midnight or one. Susannah and I went and got a bite to eat afterwards." He avoided her eyes.

"You didn't see what happened when somebody dumped the bucket of flour?"

"I saw the whole thing," Paul admitted. "It was Nadia. I saw her standing on a ladder behind the gym door in that bunny suit of hers. I even saw her dump it. I think she must have been after Cos, because whoever she dumped it on was dressed like a vampire."

"Listen!" Ari's breath came quickly. "There *was* a strange vampire at the dance last night. He asked me to dance and I'd never seen him before."

Paul shook his head. "It's not like you know everybody, though, Ari."

"He was strange," Ari said in a low voice. "He looked like one of the vampires I saw in those dreams I have. You know, the hypnagogic or hypnopompic stuff."

"How could he?" said Paul firmly. "Those are just dreams."

"I'm just telling you, he did," said Ari. The memory of her dance with the vampire made her sick, and she had to close her eyes. "I bet he was the one that got the flour all over him."

Suddenly she got up. "I'm going to go over to Sybil's house," she said. "If the buckets fell on an actual kid, Sybil may know who it was by now."

Paul squirmed. "Well, you know those buckets didn't fall on a dream, Ari. It's impossible."

"We'll see," said Ari stubbornly. "Sybil will know."

"Do you have to go over there?" Paul's face fell. "Why don't you just ask her on the phone? I don't want to be stuck here in the house all by myself."

"Come with me, then," said Ari.

"You know I can't. Sybil'd be chasing me with a butterfly net."

"Why don't you go visit Susannah, then?"

"I saw Susannah last night," Paul said sullenly.

"I don't know why you can't go out with Sybil. She's a really interesting, high-energy sort of person."

"Okay, if you pick out my girlfriends, then I get to pick out your boyfriends. Fair enough?" Paul smiled.

"I was only making a suggestion. I wouldn't think of interfering in your love life."

Paul snorted. "Yeah. I bet you wouldn't."

Ari dialed Sybil on the kitchen phone. When she hung up, Paul picked at his coffee cake, looking depressed.

"You sure you won't come with me?" Ari wheedled. "Sybil would love to have you."

"I bet she would," said Paul.

Ari took a quick a swig of milk. "Gotta go," she said. "I told her I'd be right over." She looked at her twin seriously. "If you won't come with me, I

167

wish you'd go to the mall or something, Paul. I don't want you to be here by yourself."

Paul looked up. "Don't worry," he said dryly. "Auntie Gabrielle will keep me company."

"Very funny," said Ari. "You know she never shows her face until it gets dark. Besides . . ." she hesitated, "I'm not sure how much I trust her."

Paul shrugged uncomfortably.

Ari planted a forefinger on Paul's chest. "Just suppose," she said, "that the flour got dumped last night on the mystery vampire! And just suppose that smear of flour on the floor in the hall means he came sneaking into Aunt Gabrielle's study through the garden and then across the hall and up the back stairway right to her bedroom!"

"Are you saying the mystery vampire was Aunt Gabrielle?" Paul was puzzled.

"No!" said Ari. "I saw him close up. He's got a kind of beaky nose. He didn't look a bit like Aunt Gabrielle."

Paul's eyes narrowed. "Then are you trying to tell me you think Aunt Gabrielle's got something going with some guy from our school?"

Ari seemed struck by this thought. "That's an idea! I hadn't even thought of that. Maybe it was a teacher dressed up like a vampire!"

"I hope he was cuter than that stuffed shirt she was making out with at the party," said Paul.

"I am going over to see Sybil," said Ari, "and I wish you would get out of the house until we find out what's going on."

168

Paul saluted. "Aye, aye, sir. Maybe I'll go over to Sandy's house."

Paul dropped Ari off at the corner of Twenty-ninth and Dunbarton. From there she could see Sybil's house down the block. It was a brick house rather like Aunt Gabrielle's with a Federal-style front door and black shutters. But the house on the corner had a picket fence and a front yard, an unusual feature in Georgetown, where most houses were built up to the street and jammed up close to their neighbors. The house was almost hidden by a huge tree, its leaves flaming yellow, which helped conceal a generous porch in the old-fashioned style. As Ari passed it, she was startled when a lady pushed opened the gate. She wore a broad, stiff, old-fashioned skirt, and she seemed to have appeared from nowhere with a sudden rustle of her crinoline petticoats.

Ari looked curiously after the woman. Someone coming home late from a Halloween party, she decided, dressed in Civil War style. The woman had a tiny waist but plump arms, bare to the cool autumn air. Her glossy hair was trained in unbecoming sausage curls close to the head at either temple. The woman paused at the corner of Dunbarton and Twenty-ninth, as if she hoped to hail a cab. Ari noticed with a start that she could see the fire hydrant right through the woman's skirt. Suddenly the woman vanished. Ari's heart was pounding hard, and she stumbled

169

on the uneven brick of the sidewalk as she hurried to Sybil's house and knocked on the door.

Sybil flung open the door. "Ari! What's wrong? You're white as a ghost."

"I need to sit down," said Ari. She suited the word to the deed by sitting down at once on the bottom step of the stairs. The woman she had just seen could not be a hypnogogic or hypnopompic vision, she realized, because she was wide awake. Maybe dream images were starting to invade her waking hours. The vampire at the party could have been a dream image come to life, too. "Sybil, who lives in the house on the corner?" she gasped.

Sybil giggled. "A ghost! I'm serious. That house is on all the tours. My dad could tell you all about who built it and everything—it's some important historical place—but all I remember is that's where the ghost lives. Supposedly she came to lunch sometime in the last century and never went home."

"I saw her," said Ari.

"You didn't!" cried Sybil. "It's so unfair! I've lived on this block for ten years, and I've never seen her even once."

"But other people have seen her?" asked Ari anxiously. If other people had seen the ghost, maybe she wasn't going crazy after all.

"Well, it's not like the Loch Ness monster where people come up with photographs they sell to the *National Enquirer*," said Sybil. "It's more like a legend. I don't personally know anybody who's seen her except you."

"Well, I saw something," said Ari. "It could have been somebody left over from a Halloween party except that her skirt was—" Ari wrinkled her nose "—transparent. I could see the fire hydrant right through her!"

Sybil's high, arched eyebrows rose. "Have you ever tried a Ouija board, Ari? I bet you'd be awfully good at it."

A woman with silver-frosted hair stepped into the foyer. "You must be Ari," she said warmly. She extended her hand.

Ari shook hands. "That's what everyone calls me," she said. "But Anne-Marie Montclair is my real name."

Ari felt Mrs. Barron's hand go rigid. The smile froze on her face. "Is your family from around here?" Mrs. Barron asked, her voice quavering.

Ari wondered what on earth was going on; Mrs. Barron seemed stunned by Ari's name. "My father's family is from around here," she said. "But my aunt Gabrielle is the only one of the Montclairs I know. My brother and I grew up in New Orleans."

"Oh," said Mrs. Barron. She backed out of the foyer. "Nice meeting you," she said faintly.

Sybil and Ari looked at each other a minute, and Sybil shrugged. "Search me," Sybil said flatly. "Sometimes she acts kinda weird. Want to go up to my room?"

The girls ran upstairs. Sybil's house was very different from Aunt Gabrielle's. The floor plan was similar, but the Barrons' house was full of light, air, and fresh flowers. Sybil's bedroom was a bower of white lace, with white lace pillows and billowing curtains. "You can see why I don't have many people over," Sybil said. "I tried to get Mom to let me redecorate with black walls and a tweed bedspread, but she got hysterical. She's sort of high-strung."

"I can see that," said Ari. "Does she always freak out when you introduce your friends?"

"Oh, no! She's always trying to get me to bring my friends home. 'Where are your friends?' she keeps saying. Mom wishes I were popular like she was."

"But people like you, Sybil," protested Ari. "I like you. Cos likes you."

"I don't mean that kind of popular. I mean popular like 'Homecoming Queen' and 'Sweetheart of the Key Club.' Mom doesn't quite catch on that people don't do that stuff anymore. I'm a disappointment to her. I'm surprised she froze up on you like that, though. Usually she's charming. Charming is what she does for a living. It's very helpful when she's entertaining my dad's law clients."

"Maybe it's me," said Ari, sitting down on the bed. "Maybe she simply doesn't like me."

"No," said Sybil. "I think it's your name. She was fine until she heard your name. I've got it! I'll bet she once had an affair with your dad! How about that!" She grinned.

"Very funny," said Ari uneasily. Why did her father's name have to keep turning up?

172

"They could have had a thing going back to when they were in high school," insisted Sybil. "They must be about the same age. You did say your dad's family is from around here."

Ari nodded. "My dad actually went to St. Anselm's. Isn't that funny?"

"And my mom went to the St. Anne's School for Girls, which used to be right next door." Sybil licked her lips. "I think we're onto something. They must have known each other. Of course, that was back before St. Anselm's went coed, but I think a lot of the activities between the girls' and the boys' schools were coordinated. This is so neat!" Sybil bounced on the bed. "Just think, Ari, if it had worked out a little differently we could have been sisters."

"If it had worked out between your dad and my mom, then neither of us would exist," Ari said flatly. "You're jumping to a lot of conclusions. Maybe your mother doesn't like me because she hates Aunt Gabrielle or because she doesn't like my looks."

"You are such a spoilsport," said Sybil. "I say we try to find out. Let's look for evidence." Sybil tapped her fingernail on her braces thoughtfully. "We could ask my mother," she suggested.

"*I'm* not going to ask her," said Ari. "You ask her."

"But she might lie," said Sybil promptly, "so that wouldn't prove anything. Wait a minute! I've got it. My mom's old photo albums! Wait here a minute."

Sybil crept out of the room with ostentatious stealth, like a villain in an old melodrama. It was only after she left the room that Ari remembered she hadn't had a chance to ask Sybil what she had come over to ask her. That bucket of flour—who had it landed on?

A few minutes later, Sybil returned staggering under the weight of several heavy photo albums. "I think we're onto something," she panted. "I've already taken a peek."

"You're kidding me!" Ari felt herself go cold. "You mean my father is in your mom's old photo albums?"

"Richard Montclair?" smirked Sybil. "He's there, all right."

"Give me those!" cried Ari. Her hands trembled as she took the album. "I don't even know what he looks like," she said. "When my parents split, Paul and I were too little to remember."

"Isn't this exciting!" cried Sybil. "Flip over to the picture of the third form's string quartet. That's where I spotted the name."

Sybil flipped ahead until she came to a large glossy that showed four serious teenagers. The three boys had buzz cuts and looked like recent inductees into the Army. The girl's hair was in a stiff flip. She wore a full skirt and her ankles were demurely crossed. The picture was labeled "Richard Montclair, Tom Cannon, Averill Harrison, Self."

"That's my mom," said Sybil. "The one called 'self.'"

The young Mrs. Barron was staring at the serious dark-haired boy with the cello. He looked soft with baby fat, almost pretty, but Ari thought she could make out a slight resemblance to Paul.

"Flip ahead," Sybil urged her. "I think they must have been pretty chummy."

Several pages on was another large glossy, this time a prom picture. Mrs. Barron, wearing a strapless tulle evening dress with rows of ruffles and with a corsage of carnations strapped to her wrist, was beaming at the camera. Standing next to her was a tall, dark boy with high cheekbones. He was dressed in patent leather shoes, a black jacket with satin lapels, and a black bow tie. "Richard Montclair and Self," the picture was labeled carefully. "Spring Formal."

"Isn't that weird!" Sybil breathed. "Your mother and my dad went to the prom together. Unbelievable!"

Ari stared at the picture for some time as if willing the photograph to give up the secret of what her father was like. But all she saw was a stiffly self-conscious teenager who vaguely resembled her brother. What had she expected? she wondered.

"Keep looking," said Sybil. "Maybe we'll find some more pictures."

Ari turned the page. Anyone would have imagined Richard Montclair was a member of Sybil's family, thought Ari; he was on almost every page of the photo album. Soon "Richard Montclair" was shortened simply to "Richard." Over the course of two albums, Ari watched Richard's baby fat disappear. His nose and cheekbones grew more pronounced, and his smile grew confident and charming. In swim trunks he balanced on one foot, laughing, on an anonymous boat dock. In heavy makeup with a wig he was "Richard as Macbeth." Then came a Halloween picture with him dressed as Dracula. Ari stared mesmerized at the Instamatic snapshot—the aquiline nose under the white makeup, the dark eyes. Though the features were softer, he looked disturbingly like the vampire of her bad dream, the one who had terrified her at the Boo Ball. Ari could feel that her palms were damp as she clenched and unclenched her fists. "Sybil, who did that bucket of flour fall on last night?"

"That's the funniest thing!" said Sybil. "Nobody seems to know. I must have called fifty people and nobody's got a clue. Six people told me it was Cos, but we know for sure it wasn't him."

"Paul saw the whole thing. Nadia dumped the flour," said Ari.

"That would make sense," said Sybil promptly. "Since Cos broke up with her, I've been halfway expecting she'd do something crazy like this, but if it was her, you can bet Amanda was helping her. Nadia doesn't have the nerve to do it by herself. You'd think they'd be trying to get Cos, but they must have messed up somehow."

"I think I know how. I think they got another vampire instead. I have this weird feeling," Ari said, "that my father was at the party dressed like Dracula. He asked me to dance."

Sybil looked at her blankly. "And you didn't even

recognize him? Oh, I forgot. You didn't know what he looked like, so how could you recognize him?"

"Can I borrow one of these pictures, Sybil?" asked Ari grimly. "I want to show Paul what our dad looks like."

"Sure," said Sybil. "Which one?"

Ari chose the snapshot of her father in a swimsuit on the dock. The picture was full of sunlight, and his smile was dazzling. That was the way she liked to think of him. Sybil slid her fingers under the snapshot, bending it only a little, and pulled it off the album page. "Don't lose it, though," Sybil said. "My mom never looks at these old albums, but with my luck she'll get a fit of nostalgia next week, and I'll get in a bunch of trouble."

"Hide the album," suggested Ari. "You'd better act like you can't find it, because chances are she'll dig it out tonight. Since she's run into me, I'm sure she'll be reminded of my dad."

Sybil grinned. "Good idea. You've got a natural aptitude for crime."

"I better go," said Ari. "I've got to show this to Paul."

Sybil walked Ari to the front door and waved to her. "If you see any more ghosts, let me know!" she called.

Ari hurried away down the block, averting her eyes from the haunted house. The last thing she wanted was to be known as the girl who was psychic. She wished she hadn't mentioned the ghost at all.

CHAPTER
FIFTEEN

PAUL STARED AT THE SNAPSHOT. "HE LOOKS SORT OF like me, all right."

"Sort of," said Ari. "But you look better."

"I don't know about that. He looks like the kind girls would go for."

"Sybil's mother seemed to go for him," said Ari. "She had lots and lots of pictures of him. They must have gone together for years. I wonder why they split up. You should have seen Mrs. Barron when she realized he was my dad. Anybody would have thought she'd spotted a rattlesnake."

"Maybe he cheated on her," said Paul.

The glare reflected off the water lit up her father's face and spotlighted his dazzling smile. He looked as if nothing bad could ever happen to him.

"He doesn't look like a drunk, does he?" said Paul. "He looks healthy."

"Maybe he wasn't a drunk back then," said Ari.

"I've got to get this picture back to Sybil. I only borrowed it."

"Let's take it somewhere and get it copied," suggested Paul. "I think there are camera shops that can do that. Are you pretty sure he was the one you saw at the dance, Ari?"

"I'm not sure of anything anymore," she admitted. "But it could have been. I was pretty shaken up and the light wasn't good. Besides, that snapshot must have been taken when he was about our age. By now he would have changed. It could have been him, though. And if it was, you have to admit that would explain the flour spill downstairs."

Paul chewed thoughtfully on his thumbnail. "Yeah, I guess he'd naturally come here to Aunt Gabrielle's to clean up."

"But if he's coming here to the house, why is he being so hush-hush about it?" cried Ari. "If he wants to see us, why doesn't he just come visit? What's the big deal?"

"Maybe it was him hiding behind that black mirror. Maybe he's looking us over to see if we're worth claiming," suggested Paul, with a trace of bitterness.

"All these years and not a word," said Ari. "Not even when Mamma died. The rat!" She thought of the vampire at the Boo Ball—his peremptory, overbearing manner. If that had been her father, no wonder she had hated him on sight. She clenched her fists. "I wish I'd been the one who dumped the flour on him."

"Don't you want to see him, though?" asked Paul. "In spite of all that?"

"I couldn't care less," said Ari coldly.

"Well, I'd like at least to get a look at him."

"After the way he's behaved?" cried Ari.

"I don't care," said Paul stubbornly. "At least I'd like to meet him."

"He's horrible," said Ari in a low voice.

"He's our father," said Paul. "I want to see him. I might ask Aunt Gabrielle if he's in town."

"You think she'd tell you?" asked Ari.

Paul made a face. "I don't know." He took the picture from Ari. "Anyway, we'll get the picture copied, one copy for each of us."

"Do whatever you want to with yours." Ari's eyes narrowed. "But I'm going to throw darts at mine."

Wednesday afternoon was foggy. Paul had begun training with the cross-country team and was slogging around the track with the others. He could hear ducks quacking somewhere in the mist. Probably they'd lost their way in the rain and had mistaken the school's playing fields for Rock Creek Park. He had lost sight of Sandy and was concentrating on his breathing. He was out of shape; that was for sure. He looked down at his white sweatshirt. "St. Anselm's Cross Country," it said, but he didn't feel like part of the team.

He was jogging around the track, going to class and doing his homework, but he felt as if he were holding his breath, expecting every minute that something overwhelming would happen.

Paul could hear his feet thudding against the

damp sand of the track. The back of his neck prickled as he heard a faint tuneless whistling. He stopped and listened, holding himself rigid. He could feel the cold fog settling on his bare skin and something else—a tight painful feeling in his chest.

Bryan ran by him. "You sprain an ankle or something, Montclair?" he panted.

Paul shook his head. He took a deep breath and set off running, but his concentration was shot. He had heard that whistling before, but the memory seemed just beyond his reach. He felt gooseflesh rise on his arms.

The lockers were in the activities building next to the gym. Sandy stepped out of the shower and toweled off, pink from head to toe. He pulled on his shorts. "You're going to run on Saturday, aren't you, Paul?"

Paul shrugged. "I guess." He tied his sneakers. "I'm out of shape, but it'll be good practice." He wondered if Sandy had heard that tuneless whistle out on the track. He didn't like to ask. He wasn't sure why. Maybe because it had given him the creeps.

"It's a long drive into town for me," said Sandy, rubbing his hair dry. "And the van leaves awfully early for the meet. It sure would be better if I could stay with somebody here in town the night before."

Paul barely heard him. He went on buttoning his shirt as if in a daze.

"Oh, come on, Paul. Can't you get a hint?" said

Sandy, exasperated. "Can I stay with you Friday night so I don't have to drive in for the meet Saturday morning?"

Paul laughed suddenly. He realized that Sandy was trying to get close to Ari. That was okay. Paul had seen Cos and Ari sneaking kisses around school lately, and it made him sick. "Sure. Spend the night at our place," said Paul. "That'd be great."

He had never checked out the guest bedroom across from Aunt Gabrielle's room, but when he thought of the dark shadows and the looming shapes upstairs, he suddenly was certain it would be better for Sandy to stay in his room, not down the hall. "Better bring a sleeping bag," he added. "I'm not sure what the extra bed situation is, but I know you can stay in my room." He grinned. "Ari's room is right next door to mine."

Sandy flushed self-consciously.

That evening, Paul checked with Aunt Gabrielle to see if it was okay for Sandy to stay over. She seemed to love the idea. "I'll have Carmel fix a nice roast," she said. "I know runners need good red meat to build up their blood." The tip of her pink tongue skated delicately across her lip, and Paul involuntarily took a step back. What was it about Aunt Gabrielle? he wondered nervously. When her eyes narrowed, a cold wind seemed to brush the back of his neck. With her deathly white skin and her thick black hair, she looked like an Egyptian queen just stepping out of a mummy case.

Ari seemed unaware of the chill that had fallen over her twin. She leaned serenely against the door to the kitchen and took a bite out of an apple. "Aunt Gabrielle, do you have any family albums? You know, photographs and stuff?"

Aunt Gabrielle gave a low, musical laugh that gurgled in her throat. She had an odd sort of laugh, with her lips only slightly parted. "We never went in much for photographs in our family, I'm afraid," she said. "I may have a few school photos somewhere of me as a little girl in braces, but I have no idea at all where they are. It's probably just as well. I must have been a dreadful child."

"No pictures of our dad either?" asked Ari.

"I'll look around," promised Aunt Gabrielle. "Surely I must have something of Richard. No, on second thought, he may have taken those with him."

Ari gave Paul a significant look. "Have you seen Dad lately?"

Aunt Gabrielle's hand went to her throat. "Why do you ask, dear?"

"Sybil had a picture of him in her family album," said Ari. "And I saw somebody who looked a lot like him at the Boo Ball. Whoever it was asked me to dance."

"Richard at a school dance?" Aunt Gabrielle was amused. "Oh, I don't think so. That wouldn't be his style at all."

"What is his style?" asked Paul.

"Life in the fast lane." Aunt Gabrielle made a vague, distracted gesture. "Richard never was attracted to the quiet life. He always went to extremes."

Ari thought of the serious-faced boy in the string quartet and wondered what had happened to change him into the man Aunt Gabrielle was describing. Had he suddenly hatched a new personality when he grew up? And could that happen to her and Paul, too? The idea made her uncomfortable.

After the twins went upstairs, they sat on Ari's bed talking. "Doesn't Aunt Gabrielle give you the creeps?" Paul asked.

"Sure," said Ari, surprised. "She's given me the creeps since the first night we met her."

Paul shivered. "Yeah, but just now—"

"What?" asked Ari eagerly. "What are you getting at?"

"I don't know," said Paul. "I just wish we knew what the heck was going on."

Ari stiffened suddenly. "Paul, maybe it's not a good idea for Sandy to spend the night here."

"It'll be fine," he said weakly. His imagination had gone into overdrive. Obviously Aunt Gabrielle was not some evil sorceress risen from the dead. What was he so wrought up about? "Probably Aunt Gabrielle figures Dad is a bad influence," Paul said, "so she's trying to keep him away from us." He desperately wanted to believe that nothing was wrong. "You know what a nut Aunt Gabrielle is about self-control," he said. "Maybe our dad makes a fool of himself at parties, drinks too much, wears lampshades on his head, or something like that."

"I saw him, Paul. You didn't." Ari shivered. "He scared me."

184

"You *think* you saw him." Paul paused a second, uncomfortably. "It was confusing that night. Everybody was in costume, and with that strobe light, half the people there looked like mass murderers."

"I don't care. I wish you'd tell Sandy he can't spend the night here."

Paul hesitated. Maybe Ari was right. But what explanation would he give to Sandy? "He's going to sleep right in my room," said Paul, frowning. "What can go wrong?"

CHAPTER
SIXTEEN

CARMEL OUTDID HERSELF WITH THE FEAST SHE SERVED the night Sandy came. The chandelier shimmered overhead and a splendid brown roast with little potatoes, onions, and carrots sat at the center of the gleaming mahogany table. Dinner had been served late, and it had a special, formal feeling.

"Does your aunt always serve wine with the meals?" Sandy whispered to Paul.

"Pretty much," he answered. But often he had noticed after dinner that her glass was untouched. She served wine, but she never seemed to drink it. Tonight, however, Paul had seen her lift the glass to her lips. Her cheeks were pink and her violet eyes shone.

After Sandy poured himself another glass, Paul moved the wine bottle out of reach. He didn't want Sandy to get drunk. He was beginning to wonder if he had had too much himself. The wine in Aunt Gabrielle's glass looked funny to him somehow, thicker than the wine in his own glass. It seemed to cling to the sides of the glass as if it were sticky. When she put it down, it sloshed slightly, a deep ruby-red. Paul glanced up at his aunt and was startled to see that her violet eyes were jewel-like, glowing as if they were lit from within. Paul gasped. "I think I need some fresh air," he said. He hastily pushed his chair away from the table and lurched toward the large French doors. He stumbled outside into the chill night air of the terrace. He could feel the uneven bricks under his feet, and nearby a tree creaked as it moved in the breeze. As he gulped in air, his eyes fell to the flower beds that edged the brick pavement. In the dim light, he made out a bit of brown—a small piece of fur, its hair shining in the light cast by the big windows. *That shouldn't be there,* he thought. He remembered how the man at Aunt Gabrielle's party had passed out standing in this precise spot, his fat body crumpling like a folding paper fan. Paul's head spun with formless images, swirling shapes, pinwheels, and black spots, and he felt himself sway.

Ari's voice suddenly brought him to his senses with a start. "Paul," Ari cried. "Are you all right?" He felt her grab his arm.

Wordlessly, Paul gestured toward the pathetic pelt of fur.

Ari stooped to look at it, then hastily straightened up. Her face was pale in the uncertain light. "It's all right," she said. "It's only a dead rat. It's

187

just that something has—has bitten off its head."
The twins stared at each other for a long moment.
Ari's eyes were wide and luminous in the dim
light. Her dark hair fell in glossy waves to her
shoulders. In the dim light, she looked frighteningly like Aunt Gabrielle and Paul gulped. "A cat
must have got it," she went on breathlessly. "That's
what's happened."

"Sure," said Paul. He supposed he should push
the rat's oddly flattened body under one of the
azaleas so Carmel wouldn't get an unpleasant
shock when she saw it, but he couldn't bring himself to touch it. Ari seemed in no rush to move it,
either. "I think I'd better lay off the wine from
now on," said Paul. He glanced at the big lighted
windows of the dining room. Aunt Gabrielle's
back was to them, and she appeared in silhouette,
a dark figure with a faint glimmer of jeweled
combs in her upswept hair. Across from her,
Sandy, his face flushed, drained his wineglass.

"You'd better go in and get the bottle away
from Sandy," said Ari. "If we're not careful, he's
going to be sliding under the table in a minute."

The twins opened the French doors. Aunt
Gabrielle regarded them anxiously as they came in.
"Are you all right, Paul? I hope dinner wasn't too
rich. Carmel has a heavy hand with the butter."

"Dinner was fine—delicious, in fact," said Paul.
He had to grab on to the back of a chair to steady
himself. He made his way around the table to his
place and took the bottle of wine from Sandy's
hands. "I think Sandy and me had better lay off the

wine, Aunt Gabrielle," said Paul. "We've got a race tomorrow."

"Of course." Aunt Gabrielle smiled. "It was thoughtless of me to put it out." She pressed the cork back in the bottle and it slid in with a protesting squeak. She placed it on the sideboard next to the brandy decanter.

Paul caught himself staring at his aunt. Her slender figure was encased in a clinging cashmere dress of lavender. The skirt fell in soft folds to the floor and moved gently as she turned to face them with a smile. Her arms were bare—the dress had only thin little straps—and Paul could make out the delicate bones in her chest, her skin stretched tightly over them. Paul thought the room was a bit chilly, but Aunt Gabrielle was wearing far fewer clothes than either he or Ari, and she showed no signs of gooseflesh. A chill shook him. "We have to get up early," said Paul suddenly. "Maybe we'd better turn in now."

"It is late," agreed Ari, rising hastily.

"Nice dinner," said Sandy. "Real nice."

"I'm glad you enjoyed it." Aunt Gabrielle smiled her strange half-smile.

Together the twins helped Sandy down the long hallway. His steps were uncertain as they mounted the stairs, and the twins were half-supporting him. "Ari," said Sandy, "do you know that song 'AchyBreaky Heart'?"

"I've heard it once or twice," said Ari cautiously.

"It makes me think of you," said Sandy. "All the

189

songs I hear make me think of you."

Paul wondered exactly how much Sandy had had to drink. He wasn't going to be much good to the team nursing a hangover.

"Do boys ever tell you you're beautiful?" Sandy went on.

Ari dimpled. "Constantly."

"I was afraid of that," said Sandy.

Ari watched anxiously as Paul guided his friend into his bedroom. "Better lock the connecting door," Paul told his twin in a low voice.

Paul hadn't drunk as much as Sandy, but he felt sick. He helped Sandy get in his pajamas and unrolled the sleeping bag. Sandy snuggled into it at once and made a comical snuffling sound. Paul went into his bathroom and got an aspirin for his aching head. When he got back, Sandy was snoring softly. Paul put on his pajamas, then pushed aside the curtains and stared at the terrace below. In the light cast on the terrace, he saw a slender shadow moving back and forth. Aunt Gabrielle was clearing the table, he realized. Paul felt a flash of anger. What had she meant by serving Sandy all that wine? She knew they were competing first thing in the morning.

He let the curtain drop from his hands, slid into bed, and pulled the covers up to his chin. He slept fitfully. The moonlight and the sighing night wind disturbed him. Tossing, half-awake, he felt his flesh prickle with unease.

Suddenly his eyes were drawn to Sandy's sleeping bag. A woman in a cloak had bent over him.

Paul noticed that her cloak moved and shifted easily, as if it were made of something lighter and more fluid than cloth—mist perhaps. Its folds billowed and shifted around her as she looked up. Paul was shocked to see that her face was the face of the skull hidden in the mantelpiece—the jaw hung loosely, held only with flabby shreds of rotting flesh. Bat's teeth grinned at him, and in the eye sockets, lavender eyes glowed with an eerie iridescence. It was Aunt Gabrielle! She was dead!

He sat bolt upright.

Aunt Gabrielle was kneeling beside Sandy's sleeping bag. Her dress was gray in the dark.

"Aunt Gabrielle!" Paul cried.

She lifted her head slowly, her jeweled combs glinting. Then she turned and smiled at him. To his relief, her face showed the faint pink of life. She was not a skeleton at all; he had only been dreaming. He hugged himself and shivered.

"I thought I'd better check on the dear boy," she said softly. "I'm afraid I shouldn't have let him have that wine, Paul. I blame myself." She raised a finger to her lips. "Shh—let's be careful not to wake him up." She rose and glided toward the door, passing by the foot of Paul's bed where a band of light from the window fell on her flushed face. She seemed especially lovely, and she moved with an uncanny smoothness, like a sleepwalker. "Sleep tight," she whispered. The door closed behind her.

Paul wasn't sure how long he sat in bed, staring at Sandy's still form in the sleeping bag. He could make out the spiky outline of Sandy's hair, but he was afraid to go over and look in his friend's face. He was afraid of what he might see. He leapt out of bed and rapped on the door.

It opened at once, as if Ari had been waiting for his signal. She stood before him in her flowing white nightgown, her eyes wide with fear. The windowpanes showed the first trace of the pale light that comes before dawn. "Ari," Paul gasped. "Aunt Gabrielle came in my room just now!"

Ari stared at him, white-faced with shock.

"She was bending over Sandy," said Paul hoarsely.

"Is he all right?" cried Ari.

The twins rushed back into Paul's room and Ari bent over Sandy in unconscious imitation of Aunt Gabrielle's motion. Paul could hardly bear to look.

"He's breathing," Ari said, with a frightened glance over her shoulder. "I think he's okay."

Paul sat down suddenly on his bed and wiped his palm over his damp brow. "I thought—jeez, to tell you the truth, I don't know what I thought. All kinds of crazy things! I must have been going out of my mind." He shuddered. "I was having a nightmare. When I woke up, I was actually afraid to look at him."

The alarm buzzed and Sandy stirred. Ari stood up quickly. She flashed Paul a smile as she reached for the door. "Good luck with the race!" she whispered. She slipped back into her room.

Sandy's eyes flew open. "What time is it?" he said thickly.

Paul glanced at the clock. "Five o'clock. Time to hit the road."

Sandy groaned. "I feel terrible."

Paul's heart raced, but after a second he said, "You shouldn't have drunk all that wine, man."

"I know," said Sandy, clutching a hand to his head. "Never again. Don't tell Coach, okay?"

"No problem," agreed Paul. There was a lot he didn't want to tell Coach. He only wished he had followed Ari's advice and not let Sandy sleep over.

As the team van sped along the highway, Sandy seemed dazed. He looked out the window at nothing in particular. Farm fenceposts cast long shadows on the grass that verged the highway. They were far from the city.

A teammate nudged Paul. "Look at Sandy," he said. "He's out of it. He must be in love." A couple of other guys laughed, but when Paul glanced at Sandy's glassy eyes, the laughter died in his throat.

At last they saw the fluttering flags and the large sign that announced they had arrived at the meet. A clutch of vans were already parked on the bare clay at the edge of the course.

"We're running kind of late," said the coach, frowning. "But most of you know this course. Paul, you'd better walk over it and familiarize yourself with it. It's pretty well-marked."

Paul set out alone to walk the course. The flags marking the route fluttered in the cold breeze. Leaden clouds obscured the sky, and Paul felt oppressed by the gloomy day. The race didn't seem to matter to him anymore. He turned around abruptly and walked back. He could see the bright colors of the team vans directly ahead. Coach had gathered the team into a group for a last-minute pep talk. Sandy's back was to Paul, but he was easy to recognize with his bristled reddish hair. Suddenly Sandy's head dipped and he fell forward. Two boys grabbed him and laid him on his back. Paul ran over to the group in horror.

"He's fainted," said Coach. His fingers were on Sandy's wrist, checking his pulse.

Sandy stirred. "Wha—?" he said, struggling to get up.

"You stay right there, Sandy," said Coach.

Mr. Tomlin, the assistant coach, knelt beside Sandy on the other side. "How do you feel, son?"

"Okay." Sandy tried to prop himself up on his elbows.

"No need to rush to get up," said Coach. His steady gaze met Coach Tomlin's. "We're going to have to take him in to the hospital to be checked out. You'd better go with me, Tommy. One of us has to keep an eye on the boy and one of us has to drive."

"I'll go with you," said Paul suddenly.

"You aren't going to run today?" asked Coach Tomlin.

Paul shook his head. "I couldn't," he said.

A glance at Paul's face must have convinced the coach he was in no shape to run. It was soon settled that Paul and Coach would take Sandy to the emergency room. They helped him to the van.

"I'm okay," Sandy protested. "You don't have to help me. I can walk."

"No sense taking any chances," said Coach. "You keep your arms around our necks. Have you been feeling sick, son?"

Sandy shot Paul an anguished glance. Paul knew he was worried that the coach would find out about all the wine he had drunk. "I'm okay," Sandy mumbled. "Honest."

"He seemed kind of out of it on the trip over," Paul volunteered. "And he looks awfully pale, doesn't he?"

Paul could tell by the set expression of the coach's lips that he was worried. Once they got out on the highway, Paul watched the needle of the speedometer creep steadily upward.

At last they arrived at a hospital entrance marked "EMERGENCY." Paul and Coach supported Sandy as he got out of the van. Awkwardly the three of them made their way to the lighted doors. As the automatic glass doors swung open before them, Sandy suddenly sagged against Paul. "He's fainted again," cried Paul, catching him under the other arm. A wheelchair materialized almost at once, and a moment later Sandy was whisked into the examining room. Paul had visited the emergency room once or twice and he knew that people could sit for hours there waiting their turn, but evidently being unconscious qualified Sandy to move to the front of the line. Coach and Paul went into the examining room with him. Sandy winced as a nurse pricked his finger.

"Hemoglobin count very low," a white-coated doctor said moments later, pulling on fleshy latex gloves. "The kid hardly has any blood left in him. We're going to have to do a transfusion. Can you give us permission?"

"Yes," Coach said steadily, but he was as white as chalk. "I need a phone. I've got to call the boy's parents."

The doctor glanced at Paul. "You better sit down," he said. "We don't need to have another one passing out on us."

Paul sank into a plastic chair next to the examining table. Sandy was on a stretcher now, not moving.

"Is he going to be all right?" Paul asked faintly.

"Don't worry," said the doctor. "He's in good hands. We've just got to get some blood into him."

White-coated orderlies wheeled Sandy out of the examining room. Coach talked to the doctor privately a moment over in a corner. Paul watched Coach dial Sandy's parents on the pay phone in the waiting room. It seemed he was on the phone a long time. When he returned, he placed a hand on Paul's shoulder. "No sense in you hanging around, Paul. They're going to keep Sandy overnight. Can you get somebody to come get you? I'm going to have to wait here for his folks."

"I'll have my sister come get me," said Paul. "You do think he's going to be all right, don't you, Coach?"

"You heard the doctor. He's in good hands," said Coach, but his eyes looked strained. "He's bleeding internally somehow, and it'll take them a while to figure out where. The doctor said that with as much blood as he had lost, he shouldn't have been able to stand up. Probably he wouldn't have been able to get out of bed this morning if he hadn't been a runner. Runners' blood carries so much oxygen that they can get by on less of it than most folks." Coach wiped his brow with a handkerchief. "Modern medicine is amazing. Don't you worry. They'll fix him up."

Ari got to the hospital even before Sandy's parents did.

"How fast did you drive, Ari?" asked Paul irritably. He grabbed her arm and they hurried out to the parking lot. He scowled, wanting deep inside to throw his arms around her and weep.

"I was worried!" Ari said. "Sure, I was speeding. I couldn't make any sense out of what you were saying, Paul. What's wrong with Sandy?"

"Let's get out of this place." Paul pulled the car door open. "Coach has been asking me if Sandy was acting funny, and the last thing I want is for Sandy's parents to start asking me the same thing."

"He did drink a lot last night," said Ari.

Paul shot her a scornful look as they sped out of the parking lot. "Overdoing it on wine usually doesn't put guys in the hospital," he said.

"Well, what's wrong with him, then?"

They drove for a moment in silence. "Ari, the doctor said he hardly had any blood left in him."

Ari stared blankly at the road ahead. "But what can that mean?"

"It means Aunt Gabrielle was sucking the

blood out of him last night!" cried Paul. "That's what it means. He was white as a sheet on the drive out here, completely out of it. That's why she came in my room last night—she wanted Sandy's blood."

Ari laid a hand on Paul's arm. "You're upset. You're not thinking straight."

Paul shook off her hand impatiently. "Cut it out, Ari. Sure, I'm freaking out. I've got a good reason to freak out. You know that dead rat we saw on the terrace last night?"

Ari nodded. Her eyes were frightened.

"Aunt Gabrielle bit off its head. I bet you rat's blood was in her wineglass last night. That's why it looked thicker than wine. Didn't you notice the way it sort of stuck to the sides of the glass? It was already coagulating. Usually she doesn't touch her wine, but she drank it all last night, all right." Paul laughed shortly. "She didn't like the taste of it much. I remember she sort of screwed up her face when she drank it. She probably liked Sandy's blood better. Good, oxygen-rich runner's blood." Paul shot Ari a bitter look. "Once I get back into shape, maybe I'll be the next one on the dinner list."

Large signs over the highway indicated that the junction with Route 295 was coming up soon. "We can't go back to the house now," Ari said suddenly. "Go downtown. We need to find a place we can talk."

Paul changed lanes as if in a dream. The sky overhead was dark, draining the scene of all color.

A thunderstorm would almost be a relief, he thought. Tension lay heavy in the air, and his skin felt tight. Out of the corner of his eye, he saw Ari's shirt rising and falling with her quick breath. If she hadn't been there, he would have gone crazy.

A half hour later, Paul pulled the car into a vacant parking spot in front of the National Gallery. He and Ari thrust their hands in their pockets, bent against the cold breeze, and silently mounted the tall steps. An elevator took them down to the lower level. Paul heard the soothing spattering of the artificial waterfall and headed in that direction, following the signs to the cafeteria.

Luckily, the tables were mostly empty. Only a few arty-looking people dressed in black and wearing handcrafted jewelry sipped tea and ate croissants by some potted palms. The twins found a table and turned their chairs to face the falling water. Paul hoped its white noise would help keep anyone from overhearing what he had to say.

"It all adds up," he told Ari grimly. "Aunt Gabrielle never goes out in the sun—and I mean never. We should have realized what that meant. Haven't you seen those old vampire movies when Dracula hears the rooster crow and gets real nervous? Next thing you know, he's running back to his coffin to hide before the sun comes up. Sun must be poison for vampires. When you think about it, that must be why Aunt Gabrielle couldn't come to Mom's funeral. It wasn't that she had the flu. She simply didn't dare go out in the sun."

"She took us to St. Anselm's that first day," argued Ari, "when she registered us for classes."

"It was raining," said Paul. "Remember? Not a chance of any sun. And she wore that big floppy hat even then."

"I think she's always trying to protect her complexion," said Ari.

Paul snorted. "Remember that poor guy we thought she was making out with after the dinner party? He had to be helped to his car."

"Shh!" Ari whispered. She glanced around nervously. "Don't shout."

"What other woman goes jogging around Georgetown alone after dark?" asked Paul. "Aunt Gabrielle's not jogging, Ari! She's going hunting!"

"What are you saying, Paul?" Ari's voice trembled.

"You want me to spell it out for you? Aunt Gabrielle is a vampire!"

Ari cast a glance at some people sitting a few tables away. A few words floated over the sound of the waterfall. "—tonal values—Matisse-like, don't you think?"

Ari leaned close to Paul. "But there's no such thing as vampires," she whispered harshly.

"Tell that to Aunt Gabri," said Paul. "Better yet, tell it to poor Sandy. They're pumping blood into him right this minute."

"There's got to be some kind of logical explanation," insisted Ari.

"Maybe." Paul grabbed Ari's hand and looked

her in the eyes. "But you know in your heart that this is the right one."

The twins looked at each other for a long minute.

"Ari," Paul whispered finally, "what if our dad's a vampire, too?"

Ari ran her fingers through her hair frantically. "What are we going to do?"

CHAPTER
SEVENTEEN

THE TWINS WERE SILENT AS THEY DROVE TOWARD THE town house. They gazed out the car windows. The ordinary life of the city was going on as if nothing had changed. A delivery van pulled abreast of them at a traffic light. THE LAME DUCK RESTAURANT, the lettering on its side proclaimed. LET US WOK AND ROLL YOU. A woman carrying a shiny plastic dry-cleaning bag passed by. Standing at the corner, waiting for the light, was an old man in a Stetson hat. Silver rosettes ringed the crown of his hat. Then the light changed and the traffic surged ahead. The twins moved on, oblivious to the normal world around them.

"We could search Aunt Gabrielle's room while she's out jogging," Paul said suddenly.

"Paul!" Ari was aghast.

"I hear that during the daytime vampires sleep in their coffins," Paul insisted. "If we found a coffin in her bedroom that would prove it."

"We can't search Aunt Gabrielle's room," said Ari. "She's been so nice to us! That would be an awful thing to do."

"She's probably hidden the coffin anyway," said Paul gloomily.

Ari eyed him uneasily. "Maybe we ought to call the hospital and check on how Sandy is getting on before we do anything we might regret."

"You keep thinking there's going to be some reasonable explanation for all this, don't you? We're going to call the hospital, and it'll turn out Sandy's got a bleeding ulcer, and Aunt Gabrielle is a nice lady with a sun allergy, and everything's just fine and dandy."

"No," Ari said slowly. "I guess I don't really think that." She had thought from the first that Aunt Gabrielle was strange. Nothing in the past weeks had altered that first impression.

"Remember last night in the dining room?" Paul said. "She was wearing that thin dress with the itty-bitty straps, and she wasn't a bit cold. No sign of goose bumps. She's not human, Ari!"

Ari was surprised that she didn't feel more shocked at what Paul was saying. She supposed she had suspected something was amiss all along. After all, she had noticed right off that Aunt Gabri wasn't in any way like an ordinary middle-aged woman. No bags sagged under her eyes, no crow's-feet appeared at the corners of her eyes when she smiled, and she had none of the usual comfortable padding of fat that middle-aged people have. Her lips were cold. Her eyes were that unearthly lavender. Small things, maybe, but they added up. Ari gazed out the window. Ahead she could see the gilt weather vane on top of the clock of the Crestan Bank Building. They were almost home.

When the twins drove up to the house, they were startled to see that the curtains of the living room were closed. They stared at each other a moment, not sure what to think. Paul pulled the Mazda into the garage and they got out. A cold wind drove rattling leaves down the walk as they mounted the front steps. A vase stood outside the black-lacquered front door, its mixed flowers nodding in the breeze, an incongruous splash of color. Ari slid her key into the lock, and the twins held their breath as they stepped into the house.

The big doors to the living room had been drawn back, and Aunt Gabrielle lay stretched out on the striped satin sofa. Her brow creased, her hand held to her temple, she looked as if she had a bad headache. She wore black satin pajamas and cutaway slippers that revealed bony, high-arched feet. "My darlings," she cried, sitting up suddenly. She patted a spot beside her on the sofa. "Come sit beside me. We must talk, my pets."

Paul had a sudden urge to pull the twisted satin cord and open the heavy velvet curtains to the sunlight; then he remembered that the day was so gloomy that would prove nothing. It was dim in the living room now, but it would scarcely be less dim if he pulled the curtains back.

He took a seat on one of the chairs opposite

the couch. He noticed that Ari did the same. Clearly neither of them wanted to sit next to Aunt Gabrielle. Neither even wanted to be in her reach. Paul stared at his aunt, hoping that his suspicions would seem ridiculous once he looked at her. But the more closely he looked, the more she seemed to him like a vampire. Her skin was unearthly white. It wasn't like ordinary skin at all. And her violet eyes seemed to glow as if lit from within.

Aunt Gabrielle pressed a bony hand to her head and sighed. "I loathe emotional scenes," she said. "As you know, moderation in all things is my motto. I have never cared for living from crisis to crisis the way your father does."

Paul glanced at Ari. He was in no mood to hear another lecture on the virtues of self-control. He began to speak, but Aunt Gabrielle raised a hand. "No, hear me out, dear." She took a deep shuddering breath. "I am going to have a little party this evening," she said. "A small soiree to introduce you to some intimate family friends. I want you both to be sure to be there, so don't make any other plans."

"I wish you would answer a few questions for us first," said Ari. A glint of determination shone in her eyes.

Aunt Gabrielle made a gesture with one bony hand as if she were pushing Ari away. "Not now, my dear ones, not now. I need my beauty sleep. After the party tonight, we'll talk. But please don't go all priggish and judgmental on me, my dear. I couldn't endure it if you turned into some insufferable puritan. I'm sure I don't need to say another word about that. You are such a sweet, sensitive child." She rose from the couch, and with a sad smile, she glided through the open door. A moment later, they heard the clack of the heels of her slippers on the stairs.

Paul stood up. "'Moderation in all things,'" he mocked her mincing voice. "She didn't use much moderation when she went after Sandy, did she?"

Ari cast an anxious glance at the staircase across the hall. "Hush, Paul, what if she hears you?"

"It doesn't matter if she does. She must know we're onto her. Otherwise what's that stuff about how she hates big emotional scenes? I don't see any point in waiting until after her stupid party."

Ari realized that she herself shrank from big emotional scenes. When it had come right down to it, she hadn't been able to press Aunt Gabrielle for answers. But Paul was right. They couldn't go on like this. She forced herself to unclench her fists and breathe deeply.

"I don't know," Paul continued, clutching a hand to his belly. "I feel like something's jumping around in my stomach. Maybe we shouldn't talk to her at all. Maybe we ought to clear out and run like hell."

Ari nodded. She had the sensation that the shadows in the hallway stirred with life. The wind that swept past the lacquered black door outside sighed and moaned in an unearthly voice. Even the electric sconces on the walls seemed to move a bit in her peripheral vision, as if the lights were held by unseen hands.

206

The twins tiptoed upstairs. They cast a fearful glance at the closed door of their aunt's bedroom as they passed it. Ari thought of the fanged man with the aquiline nose who had visited her room early one morning, casting his crooked shadow on her wall. He had looked like her father, she thought. But his hand had not warmed the doorknob. Had it been her father? Or a ghost or shadow of her father, similar to the ghost she had seen on Dunbarton Street of the party guest who had never left?

In Paul's room, the twins sat facing each other on the bed. "This is so awful," said Ari. "We can't tell anybody. I can't breathe a word to Cos or even to Sybil. They'd think I was certifiable if I told them what was going on."

"I'm not so sure of that," said Paul. "We can't be the only ones who've noticed that there's something weird about Aunt Gabrielle."

The twins emptied their wallets, spreading a few crumpled bills and change out on the bedspread. "That's it," said Paul. "Barely twenty dollars. But I've still got six hundred in the bank left over from my summer job. What about you?"

Ari sighed. "Three hundred, maybe. Baby-sitting doesn't pay very well."

"We could get back to New Orleans on what we've got," Paul said. "But I don't know what we'd live on once we got there, and the problem is Aunt Gabrielle would know right where to look for us. All she'd have to do is ask around and she'd find us in a matter of hours."

Ari blinked rapidly. "What if she sent the police after us?"

"I don't think she'd call the police," said Paul. "She's got too much to hide." He stuffed the bills back into his wallet. "I wish I knew more about vampires. We've got to figure out some way to protect ourselves, Ari. What about that garlic and crucifix stuff? I wonder if that would work."

Ari shook her head. "Carmel practically bathes in garlic. Think of her spaghetti sauce."

Paul nodded. "I've seen a gold cross around Carmel's neck, too, and that's never bothered Aunt Gabrielle. The garlic and crucifix stuff must not work."

"What about a stake in the heart?" suggested Ari.

Paul stared at her. "Good grief, Ari. I couldn't drive a stake into Aunt Gabrielle's heart! What do you think I am?"

Ari knew she couldn't drive a stake in her aunt's heart, either. She shrugged ruefully.

"One thing we *do* know is that Aunt Gabrielle can't take the sun," said Paul. "She never goes out in it. So that's something we can bank on."

"I've noticed something else," said Ari. "She never has a fire in the fireplace, not even on cold, gloomy days like this, not even gas logs. And she never lights any candles for dinner. All the candlesticks in the dining room are wired for electric bulbs."

"Tacky," commented Paul.

"That's why it's significant," said Ari. "Aunt

208

Gabrielle usually has wonderful taste. My guess is that vampires can't stand fire."

"Now we're getting somewhere." Paul's eyes narrowed. "Yeah, think about it. The kitchen is all-electric. She's got a microwave and the electric range. Yeah, I think you're onto something."

"But Paul . . ." Ari hesitated, "we don't really want to hurt Aunt Gabrielle, do we?"

"That depends," said Paul. "I sure as heck don't want to end up like Sandy. We have to be ready to defend ourselves. We need to be able to make her back off if things get out of hand."

"I think I've got an idea," said Ari suddenly.

The twins went together to M Street, the main shopping street of the district. When they returned, they had cigarette lighters tucked in their pockets.

The caterer was pushing open the front door when they got back to the house. His arms were full of flowers. "Ciao, kids," he trilled. "I adore your aunt's parties. No penny-pinching—everything strictly first class. Lots of times they tell me, 'Do it cheap but make it look expensive.' But no problems like that with your aunt. She pays extra for a rush job like this without a peep. And she's one who understands quality." The young man hurried down the checkerboard hallway and through the open door of the dining room. Ari saw him fussing with the flowers on the buffet table.

"I wonder what's with this party of hers," Paul said. "She came up with the idea all of a sudden.

You heard the guy—'a rush job', he said." Paul paused at the foot of the stairs. "What's she up to? I wish I knew."

"Whatever it is," said Ari, "we're ready. If we get in a tight place—"

"We'll use these," Paul interrupted, pulling his lighter out of his pocket and twirling the flint. The lighter's thin blue-and-yellow flame was a tiny spot of brightness in the shadows. Ari was suddenly terrified. How much protection could a small flame really be against a vampire? It was all they had.

CHAPTER
EIGHTEEN

ARI AND PAUL STOOD TOGETHER BESIDE THE DINNER gong at the back of the hall, watching the slender, chic party guests greet one another with shrill cries of joy. It was dark outside, but inside crystal, jewels, and shimmering satin gleamed in the lamplight.

After some anxious discussion, the twins had decided it was best to stand near the three exits at the back of the house in case anything terrible happened. Paul imagined himself giving the dinner gong a kick to create a diversion, then grabbing Ari and diving over the spread of fruit and cold cuts on the dining room table and bursting out the French doors. He had seen that sort of maneuver lots of times in movies. He was a little uncertain how it would work out in actual practice.

But as the living room and dining room filled up with guests, Paul felt the muscles at the back of his neck unclenching. He recognized a few of the guests from Aunt Gabrielle's last party—the graphic designer, Gwendolyn, for instance. Tonight she was wearing a gauzy dress in a beige flower print. Peeking out from the folds of the skirt were the toes of what looked like combat boots. The retired ballet dancer, Tippi, arrived a few minutes later with Derek, the cave-cheeked rock singer. Tonight he was wearing tight black pants and a white satin shirt unbuttoned to the navel. The familiar faces were reassuring enough to Paul that he decided to visit the buffet table. He filled a plate with frosted grapes, a wedge of Brie cheese, and some dry crackers.

Then he spotted a beautiful blonde about his age. Her straight blond hair fell in a silken fringe to her shoulders, and the black velvet scoop-necked top she wore revealed startling cleavage. Paul poured himself a glass of champagne and smiled. "Hullo," he said. "Are you a friend of my aunt?"

"Sort of," she said. "Friend of a friend, anyway." Her voice was high and flutelike.

"The reason I ask is she said something about having a soiree for her most intimate friends," said Paul. "Just an expression, I guess."

The girl smiled. "Nobody's got a hundred intimate friends, you know. Probably she tried to invite some people who were close to your age so you wouldn't be bored."

"That must be it. Can I get you something to drink?" asked Paul.

"No, thank you," she said. "By the way, I'm Verena."

"I guess you know my name," he said.

"Oh, yes." She smiled sweetly. "You're Paul."

"Where are you in school, Verena?" he asked.

"I'm not exactly in school right now," she said. "But I used to go to St. Anne's."

Paul frowned. Ari had mentioned St. Anne's School for Girls. Wasn't that where Sybil's mom went back in the old days? It had been next door to St. Anselm's, but St. Anselm's absorbed it when it went coed. "How long ago was that?" he asked.

"Oh, a while," she said. Her lovely chin had a slight cleft and a dimple teased the corner of her mouth. "School was interfering with other things I really wanted to do. It seemed like a waste of time, and it started so early in the morning!"

Paul met her eyes. "I guess you like to sleep all day."

The girl's shapely hand splayed over her mouth as she giggled. "I guess I do," she admitted. "I watch a lot of late-night TV. It probably rots my brain."

Paul looked her up and down. "It hasn't hurt your figure, anyway."

She laughed suddenly, and Paul saw the flash of her fangs. Her skin, though pale, was translucent and flawless. Tiny diamond earrings glittered in each pale earlobe, and her dress, slit up to the thigh, revealed the sort of legs featured in stocking ads.

"How long have you been a vampire?" asked Paul, trying to affect a conversational tone.

Verena looked embarrassed. "Thirty-five years. You don't think I'm too old for you, do you? You know, once vampires get made, they don't get any older, really."

Paul felt queasy. "Made?" he asked in a faint voice.

Verena leaned so close to him that he backed away. "It's great," she breathed. "Better than sex."

"No bad side effects at all?" Paul glanced over his shoulder. He wished he could get away from the girl, but he felt as if he were held to her by strong rubber bands. The girl's magnetic green eyes grew bright, then dimmed as if they were battery powered. She laid a cool white hand on his neck, and he felt himself tingle from head to foot. He glanced down and was horrified to see her fingers had left a phosphorescent glow on his skin.

"It would be beautiful," she breathed. "I'd suck out your blood until you were too weak to move and you could feel my heart beating. Then I'd bite a vein, and let my blood mix with yours. Vampire blood is eternal. You'd feel wonderful, I promise you, and you'd never, never die. You'll be sixteen forever."

"But let me get this straight," said Paul nervously. "I'd already be dead, wouldn't I? I mean, my blood would be basically gone, wouldn't it?" He ran his hand over his neck where she had touched him, relieved to see the phosphorescence was fading.

She giggled. "Well, sure, if you want to get technical about it. But you'd have vampire blood instead, and that's so much better. It's so intense—so deep."

"Sure. You get to watch all those late-night TV shows," said Paul.

"No, stupid." Verena leaned very close to him. He could see the dark sweep of her eyelashes and the fine lines of color that radiated from her jewel-like irises, and he felt himself losing his grip. "I mean, you and me," Verena said softly, "drunk on each other's blood, our hearts beating as one. Let me do it, Paul. It would be perfect."

Verena's head suddenly jerked back, and Paul was astonished to see his aunt push herself between them. Her bony hand was firmly on Verena's beautiful chest. She pushed the younger woman away. "Give the boy some air, Verena," said Aunt Gabrielle briskly.

"I find Paul so very attractive," purred Verena.

Aunt Gabrielle dusted an imaginary crumb off Paul's shirt. "I'm sure you do." She smiled. "But let's try to behave ourselves, dear. You're in a civilized household tonight. Come with me, Paul. There are some people I'd like you to meet."

"Well, nice meeting you, Verena," Paul said as he backed away.

"I'm sorry about Verena," said Aunt Gabrielle in a low voice. "She's a lovely girl, but sometimes I do wonder about her self-control. Why don't you go find Ari? Something tells me you could use a breather from my friends."

Paul found Ari by the fireplace. She was pulling grapes one by one off a bunch with her teeth. Paul

215

touched her shoulder and she jumped.

"I've been propositioned by a vampire," he said gloomily. "She wants to mingle my blood with hers. When she was talking to me, I couldn't think straight. I looked into her eyes and it started to sound good. I swear for half a second I was ready to take her up on it. I wonder if she put something in my drink."

"You're scaring me, Paul," Ari stuttered. "Are you making this up?"

"I wish." He took a gulp from his glass. "Maybe I'm past being scared." He glanced around. "When you think about it, they're all sort of like Aunt Gabrielle, aren't they? I almost feel at home. By the way, they aren't eating. Have you noticed? We're the only ones who've touched the food."

"Maybe they're on diets." Ari's eyes darted nervously around the room. "They're all very thin."

"They're all vampires, that's why. Check out the blonde over there in the low-cut velvet top."

"Very pretty," said Ari.

"That's the one that propositioned me. She's about fifty years old, I figure, and she's got fangs."

"She only looks about eighteen." Ari craned her neck to see.

"They don't get older once they become vampires. That's how Aunt Gabrielle avoids wrinkles. Check out the blonde again—see the fangs?"

"No," said Ari. "She keeps covering her mouth."

"She's hiding her fangs." Paul looked around the room. The place was so full of expensively dressed, handsome, skinny people that it looked like an ad in a glossy magazine. "Oh, what the hell." He refilled his glass from a bottle on the mantel and sipped it delicately. "Hey, what do you know? It's wine," he said.

Ari stared at him. "What did you expect?"

"You can't be too careful in a crowd like this. Could be blood," he said. "Betcha the others aren't drinking wine." He glanced around. "Since we're here, we might as well find out all we can." He downed his wine rapidly and smiled at Ari. "Well, here goes." He turned and waded out into the thickest part of the crowd.

A slender young man immediately filled Paul's place. He gazed down at Ari. "Did anyone ever tell you that you're beautiful?" he asked.

"Yes, and I'm tired of hearing it," she said firmly.

He looked hurt. "You don't have much small talk, do you?"

"I have a boyfriend," she said.

He took her hand and suddenly an electric shock froze her. A sharp pain ran through her from her head to her toes and her fingers spread out, splayed by the sudden shock. Her eyes flew open in horror. What was happening to her?

"I am sure we have so much in common," he whispered softly in her ear. Before Ari could protest, the vampire sat on her lap. She felt the cold wetness of his mouth on the flesh of her neck.

"No!" she cried, tossing her head suddenly. She

217

struggled to her feet, and to her relief the vampire slipped off her lap. She stumbled away from him, frightened by his angry glare.

A tough-looking man in a T-shirt leaned toward her. "You and Jep didn't hit it off, huh?" He smiled, showing fangs. A single gold earring gleamed in his nostril.

Ari backed away from him. She wouldn't let him touch her, she thought, her heart pounding. She would kick him. But did vampires feel pain? The mantel bit into her shoulder blades. She pictured the death's head skull in the fireplace inches away from her fingers, and her stomach heaved. "Get away from me," she said. "I hate you."

"That doesn't bother me." He laughed. "I kind of like it when girls squirm. I get off on disgust."

Ari felt herself go cold. With a sudden movement, she dipped to her knees and, taking advantage of his surprise, scooted around the couch away from him.

"Hey, I was only kidding!" he called.

She didn't turn around. She knew she could get out of the house the back way through the big doors in the dining room. But where was Paul? she wondered. She looked around desperately.

At the other entrance of the living room, Paul bumped into a middle-aged man with almond-shaped eyes. He held out his hand. "I'm Paul Montclair," he said. He noted the coolness of the man's hand, but he told himself he was past shocking. "I wonder if you know my father,

218

Richard?" Paul asked. "He's about your age."

"I'm sorry," said the man. He had a British accent. "I'm not from around here. Try Dubay over there. He seems to know everyone." The Englishman indicated a tough-looking young man wearing tight jeans and a black T-shirt. Dubay was heavily muscular—his thighs bulged under the tight jeans. He wore an earring in one nostril. He looked far too young to be a contemporary of Paul's father, but Paul was beginning to see that with vampires age was a tricky concept since they evidently stopped maturing once they became vampires. Uncomfortably he recalled that the sexy young blonde he had been talking to must have gone to school with Sybil's mother.

Paul approached Dubay cautiously.

The man smiled. It was a careful smile Paul recognized now as typical of vampires, the sort of closed-jaw smile that didn't reveal fangs.

"I was told you might know my father, Richard Montclair," he said.

"Oh, yes," said Dubay. "I know Richard." He didn't offer any further information.

"I haven't seen him since I was little," said Paul. "I was hoping you could tell me a little about him."

"We aren't close friends," Dubay began cautiously. "Richard runs in too fast a crowd for me."

Paul regarded Dubay with dismay. What sort of crowd could be too fast for this tough-looking fellow?

Dubay aimlessly scratched the corner of his eye

with a broken thumbnail. "Why don't you ask Alain about him? He probably could tell you more than I could." Dubay put his hand on a neighboring guest's shoulder and whirled him around to face them. Alain proved to be a dark and slender young man with a cynical twist to his thin lips.

"Cut it out, Dubay!" cried Alain. "Must you be so piggishly self-centered? I mean, really!"

"Tell the young man about Richard Montclair," said Dubay. "They're related but haven't met."

"Where to begin!" cried Alain. "Richard is in a class by himself. Utterly reckless. One has to admire that. There's a kind of integrity to it, a kind of primitive magnificence."

"Do you have any idea what he does for a living?" Paul asked.

Dubay and Alain looked at him blankly. "Oh, Richard doesn't work," Alain said faintly.

Paul flushed. He felt dizzy, but somehow he managed to keep talking. "Have you seen him around lately?" he asked.

"I hear he's been around rather a lot the past few weeks. I haven't actually *seen* him—that is to say, with my own eyes. But several mutual acquaintances have run into him, and I myself was coming out of a midnight movie only a few days ago, and I heard that incredibly irritating whistle of his. Richard can't carry a tune in a bucket." The young man laughed, showing gleaming white fangs. "I'd have known that off-key whistle of his anywhere. I suppose he's probably in Bombay or Singapore as we speak. He's always had a weak spot for warm, steamy nights."

Like the nights in New Orleans, thought Paul. With sickening clarity he remembered how all those corpses in New Orleans had been drained of blood. The thought made his stomach turn over. The tuneless whistling he had heard that foggy day at the track haunted his mind—his father!

Loud music had begun to play, and the vampires swayed in time with it. Paul felt dizzy. Black velvet brushed suddenly against his cheek, and Paul looked up, startled to see jewel-colored eyes in a Nordic, square-jawed face. "Want to dance?" cooed the woman in black velvet. "I simply love to dance," she said. Her fangs glistened in the dim light as she wound a pale arm around him. To his horror, he found his body swaying and moving in time to hers. He shimmied close against her. Sweat trickled down his face, and her breath stirred his hair. He stared as if hypnotized at the triangle of one of her rhinestone earrings. Impossibly bright, the jewels dazzled him, and for an instant his vision blurred so that all he saw was a mosaic of spangled light. The music held him in its grip. His pulse had become one with its beat. The coolness of the vampire's breasts pressed against his chest horrified him, yet he could not pull away. "Having fun?" she cooed.

"Y-yes," he stuttered. The sound that came out of his mouth appalled him. He wanted to get away, didn't he? Why had he said he was having fun? He listened to his heart thump loudly in his ears. He felt cool and strangely disassociated from his hot body.

"Would you like to go out with me sometime?" she cooed. "I simply adore young boys." She seized his finger and put it in her mouth, and a shudder of dread shook him. He could feel her wet lips and he cringed, expecting to feel the prick of her fangs. Instead, a tingling sensation shot through him, as if he had touched a wet battery. Then his hand fell free and she smiled mischievously at him, showing her fangs. Paul felt like a fool. What had he thought? That she was going to suck the life-blood out of him through a single finger? The cold dampness of his finger mocked him.

"I . . . I'm sorry," he said, backing off suddenly. "I have to go."

She pursed her red lips and mouthed something, but he couldn't hear her over the loud music. She looked more sinister than sexy in that black dress, and Paul was afraid to meet her gaze. With a sudden dread, he remembered Ari. He should have stayed with her.

No wonder his mother had been drawn to his father, he thought uncomfortably, recalling the wiles of Verena and the tall vampire in black velvet. He stumbled to the dining room and poured himself another glass of wine. The room seemed stiflingly hot, and he knew he was getting drunk, but he couldn't stop himself.

He wasn't sure how long he stared out the French doors. He felt as if he were floating through a universe of stars and blackness with nothing to hold him in one place.

Ari's voice startled him. "Paul?"

222

Paul blinked. He hadn't seen her standing there in the shadows, her back against the French doors. "Jeez, Ari, I'm glad to see you. I've been worried about you." Guilt pricked him. He should have been protecting her, he thought. He had been shimmying with vampires when he should have been looking out for his sister.

"I thought about going out to the garden," said Ari in a small voice. "But then I started to worry. What if I met one of them out there? Or on the garden path? That would be even worse." She shuddered. "At least it's quiet here. None of them go near the food table." She peered at him closely. "Are you all right? You haven't been drinking again, have you?"

"What if I have?" he said. "I'm entitled."

Ari put her hand on his arm. "Listen," she said. "I'm counting on you. You've got to keep sober. You're all I've got!"

Suddenly Paul felt ashamed of himself. How could he feel cut adrift when he had Ari? He glanced over his shoulder down the long hallway. The music was playing softly now, and he could see that people were leaving.

"I think the party's starting to break up." Ari took a deep breath. "Good."

Paul shot her an uneasy glance. "None of those vampires gave you a hard time, did they?"

"A couple tried." Ari's eyes flashed. "But I didn't let them get away with anything."

Paul felt sick with shame. The dim thought had crept into his mind that maybe he hadn't wanted

223

to get away from that tall blond vampire as much as he imagined. Maybe she had sensed his ambivalence and sucked up his strength.

"Did anybody else try anything with you?" asked Ari.

Paul felt himself go scarlet. "Same as with you," he said gruffly. "I fought them off." Remembering the way he had danced so close to the vampire's cold, vulpine body, he felt unclean.

Ari lowered her voice. "It's scary, though, Paul. They don't feel any pain, and they're already dead so you feel so . . . weak. And something strange happens when they touch you." The color drained from her face at the memory.

"You don't have to tell me about it," said Paul quickly. In a quick flash of comprehension, he sensed that Ari, too, despite her brave words, was badly shaken. At least, he thought, the party was breaking up.

Paul and Ari pulled up chairs to a corner of the dining room table, and comforted by the other's presence, they began companionably eating off each other's plates. "The lobster's good," said Ari after a minute.

"I'm sick of lobster." Paul gave his familiar crooked smile. "I'm sick of this whole scene." He gave Ari a sip out of his wineglass.

The elaborate buffet with its frosted grapes, its cold seafood, dip, and crackers was as symmetrical and as carefully arranged as when the caterers had left.

"I wonder what happens to all this food," Ari said.

Paul shrugged. "Donation to a soup kitchen? Compost heap? Caterer's cleanup crew gets to pig out? Dunno."

Finally, they became aware that the house had grown still. Even the music had stopped. "I bet they've gone on to other parties," said Paul. He remembered the bar he had gone into looking for Aunt Gabrielle. The woman at the bar had had fangs—he hadn't imagined it. The place must have been a vampire hangout. "I have the idea this bunch does a lot of partying," he said.

Together they tiptoed up the marble hall and peeked in the living room. Everyone was gone. Ari popped a last grape in her mouth as she sat down. "One thing about vampires," she said calmly. "No cigarette stubs all over the Oriental carpet after the party."

"Great," said Paul. "That makes it all seem worthwhile."

They heard squeals of delight and the front door closed. Aunt Gabrielle was radiant as she stepped into the dining room. "There!" she cried. "Aren't they charming? My dear, dear friends. I wanted you to see that we aren't a bunch of losers." She clasped her hands together. "I wanted you to have some real appreciation of your heritage."

Her words lay in Ari's stomach like cold stones. For the first time, it struck Ari as sinister that her name seemed to echo her aunt's—Ari, Gabri. Too close for comfort. "What do you mean, 'our heritage'?" she choked.

Aunt Gabrielle perched on the striped couch,

leaning slightly toward the twins. "My dears, haven't you noticed that you see the world in a more intense and colorful way than ordinary people?"

Ari's gaze met Paul's. She and Paul saw letters and numbers in color. Was that what Aunt Gabrielle was talking about?

"Haven't you noticed the awakening of a feeling that there's more to the world than simple everyday life?" prompted Aunt Gabrielle gently. "You have visions, perhaps. See things that other people can't see?"

Ari thought of the ghost she had seen near Sybil's house. No one else had seen it, Sybil had said. At least not for years. And the morning visions that Paul had assured her were normal. She stared at Aunt Gabrielle, appalled.

"It's a sign of the potential that's there inside you," Aunt Gabrielle went on. "You must have noticed how some families produce musicians, others mathematicians. We tend to produce vampires," she said with modest pride.

"No!" cried Ari. "I'm not a vampire." She and Paul stared at each other in dismay. Paul's hand was in his pocket on the cigarette lighter, but all of a sudden he was unsure what to do with it.

Aunt Gabrielle reached for her purse and struggled with the clasp a minute. Then she produced a gold compact and flicked it open before Ari's face so that its mirror cast a circle of light on Ari's mouth. "But you are a vampire, dearest," she cried. "See your cute little baby fangs?"

CHAPTER
NINETEEN

THE TWINS RAN UPSTAIRS ALL AT ONCE, SLAMMED THE door, and fell into each other's arms on Ari's bed. "It can't be true," Ari sobbed. "No! No! It can't be."

Paul stroked her hair, but a moment later the twins found each other gazing in horrified fascination at the other's mouth, the soft pink of the parted lips, the white gleam of teeth, and the pointy incisors. "Whatever it is, Ari," he said, "we're in it together. You and me. From beginning to end, we'll never be alone."

Ari turned and pinched her arm, reassured by its pink fleshiness. Lots of people had pointed incisors, she told herself. It didn't mean she and Paul were vampires. But she knew that she was changing. Every week she felt stronger and more grown up. Was she somehow also changing into a vampire without realizing it? "How can we be the children of a vampire?" she cried. "Vampires can't have children. They don't have sex. They aren't even alive."

"I've thought about that," said Paul. "Maybe our parents got together before Dad became a vampire."

Ari jumped up from the bed and began pacing tight circles on the floor. "I don't feel a bit like a vampire, do you? The sun doesn't bother me. I don't even like my steak rare!"

Paul regarded her cautiously. "Maybe it's just that the tendency runs in the family," he said. "Some families have a lot of musicians or scientists. Stands to reason all of them aren't musicians or scientists. Some of them end up working in convenience stores, right? Nothing is a hundred percent. Maybe we'll be the lucky ones who don't make it as vampires."

Tears streamed down Ari's cheeks. "I'm scared, Paul. Maybe we're turning every minute. Maybe we're already becoming vampires."

A clap of thunder sounded. The floor trembled and the prisms of the bedside lamp jingled. Ari ran to the window and threw it open. A wind blew in, ruffling her hair. A sheet of paper was swept to the floor. Ari heard a rustling sound and knew without turning around that the fanged creatures were in the room. They were nosing in her things while her back was turned.

"Ari?" She could hear Paul's voice coming as if from a great distance, but she couldn't turn around. She stared out the window in a trance.

A black cloud rose before her, swallowing up

the terrace below in a roar, and the hot sweep of wind brushed against her cheeks. Flames licked at the brick buildings of the courtyard, and through the flames she saw a dark figure in a cape on the fire escape of the tall building behind the terrace. Somewhere people were shouting and Ari heard the sound of sirens. Bits of ash floated aimlessly in the air. The dark man's cape was swept out balloon-style by the holocaust of fire, and someone screamed. Ari's flesh crawled. Through the flames, she could see that blood was streaming down the buildings. It lay in pools on the terrace.

"No!" Ari cried. She squeezed her eyes closed and covered her ears. "It's not going to happen to me. I won't let it. No! Never!"

"Ari? Are you okay?" She felt Paul's arms around her. Ari turned to meet his gaze and felt her heartbeat slowing down and becoming more steady.

"Paul," she sobbed, "something horrible's about to happen."

"Something horrible's always about to happen," he said wearily. "We can't worry about that right now. We've got to figure out what to do."

Ari gazed out the window once more and saw that the fire and the blood were gone. She gulped for air. It had been a vision, she knew. But it had been so real—like a window into the future.

"Paul," said Ari in a calmer voice. "The man is still there. The one that was on the fire escape in my vision."

"What man?" Paul peered out the window. A

black-caped figure stepped across the petunias and walked deliberately across the bricked pavement of the terrace. So foreshortened was the figure below that they saw only a suggestion of white face and white—gloves, perhaps?—against the black of darkness, clothes, and cape.

Ari held Paul's arm in a tight grip. "It's our father."

A chill slithered up Paul's spine. "Maybe not," he said.

A tuneless whistle floated up to them as the doors of Aunt Gabrielle's study were thrown open.

"He's come for us," cried Ari. "He's going to make us into vampires."

Paul had an uncomfortable flashback to the girl at the party. She wanted to mix her blood with his. Suddenly Paul was sure Ari was right. Their father was going to make them into vampires so they would be with him forever.

"I won't let him!" cried Ari. She slammed the window shut and fastened the catch. "Lock the doors, Paul."

Paul leapt to the connecting door and slid its lock into place. He heard Ari turn the big key in the door to the hall. She took the key out of the lock and dropped it on the floor.

"The bathroom," she said breathlessly. "I'll get the window. Then we'll be locked in. We've got water. We can last in here a long time."

Paul was miserably conscious of the flimsiness of the latch on the connecting doors. The lock to the hall door was sturdier, but he doubted that

230

either door would stand up if a grown man threw his weight against the frame.

Ari spoke in a low trembling voice. "Don't let him talk you into anything, Paul. We don't open those doors no matter what, do you hear me? Promise!"

Paul nodded.

They heard rapid heavy footfalls in the hallway, and suddenly the door rattled with heavy and insistent banging. Someone was trying the doorknob. "Open up!" someone muttered. The frame of the door shuddered as a heavy weight was thrown against it. Paul heard the splintering of wood and gazed at Ari in terror.

NIGHTMARES

Vampire Twins 2

BLOODLUST

Janice Harrell

CHAPTER
ONE

PAUL MONTCLAIR COULD HEAR CURSING AS THE bedroom door shuddered from the weight of a heavy body being thrown against it.

"We could climb out the window," said his twin sister, Ari.

Paul peered out the second-story window. Light from the French doors in the dining room illuminated the raised brick beds and the stone paving of the terrace far below. "We'd break our necks," he said.

The note of resignation in Paul's voice seemed to fuel Ari's panic. "Stay here if you want!" she cried. "Let him kill you. He's not going to get me." She shot a glance over her shoulder. The door looked solid, but already Paul could hear the ominous sharp crack of splitting wood.

Ari threw the window up, and biting her lip,

she looked down. Paul followed her gaze. The sight of the pavement in the shadows below made him dizzy. He tried not to think of his twin's broken body lying limp on the paving stones. Ari put one foot on the sill and took a quick breath.

Suddenly the door flew open, sounding like a pistol shot as it struck the wall behind it. A tall man strode angrily into the room. The black cape that billowed behind him made him look frighteningly huge. Paul gasped.

Richard Montclair's face was inhuman, as white and as glossy as a skull. Tight flesh arched over a handsome aquiline nose, and his jewellike eyes were startlingly dark. His black hair was combed back behind his ears, curling slightly where it brushed his collar. His lip was lifted in a sneer that showed glistening ivory fangs. Paul and Ari shrank from him. *He's going to kill us,* thought Paul with cold certainty.

Ari grabbed the lamp beside the bed and brandished it. "Don't come one step closer!" she warned.

Their father laughed harshly. "Put that down. Do you think you can stop me from doing anything I want with you? Don't make me laugh."

"Can't we discuss this?" whispered their aunt Gabrielle. Paul had not noticed her until then.

His father was so huge and frightening he had completely overshadowed her.

"Back off, Gabrielle," Richard snarled. Paul heard his father hiss an animal sound like a cat preparing to attack. Aunt Gabrielle's slim, elegant body crumpled against the door, her face streaked with tears.

Suddenly Paul remembered the cigarette lighter he and Ari had bought. He doubted that the tiny flame would offer any protection, but he had to try. He pulled it out of his pocket and flicked the flint with his thumb. A tiny flame leapt into life and in an instant everyone in the room froze. Paul glanced up at the dark figure looming threateningly over him and saw the flame reflected in his father's deep black irises.

His father took a step back.

"Put out that flame, Paul!" whispered Aunt Gabrielle. Her lavender eyes glowed.

It's true, Paul thought with a rush of elation. *Vampires can be destroyed by fire—they're even afraid of this tiny flame.*

"Put it out," Aunt Gabrielle pleaded. "What if something in the room catches on fire?"

"That would be too bad, wouldn't it?" cried Ari defiantly. "Then you'd both turn to ashes."

The twins' father folded his arms across his broad chest. "Maybe," he said. "Or maybe not. Don't be a fool, Anne-Marie." When Paul heard

3

Ari called by the formal name on her birth certificate, he saw with sudden clarity that his father was an absolute stranger to them. Yet even as he held his father at bay, Paul felt a strange connection to him, as if some terrible blackness was seeping from his father's soul and into his.

"We need to talk!" cried Aunt Gabrielle, wringing her hands. "There's so much to discuss, and I can't think straight with that flame burning, Paul. Put it out, I beg of you!"

Paul shot an uneasy glance around the room. Should he try to set the bedding and the curtains on fire to give him and Ari a chance to make a break for it? But he knew his father would overpower him before he could get a fire going.

"Please, Paul!" said Aunt Gabrielle. "Put it away. Do it for me."

"Don't plead with him, Gabri," snapped Richard.

"Ari and I want the lighter turned on, don't we, Ari?" asked Paul.

Ari nodded vigorously.

"We're not ready to put it out," said Paul.

"Do you think I came up here to murder my own flesh and blood?" Richard snarled.

Paul's eyes met his twin's. He couldn't reply.

Their father eased himself into a chair by the door, then crossed his legs and looked around the room. Paul sensed tension behind the relaxed pose. His father wasn't used to meeting up with resistance, he guessed. A spoiled, petulant cast to Richard's lips suggested he was accustomed to getting his way.

"This used to be my room," he said, looking around. "Some of the furniture is still the same."

"Of course, you had a coffin instead of a bed," said Ari sarcastically.

Anger flashed in their father's eyes and for a moment he didn't move. Then he smiled. "I wasn't always a vampire," he said. "Once I was an ordinary teenager just like you and Paul."

"You were never ordinary," said Gabrielle.

"No," admitted Richard. "I always was sensitive to the supernatural. My destiny was calling to me."

Gabrielle's finger tenderly brushed her brother's face, and she murmured something in French.

Suddenly, to Paul's horror, the flame in the lighter flickered out. He stared at it. The muscles at the back of his neck tensed. He expected to feel his father's teeth there any second.

"Don't worry, my children." Richard surveyed them through half-opened eyes. "I did not come here to hurt you." He studied his cuff, a snowy expanse of starched cotton in which a gold cuff-link glittered. His hands were so white it was hard to see where the flesh ended and the cuff began. A large signet ring gleamed on one

5

finger. "Of course, I was angry when I came in the house and found Gabri in tears. After all she's done for you, taking you in when your mother died, you suddenly treat her as if she's a monster."

"It was the shock, Richard," put in Aunt Gabrielle. "They didn't mean to hurt me. It's just that they had no idea of the truth."

"I would have told you the truth in the beginning," said Richard, "but your mother was determined to keep me from seeing you, and I decided it was best to go along with her wishes and stay away until you were older. And Gabrielle thought it would be unwise to spring a lot of unexpected news on you right after the blow of your mother's death."

"You've been watching us," said Ari harshly. "Since we came here you've been watching us through that two-way mirror in the hall."

Richard laughed. "You felt my presence. You take after me."

"No!" cried Ari. "I'm not like you at all!"

"You've been sneaking up the back stairs, haven't you?" asked Paul. He realized then that his father had never been far away, but had been brooding over their upbringing like an evil angel. Childhood memories stirred of a dark shape and glittering eyes watching him at dusk when he came in from the playground. Their father had always been there—standing in the shadows, watching them grow up.

"Naturally, I've been visiting my sister." Richard flicked an imaginary speck of dust off his pants leg. "This is, after all, the house where I grew up. I prefer to slip in and out quietly, because, as you know, Gabrielle attempts to pass herself off as human and I don't want to"— he smiled—"blow her cover. It was clever of you children to sense my presence. You must have second sight." He lifted an eyebrow at Ari. "Do you see ghosts, or colors other people can't see?"

"No!" Ari flushed and glanced at her twin. Paul knew that she was lying, and he supposed their father knew it, too.

"I want to get to know you," their father said softly. "It's important to me that we get acquainted. I want to be part of your life." As Richard spoke, he worked the long white fingers of his left hand into a fine leather glove. "I am about to go out for my evening walk. I'd like Paul to go with me."

"No!" protested Ari.

Richard gave her a chilling look. "Don't speak to me in that tone, Anne-Marie."

"Don't go, Paul," pleaded Ari.

Richard stood up, smiled, and reached out. Paul was appalled by the strange shiver that seized him when his father touched him. His entire body shuddered as if he had touched an electric wire and all his muscles contracted painfully. As if he were watching the scene from a distance, he was conscious of Ari's horrified gaze. It made him sad, yet neither his own pain nor Ari's obvious horror seemed to matter. He realized with a deep, inexorable conviction that he had waited all his life for this moment. "I'd like to go with you," he said calmly.

Richard laughed, and his fangs gleamed white in the dim light. "Anne-Marie thinks I'm kidnapping you so I can suck your body dry and fill you with vampire blood, don't you, Anne-Marie?"

Ari stared at him with a look of intense hatred.

"I said I wouldn't hurt either of you," he said silkily. "But you must realize that as a vampire, Paul would live forever."

"If you do anything to Paul," Ari said passionately, "I'll hunt you down, I promise you. I'll burn you to ashes."

Richard raised an eyebrow. "Such a temper. You're my daughter, all right."

Ari saw Paul leave with their father through the red mist of her anger and only slowly became conscious of Aunt Gabrielle fidgeting uncertainly in the doorway.

"Now, dear, try to get some sleep," her aunt said. "It's natural Paul would want to go with his

8

father." The door closed behind Aunt Gabrielle then, and Ari was alone.

Her fists clenched, Ari rushed into Paul's room and went through his drawers. She pulled his baggiest sweatshirt over her head and then stuffed her hair under his dark knit cap. Her mind was racing. She needed something like gasoline or kerosene and plenty of matches. The other lighter! She felt the pocket of her jeans. Still there. But she had to hurry. Maybe she should take the car. But she was afraid that if she took the time to get it out of the garage, she would lose them.

Her heart pounding in her throat, she rushed to the door of her bedroom and peeked anxiously outside. No sign of Aunt Gabrielle, at least.

Ari darted out into the dark hall and opened the door to the servants' staircase. She had never been down those narrow back stairs, but she knew her father came and went that way without being seen. She felt her way down in the darkness. When she reached the service hall at the bottom, she listened carefully. Hearing nothing, she ran up the mansion's main hallway, her sneakers squeaking on the marble floor. Then she slipped out the front door.

Glancing up the street, she saw Paul, and her heart gave a thud of relief. She hadn't lost them. Next to Paul was the dark figure of their father.

The traffic light at Wisconsin Avenue cast a lurid glow on father and son for the instant that they paused at the curb. It seemed incredible to Ari that people strolled past them without realizing her father was a vampire, but then she remembered that he had pulled on leather gloves to hide his glassy nails and the ghostly white flesh of his hands. At night, with a hat shadowing his face, he might be able to pass as human. The two turned down Wisconsin Avenue and Ari ran after them. She slowed her pace when she turned the corner onto the avenue.

Staying a block or so behind them, she followed the pair through the streets of Georgetown. It was a shock to see how much they resembled each other from behind. They had the same loosely curling black hair, the same long-legged gait, the same tall, slim figure.

I won't lose them, Ari swore silently.

Richard Montclair glanced over his shoulder, then narrowed his eyes and quickened his pace. "Paul," he said, "you remind me very much of myself when I was your age."

Paul looked at his father. "How?" he asked. "We aren't a bit alike."

His father shook his head. "Of course, in some ways, you remind me of your sister—your tactlessness, for instance. But there's a resemblance between us—you must see that. At your

10

age, I suffered from not understanding the pull of my vampire nature. I tried music, then Tarot cards, and for a time I took up with spiritualists and hung around dubious bars. I was looking for something, but I didn't know what. Searching, always painfully searching." He sighed. "Costume parties were a passion with me—I suppose because I didn't know who I really was. The problem was that I didn't have a father's guidance." He smiled at Paul. "At your age I didn't yet realize that it was only as a vampire that I would fulfill my deepest, darkest self."

Paul stared at him in dismay. "I'm not like that at all. I'm just an ordinary guy."

His father's smile was unsettling, and Paul felt the flutterings of an obscure fear in his stomach. He began to wish that he hadn't come.

"I tried to deny the truth," said his father, "yet always I sought out vampires, not knowing quite what I wanted." He shrugged. "In a city like this, it's easy to find them near bars where they go to pick off drunken stragglers. With my special sensitivity, I could feel them hiding in the shadows, and I experienced a thrill that at the time I scarcely understood.

"When I was not much older than you are now, I began sneaking out nights to walk the dark streets alone, watching for them. One night, a vampire leapt on me. He drew blood— he was very powerful, but I was a match for him and succeeded in throwing him off. But I was terrified by my close brush with death. I fled to New Orleans swearing I would lead a normal human life. No more lonely midnight walks and waterfront bars. I would marry and raise a family. I would be normal."

In spite of himself Paul felt his interest growing. This was the story of how he had come to be born. Ever since he had met Aunt Gabrielle—and even more since he had seen his father—he had been curious about how his parents had met. His mother had liked silly rhymes and crossword puzzles, and her worst sin was eating too many chocolates. No one could have been more different from the sinister Montclairs with their sophistication and taste for luxury. What had brought his parents together?

"Your mother and I shared a love of music," said his father, seemingly reading Paul's thoughts. His dark gaze met Paul's eyes and held them. "That was how we met. We played together in a community orchestra. For my part," he went on, "I was determined to put my yearnings for the dark world behind me. But I didn't realize that New Orleans, too, is a city haunted with vampires. Soon I could feel them—sitting on dark, ruined balconies, living in decayed mansions. Their presence excited me. Even before you were born, I began to walk the streets at night again, feeling that familiar mounting excitement." His father put his arm around him, and though Paul cringed, he was unable to pull away. The tale had a strange magnetism. He felt he needed to know what happened next.

"How can I describe for you the thrill of what happened then?" said Richard dreamily. "A vampire stalked me. I teased him and pretended to be afraid. That only excited him the more—he was cruel and loved preying on those who were terrified. Pretending fear, I bared my throat to him and gave myself up willingly to death. Our hearts beat together as he sucked the blood from my pulsing flesh." Richard sighed. "Two hearts beating together like stars burning in the black sky." He had stopped walking, as if overcome by the memory. "When at last I came to myself again," he went on huskily, "I was a vampire."

Paul was having trouble breathing, and he stumbled on the brick sidewalk. He felt his father's cold hand grab his arm and steady him. The neon lights on the street had a strange intensity. Paul began to feel as if he had been drugged.

Ari was vaguely conscious of her feet passing silently over the brick sidewalks. Overhead, the streetlamps were shrouded in mist.

What had their father done to Paul to make him come along? She remembered once when a

13

vampire had touched her at a party of Aunt Gabrielle's, she had trembled with the shock. Yet she had managed to fight him off. Why hadn't Paul tried to fight off their father?

A sick feeling grew in her that Paul had wanted to go with his father. For years he had longed to have a father, and that longing was probably still alive, in spite of all the terrible things they had found out. Ari wasn't sure what she could do to help her twin, but a fierce protective instinct made her follow him.

Suddenly Richard and Paul turned off the thoroughfare and Ari found herself following them on a twisted path through narrow, dimly lit streets. Water dripped softly from the lamps and trees. The streets were deserted. Soon Ari was no longer sure where she was, and she felt the first stirrings of fear. Determinedly, she kept her eyes fixed on the two figures walking faster and faster ahead of her. Then they disappeared as completely as if the mist had swallowed them up.

Ari ran ahead and peered down narrow alleys and dark passageways. Broken glass. Discarded cigarette packets. Suddenly a dark shape darted past her feet and she held her breath. A cat's fur glimmered briefly under the blurred lamplight and then disappeared into a nearby alley. But there was no sign of either Paul or their father.

Frozen with indecision, Ari realized the sky

over the dark hulks of the buildings had the glow of light. M Street must be straight ahead. But why, then, had they taken such a circuitous path when it would have been easier to go straight along Wisconsin Avenue? Did her father suspect she was following them?

Her anxiety flared. The buildings around her reeled and Ari gasped for air, dizzy and helpless in her panic. Why would her father try to lose her unless he didn't want her to see what he was going to do to Paul?

CHAPTER
TWO

PAUL REGAINED HIS BALANCE WITH DIFFICULTY. HIS father had suddenly jerked him off the sidewalk. A moment later he realized he was in the same alley where he had landed on his face the night he had tried to follow Aunt Gabrielle on her jog. He recognized the rotten cabbage that lay at the back entrance of the noisy bar, the same sodden newspaper on the ground. Paul shot an anxious glance at his father. "Why are we going in this way?" he asked. The next minute he felt the pressure of his father's hand on his back, pushing him in the back door of the bar.

"Inside," said Richard, stepping in after him. The colored light rotating at the back of the bar disoriented Paul and reminded him of the night he had come to this bar. Someone had mistaken him for his father and had socked him in the jaw.

"We're being followed," said his father, closing the door behind them.

"Why would anybody be following us?" asked Paul. He went on in and suddenly was stunned to find himself face-to-face with a classmate from his school. Jesse Driscoll's blond hair was as bright as a candle in the darkness.

"Jesse!" gulped Paul. "What are you doing here?"

Jesse turned his blue eyes on Paul. "Getting a beer. What are you doing here?"

"I came with my father." Paul glanced over his shoulder, but his father had gone. Paul felt a rush of relief. The light in the bar was dim, but not dim enough to hide his father's gruesome face.

"They don't check IDs here." Jesse leaned on the bar and signaled the bartender with an upraised finger. "Another beer," he said.

The bartender, whose bald head contrasted dramatically with his hollow eyes and cadaverous thinness, silently slid a frosted glass of beer down the counter. As Jesse raised the mug to his lips, Paul glanced around the bar nervously. All of the patrons—pale men with chiseled cheekbones, skinny women with bony jeweled hands and strange eyes—looked nightmarish in the noisy darkness of the bar. *Vampires! All of them!*

"Did you come here alone?" Paul asked Jesse, trying to sound normal.

17

"Nah," he said. "I dragged Cos along. Hey, here he is."

Paul's heart sank. Cos Cosgrove, Ari's boyfriend, was making his way through the crowd toward them. Paul watched as Cos bumped against a flaxen-haired vampire and apologized. The vampire giggled, covering her mouth to conceal her fangs. "Don't mention it, I'm sure," she said in a cockney accent.

Hiphugger jeans showed her perfectly flat stomach, and Paul could see the ribs of her bare midriff. Cos was having a hard time wrenching his gaze from her. When he reached the bar he was still blushing hotly, but he stopped dead still and went pale when he recognized Paul.

"Jeez, Paul. Don't tell Ari you saw me here," he pleaded.

For a full second Paul stared at him. He intensely disliked Cos. But he had bigger things on his mind right now than tattling on his sister's boyfriend.

"I just came along to keep Jess company," Cos went on nervously. "I don't want Ari to think I'm out cruising the bars to pick up college girls."

"She won't think anything like that," Paul said. His eyes searched anxiously for his father. Where had he gone?

"Don't tell her you saw me," urged Cos.

Paul smiled. "Heck, Cos," he said, "I can't

keep anything from Ari. You ought to know that. She can read my mind." How could Cos be stupid enough to ask him for a favor? But then, Cos was the sort whose self-assurance was un-flinching. He thought everybody liked him.

"Don't you want something to drink?" Jesse asked Paul.

"Go ahead," put in Cos. "They don't card anybody here. We'll have to spread the word."

Paul passed a hand across his brow. "Don't do that," he said. He had a horrible vision of kids from school hanging out at this strange bar and picking up gossip about his dad and Aunt Gabrielle. Suddenly he realized Cos and Jesse were staring at him. "I mean, it could be a sting operation or something," Paul explained weakly.

Cos smiled. "You worry too much." He gulped down some beer. His hair looked damp and rumpled, as if he had run wet fingers through it. "So what do you think of our chances against St. Alban's this weekend?"

Paul sat at the bar with Cos and Jesse talking sports for what seemed like hours but was prob-ably no more than twenty minutes. He felt like a wind-up toy. He was making all the right sounds, but he kept casting anxious glances over his shoulder, scanning the crowd behind them. He wondered if his father had left the bar. More likely, Paul decided, he was hiding somewhere waiting for Jesse and Cos to leave.

Suddenly, his father's face loomed out of the darkness and he stood beside them. In the dim light he simply appeared to be a well-dressed man with pale good looks. "My father," Paul explained in a faint voice.

Jesse and Cos slid to their feet and Paul heard Cos murmur a polite "How do you do, sir."

Paul could not take his eyes off his father's face. Richard's smile was carefully moderated to conceal his fangs, and except for the extraordinary plastic smoothness of his skin, he looked lively—almost human.

"Sit down, boys, sit down," Richard said. "Have one on me?" He signaled the bartender and three beers materialized. "A Bloody Mary for me," said Richard.

It slowly dawned on Paul that his father's skin had taken on the warm glow of life. That was why he looked different.

Cos glanced at Paul and then at his father. "I thought Ari said that you lived out of town, sir."

Paul knew Ari must have told Cos that they had never even met their father. Naturally Cos was wondering what was going on. "I'm visiting my sister," Richard explained. "I haven't seen much of my children in the past, but now I'm hoping to make up for lost time. Right, Paul?" He clapped Paul on the shoulder.

The bartender put a Bloody Mary in front of them. Paul regarded it with horror. Was it only his imagination, or did the tomato juice look like blood?

"Let me show you something curious," Richard said. He laid a small, snub-nosed pistol on the bar. The gun's handle was jeweled, and the gems winked in the shifting light. Before Paul's eyes they took on the shape of a skull with ruby eye sockets. He blinked and took another look. He hadn't imagined it. The handle of the gun was inlaid with a jeweled skull.

"Cool!" said Jesse. Paul remembered that Jesse had a large collection of firearms. "Where'd you get it?" Jesse demanded. "I've never seen one like that."

Richard's pale vampire lips curled into a grin. "I got it from a man who . . . won't be needing it anymore."

Jesse touched the jeweled handle. "It looks custom made," he said. "Maybe one of a kind. It's like a toy, though. I bet it isn't too accurate."

Richard reached out to take the gun back, and Paul was horrified to see that his father's shirt cuff was wet with a dark red liquid. The cuff was dripping with blood!

"Jeez," cried Cos. "What happened to you?"

Richard turned his gloved hand over and regarded his cuff in surprise. "I must have cut myself." He thrust the hand into his pocket. "Want to take the gun out back and try it?" he asked Jesse.

21

"Sure," said Jesse eagerly.

"Oh, come on." Cos shot Paul an uncomfortable glance. "I don't think that's such a hot idea. What if the bullets ricochet and somebody gets hurt?"

Richard smiled. "Don't worry. I'll take good care of him."

A chill ran up Paul's spine. He understood now why his father's cheeks were faintly flushed. Paul recalled that Aunt Gabrielle, too, always looked pink and healthy when she came back at night from her jogging. While Paul and the two other boys had been talking about sports, Richard had been ripping some poor fool's artery open. Maybe he hadn't had enough blood to satisfy him. Why else would he be luring Jesse out into the dark alley in back of the bar?

Paul slid off his bar stool. "We ought to be getting home," he said uneasily.

His father laid a gloved hand on Paul's shoulder. He looked deep in Paul's eyes, and suddenly Paul felt disoriented. The light over the bar glowed and its dazzling reflections in the barman's silver pitcher were spinning.

"I won't be long," said Richard. "You wait. We'll be back soon."

Paul watched impassively as Richard and Jesse slipped out the back door. He realized dully that his father might kill Jesse, but for some reason, it just didn't seem to matter.

22

"It must be weird seeing your father again after all these years," Cos said.

It took Paul a moment to collect himself enough to reply. "Yes, it is," he said finally. "You can't imagine how weird."

"Ari told me she wouldn't recognize her dad if he walked in the door. I wonder why he suddenly decided to look you guys up."

Paul shrugged.

"It must have been pretty sudden," insisted Cos. "Ari didn't mention that you were expecting him."

A muffled gunshot sounded. The boys' heads turned toward the back door, but the loud music almost drowned out the sound and no one else noticed.

"It was a surprise when he showed up," said Paul. "A really big surprise."

Cos asked, "Does he dye his hair?"

Paul shrugged. He couldn't very well explain that the reason his father looked so young was that he hadn't aged since he became a vampire. "I don't know," said Paul. "Ari and I don't know him very well."

"Weird," said Cos. In the silence that followed, another shot popped. It sounded unreal, like a sound effect of the music. The music was so loud now that Paul could feel its vibrations in the bar stool. "Is your dad a hemophiliac?" Cos asked curiously.

"I don't know," he said quickly. "Like I said, we really don't know that much about him." He found himself struggling to maintain the illusion that everything was normal. All of a sudden he realized that he was desperately afraid that the kids at school would find out the truth.

When Richard and Jesse returned, Paul caught his breath sharply. There was a confused, vacant look in Jesse's blue eyes that frightened him. When Jesse reached them he leaned heavily against the bar. "I don't feel so great," he said. His face was pale and his eyes rolled as if he were about to pass out.

"Maybe you're coming down with the flu or something," said Cos. "You'd better sit down."

"It's probably something you ate," said Paul's father. "I'm sure you'll be all right tomorrow. Well, boys, we'd better be going." He shook hands with Cos and Jesse, but Jesse's arm was as limp as a rag doll's.

Paul wasn't sure that Jesse even realized where he was. But all he wanted to do was to put as much distance as possible between himself and Jesse. He didn't even want to think about what must have happened out in that alley.

As Paul followed his father through the crowd, he heard a shrill voice call out Richard's name. Richard smiled into the crowd and waved a gloved hand, but he did not stop. A minute

24

later they were on the sidewalk, where the night air was tinged with neon. Paul could see his own breath coming in cloudy puffs. He shoved his trembling hands in his pockets. "What did you do to Jesse?" he asked abruptly.

Richard fastened his cloak. "I let him fire the gun." He raised a black eyebrow. "That was what he wanted."

"You're telling me you didn't drink his blood?" he said in a voice he scarcely recognized as his own.

Richard threw back his head and laughed. "What if I did? What are you going to do about it? Tell on me?" He bent over and laughed helplessly. Paul felt nausea sweeping over him. His father was drunk on Jesse's blood. When Richard straightened up, his cheeks were flushed and his dark eyes sparkled. He looked vividly happy, ecstatic, in fact, as if he might burst into song.

Richard whistled tunelessly as they passed Dean and Deluca's grocery store. Paul felt certain that people were looking at them. He turned his head, and through the big windows of the store, he could see stuffed pheasants and chickens perched on top of the coolers. The sight overwhelmed him with the sense that he lived in a cruel world where foxes preyed on chickens, butchers stunned bulls with an electric prod before cutting their throats, and where

25

vampires drank the blood of the unwary. It seemed horrible—and yet at the same time inevitable. Didn't the strong always prey on the weak?

Suddenly a woman came out of the grocery store and collided with them. "Richard!" she gasped. Her face was so shrunken and strained with shock that it took Paul an instant to recognize her as Sybil Barron's mother. Her frosted hair was silvery in the artificial light, and her hands, clutching a string bag of groceries, were rigid like a bird's claws.

"Anne," said Richard softly. "How are you?" He smiled incautiously, and Paul saw his fangs. The whites of his eyes glittered as he stared at Mrs. Barron. He seemed to be struck dumb by the sight of her.

Mrs. Barron's mouth was foolishly agape. Without saying a word, she turned and ran. She looked grotesque, awkwardly fleeing with her string bag banging against her tweed skirt. Paul saw her fumbling with the keys to her car. She was obviously crazy with fear. An instant later she slid into her car and pulled away with a screech of the tires. Angry horns honked. Paul saw that the string bag of milk and bread sat forgotten, sagging against the parking meter.

"She knows about you, doesn't she?" Paul asked. He felt detached, as if he were watching

26

the scene from a rooftop. The night had been so full of horror, he had gone numb.

His father turned his face away. "Yes," he said in an odd voice. "We used to be in love once when we were very young, and when I left your mother I was so lonely I went to Anne, told her the truth, and asked her to come away and live with me forever." He paused. "She acted so idiotic that I changed my mind. To have her hanging around my neck for eternity would be a punishment." He spat out the words.

Paul knew his father was lying. Mrs. Barron had violently rejected his father once. It was clear that the old rejection still hurt.

"Did you see how ugly she's grown?" Richard said venomously. "Her jowls sag and her stomach is slack. Next her neck will go scrawny, and hairs will sprout on her chin. Her eyes will cloud over, her brain will shrivel, and then she will die." He took a deep breath and his dark eyes glittered. "Let's take a turn down by the canal," he said. "It's a beautiful night." He peeled off his gloves.

Paul's flesh crept. The night was cold and foggy. Why would anybody want to go down to the canal? "No," he said. "Let's go home."

His father grasped Paul's arm with startling power. Paul saw he would be unable to resist.

The side streets were scarcely lit as they turned the corner and walked away from the avenue, plunging into darkness. A parking garage loomed directly ahead of them. Cement layers of cars rose several stories against the sky. Some yards ahead stood the lighted booth of the attendant, a black man in uniform who was talking on the telephone.

Paul heard the sharp clack of high heels on the pavement behind him and turned around. A blond woman with a briefcase was walking in their direction. Just as she reached them she opened her purse, groping for her keys.

"Excuse me," said Richard.

The young woman jumped, but then her face relaxed. Richard smiled warmly. "Do you have the time?" he asked.

"Yes," she said, arching her wrist to read the dial of her gold watch. Paul was entranced by the faint shading on her cheekbone and the delicate arch of her blond eyebrows.

His father leapt on her, and Paul saw the woman's eyes widen in horror as Richard buried his face against her neck. Paul was never sure whether he heard her flesh rip or not—it seemed impossible—but afterward his memory retained a soft tearing sound and a kind of choking gulp. The woman crumbled beneath Richard, both of them falling as one to the sidewalk. Paul saw her foot protruding from his father's cape. The blue veins of her arch looked pathetically frail and her high-heeled shoe lay on the sidewalk beside her.

28

Sick with nausea, Paul stared as his father tore at her neck like a wolf.

Finally he sank to his knees and pulled desperately at his father's shoulder. His father hissed and turned to face him. His cheeks were streaked red and his lips were ruby.

"Stop!" Paul whispered. "Stop it. You'll kill her."

His father gulped. His dark eyes were glazed, and Paul was not even sure his father saw him. Richard's right hand was pressed tightly against the woman's neck as if to stanch the jetting blood. "Go away," he said thickly. "Leave us."

Paul shot a desperate glance at the lighted booth. Incredibly, the attendant had propped his feet up on his desk and was still talking on the phone.

How long did it take someone with a severed artery to die? Paul wondered. Was it possible the woman was still alive? "We've got to get out of here," he gasped.

Richard hesitated, then stood up. In shock, Paul realized that even Richard's eyebrows were wet with blood. Yet the exposed white expanse of the woman's neck was unblemished. His father had somehow sealed her neck with his hand. Richard pulled a handkerchief out of his pocket and began swabbing the blood off his face.

Paul could see a slight movement of the woman's chest. She was breathing, but was in bad shape. With his father there, he couldn't very well call for an ambulance. Paul felt in his pocket for the lighter. He scrubbed it briefly on his pants leg, then threw it with all his might at the lighted booth.

"Hey!" the attendant cried, turning in their direction. Paul grabbed his father's arm. Crouching in the shadows of the building, they ran.

CHAPTER THREE

WHEN PAUL STEPPED INTO HIS ROOM, ARI WAS WAIT-
ing for him in the darkness. "Paul!" Suddenly
her arms were around him and he could feel the
dampness of her tears on his face. Her warmth
sent a comforting calm over him. At least he had
stopped shaking, but his mouth was sour—he
had vomited on his way back to the house. He
pulled away from her and sat down heavily on
the bed.

"Are you all right?" Ari asked.

"I guess. I mean, he didn't attack me, if that's
what you're worried about."

Ari sat on the bed. "I tried to follow you,"
she said. "But he must have guessed I was behind you. Suddenly you both disappeared.
Where did he take you?"

"To some vampire bar on M Street." Paul

31

turned on the light. "And guess who else was there," he said bitterly. "Jesse and Cos!"

"Cos!" Ari covered her face. "Oh, no! What was he doing there? You aren't saying that Cos—!"

"No, no," interrupted Paul impatiently. "You know that Cos isn't a vampire, Ari. I'm not saying I like the guy, but it's not as bad as that."

"Of course not." Ari caught her breath. "I don't know what's come over me. I feel like I'm going out of my mind. I've been so worried. It was awful to sit here in the dark wondering if you would ever come back."

"I don't know what Dad is up to," Paul said, frowning. "He's hard to figure." Paul remembered his father's attack on the woman at the parking garage. He had been crazy with bloodlust, like a wolf or a hyena. Paul didn't want to tell Ari that. He shivered. He didn't even want to think about it.

"He's got some kind of power," Paul said slowly. "When I'm with him, it's like I find myself doing things that don't make that much sense." He thought of the way he had let Jesse go back to the dark alley with his father. He'd felt strange—as if he had been in a trance.

Ari grabbed her brother's hand. "You've got to hate him, Paul. Hate him the way I do. Then he won't have power over you."

"I can't hate him," said Paul slowly. "Do you hate a wolf? Or a weasel when it goes after a rabbit? That's just the way he is, Ari."

"I hate him," Ari said in a low voice. "I hate him enough for both of us." She held Paul's gaze with her own, and he knew he wouldn't be able to lie to her. "What happened at the bar?" she asked. "Did Cos get a good look at him?"

"Yeah, he got a good look. But I don't think he guessed anything was wrong." He hesitated. "I hope not, anyway."

"What happened?" she asked. "Tell me the truth."

"The only thing is," said Paul reluctantly, "Dad took Jesse out in the alley behind that place and he did something to him."

Ari's hand flew to her mouth.

Paul's heart was pounding at the memory of what had happened, and he wished he didn't have to tell her. "Jesse looked just like Sandy did, Ari, after that night Aunt Gabrielle sucked his blood."

Ari's eyes widened with fear.

"Maybe he's not as bad off as Sandy," added Paul. "I hope not. People are going to ask questions if this keeps up."

"What do you mean, 'if this keeps up'?" cried Ari. "We can't stay here. We've got to get away. We've got to escape."

"Where would we go?" asked Paul, turning up the palms of his hands helplessly. "When you think about it, we need to hang around to figure out where we stand. I mean, our father is a vampire. We've got to figure out what that means."

"Don't start talking about our vampire nature." Ari covered her ears. "I'm like my mother," she cried. "He's got nothing to do with us!"

Paul gently pulled her hands down and held them. "The point is, we don't know where we are with this vampire stuff. When I was walking with Dad to the bar, he kept telling me how his vampire nature called to him for years before he turned. While he was in high school, even."

"That's stupid," said Ari. "That junk about his destiny is just stupid. People do what they want to do. There's no such thing as destiny."

"Maybe. But I think it makes sense for us to hang around here and try to find out as much as we can about our family. At least until we're sure what's going to happen to us."

"But what if Dad or Aunt Gabrielle tries to make us into vampires!" gasped Ari.

Paul was silent for a moment. "Aunt Gabrielle?" he said at last. "No. I can't see her doing that. Besides, look at all the chances she's had to attack us already. I can't see her forcing us to do anything. But with our dad—I'm not so sure."

"Don't go out with him anymore, Paul," cried Ari. "Promise me you won't."

"Don't worry. I've got all that out of my system." Paul remembered the body of the young woman crumpled on the sidewalk by the parking garage and shuddered. After a moment he added, "There's something else you ought to know, though."

"What?" gasped Ari, clinging to him. "Tell me!"

"Sybil's mother knows about Dad," admitted Paul reluctantly.

"I can't stand it!" cried Ari. She leapt up from the bed and began pacing the floor. "We can't go on acting like everything is okay. Don't you realize that Aunt Gabrielle and our dad both grew up in this very house? Other people who live around here must know that they've killed people! They've attacked kids we know! Nadia and Amanda must have seen him when he came to that Halloween dance at our school! And that's just since we've been here. People are going to figure out something is wrong." She stared at her brother. "Paul, the next thing we know a mob could be storming the house looking for them!"

Ari stared out the window for a long time, clenching and unclenching her fists. The window was open and a light breeze stirred the curtains. Paul had gotten home safely, she reminded herself. That was the important thing. But she had seen the shadow of horror on his face, and she felt cold. How could they protect themselves? she wondered.

35

Her instinct was to run—but Paul was right. They had nowhere to go.

"Listen, Ari," Paul said at last.

Ari turned to face him. "So what are we going to do?"

"Maybe nothing. Our dad is the rootless type. That's one of the things I found out at that party of Aunt Gabrielle's when I asked around. He never stays anywhere long because he's too restless. It's possible that he could be out of here before he causes any more trouble for us."

"I hope you're right about that."

"As for Aunt Gabrielle," Paul went on, "she's been passing as human for years. She's even got a job. Maybe we can go on living here with no more problems."

"We'd better bolt our doors and not go out alone at night." Ari licked her lips. Was it possible tonight's horror was going to fade away the way Paul hoped it would? "We've got to stick together and try to protect each other."

Paul nodded. "Don't worry. After this, I'm going to be careful to stay clear of him."

Suddenly the phone rang. Ari gasped at the sudden noise and grabbed the receiver. "Hullo?" she said.

"Ari? It's Cos. I didn't wake you up, did I? I know it's late."

Ari fell onto the bed. "No, no," she said.

"We're—I'm not asleep yet." She mouthed "Cos," and Paul made a face.

"Did your brother tell you we ran into each other tonight?" asked Cos.

"Yes," said Ari. She bit her lip. "Yes, he mentioned it."

"I got a chance to meet your dad. I didn't know he was in town," Cos said.

"We weren't expecting him," said Ari. "It was kind of a shock."

"He really looks good for a man his age," said Cos. "Good looks run in your family, huh?" She could hear the smile in his voice. "Do you think he's had a face-lift?"

"I don't know," said Ari desperately. "How's Jesse getting along, Cos?"

"I guess Paul told you he nearly passed out on us. I drove him home and helped his mom put him to bed. If it's the flu, I hope I'm not going to get it." Cos began talking about school, but it was hard for Ari to keep her mind on what he was saying.

"Are you okay, Ari?" Cos asked.

"Sure!" she said. "Why do you ask?" Her eyes darted to Paul's face in alarm.

"You seem kind of quiet. You're pretty upset about this visit from your father, aren't you?"

"Yes," said Ari in a small voice. "I am."

"Do you want to talk about it?"

"No," she said. "Not now."

"Okay, okay. That's cool. But if you want to talk about it—well, you know I'm ready to listen."

"I know." Ari felt her throat constrict painfully.

"Okay, then," said Cos. "Forget that. Change of subject. Want to go out to dinner Friday night? I just got my allowance and I'm rich."

"That sounds good." Ari suddenly remembered that she and Paul had agreed to stick together after dark. "But let's double with Paul and Susannah, okay?" she added.

"If that's what you want to do," said Cos. He didn't sound thrilled about the idea.

"I think it'd be good for you and Paul to get to know each other better," said Ari.

When she hung up, Paul protested. "I don't want to double with you and Cos, Ari. You know I can't stand him. He's so darn sure of himself."

"I know—but we said we weren't going to go out at night by ourselves, remember?" she reminded him. "We agreed to stick together."

"You're right. I couldn't stand it if anything happened to you, Ari," said Paul hoarsely. He was suddenly pale. "We'll stick together," he agreed.

CHAPTER
FOUR

A BLUE SKY ARCHED OVER THE GOTHIC ROOFTOPS OF St. Anselm's school. The old buildings glowed in the bright sunshine. Cos had backed Ari up against the uneven stone wall of the administration building and she was happily looking up at him. She loved the way his brown hair feathered at the back of his neck. He had a way of wearing his tie half undone that gave him a sexy, unkempt look.

"I'm crazy about you," he whispered in her ear. She felt his lips brush her neck.

"Stop it," she said, squirming. "That tickles."

"Sorry." He grinned. "Am I boring you by saying how crazy I am about you over and over?"

"No." Ari laughed. "Keep at it. I need all the good stuff I can get." Suddenly she kissed him. They held each other close for a long time.

"Mmm," he said, squeezing her close to him. "Let's do that again." He nuzzled her.

Ari could smell his hair and feel his warmth, and she burrowed against him like a small animal hiding from a storm.

"Wow," he murmured after a moment. "Are we sure we want to double with Paul and Susannah? Don't we want to go to some quiet little restaurant and find a dark corner—"

Ari's eyes flew open suddenly. "No! I mean, I want you to get to know Paul." She stretched her lips into a smile.

Cos's finger touched the corner of her mouth. He gave her a puzzled look. "Are you okay?"

"I'm fine." Ari felt hot color rise to her cheeks. "It's only that I guess this stuff about my father is getting to me."

Cos frowned. "Look, Ari, forget him. If he hasn't paid any attention to you up till now he's not worth worrying about."

"You're right." She sighed. "I know you're right."

It was time for class, and kids were beginning to go inside. Ari turned to go, but Cos caught her around the waist and pulled her close to him. "Don't be sad," he said softly. "Don't let your dad ruin everything."

She lifted her chin determinedly. "I won't," she said. She turned around and smiled up at him. "I've got to get to class. See you later," she said.

"You bet." Cos's smile lit up his face.

As Ari walked into the classroom building, she overheard Amanda saying spitefully, "Whenever I see people making out in public, I wonder what they're trying to prove."

Ari glanced over her shoulder. She knew she was supposed to overhear Amanda's remark, and she hated that she couldn't stop herself from blushing. The problem was she *had* been trying to prove something, but only that she was a warm and loving human being and not a vampire. How could she tell that to Amanda?

It seemed to Ari that she went through the day in a daze. When she glanced out the window of her first-period classroom, a pink hairless creature with bat ears clambered up on the windowsill. Its ribbed wings flapped clumsily behind it, and Ari could hear the scratch of its nails on the wood. It clung to the window, then opened its mouth, and she saw its sharp fangs. Cold sweat prickled her forehead as she looked away. *It isn't real,* she reminded herself.

Later in the morning Ari noticed that Jesse wasn't in English class. Her heart sank. Her friend Sybil tossed her mane of frizzy red hair and waved. But all Ari could think now when she looked at Sybil was that Sybil's mother knew the truth. No wonder Mrs. Barron had acted so strange when Sybil took Ari to their house!

After class, Sybil touched Ari's arm. "Is something wrong? You look terrible."

"My father showed up last night."

Sybil raised her high-arched eyebrows. "Did he happen to explain what he's been doing the last sixteen years?"

"He's been busy," said Ari dryly.

"Well, he's not going to take you off with him, is he?" asked Sybil, alarmed. "You aren't moving, are you?"

"No," said Ari. "Paul and I aren't going to have anything to do with him."

"That bad, huh?" Sybil was soon breathless with the effort of keeping up with Ari. "What is he like? Is he a drunk or something like that?"

Ari hesitated. "He's just bad news, Sybil. Let's talk about something nicer."

"My brother Rab," said Sybil promptly. "He's nice. And he's coming home from college this weekend. I want you to get to know him."

"Sure," said Ari. "I'd like to."

When Ari got to her chemistry class, it turned out their teacher had been called away by a death in the family, and Ari had an unexpectedly free period. She decided to go to the library.

St. Anselm's library had tall windows that looked out on the school's green lawns. A globe stood in front of the rows of book stacks, and by

42

the entrance was a collection of comfortable chairs whose shapes were reflected in the screens of the nearby computers.

Ari plucked a book off the shelf and sat down. Soon she realized that Nadia, Cos's old girlfriend, was at a table nearby. Nadia was a pretty, shy girl with large brown eyes. Her dark hair was pulled back with pink ribbon and tumbled in a cascade down her back. A stack of books stood at her elbow. One was *Malus Malefacorum*, an old book on witchcraft. Suddenly a chill ran up Ari's spine. Nadia was reading a book called *Vampires and Their Kin*.

The title burned into Ari's eyes as she watched Nadia turn a page. She wondered what accounted for Nadia's sudden interest in vampires. Ari knew that on the night of the Halloween party, Nadia and her friend Amanda had accidentally dumped buckets of flour and water on Ari's dad. Nadia might have gotten a good look at him. Had she somehow stumbled onto the truth?

Unable to stand the tension any longer, Ari leapt up from her chair and went over to where Nadia was sitting. She rested her fingertips on the table and smiled self-consciously. "Hullo," she said. "Getting a head start on your research paper?"

Nadia's book fell to the table with a sound like a slap. She crossed herself. "Don't touch me!" she whimpered. "Please, don't touch me."

Ari backed away. "I'm not touching you," she said. "I—I only asked if you were working on your research paper."

"I won't let you cast a spell on me," Nadia whispered.

"Cast a spell? What are you talking about?" Ari glanced around uneasily, wondering if anyone was standing behind the nearby book stack overhearing this conversation.

"You cast a spell on Cos," said Nadia. Her liquid eyes were open very wide and their whites stood out in stark contrast to her skin. "You enchanted him. I've always known there was something strange about you," she whispered. "Your teeth are pointed like an animal's. Get away from me or I'll scream."

Ari could feel her face burning as she backed away. "Well—good grief!" She turned suddenly and fled the library in tears.

She hurried through the empty halls of the building conscious of the cool air on her hot cheeks. Her book bag was in the library somewhere, but she couldn't go back there.

Finally she stopped and leaned against a wall, breathing heavily. Her temples were pounding with a terrible headache. She was not turning into a vampire, she told herself. She was not!

* * *

"Come on, Ari," Paul said that afternoon as he steered the car down Massachusetts Avenue. "What's the big deal? You know you didn't cast a spell on Cos." If anything, Paul thought bitterly, it was the other way around. "Nadia's only freaking out because Cos dumped her."

"I know that," Ari said, gazing out the window. "But you can't imagine what it's like to have someone treat you like that. Nadia acted as if I were the Creature From the Black Lagoon crawling out of the slime. It was awful!"

Paul glanced at her sympathetically. "You really got shook up, huh?"

Ari nodded. Her eyes were shiny with tears.

Paul was glad she hadn't been along with him when he went out with their dad. Compared to what he'd gone through, seeing Nadia freak out in the library didn't even rate a mention. "Look, stop brooding about it," he said. "You're fine! And quit worrying about your teeth. They're just like mine. Lots of people have pointed canine teeth. You know you aren't casting any spells, so forget about it."

Ari wiped her eyes. "You're right," she said. "I've got to calm down."

"That's right. I know that little chat with Nadia wasn't any fun, but we can't afford to worry about the small stuff. We've got bigger problems." Paul glanced at her. "Can you get a ride home with Sybil tomorrow?" he asked.

"I guess so," she said, looking at him curiously. "Why?"

"I'm going to see Sandy in the hospital," he said gruffly.

"Oh." She went pale. "Of course. You ought to do that."

That night at dinner, Aunt Gabrielle's eyes sparkled. Paul stared uneasily at her wine-glass. He didn't even want to think about what filled it.

Overhead, the chandelier's shower of prisms cast an uncertain glow over the long mahogany table.

"It's so nice to have Richard around again." Aunt Gabrielle's musical voice seemed to echo in the large room. "When we were young, you know, we were very close."

"Is that why you became a vampire, too?" asked Ari. "Because you were so close to him?"

Aunt Gabrielle was reaching for her glass, but her hand froze for an instant. "Yes, dear," she said quietly. "It is. When Richard told me what had happened to him, I pleaded with him to make me a vampire, too—so we could be together forever."

"I bet he didn't take much persuading," said Paul in a low voice. He shoveled a forkful of food into his mouth.

"Do you have any regrets?" asked Ari, with a

46

quick darting look at her aunt's face.

Paul saw that Aunt Gabrielle's eyes were empty of all expression. He couldn't guess what she might be thinking. "I suppose regrets are only natural," she said finally, "but I do my best to look on the bright side." She made an impatient gesture. "Of course, living as a human being, as I do, presents unique challenges."

Paul didn't have to ask if Carmel, the housekeeper, had left for the day. He knew this frank conversation would not be taking place if Carmel were still pottering around in the kitchen.

He noticed that Gabrielle's fingernails had been carefully enameled pink to hide the telltale vampire glassiness.

"Of course, I haven't eaten food in years," said Aunt Gabrielle, toying with the helping on her plate. "You can't imagine the discipline it takes to be sure that the proper amount of ordinary garbage goes out to the curb twice a week!"

"I guess you do your real feasting at night when you go jogging," said Paul.

His aunt frowned at him. "You aren't going to get all sanctimonious on me, are you, darling?"

Paul split open a biscuit and stabbed a pat of butter with his fork. "Just asking. You don't have to answer, if you don't want."

47

Aunt Gabrielle looked down, and her dark lashes made a soft shadow on the white flesh. "I do usually feed while I'm out jogging," she admitted finally. "Georgetown has so many bars. It's easy to find an unwary drunk." She glanced mischievously up at the twins. "I often jog along the canal path, and once a mugger got the surprise of his life when he went after me thinking I was a defenseless woman."

Paul noticed that Ari had not touched her food. "You'd think people would get suspicious," he said. "All those bodies littering the streets of Georgetown."

"Nothing causes more questions than a rash of bodies." Aunt Gabrielle raised her napkin and patted her pale lips. "I've said it a hundred times—better to drink a little from several victims. It pays in the end to be careful."

"You weren't exactly careful with Sandy, were you?" asked Paul harshly. "He ended up in the hospital with doctors pumping blood into him all night. Did you have to attack a guest in our home?" He was surprised at how quickly his anger had flared up.

Aunt Gabrielle's pink tongue showed briefly as she licked her lips. "I do feel a little embarrassed about that." Her lavender eyes glowed brighter and then dimmer, as if they were lit by some unseen source. Paul couldn't take his gaze off her. He was suddenly struck by a horrible memory—he had dreamed about a glowing skull and then had awakened to find Aunt Gabrielle bent over Sandy, sucking his blood. "I only intended to have a little sip," Aunt Gabrielle went on. "But I had never tasted blood from a young cross-country runner before. It was so good."

"May I be excused?" Paul rose from the table abruptly.

"Of course, dear," said Aunt Gabrielle. She smiled a bright little smile. "Isn't it nice that we can be completely open and honest with each other now?"

"Just terrific," said Paul in a hollow voice. He stood up and stumbled out of the room.

In the hallway he could hear Ari's voice clearly. The marble floors carried the sound. "Our father doesn't keep a house here, does he?" she asked.

Aunt Gabrielle heaved a loud sigh. "Richard doesn't keep a house anyplace, Ari. He can't be bothered. Discretion and restraint, I'm sorry to say, form no part of his vocabulary. He prefers to drink his fill and move on."

"Leaving bodies everywhere," said Ari in a thin voice.

"As you say," said Aunt Gabrielle.

Not wanting to hear more, Paul fled upstairs.

CHAPTER
FIVE

ARI CAUGHT A RIDE HOME FROM SCHOOL THE NEXT day with Cos. Paul was visiting Sandy in the hospital. At least Jesse had recovered from their father's attack. She had seen him in English class yesterday looking a bit pale but otherwise fine. Ari glanced out the window. Some men in hard hats were getting ready to pour a sidewalk. To Ari's horror, a skeleton strolled into the workers' midst, leaned on the bumper of the cement mixer, and lit a cigarette. He looked at her, white smoke curling in a corkscrew over his head. She clenched her eyes shut. *Go away*, she whispered to herself. *Leave me alone. Please, leave me alone.* The car jerked ahead, and she felt Cos's hand on her knee.

"Are you okay?" Cos asked. "I feel like you're

here but you're not here, if you know what I mean."

She opened her eyes, and to her relief the skeleton had disappeared. "I guess it's all this stuff about my dad," she mumbled.

"Confused feelings, huh?" He shot her a sympathetic glance.

"I hate him," she said simply.

"That's tough." Cos's car rolled past the dark masses of trees at Rock Creek Park. Ari shuddered, wondering what horrors were hiding in the darkness—horrors only she could see.

"I guess I can't really imagine what it's like for you," Cos said. "I've got such a normal family—a dad who works all the time and expects me to make straight A's, and a mom who thinks I'm wonderful and treats me like I'm a five-year-old." He laughed.

Ari gazed at Cos, loving the look of his friendly face, the flecks of gold in his dark eyes, the untidy hair. Her eyes filled with tears. "You are so lucky," she choked.

"I'm sorry, Ari," he said softly. "Maybe things will get better. Maybe he'll go away and you'll never have to see him again."

"Maybe." Ari pressed her fingertips against her closed eyelids. Her head felt hot. Cos couldn't possibly imagine what she was up against. How could he?

He glanced over at her and handed her a tissue.

She blew her nose noisily. At least she had Paul. If anything happened to Paul, she thought, blinking away her tears, she would be lost.

Paul had never felt so uncomfortable, so heavy-footed, or so awkward as when he walked into Sandy's hospital room. A screen stood beside the bed, shielding the rest of the room from view. Sandy's head rested against the pillow, eyes closed, and his freckles stood out against his bleached skin. The television flickered, playing without sound.

"Sandy?" Paul whispered.

Sandy's eyes flew open and he smiled broadly. "Boy, am I glad to see you, Paul. If I watch another television game show I'm going to lose it."

Paul pulled up a chair and uneasily eyed the tray beside Sandy's bed. "How are you getting along?" he asked.

"I'm perfectly okay, but they won't let me shower unless somebody's in here with me. It's so stupid. They won't even let me leave the room unless I'm in a wheelchair. It's like being in jail, except the food's worse here."

"When are they going to let you go home?" asked Paul.

Sandy made a face. "I don't know. They've run a hundred tests and they haven't been able to find a thing, but the doctor thinks I must have some kind of break in this extra loop of the small intestine."

Paul gazed at him in astonishment. Aunt Gabrielle had sucked Sandy's blood. She had confessed it!

"I don't need that extra loop," Sandy went on, "so they're going to go in and take it out."

"You mean they're going to operate!" cried Paul.

Sandy's head fell back against the pillow. "Jeez, don't say it that way. It's supposed to be a very simple operation. Like an appendectomy. I'll be back in school in a week." He smiled wanly. "No more cross-country for me this term, though."

Paul knew he should go straight to a nurse and tell them it was all a mistake—Sandy didn't need an operation. But how could he? He couldn't tell anyone the truth. "Shouldn't they run some more tests first?" he asked, running his finger around the inside of his collar.

"They say it's better to go ahead and take it out. So, was the chemistry test hard? Want to give me some clues about what's on it?"

Paul felt so guilty he would have given Sandy a complete copy of the chemistry test, but he couldn't remember the first thing about it. His mind was blank. "You don't want any hints from me," he said. "I probably bombed it."

Sandy's gaze shifted. "How's Ari?" he asked.

Paul slumped in his chair. If Sandy hadn't had a crush on Ari he would never have come to spend the night at their house in the first place. "She's fine. She said to say hello for her," he lied.

"Maybe she can come visit," Sandy said, glancing at him hopefully.

"She hates hospitals, Sandy," said Paul, avoiding his friend's eyes.

"She's got a thing about pain and blood, huh? I don't blame her. Me, too. Only thing is, I've *got* to be here." Sandy fell back against the pillow. "Ari and Cos are getting pretty tight, aren't they?" he asked wanly.

"I guess they are," admitted Paul.

"I never had a chance competing with Cos anyway," said Sandy. "I don't know what it is he's got, but girls seem to love it. He's not even that good-looking, is he?"

"Well, *I* don't think so." Paul smiled a little.

"I mean, lots of guys look better than him. Who can figure girls?"

They talked a while longer about school. For some of the time Paul was even able to forget about Sandy's impending operation. Then the awful memory of what Aunt Gabrielle had done to him would coming flooding into his mind.

"I guess I'd better be going," Paul said finally.

"Well, thanks for coming by. Say hello to Ari for me." Sandy smiled at him.

"I will," said Paul, backing out of the room.

Halfway down the hall, he spotted Jesse Driscoll approaching, dressed in army fatigues. His heart sank. He had no idea how much Jesse remembered of what happened that night in the bar. What would happen if Jesse and Sandy started comparing notes? Paul forced himself to nod pleasantly.

Jesse frowned at Paul as if he were trying hard to remember something, and Paul felt himself go cold. He was aware that he bore more than a passing resemblance to his father. What if Paul's face triggered Jesse's memory and he suddenly recalled what had happened that night? Gulping hard, Paul hurried past his classmate, but he was conscious of Jesse's curious gaze as he fled.

Outside, in the parking lot, Paul stood by his car, immobilized. He was so weighed down by guilt that it was as if his own body were a heavy burden. Perhaps he would stand in the parking lot, still as a statue, while the afternoon shadows grew long and the sun sank below the horizon.

A crow flew over him, casting a moving shadow on the pavement, then landed in a tree by the curb. From its perch, it cocked its head and regarded Paul with a glitteringly intelligent black eye. Paul wished he could change places with the bird. He imagined lifting himself effortlessly into the blue sky, leaving behind all his guilt and his painful self-consciousness.

The feathers at the bird's neck ruffled and it uttered a harsh caw. Paul had the unnerving sensation that the crow was trying to warn him. With a sudden movement Paul jerked open the car door and got in, his heart pounding as if he had been running.

"I'm okay. I'm going to be fine," he said aloud, and the sound of his voice startled him. He stared into space for a full minute before he could bring himself to start the car and drive out of the parking lot.

Jesse sat down in the chair by Sandy's bed. "Sorry I wasn't able to come sooner," he said, "but my mom said I'd better stay away until I was sure I didn't have anything contagious that you might catch."

"I didn't think you ever got sick, Jesse." Sandy grinned. "I thought germs were afraid of you."

"Damn straight. I stomp on 'em," said Jesse, scowling. Running into Paul in the corridor reminded him that he still hadn't quite figured out what had happened to him that night in the bar. His memory was clear up to the point that he had gone out in the alley.

He remembered that Paul's dad had been standing close behind him to show him how to put on the safety catch of the gun—and after that things had gotten weird. Maybe somebody had put something funny in his drink. He had vague images and feelings—a blinding pain, a thumping sound like a savage kind of drum, and then darkness had enfolded him. The next thing he knew Paul's father was shaking him. "Can you stand up?" Mr. Montclair had asked him. "You look a little wobbly." And then he had laughed. The memory of that laugh chilled Jesse.

"I said," repeated Sandy, "how was the chemistry test?"

"Oh. Sorry." Jesse shook his head. "I guess I went blank there for a minute. It was easy. You don't have a thing to worry about."

"I tried to get some clues about the questions from Paul, but he acted like he had total amnesia."

Amnesia, thought Jesse with a jolt. *That's what I have. A strange kind of amnesia.* He could remember some things, but none of it jelled or made sense. The more he thought about it, the more he thought somebody must have put something in his drink. He glanced at the open door. "Don't you think Paul is kind of strange?"

"Paul?" Sandy looked at him in surprise. "Nah. You don't know him very well, that's all."

"Do you?" asked Jesse bluntly.

"Well—sure!" Sandy looked at him in surprise.

"I met Paul's dad the other night," said Jesse.

"And he was—weird. There was something about his face . . . I can't quite put my finger on it, but it looked hard, you know, like plastic."

"Relatives," sighed Sandy. "Everybody's got weird relatives. You can't blame them for that. You should meet my great-uncle Julius. He's been stashing guns in abandoned mines for fifty years because he's convinced the Russians are going to take over the country." Sandy suddenly stopped talking and blushed.

Jesse smiled. He supposed Sandy had remembered that he, too, collected guns and that the remark about his uncle being weird wasn't exactly tactful. "He must have an interesting collection of guns," Jesse said. "Lugers, derringers, and everything. All the good old stuff."

"Probably all of them are rusted out by now," said Sandy. "So, what's going on at school?" he went on casually. "I get the idea Cos and Paul's sister are sort of an item."

"Going at it hot and heavy right in front of the Schuler Building this morning," Jesse confirmed. "Saw them myself."

Sandy sighed and sank deeper into his pillow. "Yeah, I figured Paul was trying to let me down easy."

"Cos is nuts about her," said Jesse, frowning. "Beats me why."

"Jesse, man, she's beautiful!" cried Sandy, staring at him in astonishment. "Are you blind?

And her smile! She's beautiful inside and out."

"You've been over to their house, haven't you?" asked Jesse. "What's their aunt like?"

Sandy shrugged. "Pretty. Dressed to kill. She seems just slightly out of it. Or maybe it's the house." He laughed. "It's one of those gloomy old town houses on N Street. You keep expecting to find the bride of Frankenstein in the basement."

"That so?" Jesse scratched his head thoughtfully.

"So what are you doing with your life while I'm rotting up here in a hospital bed?" asked Sandy.

"Nothing much." Jesse propped a shoe on the rim of the bed frame.

"You must be doing something besides studying for chemistry," said Sandy.

"Well, I've asked Nadia to go out with me."

"Aw-right!" said Sandy. "But say—isn't that kind of sticky since she just broke up with Cos?"

"Nah. It was sticky when she was *going* with Cos. But now it's smooth sailing." Jesse tapped on his teeth with a thumbnail. "Yeah," he said finally. "I guess I've sort of liked her for quite a while. The trouble is I never noticed her much till Cos took up with her, and then it was hands off, if you know what I mean."

"Yeah," said Sandy, heaving a sigh. "I know what you mean. Cos has all the luck."

CHAPTER
SIX

THE ETHIOPIAN RESTAURANT'S NAME WAS PAINTED on the glass of its front window. Inside, the place was narrow and dark, and the scent of unfamiliar spices filled the air.

"Let's sit in the front," suggested Ari with an anxious glance at Paul. "The light is better there."

"Whatever you think," said Susannah.

Ari rolled her eyes. Paul knew that Susannah's sweetness annoyed Ari. She had complained to him about it often enough. She also didn't like Susannah's long manicured nails, her dreamy manner, or the way she let strands of her hair escape and fall around her face to give that careless, artistic look. Paul had a good idea how Ari felt because he couldn't stand Cos, either. Under the circumstances, it wasn't too surprising that there had already been some long, uncomfortable silences.

A beaded curtain separated the restaurant from the kitchen. The beads swung gently and a waitress in a sarong appeared and handed them plastic menus.

"Did I tell you Jesse visited Sandy at the hospital?" asked Cos. They sat down.

Ari darted a glance at Paul. "I know. Paul ran into Jesse there, didn't you, Paul?"

Paul nodded, shifting uncomfortably in his seat.

"Yeah," Cos smiled, "but Paul probably went by, handed Sandy some flowers, then went home and didn't give it another thought. Jesse goes to the hospital and all of a sudden he's convinced something sinister is going on."

"Jesse ought to go into therapy," Susannah said. "I know he was kidnapped when his family lived in South America and all that, but that was years ago. It's time he got over it. He's not normal."

"Jesse's okay," insisted Cos. "He's got one or two blind spots, just like anyone else."

"I think we ought to order, don't you?" put in Ari, eager to change the subject.

But Cos was still intent on defending his friend. "It's not so crazy of him to be paranoid, you know," he told Susannah. "There are conspiracies and murders and kidnappings all the time right under our noses."

"Cos." Susannah's eyes widened. "If you aren't careful you're going to end up thinking like Jesse. I'm serious."

"I'm just saying bad things do happen to people—especially here in this city," he replied.

"That's true," agreed Susannah softly, "but you can't let that poison your mind. There is so much beauty in the world." She smiled and touched Paul's hand.

Paul was unable to smile back. Cos's announcement that Jesse thought something sinister was going on had struck him like a lightning bolt. He would have given anything to know exactly what Jesse suspected, but he couldn't bring himself to ask Cos any questions. "I guess we'd better order," he said reluctantly.

The food was served on a tray-sized piece of thin bread that was like a giant pancake. The orders—lamb, mixed vegetables, chicken stew—had been heaped directly onto it.

"Isn't this interesting!" Susannah cried. "So authentic!"

Cos tore off a bit of the bread and scooped some lamb onto it. "I'm going to have a big party next weekend," he said. "You'll all have to come. My parents are going to be out of town."

"Great," Ari said, smiling.

Paul remembered how Ari used to hate big parties. But it seemed that anything Cos did or said was just great.

"Should we bring anything?" Ari asked. "Do you need help getting ready?"

"Nope. I'm going to order a keg and lots of tortilla chips. That should take care of everything."

"Did you say next Saturday?" asked Susannah, disappointed. "I'm going to miss it. I'm going to be at my grandmother's."

"You come anyway," Cos urged Paul. "Bryan's going to bring his new amplifiers. Do you play an instrument?"

"No," said Paul shortly.

"You never told me you were a musician, Cos," said Ari.

"Oh, I fool around with the guitar a little." Cos made an unsuccessful attempt to look modest.

Paul knew he was scowling, but he couldn't help it. The guy was so full of himself!

Suddenly the door of the restaurant flew open, and to Paul's horror, he heard a familiar flutey voice calling his name. He glanced up in alarm. It was Verena, the vampire who had been putting the moves on him at Aunt Gabrielle's party! Behind her stood a tough-looking, muscular vampire that Paul knew he had also seen before.

"I thought I saw you," cried Verena. "It's so cool to run into you again. Do you remember me?"

Paul closed his eyes, feeling slightly dizzy. He remembered her all too well.

"I'm Verena," she reminded him helpfully. "We met at your aunt's party."

"Why don't you join us?" said Cos, his eyes glued to Verena.

"Thanks," Verena said, hooking a chair from the next table. She shed her jacket, and Paul could see that her unbuttoned satin shirt barely covered her cleavage. Her blond hair fell in a silken fringe to her shoulders.

The muscular vampire straddled a chair backwards. He looked amused as he surveyed the table.

"You like lamb curry?" asked Cos, offering her a taste of his.

Verena tucked her feet demurely under her chair and shook her head. "No, thanks. Dubay and I have already eaten."

I'll bet, Paul thought. With a sinking heart, he noticed that Verena's pale skin had the faint pulse of life under its porcelain smoothness. She and Dubay looked sleek and well-satisfied. Paul knew with a sick certainty that they must have been sucking the blood out of some poor victim only moments before.

Verena pushed her hair behind her ears, and her tiny diamond earrings glittered in the dim light. Her eyes were the green of glowing emeralds. Paul found he couldn't take his eyes off her. Dimples played around the corners of her mouth. She wiggled provocatively, and her silken hair moved over her shoulders as if in slow motion. She was humming a tune under her breath.

Cos snapped his fingers. "'You'd be Nothing Without Me,'" he said.

Ari blinked at Cos. "Excuse me?"

"That tune she's humming," said Cos. "It's from the musical *City of Angels*."

"I have the sound track," Verena confided. "I just adore musicals, don't you?"

"But not Andrew Lloyd Weber," said Cos.

"Oh, no!" agreed Verena. "Real musicals. The old-fashioned kind."

Cos and Verena grinned at each other. Paul began to feel sick.

"Hey, you guys have got to come to my party!" Cos said brightly.

Ari choked on her food. Her face was turning purple.

"Are you okay, Ari?" Cos pounded her on the back.

She nodded vigorously and reached for a glass of water. *These vampires can't come to Cos's party!* Paul thought in a panic. What was to stop them from leaving the Cosgroves' lawn littered with dead bodies?

"A party!" Verena cried. "That sounds like so much fun! I *love* parties. When is it? You'd better give me your address."

Cos jotted down his address for her, and Paul noticed that he let his fingers touch Verena's when he handed her the note. Paul wanted to scream, "How can you flirt with her? She's a vampire! And she's older than your mother!"

Paul had been only vaguely aware of Dubay, but suddenly he realized that Dubay had pulled his chair up next to Susannah and was talking to her in confidential tones. It sounded as if they were talking about art. Paul would have figured Dubay to be more interested in boxing or hunting—some kind of blood sport. Paul grabbed the edge of the table as he felt fear welling up in him. A vampire was putting the moves on his girlfriend, and he had no idea what to do about it.

Verena stood up abruptly. "Hate to run, guys, but Dubay and I are on our way to the movies and I just hate to come in after it's already started." She wiggled her fingers at them. "Ta!"

When the door closed behind the vampires, silence fell over the table. Finally Susannah spoke. "Where did you say you know her from, Paul?"

"She's a friend of my aunt's," Paul explained nervously. "We only met one time."

Susannah looked down and tore off another bit of bread. "She's very pretty, isn't she?"

"Not as pretty as you," said Paul quickly. He laid his hand over Susannah's.

Susannah made a face. "It's too bad I have to go to my Nana's next weekend."

Paul met Ari's disconcerted gaze. Why did Cos have to ask Verena to his party? Paul was worried, and he knew Ari was, too. Susannah wasn't too happy either, for that matter. She obviously wasn't crazy about the idea of his being at a party where Verena could direct those glittering green eyes at him. If she only knew the truth.

CHAPTER
SEVEN

AFTER DINNER, COS DROVE BY SUSANNAH'S HOUSE
first and Paul walked her up to her door. She
smiled sweetly, then leaned forward and
pressed her nose against his. "My sweet wittle
Paul is going to be good while I'm at Nana's,
isn't he?" she said in a little-girl voice.

Paul pulled her toward him and squeezed
her tight. He could smell a faint flowery
scent when he pressed her close. Her lips
were soft against his. "Jeez, Susannah," he
muttered thickly. "Do you have to go to your
grandmother's? Why don't you just stay here
with me."

"I have to go," she said. "My Nana's not well.
Besides, my parents would never let me stay
here by myself."

Paul pulled away from her and thrust his

hands in his pockets. "Sure. Well, that's the way it is."

Susannah made a wry face. "I'm sorry. I wish I could stay,.too," she said. "Really." She touched him gently on the shoulder and then went in.

As Paul walked back to the car, he glanced over his shoulder at the porch light shining in the front of the house. It was just as well Susannah couldn't go to Cos's party, he told himself. What if Verena showed up? He was going to have enough on his hands dealing with that without the problem of having to hide the truth from Susannah.

"I hope you're not jealous of Verena, Ari," Cos was saying as Paul got into the backseat. "I was only being friendly."

"I know," said Ari.

"She's not really my type," Cos went on. "She's kind of brassy, don't you think, Paul? Verena, I mean."

"She comes on pretty strong," agreed Paul. He locked the car door with a sharp click. As they drove off, Paul had a vivid flashback to Aunt Gabrielle's party. He could hear Verena whispering in his ear as clearly as if she were sitting in the dark next to him. *"Let me make you, Paul. It's great,"* she whispered. *"Better than sex."* When she had laid her cool white hand on his neck he had felt himself tingle from head to toe. *"It would be beautiful,"* she had said. *"I'd*

69

suck out your blood until you were too weak to move, and you could feel my heart beating. Then I'd bite a vein, and let my blood mix with yours. Vampire blood is eternal. You'd feel wonderful, I promise you, and you'd never never die. You'll be sixteen forever."

Paul gazed vacantly out the car window. Shadowy trees and shrubs rose to meet them. Even this prim suburban street swam with the dark softness of shadows deep as velvet. *If only I could sink into the darkness and disappear.* Suddenly the thought frightened him. His heart beat so violently it felt as if a fish were leaping inside his chest.

"That guy Dubay looked a lot older than Verena," observed Cos. "I wonder if her parents know she's going out with him."

"I doubt that Verena worries about what her parents think," said Ari in a muffled voice.

"Jeez," muttered Paul.

Cos looked around. "Did you say something, Paul?"

Paul shook his head. He felt he could hear vampires moving in the bushes, rustling the trees with the wind. He wiped his damp brow with his hand.

As soon as Cos pulled up in front of the town house on N Street, Paul said a quick good-bye and hurried inside. The last thing he wanted was to hang around while Cos and Ari were kissing each other goodnight. It was bad enough to catch glimpses of them making out at school.

Once inside, Paul looked around for any sign of Aunt Gabrielle. The house seemed empty. She would be teaching one of her night classes, he thought. Or else she was out jogging. "*Maybe we can go on living here with no more problems*," he had told Ari. His own words echoed with irony in his mind. Who was he kidding? He couldn't go on this way—he felt as if he were suffocating. He was losing Ari to Cos, he couldn't talk to Susannah, and Sandy, the only friend he had made, was lying in the hospital, a victim of his aunt's thirst for blood.

Paul found himself walking toward Aunt Gabrielle's dark library. He hesitated at the door. As he scanned the shelves of books that rose to the ceiling, he began to feel an odd, familiar tingle in his fingers. His hand moved seemingly of its own will toward the west wall of the room—to an old book bound in a wooden cover. It was the same book that he and Ari had seen when they first explored Aunt Gabrielle's house.

He had known he wouldn't have to look for it. All he needed to do was to step into the room and his fingers would be drawn to it as if they were being pulled by a strong elastic band.

He opened the book, noticing that shreds of light-colored fabric clung to the wood. Perhaps

it had once been covered with velvet. The bookplate was splotched with blood and he couldn't
make out the name of the book's owner, but it
was a vampire's diary—Ari had been able to
understand that much of the French. His fingers caressed the smooth velum of the large
pages, and he stared intently at the strange
block writing that covered the page.

"Je m'appelle Blanche," said a voice in his ear.

He wheeled around and suddenly found himself facing a woman in a green velvet gown. She
was close enough that he should have been able
to feel her breath on his neck, but he couldn't.
He had seen her once before—in his own room—
and he recognized her immediately. Her eyes
looked feverishly hot, and her forehead was unnaturally high, as if she had plucked out the first
inch or so of her hair. She stepped away from
him and smiled. Her odd headdress, a soft white
cloth draped over a tall twin-peaked frame,
moved softly as she stepped back. Her skin was
the white color of her headdress, and long blond
hair streamed thinly to her waist.

She stopped moving and began speaking in
French.

"I don't understand you," Paul said.

"Listen with your heart," she said. "And you
will understand." She was still speaking French,
but somehow he understood the meaning of the
words as well as if she were speaking in English.

He shut his eyes, but still he saw her. It was as if his eyelids were transparent.

"You are mine," she murmured softly. "I am yours. This is the answer you are looking for. Reach out and take it. It's so easy—so very, very easy. Why do you struggle? Peace is in perfect darkness. Life is too hard. Only death is easy." She smiled then, and he saw her fangs. Her skin was pale and thin; he could see the blood vessels pulsing at her temples. Her feverish eyes were deeply set and her face became gaunt before his eyes. Her clothes grew loose as if she were shrinking. He gazed at the baggy green velvet dress in horror—she was turning into a skeleton.

"No!" he cried.

He heard the front door open, and his head jerked. "Paul!" Ari called.

When he looked back to the shadowy corner of the room the woman was gone. With trembling hands, he pushed the book back into its place on the shelf. "I'm in here," he called.

He heard Ari's footsteps on the marble. He knew she heard the fear in his voice, because she was running.

"Paul!" Ari cried, bursting into the dark room. "Were you looking at that book? It's awful! It's horrible!"

"Well, you were taking your time out there

73

with Cos, weren't you?" He looked pale. "I was only passing the time."

"Look, Paul, Cos makes me forget this horrible old house." She glanced around the room. "I'm entitled to a little fun, so don't try to make me feel guilty."

Paul covered his face with his hands. "I'm sorry, Ari. Jeez, I'm so shaken up, I don't know what I'm saying."

"What happened?" she asked, suddenly alarmed. She reached out and touched him. "Tell me."

"The book—I think it belonged to some ancestor of ours."

"So what? It doesn't have anything to do with us!"

"But I've seen her. . . ."

Involuntarily, Ari looked around. "Here?"

He nodded. "And up in my room, too, one morning. Only, this time she talked to me. She was speaking a funny kind of French, but somehow I could understand what she was saying."

"It isn't real, Paul," cried Ari, suddenly terrified. "It's only one of those stupid visions. It doesn't mean anything." She hesitated. "What—what did she say?"

Paul made a helpless gesture. "She said I should give up."

Ari gulped. "It's your subconscious talking, Paul. That's all. You're stressed. You need something to take your mind off all this." Ari was suddenly glad she hadn't told anyone, not even Paul, about her own visions. She saw clearly now that when you talked about visions out loud you sounded insane. "I think we ought to turn in early," she said uneasily.

Just then Ari heard Aunt Gabrielle come in. She stuck her head in the library and waved. "Hi, kids," she said brightly. "Did you have fun?" Her lavender eyes gleamed with an unearthly light. She pulled off her cap and her abundant black hair swirled free around her shoulders. "Do you want a cup of tea or something?" she asked.

The twins gazed at each other in dismay. Her face was flushed and lovely. All too evidently, Aunt Gabrielle had just been feeding.

"Sure," said Paul in a flat-sounding voice.

Ari looked at him in amazement, but when he followed Aunt Gabrielle to the kitchen, she went along. After what he had told her about his vision, she was afraid to leave him alone.

With a clatter of pans, their aunt pulled out a teakettle. Her skeletal white hands gave a macabre cast to the homely routine as she ran water into the kettle and slid it onto the electric burner. "Isn't this nice," she said. "Family time together." She smiled a tight little smile that did not show her fangs. Her strange eyes glowed.

"Aunt Gabrielle," Paul asked, "were our grandparents vampires?"

Pottery clinked as Aunt Gabrielle took mugs out of the cabinet. "Our mother was widowed young," she said, "and Richard and I don't remember anything about our father."

"But our grandmother?" insisted Paul. "Was she a vampire?"

Aunt Gabrielle hesitated. "Yes, I'm sure she was. Richard and I didn't realize it, but looking back, that's the only thing that makes sense. She was an invalid and never went out." She sighed. "It was a lonely way to grow up. I suppose that's why Richard and I were so close— we had to depend on each other. All day long our mother would be locked in her room, her curtains drawn, while our care was left to servants who came and went in a most erratic way. We saw very little of our mother, but I remember her propped up in bed, so pale and thin, in her lace bed jacket." Dreamily, Aunt Gabrielle poured the tea into the blue crockery mugs.

"Maybe she was anemic," said Ari.

Aunt Gabrielle gave her a careful little smile. "I believe that was the problem, dear."

"That she was anemic?" repeated Paul.

"Not enough red blood." Aunt Gabrielle's strange eyes darkened as if a storm were passing over them. "She didn't feed regularly. Looking

76

back, I'm sure that was it, though of course at the time, I hadn't a clue."

Ari stared. Even the loose pink jogging clothes could not hide her painful thinness. Her cheekbones stood out in sharp relief under the tightly stretched skin and her eyes burned bright, then dim, with a heat from some unknown internal fire. How could she even try to pretend to be human?

"But how can you be sure?" cried Ari. "Did you ever see—?"

"Oh, no. She was discreet to a fault," said Aunt Gabrielle. "But one night I had a terrible nightmare." Aunt Gabrielle's lips were white under her red lipstick. "I was rather troubled with visions and nightmares in those days." She shrugged. "You know how it is. I ran shrieking to my mother's room and banged on the door. To my surprise, the door flew open and she wasn't there. The window curtains flapped in the breeze, I remember. And her nightgown and bed jacket lay in a heap on the bed as if she had simply shrunk up to nothing and disappeared." Aunt Gabrielle leaned heavily on the counter. "I was terrified."

"She was out hunting, wasn't she?" said Paul.

Aunt Gabrielle nodded.

"But if she were a vampire, she'd still be around, wouldn't she?" cried Ari. "So that doesn't make any sense. She *couldn't* have been a vampire."

Aunt Gabrielle dabbed at her eyes with a tissue. "She perished in a dreadful fire at our mountain cottage," she said. "Not a trace of her remained. The place was burned to the ground while Richard and I were off at college." She pushed the mugs toward them, smiling through her tears. "There, now," she said. "The tea is all nice and hot."

Ari stared in dismay at the steam curling up from the cup. "That's horrible!" she cried.

"It was a terrible tragedy," agreed Aunt Gabrielle. She seemed unaware that what appalled Ari was not her grandmother's death but her life as a vampire.

"Aunt Gabrielle, have you talked to our father lately?" asked Paul.

Aunt Gabrielle twirled a ring on her bony white finger. Her eyes darkened with unhappiness. "No, but I'm sure we'll hear from him eventually. There's no use asking him to stay in touch. Richard hates to have the feeling he's tied down." Aunt Gabrielle smiled tremulously. "But he loves you both. I'm sure he'll return."

"We don't want to see him." Ari clenched her fists. "Even if he comes back, we won't talk to him."

"Of course, dear." Aunt Gabrielle's eyes shifted uneasily. "Whatever you wish."

The twins fell onto Ari's bed. "She doesn't have any control over him," said Paul. "It's hopeless."

"Paul!" Ari cried. "Stop talking that way." She suddenly leapt up and bolted both doors.

"What's the point, Ari? We know he can break down the door if he wants to. He already has."

"I'm going to get a rope ladder," said Ari breathlessly. "Then, if he starts banging on the door again, I'm going out the window. But I really think he may not show up again for a long time. You heard how sad Aunt Gabrielle sounded just now. She knows he's a here-today-gone-tomorrow type."

"Maybe so," said Paul listlessly. He didn't see how it mattered anyway. Even if their father didn't show up, vampires would manage to find them. That incident at the restaurant tonight proved it.

"I don't care about our stupid father and our stupid ancestors." Ari went over to the window and leaned on the sill. Paul could see her reflection in the window glass, but somehow he didn't think she was looking at her reflection. "Nobody's going to make me into a vampire," said Ari in a hard voice. "I won't let it happen."

CHAPTER EIGHT

PAUL KEPT UP WITH HIS USUAL TRAINING SCHEDULE during the following week. It was easier to show up for practice than to explain his absence to the coach, but his feet seemed heavy as he jogged around the track, and he knew his concentration was shot. More than once he stopped and strained to listen for his father's off-key whistling. He heard only the sighing of the wind in the trees.

After Thursday's practice, Coach asked Paul to stop by his office. Paul tried to remember if he had done anything wrong. He wasn't conscious of having broken any rules lately, but half the time he was so out of his mind with worry he wasn't sure what he had done.

Paul stepped into Coach's office and glanced at him apprehensively.

"Close the door, Paul." Coach gave him a grave look.

Paul's chest felt as constricted as if it were bound with iron bands. For a horrible instant, he was sure the coach had found out the truth about what his aunt had done to Sandy.

"Sit down," said Coach.

Paul sat down and shifted in the chair uneasily.

"I can tell you haven't been yourself since Sandy ended up in the hospital," said Coach in a heavy voice, "and I want to remind you that you're not responsible for what happened. It's nobody's fault—it's just one of those things. Sometimes the body doesn't work the way it's supposed to. But modern medicine is wonderful. I've talked to Sandy's parents. The operation he's going to have isn't serious, and he's in tip-top physical condition going into it, so he's in pretty good shape, all in all. There's nothing you need to worry about."

Paul stared at him blankly, unable to take in what he was saying.

"You believe me, don't you, Paul?"

Paul nodded. He wished he could get up and run out of the office. Not his fault? If only Coach knew!

"I know what it's like to grow up without a father." Coach bent a paper clip into an S shape. His face was heavily creased from years in the sun. "My own dad was an alcoholic, and I'm here to tell you, that's worse than having no dad at all."

Paul nodded. He had been thinking something along the same lines himself since learning his father was a vampire. He hadn't realized that he was better off being fatherless.

"I had no other man to depend on," Coach went on. "No one to ask those questions that you don't like to ask your mother."

Paul wondered if Coach was working up to talking about sex. He felt his face growing warm.

"Of course, you've had a double loss, losing your mother so suddenly. It's tough. Life isn't fair. But I want you to know, Paul, that if you need to talk to somebody, I'm here. You can tell me anything and you can be sure it will go no further."

Paul nodded. Tears stung his eyes. All he wanted to do was to get out of the office without breaking down.

He stood up, and Coach clapped him on the back. "We've got some real good folks at the counseling office, too," he said. Then he added heartily, "It's no disgrace to get help. Everybody has to lean on somebody sometime. Do you hear what I'm saying, son?"

"Yes, sir," Paul choked. He felt as if he were drowning. He turned around and groped for the door handle. Why did Coach have to mention his mother? He suddenly recalled sunlit days playing with Ari in the neglected garden behind their house. Easy summer days that had faded into dusk when the sound of his mother's voice would call them to dinner. He'd had it all then, and he hadn't even appreciated it.

He ran down the hall. Outside the building, the cold air on his face felt good. "Jeez," he muttered, closing his eyes.

Ari was surprised the next morning to spot Jesse and Nadia holding hands as they walked to class.

At lunchtime Ari found Sybil. "Hey, are Jesse and Nadia . . ." Ari made a waffling gesture with her hand. "You know?"

"Weird, isn't it?" Sybil's gaze swept the refectory. "But think about it. There's a kind of logic to it." She ticked off on her fingers. "First, Nadia's afraid of her own shadow. Second, Jesse's got an arsenal."

"That sounds like an extremely weird relationship you're describing."

Sybil grinned. "What can I say? They're weird people. They probably spend their spare time oiling guns and making plots to get rid of their enemies. And don't forget the secret bond they have—they're both crazy about Cos."

"Nadia's not crazy about Cos anymore," said Ari. "She hates his guts."

"Don't you believe it," said Sybil. "When a person falls hard, that feeling never goes away. Not really."

"Is this true confessions time, Syb?" Ari remembered that Sybil had once had a fling with Jesse.

"I'm basing my observations purely on scientific study," said Sybil, raising her eyebrows. "I'm not speaking personally, of course."

Ari watched Jesse make a beeline for Nadia's table. "It must be kind of awkward, wouldn't you think? With him and Cos being such good friends? I mean, basically I have the impression Nadia spits at Cos every time she sees him. That's what he told me, anyway."

"It's always tough when people break up in a school like this." Sybil shrugged. "Pretty much everybody knows everybody else, so it isn't like you can avoid people. You have to cope."

Ari couldn't take her eyes off Jesse and Nadia. Their heads were bent close together and they were engrossed in conversation. "I wonder what they're talking about," she said uneasily.

"Guns? Ammunition? Vampires?" suggested Sybil.

Ari jumped and stared at her friend in alarm. "Why do you say that?"

"What? Guns? You know Jesse's a gun freak."

84

"No. I mean, yes, I knew that." Ari licked her lips. "I wondered why you mentioned vampires."

Sybil lowered her voice. "Remember how I told you Nadia's family has this old castle in Romania? Well, I don't know if that has anything to do with it or not, but Amanda told Stephanie in strictest confidence—"

"So she right away told you about it, huh?"

Sybil looked at her pityingly. "There's no such thing as in strictest confidence, Ari. It's like a politician saying 'don't quote me.'"

"Right," Ari agreed. "So, what did Amanda say?"

"Nadia actually believes in vampires," Sybil whispered.

Ari stared at her friend in shocked silence.

"Amanda is really upset," Sybil went on. "The girl needs help. Get this—Nadia has the idea that an actual vampire was at our school Halloween party."

"Really?" said Ari weakly.

"What I can't figure out is whether this is some sort of cultural thing—like is it normal to believe in vampires in the Transylvanian part of Romania? Or has Nadia become completely un-hinged?"

"Maybe she's just putting Amanda on," said Ari desperately. "Or maybe Amanda misunderstood her."

"Face it, Ari. Some people are strange. It's a

fact of life. Not everything that happens around this school is subject to rational analysis."

"I know that," muttered Ari.

Sybil shrugged. "Why don't you ask Cos if Nadia ever talked to him about vampires?"

"I can't do that!" she cried. Feeling her friend's curious eyes on her, she added hastily, "I mean, I don't like to bring up Nadia with Cos. It's kind of a sensitive subject." Ari stared at Nadia and Jesse. Were they comparing notes about vampires? She felt that a wall was closing around her.

"Why don't you come over to my house this afternoon," said Sybil. "And we'll study for the English test together."

Ari hesitated. She didn't like to leave Paul alone. But it would be broad daylight, she reminded herself. Aunt Gabrielle never showed herself until after dark, and it was the same with their dad. What could go wrong?

Paul hated being alone in Aunt Gabrielle's old house. He paced nervously up and down the hall, angry at Ari for going over to Sybil's without him.

Most afternoons he could hear the reassuring sounds of Carmel running the vacuum cleaner or rattling around in the kitchen, but it must have been her day off, because the house was still. Paul looked down the hallway at the dining room and glimpsed the garden through its big French doors. Limp petunia leaves and bare roses looked colorless in the cold autumn light.

The utter silence in the house reminded Paul that he wasn't alone. Upstairs, Aunt Gabrielle was sleeping in her coffin.

Fed up with walking around restlessly, Paul stepped into the living room. The glass-domed French clock on the mantel, decorated with blue and gold signs of the zodiac, ticked softly. Heavy velvet draperies stifled all street sounds from outside. Paul shivered. He felt as if he were entering a tomb. The dim light and the heavy silence, punctuated by the sharp ticking of the clock, gave the room an eerie quality. He knew Ari didn't like to go in this room since they had discovered the secret of its fireplace. But now that she was over at Sybil's, Paul figured this would be a good time for him to have another look.

The pale marble below the huge mantel had been carved into the shape of a simperingly sweet woman's face wreathed with curly acanthus leaves. Holding his breath, Paul let his fingers slide over the surface of the cold marble face. Then he nudged it gently with the heel of his hand until he heard a click. The face pivoted easily in its stone socket to reveal its other side—the carving of a macabre skull, its jaw held on by shreds of rotting flesh. Paul knelt and stared at it.

Empty eye sockets stared back at him. The

skull had the wide grin of death, but the most curious thing was that its teeth were bat's teeth—jagged, with two long fangs. Paul heard a sharp intake of breath and realized with a strange detachment that it was he who had gasped. The skull was even more grisly-looking than he had remembered. With trembling hands he pushed it back so that the beautiful, smiling face was showing once more. Paul gazed at its empty prettiness, then turned the skull back toward the front. Knowing that the face hid the rotting flesh and bones of a vampire gave it an allure it did not possess alone. The image was double-edged, powerful.

Strange, Paul thought, smiling. He knew Ari would have been nagging him to leave it alone by now. She shied away skittishly from anything connected with vampires.

He twirled the face around a couple of times, first one way and then the other, simply for the pleasure of seeing the startling change. But suddenly, to his alarm, he felt the mantel move. "Don't do this to me!" he pleaded with it. Somehow he had jarred the valuable antique mantel loose from its moorings. He felt a rush of panic. Aunt Gabrielle was going to come downstairs and see what he had done!

Paul got to his feet, scarcely breathing for fear the marble would fall and shatter. He anxiously surveyed the fireplace, trying to assess the damage. A dark crack had opened along the side of the mantelpiece—like a door! It wasn't broken, he realized with excitement. It must be some kind of secret passage! Paul grasped the edge of the marble in his hand and pulled very carefully. The marble slab swung slowly, as if it were on a hinge. The vampire's marble head must be like a combination lock; by twirling it around first one way and then the other he had inadvertently dialed the combination.

He saw that behind the fireplace, a secret chest of drawers had been shaped to fit the wall. Paul's breath was coming in gasps. He pulled a drawer open and saw the glint of gold. Drawer after drawer he opened in a frenzy of nervous excitement. They were filled with gold coins of a type he didn't recognize. He picked up small jeweled bottles and unscrewed their tops. They smelled of odd perfumes. Even stranger, in a long shallow drawer at the center, he found a thin, flat mask of gold and some thin gold disks. Very old, Paul judged. They reminded him of pictures he had seen of goods stolen from the graves of ancient Greek kings. There were also several gold chalices and a number of gold plates inlaid with jewels, each wrapped in its own soft black cloth. Paul unwrapped a chalice and gazed at it. Birds of prey, their talons gripping small mammals, had been etched in an elaborate design around its rim.

Suddenly a wave of terror swept over him. He took the corner of the cloth and scrubbed his fingerprints off the shining surface. He was sweating now, anxious to close up the fireplace. He quickly wrapped the chalice in black cloth and put it back in its drawer.

Holding his breath, he gripped the marble mantel and pushed it back gently toward the wall. To his relief it moved easily. When the marble slab met the wall, he heard it click. He stepped back. No one could possibly guess that the fireplace hid a treasure trove. All that was visible was the bland surface of the mantel. "Gold!" Paul whispered.

He looked around the elegant living room until he found a pad and pencil. He jotted down what he could remember about which way he had turned the stone head. Twice to the right and then once to the left, and then once to the right. He thought that was the way he had done it, but he couldn't be sure. He would have to experiment again later.

Paul parted the living room's heavy velvet curtains and peered out at N Street. Normal life continued outside, but in this dim room Paul kept uneasy company with the treasure of his ancestors. Had they robbed a museum? he wondered. Or had they instead, for countless generations, been robbing graves?

CHAPTER
NINE

SYBIL TOOK A FRAMED PICTURE OFF HER DRESSER and showed it to Ari. "My brother Rab," she explained. "Remember? He's coming home next weekend."

Ari took the picture in her hands and stared at the face.

"He's not exactly handsome," said Sybil a bit anxiously, "but he's really nice."

"I like his face," said Ari. "He's very striking."

Sybil beamed.

Ari noticed that Rab's hair was crinkly like Sybil's, and he had her high arched brows. But while Sybil's eyebrows were a soft strawberry blond, his were black and almost V-shaped. He was dark with a strong, hooked nose and a solid jaw. The long line of his mouth looked mobile and amused. Sybil was right. He was not handsome, but somehow Ari felt she would like him.

"He goes to the University of Virginia," Sybil said.

Ari glanced at her in surprise. "That's so close by. He could drive home every weekend if he wanted to."

Sybil shrugged. "Yeah, but he doesn't want to. There's nothing much for him to do here. He went away to boarding school when he was really young. That's why none of his friends live around here. He's spent so much time away, it's like this isn't really his home."

Ari couldn't take her eyes off the photograph. Rab was like Sybil, and yet he wasn't. Something about his expression tugged at her mind like a melody that she couldn't place. "I wonder if I've met him," she said.

Sybil took the picture from her. "How could you have? He hasn't come home since you got here. You'll get to meet him this weekend, though. Maybe we can all go out to dinner together Saturday night."

"Oh, I can't, Sybil!" cried Ari. "Cos is having a party Saturday night."

"You could go to the party late," Sybil pointed out.

Ari remembered that Verena might be showing up at the party. "I'd better not," she said uneasily.

Sybil looked disappointed.

"Get Rab to come home next weekend and we'll go out then," suggested Ari. "He could drive home next weekend if he wanted to."

"I'll tell him. But remember, if he does come home, I'm going to hold you to your promise to go out to dinner with us."

"I do want to meet him, Syb. I'm not trying to get out of it."

"Oh, I know that," said Sybil. She put the picture back up on her dresser. "I wish Rab had a girlfriend here in town. I bet he'd be home every weekend then." She smiled suddenly. "I've told him all about you."

Ari understood now why Sybil was so interested in introducing her to Rab. "Well, I can't be his girlfriend," she said. "I'm in love with Cos, remember?"

"I just know you and Rab are going to hit it off, though." Sybil plopped down on her bed and sighed. "Why can't life be easy and neat?"

"I don't know," said Ari, frowning. Sybil's foolish attempt at matchmaking might have annoyed her a few weeks ago. But now she had much bigger things to worry about.

When Ari got home, the silence in the house alarmed her. Her heart began to race in fear. "Paul?" she called faintly. She dashed into the kitchen. A few cookie crumbs on the counter showed he had come in and had a snack after school. Ari dashed up the servants' staircase. She had the uneasy feeling she could see traces of her father's phosphorescent handprints on the wall as she groped her way up the narrow, unlit stairs. At the top landing were two doors, one of which opened onto Aunt Gabrielle's bedroom. Ari pushed open the other door and found herself in the upstairs hallway, only steps from her room. She ran into Paul's room and saw that his book bag had been tossed unopened on the bed. "Paul?" she cried desperately.

She peered anxiously out the window. The thin autumn sunshine cast long blue shadows on the garden below. Everything looked the same as usual—except Paul had vanished.

Suddenly she remembered the car. Paul might be enthusiastic about cross-country running, but she knew he would never walk if he could take the car instead. She ran down the gloomy hallway. Their father! But he couldn't have kidnapped Paul, she told herself. Not on a bright, sunlit day.

Downstairs, Ari threw open the front door and was startled to find herself facing her twin. "Paul!" she said. "Where have you been?"

He smiled. "The library." She noticed then that he was carrying several books under one arm.

"You might have left a note or something,"

she said. "I was worried sick. How would you like it if I took off without saying a word?"

"I didn't think you'd miss me," he said. "You were over at Sybil's."

Ari bit back a bitter retort. "Next time leave me a note," she muttered.

He took her arm, motioning toward the living room. "Come in here, Ari. I want to show you something."

"No!" She held back. "I'm not going in there."

"That vampire skull on the fireplace isn't just a weird antique, Ari. It's a combination lock! I was playing with it this afternoon and the fireplace swung right away from the wall. I almost passed out."

Ari drew closer to the fireplace, but she couldn't bring herself to touch it.

"I thought I had broken it," Paul went on excitedly, "but right behind it are drawers and drawers full of *treasure*. Look what I've been doing at the library."

Ari glanced at the titles of the books he was holding. *Schliemann's Treasure. Treasure and Treasure Hunters.*

"Gold is hidden in there," Paul said. "Stuff like you see in museums. It must be worth a fortune. I just hope I can figure out the combination."

His words filled Ari with dark foreboding.

95

Instinctively, she backed away from the sinister fireplace. She eyed Paul uneasily.

"I sort of dialed it by accident," he went on, "and I'm going to have to experiment to make sure I can do it again. I thought I'd give it another try right now. This is a perfect time because Carmel's not around. I can't wait for you to see it!"

"I have to do my calculus," Ari said.

Paul stared at her incredulously. "I tell you that the wall behind the fireplace is full of priceless treasure and you say you're going to go do your homework? Are you insane?"

"It's vampire treasure," Ari said hotly. "I'm not going to touch it, Paul, and you'd better not, either. It might turn out to have some kind of awful power over us."

Paul frowned. "You don't get it. This isn't ordinary gold. It's ancient stuff. It's like nothing you've ever seen."

"It was probably stripped off of dead bodies." Ari could hear her voice growing shrill. "Or robbed from graves."

Paul hesitated.

Ari jerked free of him and headed toward the stairs. "I'm going to do my homework."

As she mounted the steps she heard Paul swearing angrily under his breath.

When she got to her room, Ari sat on her bed, opened her calculus book, and stared at it sightlessly. She kept listening for Paul's foot-steps, but he didn't come upstairs. All she could think of was how he must be standing at the fireplace right now, twirling the marble vampire head around.

Suddenly, before her eyes, a shower of gold coins tumbled from the ceiling. Ari heard the thump and tinkling of the coins as they fell to the floor. Horrified, she stared down at the pile of gold that lay beside her bed. As she gazed at it a bony, sparsely haired arm extended from under her bed and grasped a gold coin with its claws. Ari drew her feet up under her and squeezed her eyes closed. "It's not real," she said aloud. And when she opened her eyes, it was gone.

She jumped up and peered under the bed. A couple of wispy balls of dust stirred slightly in the darkness. Her heart was racing.

Ari threw the window open, hoping that the rush of cold air would clear her head. She wanted nothing more than to bury herself in the solid realities of calculus. In calculus, at least, she could always find the answers. There the truth was solid. No visions. No hallucinations. No vampires.

A bit later, she heard Paul come into his room. "So, did you get the combination to work?" she called through the connecting door.

Paul came to the door and stood there. "I thought you weren't interested."

Ari stamped her foot. "Don't be a pain, Paul. We've got enough problems without fighting."

"No," he admitted. "I couldn't get it to work. I'm going to try again, though. There's some trick I haven't figured out yet. Maybe I need to stand in just the right place to do it or something like that."

Ari perched on her bed. "Paul, forget the treasure for a minute and listen to me."

He rolled his eyes. "Jeez, Ari, how can I? Heaps and heaps of gold are just sitting there in the living room. You're the only person in the world who could sit up here doing calculus homework and forget about it."

"This is serious, Paul. Listen. Have you noticed that Jesse and Nadia have gotten awfully tight all of a sudden?"

"Why would I notice something like that? Who cares?"

"Sybil says Nadia believes in vampires and that she told Amanda that a real vampire was at the school Halloween party. Think of what could happen if she puts her head together with Jesse. They could figure out who that vampire was!"

Paul sat down suddenly on the bed. She knew from the desolation in his eyes that he realized how serious this development was. "I had this feeling Jesse was giving me a funny look when I saw him at the hospital," Paul said. He glanced at her helplessly. "Why did Dad have to jump Jesse? Why did he have to pick somebody from our school?"

"You don't think Jesse knows what happened, do you?"

Paul threw up his hands. "Who can tell? When people get concussions, lots of times they don't exactly remember what happened. Maybe this is like that." He hesitated. "I didn't want to tell you this, but the night I was out with Dad, he attacked someone else."

Ari stared at him in mute terror.

"We had just turned off M Street in front of a parking garage." Paul took a deep breath. "It happened so fast I hardly knew what happened. Dad asked this woman what time it was, and before I knew it he was on top of her ripping her throat open." He shuddered. "I swear, it seemed as if I could hear the flesh tearing. That's not possible, is it?"

Ari shook her head numbly. "I don't know what's possible anymore, Paul. Did she—die?"

"I don't think so. I checked in the newspaper for the next few days and didn't see a story about any body being found. I must have pulled him off her in time. He was in some kind of frenzy. He turned around and snarled at me like an animal." Paul hesitated. "And this is the strangest part—when I looked at the woman to see if she was still alive, her throat looked fine! He had blood all over his face, but when he took his hand away from her neck, I swear there wasn't a scratch on it. Of course, she was pale and barely breathing. He'd gotten a lot of blood out of her, all right. "

Ari gave him an anxious look. "You think that he has some way of sealing up the break he makes in the skin?"

"We know there's something weird about vampire hands, don't we? I remember at Aunt Gabrielle's party, Verena touched me and my skin started to glow." He glanced uneasily in the mirror as if he needed to reassure himself that the mark was gone.

"Maybe Jesse doesn't know what happened to him, then. Maybe Dad did something to Jesse to make him forget—just the way he did something to seal up torn flesh."

"What bothers me is . . ." Paul hesitated. "If Jesse doesn't remember anything about what happened, then why is he looking at me funny?"

Ari chewed on a thumbnail anxiously. "We can't know for sure. That's the trouble. This is all guesswork. Maybe he doesn't remember a thing—or maybe he does remember but because what happened is so bizarre he thinks he was hallucinating."

"You could get Cos to find out how much he knows."

Ari stared at him. "How? Am I supposed to go to Cos and say, 'Hey, I have this little problem. My father the vampire sucked Jesse's blood the other night. Would you just check it out for me and see whether Jesse has any idea what went on?'"

"You could ask him if Jesse's been talking crazy lately. You could do that much."

"I won't," cried Ari, pressing her lips together firmly.

"You won't!" Paul mimicked her tone. "What's going on with you, Ari? We used to be able to count on each other."

A tear trickled down her cheek. "I can't, Paul. I'll die if Cos finds out about Dad and Aunt Gabri. He'll hate me. And I need him."

"I don't see why you need him," muttered Paul. "You've got me."

"It's not the same thing." Ari squeezed her hands together tightly. "Cos doesn't have anything to do with all this junk—Aunt Gabrielle, our dad, the vampires. He's—normal."

"Thanks, Ari," said Paul. "That really makes me feel great. Thanks a whole bunch."

"Don't be that way, Paul. Don't you understand at all what I'm saying?"

Of course, thought Paul. That was the trouble. He understood perfectly. They used to be able to count on each other, and now they couldn't anymore. Ari was drifting away from him. He was losing her to Cos.

CHAPTER
TEN

COS'S HOUSE WAS A RAMBLING, MODERN PLACE ON a big wooded lot near Silver Spring. It had rooms on four levels, all connected by stairs. On the ground level were bicycles, sports equipment—even a weight room.

Ari and Paul followed several other kids inside. The stairs at Cos's house were not closed up in a stair hall, like at Aunt Gabrielle's. They were cantilevered somehow so they seemed to float in space. Ari could see right through the stairs to the downstairs and then could glance up at the kitchen and living room overhead. The walls were done in natural wood with large plate-glass windows.

"Isn't this place great, Paul?" Ari's eyes shone as she looked around. "I love it."

Paul knew what Ari liked about it. It was like

Cos—wholesome, all-American, and as clear as glass. Nothing could have been more different from Aunt Gabrielle's mansion.

The living room had a grand piano, modern screen prints, and sliding glass doors that opened onto a porch that overlooked the woods surrounding the house.

"He invited enough people," said Paul sourly. The house was already filled.

Ari laughed. "You don't invite people to a party like this, Paul. They hear about it and they come. Cos explained that to me." She put her grocery bag of corn chips on the kitchen counter. Then she went to find Cos—first scanning the crowd anxiously for any sign of Verena and Dubay.

"Ari!" Cos threw one arm around her. His other hand held a Styrofoam cup of beer. "You're here! That's great. We're trying to get the amplifiers hooked up. Do you know anything about electric wiring?"

She grinned. "Sorry, Cos. I know absolutely nothing about electric wiring." The smile left her face when she spotted Jesse setting up drums near the piano. Instinctively, she looked around for Nadia. Surely Jesse wouldn't have brought her, Ari thought, since Nadia and Cos had had such a bitter breakup. But then she spotted Nadia perched on a hassock by the sliding glass door. She was talking to Amanda.

The piercing sound of feedback filled the room, and Ari covered her ears.

"I think they've got it hooked up now," shouted Cos. "Come take a look."

Paul wished he hadn't come. Big parties had never been his idea of a good time, and he didn't know enough people at school yet to even have a shot at enjoying this one. He came only because he and Ari had made a solemn pact not to go out alone after dark. But now that seemed like a stupid reason. This house and this party were a world away from vampires. Only the thick woods near the house gave him a slightly uncomfortable feeling. He found a keg in the breakfast room next to the kitchen. On the floor stood a couple of coolers full of ice and cold drinks. Paul turned the tap and watched the beer foam up in his Styrofoam cup. Then he moved back toward the living room.

"Hi, Paul."

He jumped. A girl he vaguely recognized was smiling at him. She was tiny, cave-chested and slightly built, with mouse-colored hair, a baby face, and a faint sprinkle of freckles over her nose. The glazed look in her eyes worried him. He hoped this wasn't one of those situations where a few beers was going to make some neurotically shy girl do something that was completely and totally embarrassing.

"You're cute." Her eyes crossed slightly when she smiled at him. "Do you think I'm cute?"

"Uh, I think I'd better get some chips," he said nervously.

"Hi, Paul!" Paul's heart pounded when he heard the voice. Verena!

She was coming up the stairs, her burning emerald eyes fixed on him. He saw that she was wearing a flimsy silver tunic that fell to mid-thigh. Underneath, a pair of thin pants shimmered over her legs. Strappy silver sandals encased her white feet. Paul couldn't take his eyes off her. Her face was deathly pale under the fringe of blond hair.

"I was hoping you'd be here," she whispered, stepping up close to him.

The mousy girl's mouth fell open. Suddenly she turned and ran. Paul had the vague sensation he heard sobs in the kitchen, but it seemed to be happening somewhere far away.

Verena put her hand on Paul's shoulder. "I have a new Jaguar," she said. "Want to see it?"

"Are you serious?" he asked. "Sure I'd like to see it." He glanced around uneasily. Somehow he felt he should tell Ari that Verena had shown up.

Ari was sipping a glass of diet cola when she spotted Paul standing at the top of the stairs. His back was to her, and over his shoulder she saw the tip of a blond head. Then Paul shifted his position a little and she saw Verena.

In a panic, Ari rushed over to him and grabbed his hand. "Hello, Verena," she said. "I need to take Paul to show him something. Will you excuse us?"

Paul followed Ari into the living room. She turned to him, anguish in her eyes. "She's here, Paul! What are we going to do?"

"I don't know, Ari." Paul shrugged. "The situation already seems out of control to me."

"We've got to do something. Have you seen any sign of the other one?" Ari asked. "The guy, Dubay?"

"Not yet." Paul glanced back at Verena. "Maybe she came by herself."

"None of these kids would ever imagine she's a vampire," cried Ari. "They're all sitting ducks."

Paul glanced around. "So far everybody's pretty much staying in the kitchen or the living room. Nobody's even very drunk. People will be okay if they stick with the crowd, don't you think?"

"I don't know what I think," said Ari desperately. "We ought to keep an eye on her, Paul. We have to keep her from luring anybody outside." She shot a glance over at Verena. A couple of boys were crowding around her. "I can't believe this is happening. What if Nadia sees her?"

"Everybody's going to see her," said Paul.

"She's not exactly inconspicuous in that outfit."

"Ari!" Cos skidded to a stop next to her. "Come on! I've been looking all over for you. You're supposed to be our lead singer!"

Ari shot a desperate look at Paul as Cos pulled her away.

Paul could hear the steady thump of drums and the shrill shriek of the feedback. Soon an electric guitar was strumming and a wall of sound filled the room. To his astonishment, Ari's uncertain voice blared out of the speakers. She was singing a song he'd never heard before. It was about love and it had a lot of stupid rhymes. Cos probably wrote it, he figured.

Paul made his way over to the crowd of guys who were standing in a circle around Verena. "Oh!" exclaimed Verena with delight. "Here comes Paul!" She threw her thin arms around his neck. "Paul and I are very special friends." She shimmied suggestively.

In spite of his better judgment, Paul was flushed with triumph when the other guys slunk away.

"You aren't afraid of me, are you, Paul?" Verena's whisper tickled his ear.

"No, I'm not afraid of you." Paul's voice was steady. It was funny, but he was less afraid of Verena than of the mousy little girl with the glazed eyes. He instinctively knew that Verena would not embarrass him. In a strange kind of way, he felt as if he understood her.

"I wasn't lying just now, you know," she said softly. "You are very special to me. I want you, Paul." She stroked the small hairs at the back of his neck. Then her cool hand touched him and Paul felt an electric charge shake him. He gasped. All at once he was a little unsteady on his feet. He closed his eyes to shut out the sight of Verena, but the feeling remained that the solution to all his problems was very simple.

"No vampire stuff," he mumbled, no longer seeming to be in control of himself. It was as if he were watching someone else from far away. He found himself bending to kiss her.

She pulled away. "Not here," she said. "Aren't you afraid your girlfriend will find out?"

The thought jolted Paul to his senses. Susannah! The room was full of people from school who would be bound to tell her if he kissed Verena here.

Seeing Paul's hesitation, Verena smiled sweetly. "Want to see my Jag? We could go out and take it for a spin." Her skin was translucent and flawless. Tiny diamond earrings glittered in each pale earlobe. It struck Paul suddenly how small she was. He could easily pick her up and throw her over his shoulder if he liked. What was he so worried about? Verena could never make him do anything he didn't want to.

"What model is it?" he asked.

"An XJS." Verena spoke knowledgeably about the car's motor as they went downstairs. Envious gazes followed him, and Paul had the feeling he had scored one over the other guys. It was a relief to walk away from the booming noise of the party. He never knew what to say to anybody at these things anyway. He usually ended up standing around by himself, feeling like an idiot.

Verena had parked under a streetlamp, and the Jaguar's sleek black finish shone. Paul ran his hand lightly along the satiny smooth fender, then skated his index finger along the hood—the engine was still giving off heat. He smiled at Verena. "You like to drive fast, don't you?"

"Very fast," she said softly.

"So do I," he said. He had spent too much time being careful, he decided. What good had it ever done him?

Verena laid the keys in the palm of his hand. Paul hesitated a second, then closed his fingers over them and got in the car.

The big motor purred as they drove out of the neighborhood. Paul glanced over at Verena. "Buckle your seat belt," he said.

A laugh welled up from her throat. "I don't have to worry about that anymore." Her emerald eyes sparkled mischievously.

"No, of course you don't," he murmured. It

suddenly seemed to him that it would be great to be like Verena and not worry about anything. He let his fingers slide along her silver-clad thigh. It was smooth and silky like the hood of her car. She laughed, and her emerald eyes gleamed in the dark.

Paul pulled the car onto the beltway. The exit signs whizzed by—Chevy Chase, Rockville, Bethesda, Wolf Trap. "Where are we going?" he asked.

"We could go to the Jefferson Memorial," she suggested, "and park."

Paul felt intoxicated by the way the steering responded to his touch. His face was numb from the wind coming in the open window.

Somehow he felt older and more in control than usual. He wasn't sure whether it was the car, or Verena, or his sudden decision not to worry.

He turned the car around and headed downtown. The lights of the deserted city streets sped by him with an unreal, dreamlike quality. Paul pulled the car up at the Reflecting Pool, his heart pounding wildly. A feeling not unlike stage fright stirred in his stomach—he was sure that something important was about to happen.

Verena slid her arm along the back of his seat. She laid her other hand on his stomach, then let her fingers inch inside the shirt until he felt her cool touch. "You've been waiting for this, haven't you?" she said softly. "You want it as much as I do."

"I don't know." He squirmed uneasily at her touch. "Maybe we'd better not," he said. "I don't want to get in over my head."

"You worry too much." She smiled sweetly. "When you get in over your head is just when it starts being fun."

He felt her cold lips press wetly against his neck and then a sudden sharp pain. "Jeez," he said thickly. A sense of languor stole over him. It didn't seem worth struggling against her. He felt light-headed and unsteady, and a swirling blackness swept over him. Brilliant pinwheels and starbursts flared in his brain. A fluttering drumbeat sounded in his ears. The beat slowed to a hypnotic thump that echoed in the farthest corner of his being, rocking him with its powerful, body-shaking rhythm.

Slowly he became aware that another, smaller drum was keeping time with his—two hearts, he realized with a surge of emotion. His and Verena's beating together. His sight cleared and he saw the Jefferson Memorial shining with a wondrous brightness, its image reflected in the water.

Suddenly a wave of nausea hit him and he felt himself tremble all over. He was too weak to move or even breathe. He had never been so tired, too tired even to lift a little finger. Fatigue weighed him down, pressing him against the seat cushion. Verena whispered in his ear, "Do you want to be immortal? This night could last forever, Paul, like an eternal jewel." A police officer walked by the car, his hands folded behind his back, and smiled at them. Paul stared blankly at the police officer and the luminous monument ahead of them.

Around him the soft night of the city enveloped countless sweet-smelling herbs, the scent of crushed grass, the smooth bronze surfaces of statues, the cold inexorable flow of fountains and pools. Paul could have sung with ecstasy over the beauty of it. "Yes," he whispered. "I want to live forever."

The viciousness of her bite startled him, and he cried out. He struggled then, but he was too weak to fight her. The pain was like a burning iron pressed against the flesh. He tried to scream but couldn't. He heard his blood welling up in her throat, gurgling loudly, the sickening sound of her tongue slurping it. The suction was frighteningly powerful. She was sucking greedily as if she were trying to turn his arteries inside out.

A shrill whistle of fear sounded in his brain and Verena's pale face swam before his eyes. He had thought she was small, but now she seemed as large as the moon. Her emerald eyes burned, and when she drew away from him, her face was flushed with color.

Verena threw back her head and drew a deep shuddering breath of satisfaction. He realized then that she had gripped his shoulder so hard that her long nails had bitten into the flesh. Her grip loosened and she looked directly into his eyes, smiling a little. She held up her slender wrist so that he could see the pale blue veins under the translucent skin. She snarled at him, baring her fangs, and he cringed, terrified. In a quick, vicious movement she tore at her own flesh—making an angry red slash across the soft white skin at the base of her hand. Dark blood welled up in a fat bead at the center of the cut. She grinned at it with a peculiar satisfaction. Then she pressed her wrist hard against Paul's mouth.

He was too weak to draw away from her. But he didn't want to. He was thirsty. Very thirsty. He licked the blood and suddenly he was sucking, pressing his lips close against her white flesh, greedy for her blood. The sound of traffic behind the car grew to a deafening clamor like a clash of grinding metal. Verena's breath sounded like a typhoon in his ears. The stars over the monument pulsed and grew unbearably bright. All of a sudden he felt sick and dizzy and closed his eyes. The car seemed to be whirling around and rocking. At last, mercifully his senses went black.

*   *   *

When Paul finally came to, he was aware first of the silence around them and then of an overwhelming sickness in his stomach. He faded in and out of consciousness. At last he was able to open his eyes. Verena was sitting in the passenger seat next to him, calmly painting her nails with pink nail polish.

"I have to keep my nails polished," she said, holding her splayed fingers out to check her work. "If I don't they look so weird—slick and clear like glass."

Paul looked down at his own trembling hands. His nails were like glass. In a panic, he pinched his arm hard. Nothing. He felt nothing. He looked at Verena. "I'm asleep. This is a dream."

Verena laughed. "No, love. Guess again."

"I'm a vampire," he gasped.

"You've got it!" She rested her cheek against his and stroked his hair. The smell of the nail varnish made him feel as if he might pass out.

"We're going to have such fun together." Suddenly she drew away from him and smiled brazenly. Her glistening white fangs gleamed in the darkness.

CHAPTER
ELEVEN

WHEN ARI HAD FINISHED SINGING, SHE SLIPPED away from the band and went to look for Paul. The music boomed as she peered in the kitchen. With increasing uneasiness, she opened the sliding glass doors and peered out onto the porch. The entire house was crowded with kids she had never seen before. There was no sign of Paul. Stepping around a couple that was making out on the stairs, she checked the upstairs bathroom. Nothing. Then she went downstairs and knocked on another bathroom door. An annoyed-looking boy came out. She opened the door to the weight room. Rolled-up mats, benches, and heavy rings of metal. Finally she went outside and saw that their car was still parked out front. Panic swept over her. Where could he be? Was there someplace she hadn't looked?

"Hey, Ari!" Cos was coming toward her, a Styrofoam cup in one hand. "You aren't going home already, are you? The party's just getting going."

"Cos! Paul is gone!" she cried. "I've looked everywhere."

"Hey, this is your car, isn't it?" He rested his hand on the fender.

Ari nodded mutely.

Cos smiled. "Well, he didn't head home, then. I saw him going downstairs with Verena. They must have left in her car."

"Oh, no!" Ari could have sunk to her knees, so overwhelming was her sudden despair. "That's terrible." Her eyes filled up with tears, and it took her a moment to realize that Cos was giving her a strange look.

"You don't have some sicky thing going with your brother, do you?" he asked, looking uncomfortable.

Suddenly Ari realized how strange her distress must look to him. But she knew she had to hide her feelings no matter what it cost her. "I—I don't trust Verena," she said. "I'm worried about him."

Cos grinned. "Come on, Ari. Paul is a big, strong guy. He's a heck of a lot bigger than Verena. It's not like she's going to force him to do anything he doesn't want to do."

"She's sneaky," said Ari miserably. "Oh, I don't know. Maybe he didn't leave with her.

116

Maybe he caught a ride with somebody else and didn't want to leave me without the car. He's never liked parties."

"You can't spend your life worrying about your brother." Cos put his arm around her. "Don't get so wrought up about it. Verena didn't look drunk to me, and if she doesn't crash the car, what's the worst that can happen?"

"Don't ask," she muttered under her breath.

"Brighten up." He bent his head to give her a kiss. "Show me a smile, huh?"

Ari had a strong impulse to jump in the car and go look for Paul. But how would she ever find him? It was a big city, and she didn't even know what Verena's car looked like. She stole a glance over her shoulder as they walked back to the house. "Cos, did you talk to Paul?" she asked anxiously. "Had he been drinking much?"

"When I saw him he was walking a straight line," Cos assured her. "He got downstairs without falling on his face. Besides, they left kind of early, so he couldn't have had time to get really drunk. Calm down, Ari. I swear, sometimes you sound like my mother."

He drew her close to him again, and the smell of beer on his breath made her feel sick. She pulled away and glanced up at the few bright stars that could be seen through the faint hazy glow of the city sky. It seemed amazing to her that the stars didn't cry out. But horrible things never left their mark on the world, she thought in despair. An oak tree where a murder took place looked no different from any other oak tree. The earth was amazingly indifferent. "I hope he's all right," she whispered.

Paul felt too weak and sick to drive. Verena got out, shoved him over into the passenger seat, and slid behind the wheel. His head lolled back until he felt the strain in his neck muscles; then, gasping, he forced himself to sit up. Instinctively, he groped for the metal catches of the seat belt to fasten it, but then he caught himself. Seat belts didn't matter to him anymore, he reminded himself. Nothing mattered.

"Fun, isn't it?" shouted Verena. She had put the top of the Jag down, and as they pulled out on the beltway the wind whipped her hair like a blond flag behind her head. The Jag's shiny hood stretched before them, swallowing up the road. The lights of the city sped by, points of light each with its own halo of mist. Overhead the moon was as bright as a searchlight and the stars pulsed through the golden haze that cloaked the city. The beauty of the night was overpowering. Paul closed his eyes, afraid he would faint with the ecstasy of it.

"We'll go to my place," Verena said. "*Casablanca*'s the late-night movie."

Paul fell back against the seat. His sensations were confused; he thought he could hear voices, violin music wailing with the wind, the rustle of leaves. Someone was crying and he glanced in surprise at Verena, but her usual mindless smile stretched across her face.

She looked at him and pressed her fangs against her bright red lips. With a shock he realized her lips were red with his blood. "You're sort of mine now," she said a bit shyly. She licked her lips, then sighed in satisfaction. "I made you, and that means you're mine."

He was surprised he hadn't noticed before the emptiness of her emerald eyes and the vacancy of her smile. He shook his head. A wave of sickness swept over him, and he had to close his eyes. "I don't know what you're talking about," he whispered. "Shut up. I feel sick."

"Don't talk to me that way." Verena laughed. "You *need* me, man. You can't go out in the sun. You'd shrivel up and die. As soon as the sun comes up, you sleep with me in my coffin or else. Believe me, you'll be grateful for the privilege. I should make you beg for it."

He glanced at the speedometer and saw that she was going 130. He wondered what she would do to any police car that stopped her. He could guess. Cop for dessert.

"You're going too fast," he said.

She frowned. "I don't want to miss the beginning of *Casablanca*. I hate to come in after a movie's already started."

119

She turned off the beltway and soon they were driving on Wisconsin Avenue. Paul had the feeling he had forgotten something important, but it was hopeless to try to remember it. He was far too tired. Verena turned off Wisconsin, and he gazed around him at the vaguely familiar leaf-clogged gutters, and overhead at the old-fashioned street-lights glowing in the night. The Jaguar pulled up in front of a brownstone apartment building. A maple grew by the sidewalk, its leaves burning as brightly as neon. Paul blinked at the golden glare. "Home," Verena announced. "And move fast. I don't want to miss the start of the movie."

Meekly, he followed her upstairs and into her apartment. To his surprise it was furnished with antiques. He wouldn't have thought Verena was the type to appreciate antiques. "It's kind of crowded with all this old junk," she explained, "stuff that was in my parents' house. I wished I didn't have to sell the house and crowd the furniture in here." She grinned. "But I was afraid the neighbors might start to wonder why I never got any older and why I only came out at night."

She switched on the set and sat very close to it. The light from the television flickered white on her face. She seemed to have forgotten about him.

Paul took off his jacket and sat down. He wasn't sure how long he sat there, annoyed with Verena for acting as if she owned him. He didn't even like her, he realized.

120

At last he got up without speaking and walked out the door.

When Ari got home from Cos's party, she saw that Aunt Gabrielle was in her study. The doors had been left ajar and light spilled out into the dining room. Ari ran upstairs first, to check if Paul had gotten home. But there was no sign of him in his room. She went downstairs then and stepped into Aunt Gabrielle's study. Her aunt sat at an antique inlaid writing desk. She looked up when Ari came in, and her ghastly white face made Ari's heart stop momentarily. Now Ari could never regard her aunt's fine-drawn beauty—the tightly stretched white skin, sharp, high cheekbones, and violet eyes—without thinking of the stolen blood that gave it life. "Is something wrong?" Aunt Gabrielle asked sharply.

"Paul left Cos's party with Verena," said Ari. "And he's not home yet."

Aunt Gabrielle was visibly jolted. "Oh, dear."

Ari pressed her fist to her mouth. "I'm worried," she whimpered.

"Try to get a grip, Ari," Aunt Gabrielle said firmly. "Hysteria won't help."

"You don't trust her either, do you?" None of this would have happened, Ari thought bitterly, if Aunt Gabrielle hadn't asked Verena to her party.

"Maybe I don't trust Verena," said Aunt Gabrielle. "But Paul is a big boy and he's very fit.

If he wants to fight her off, he's perfectly capable of doing it."

"What if he'd been drinking?"

Aunt Gabrielle blinked at her. "Do you think he was drunk?"

"I don't know. I don't think so. He'd only had maybe one beer. I'm so worried," said Ari miserably. "Isn't there anything we can do?"

Aunt Gabrielle rubbed her eyes thoughtfully. Just for an instant, she looked owlishly intellectual, like the college teacher she pretended to be. "Probably not," she said finally. "People have to live their own lives, Ari. Maybe you don't want to be a vampire, but it's quite possible Paul sees things differently. He is his father's son."

Ari turned away from her and ran upstairs, her eyes blurring with tears. What a fool she had been to think Aunt Gabrielle would understand her terror! But she had no one else to turn to. When she got to her room, Ari threw the windows open and stared out at the night. A feeble hope flickered inside her. She thought of the afternoon she had panicked when Paul had only been at the library. Maybe this was going to turn out like that. For once, she longed for a vision—anything that would give her a clue. If she truly did have second sight, the screen had gone blank. Ari's heart twisted painfully inside her.

Come home, Paul. Please, come home.

CHAPTER
TWELVE

PAUL REALIZED WHEN HE REACHED THE STREET that he had forgotten his jacket. But he wasn't cold. He laughed, and the sound seemed rich and bell-shaped, like the laugh of a well-trained actor. There was a faint ripping noise, and Paul glanced up to see a golden leaf pirouetting downward in the still air. He picked it up off the brick pavement and crushed it in his hand. It glowed phosphorescent as he tossed it to the ground.

The lights of M Street burned in the distance, and Paul turned in their direction. Thrusting his hands in his pockets, he began whistling. The melody sounded as if it were being played on a silver flute. He could hear his steps on the pavement, a rhythmical underbeat to the music. The stars were orbs of light set in the endless nothingness of interstellar space. He could feel the whirring of distant planets and the rocking of ocean waves against the shore. But at the same time, he sensed the presence of slugs leaving shiny paths behind them as they crept along the cold stones of nearby gardens. Flower bulbs were sending out tender roots into the soft leaf mold. He felt he could burst with joy. It was marvelous!

When he reached M Street, he glanced in a dark shop window and saw his reflection. His face looked black in the glass, but the image was clear. He took his driver's license out of his wallet, stared at the picture, and compared it to his reflection. He looked the same, he decided. But he wondered why he had never before noticed that he looked good—those strong dark brows and marked cheekbones. Odd that he could look the same when he felt so different.

He crossed the street and turned in the direction of the old C & O canal. He wasn't afraid of dark neighborhoods now. No one could murder him, he thought, smiling a little.

As he drew closer to the water, Paul noticed a shop on the street nearby. A single light burned inside, illuminating a sign that read *WILEY HOBAN, COSTUMER AND DESIGNER*. Paul looked curiously at it. It had been a part of his old life, and he could feel the past floating up in his consciousness like a soap bubble. He had been in this shop before with his sister. He smiled suddenly. That was what he had forgotten—his beautiful sister, Ari. Memories were crowding back now: many memories, like apples ready for the plucking.

He made his way down stone steps to the narrow cement path that went along the canal. Suddenly he was hit by a wave of nausea and weakness that doubled him over. Cold sweat beaded on his forehead. He gasped. Was this horrible feeling the price he paid for his heightened senses? Or was he only adjusting to his new vampire body? He didn't care, he decided, lying down on the cement until the nausea waned.

He gazed at the stale black water next to him a long time, only vaguely aware that the light had finally gone out in Mr. Hoban's shop. The water was black and beautiful, he thought—black as Verena's heart, black as Ari's hair, black as black satin and hopeless love. He dipped his fingers into it, relishing its cool wetness. But slowly he became conscious that the water was no longer as black as it had been, and a spur of panic pricked him.

He leapt up suddenly and staggered, teetering at the edge of the canal on one foot. After what seemed like an eternity, he managed to recover his balance and run for the stairs. The metal handrail felt reassuring under his tight grasp. He knew now that he couldn't trust his strength.

When he reached the top of the steps he cast an anxious glance at the sky, which was the deep violet blue that comes before dawn. Morning must be hovering at the verge of the horizon. Fear welled up like bitter bile in his throat. How could he find his way back to Verena's?

Choking with fear, he charged blindly across M Street. Suddenly he felt a sharp blow at the knees. His body glanced off the bumper of a gray Mercedes, but instantly the speeding car scooped him up on its hood and threw him flat against the windshield. He placed his hands on the windshield and gazed in through the glass, pressing his nose against it, his face inches away from the driver. She was a woman with a slackly pretty face and bleached hair. He heard the squeal of tires as the car skidded wildly along Wisconsin. The woman's mouth suddenly fell open and her grip on the steering wheel loosened. Paul smiled, wondering if she had noticed his fangs.

The Mercedes slowed and began to weave. Paul lost interest in the woman. Turning around, he slid down the hood and sat on the edge of the car, perched there like an oversized hood ornament. He decided he must be near Verena's. He leapt off and landed with surprising ease. Behind him the car crashed. Paul glanced briefly over his shoulder and noticed that the Mercedes's front end was crushed against a tree.

A faint frosting of light showed at the horizon, and once more Paul's fear flamed hotly. He broke into a run. He was terrified now, ready to burrow under dirt and leaves or dive into a Dumpster to escape the light that seemed now to be thundering toward him.

Just then, his heart gave a sharp squeeze of relief. Verena's apartment! He bolted up the stairs.

"Let me in!" he pleaded, pounding furiously on the front door. "Hide me!"

Verena opened the door and smiled vacantly. "Where'd you go? You missed a good movie." She yawned, and Paul gaped at the surprising length of her curved fangs.

"What do we do now?" he cried. "You've got to help me."

"Oh, come on." She grinned. "Beg me a little."

He sank at once to his knees, grabbed her hand, and pressed his cold lips to it. "I'm begging you, Verena," he muttered. The nausea swept over him again and blackness gripped his brain long enough to make him shudder. "Save me," he begged. "Tell me what I've got to do. I'll do anything. Save me!"

"Jeez, I was only kidding." She shook her hand free of his grasp. "You don't have to kiss my feet or anything. Don't be disgusting, Paul—you're embarrassing me. Get up."

Paul was too desperate to be embarrassed. Meekly he followed her into the bedroom. The room had heavy dark curtains and, he noticed, a businesslike brass bolt on the door. There was no bed, but in the middle of the oak floor lay a polished coffin.

"Sleeps two," Verena said brightly. Grasping a brass handle, she pulled it open. The interior was padded with cheap white satin. Verena kicked off her silver slippers, climbed in, and tucked her arms in close at her side so she would fit.

Horrified, Paul regarded her prone figure, so tightly encased in the coffin. "You stay in there all day?"

"You get used to it," she said. "Get in on top of me. And hurry. The sun is coming up. I can hear it."

Awkwardly, Paul lay down on her, repelled by her closeness. Her breath blew noisily in his ear and she smelled of synthetic perfume. He was pressed tight against her now, sharing her every breath in the terrible, stifling darkness. Her voluptuous breasts flattened under the weight of his chest and the sharp bones of her hip bit into his belly. He was surprised that he felt only disgust. Then he remembered that he was a vampire. Vampires were not interested in sex. Only blood.

She reached out, and her skinny arm grabbed a satin strap. The coffin lid fell down on them, closing them into perfect blackness with a loud and final clap of wood.

"No!" screamed Paul.

Ari uneasily sensed the coming of dawn. She woke suddenly. The dresser and bedside table were only black shapes in the darkness. The faint glow of the city lights bleached the bit of sky she could see from her window. Her skin felt too tight and her teeth were clenched. Something was terribly wrong. As the minutes ticked by, the scrap of sky turned violet blue. A bird rasped out a song. Ari suddenly leapt up from her bed and ran to the connecting door, throwing it open.

"Paul!" she cried, staring at the neatly made bed in disbelief. "Paul!" She threw herself on his bed, then grabbed his pillow and hugged it, burying her face in it. Paul's familiar smell on the pillow brought tears to her eyes. She lay there sobbing helplessly.

How could he be gone? What was she going to do without him? If only she hadn't left his side to sing that dumb song for Cos. She wished she had thrown her arms around her twin, held him tight, and never let go. What haunted her most was the thought that maybe he had needed her, he had called for her somehow, and she hadn't heard him.

They had promised to stick together and protect each other no matter what, and she had let him down. She sat up and stared blankly out the window. The sky outside was white now, which meant Aunt Gabrielle must be locked up tight in her room.

Ari slid off the bed and began pacing the floor, wiping her eyes with the sleeve of her nightgown. She felt she had to act, though she wasn't sure what to do. She glanced at the clock. Seven A.M. Taking a deep breath, she picked up the phone beside Paul's bed and dialed the police.

"I want to report a missing person," she told the switchboard operator.

"I will connect you," said a nasal voice.

A weary-sounding male voice picked up on the line. "Sergeant Harper here," he said.

"I want to report a missing person," Ari repeated. "My brother didn't come home last night. He's disappeared."

"How old is your brother, miss?" the voice inquired cautiously.

"Sixteen," said Ari. "We're the same age. We're twins."

"Sixteen, huh?" Sergeant Harper sounded amused. "You can't report a missing person for five days unless it's a child."

Ari was silent.

"Unless you have reason to suspect foul play,"

added Sergeant Harper. "You don't have any reason to suspect foul play, do you?"

"I don't know," said Ari in a small voice.

"When did you last see your brother, miss?"

"We were at a party together last night in Silver Spring," she said. "He just disappeared. And his bed hasn't been slept in."

"When you say he just disappeared, what do you mean by that? Is his car missing? Did he leave with someone?"

"I guess he must have left with someone," Ari admitted reluctantly.

"Do you know who?"

"A strange girl." Ari added, "I don't know her."

Sergeant Harper laughed. "I understand your concern, miss, and believe me I don't want to make light of it, but boys will be boys, if you follow me. You'll be hearing from your brother, and you can give him a piece of your mind when you do. But I'm sorry, it's not a police case."

Ari heard a dial tone. The police officer had hung up on her.

CHAPTER THIRTEEN

PAUL COULD SENSE THE LIGHT EVEN THROUGH HIS closed eyelids, and he was frightened. Verena squirmed underneath him, reaching up to open the lid of the coffin.

"We left the light on," said Verena. "Get up, Paul. You weigh a ton. Get off of me."

Awkwardly, he scrambled up and breathed a deep sigh. It was a relief to be out of the tiny space, but he glanced at the window anxiously. "How can you be sure it's already dark outside?" he asked.

"I just know, that's all." Verena climbed out of the coffin. "I've been a vampire a while, you know. I've learned a few things. The summertime is really bad because the nights are so short. I get stir-crazy being in the coffin that long." She looked down at her sheer silver tunic, which was heavily wrinkled from Paul's weight resting on it. "Jeez, I'm a mess. Look at me," she said. She lifted the tunic over her head, dropped it on the floor, and then stepped out of the sheer trousers as well. She was naked then except for sheer bikini panties.

She walked casually across the room and began leafing through her tightly packed closet. She was far too thin, he observed. Her skin was like paper over her hipbones, and Paul could count every one of her ribs. But her breasts were large and pendulous. It occurred to him that she looked almost cowlike. He could only barely recall the passion her body had stirred in him the night before; it somehow made him sad. She stepped into a pair of jeans and continued searching for a blouse, frowning in intense concentration. At length she found a skinny, cropped T-shirt and pulled it out from the other clothes with some difficulty. Wiggling, she pulled it over her head. Paul hadn't noticed before that she had a very cheap style of dressing.

He sat down on the floor and steadied himself by bracing his hands behind him. "Verena," he said, "who made you?"

"That's a pretty personal question." She had opened a jewelry box now and was rattling around in it, trying on bracelets.

"You've drunk my blood and we've shared a

133

coffin, and all of a sudden I'm not supposed to get personal?" said Paul.

Verena giggled. "Oh, yeah. Sorry. I forgot." She slipped on a bracelet. "I think accessories are really important, don't you?"

Paul had a feverishly urgent need to know about "being made." Did it mean he was stuck with Verena forever? He had a horrible and overwhelming fear that he was going to have to listen to her inane conversation for all eternity. But he felt he needed to be tactful about finding out what the situation was. The truth was that he was afraid of her. He remembered her attack on him with painful vividness, and it was hard for him to believe that she couldn't hurt him anymore. "So, who did it to you?" he insisted. "Who made you?"

"Dubay," she admitted. "We're still just like this." She held up two fingers squeezed close together. "Really tight."

"But he doesn't live here, does he?" asked Paul, relieved at this clue that there might be some way for him to escape from her.

"Nah. We tried sharing his place, but it didn't work out. He's a pig. Leaves his stuff all over. And you should see his toothbrush. It's got fungus and everything. Yech."

Paul remembered that Dubay, despite all his muscles, had slightly thinning hair. He must have been pushing thirty when he had become a vampire. And Verena had been only sixteen when she was "made." Something about that bothered him. It didn't seem fair. "Did he—did he force you?" he asked tentatively.

She shrugged. "Well, not exactly."

"But sort of?"

"I have to be honest with you." She laughed. "It was my idea. Does that shock you?"

Paul shook his head. Nothing could shock him now, he realized bitterly.

"I always liked living on the edge back when I was human," admitted Verena, hugging herself tight. "I'd done sex, I'd done drugs—and this was back in the days when nice girls didn't even kiss, remember. I've always been a free spirit." She threw out her arms and the tiny white T-shirt strained to contain her. "I wanted to do it all! And now I have."

Paul took a deep breath. "You sure have."

Verena perched on the closed coffin and tapped her fangs with an enameled fingernail. "Had to give up smoking, though," she said. "I used to always sneak smokes in the bathroom at school. It was tough giving it up. Now, half the time I don't know what to do with my hands."

Paul remembered that she had been to St. Anne's School. And that school had been absorbed into St. Anselm's when it went coed in the sixties.

"I guess you used to know Sybil's mom, didn't you?" he suggested.

"You're not going to start on me about my age, are you?" She frowned. "I'm always going to look sixteen. I'm in very good shape and I keep up with all the latest fashions."

He could see this was a sensitive subject with her. "No, no," he said. "I just wondered what Mrs. Barron was like when she was young."

"She was a real pill." Verena stood up. "Miss Hoity-toity, holier-than-thou. Boy, it burns me. I could tell you things about her, believe me. She wasn't nearly as innocent as she made out."

"So tell me about her." Paul's curiosity had been piqued when he found out his father had been in love with Mrs. Barron. It was hard for him to imagine how two normal, ordinary women—his mother and Mrs. Barron both—had fallen in love with a man like his father. It seemed an unfathomable mystery. And now that Paul had opted out of the human love scene so early, it looked as if he wouldn't likely get much more insight into the way it worked.

Verena dimpled. "I don't want to sit here talking about Sybil's mom, Paul. For one thing it's ugly, and for another thing it's boring. Tell you what, are you hungry yet?"

Paul's heart began to pound uncomfortably. "No!" he said too loudly. "I'm not."

Verena looked at him under her lashes.

136

"Don't have a cow. I was only going to take you hunting. How are you going to know what to do unless I show you? You'll be completely helpless." The prospect of that seemed to please her, and she smiled as she got up and moved toward him.

Paul backed away from her.

She giggled. "Don't worry. I got all your blood last night." Suddenly she bent over, laughing until tears streamed down her face. "I'm sorry," she said, wiping her eyes. "But the look on your face was priceless. I mean, you wanted it but you didn't want to admit it. What a scream! I love it when they struggle with their pitiful little consciences. It *kills* me."

Paul felt sick. His heart was beating so hard he could feel it in his stomach.

She kneaded his cheek with her bony fingers. "Wow! It was great, wasn't it?" She smiled.

"Do you—do you do it every day?" He remembered that Aunt Gabrielle went out every night faithfully on her jog. He couldn't do that. He knew he couldn't.

Verena cocked her head and thought about it. "You mean do I have to? Nah. A whole bunch of blood like I got last night will set me up for a week, if I don't get around to hunting. You know, if I'm too busy shopping or something."

Paul felt the wall pressing against his back. She put her hands on his shoulders, squeezing them so her nails bit into his flesh. It didn't hurt, but the memory of when she had held him helpless in her grip made nausea sweep over him again. He could feel himself trembling.

"It's not that I have to do it every night," Verena said softly. "It's just that I *love* to do it." Suddenly she buried her face against his neck and he felt her fangs dig sharply into his flesh.

He looked down at her blond hair, repelled by the smell of her perfume. "Cut it out, Verena," he pleaded. "Give me a break."

"Didn't you feel anything?" She drew away, looking hurt.

Paul glanced down at the gash in his flesh, the glistening blood welling up in it. Panicking, he clasped his hand over the cut until he felt a strange warm feeling. He took his hand away and the gash was gone. He stared at it incredulously for a moment, then he blinked at Verena.

"Leave me alone," he begged her. "Just leave me alone."

She laughed. "Come on! A girl's got to have some fun!" She stooped and picked up the car keys off the floor.

"Where are you going?" he asked.

"Out," she said, lifting her chin. "You don't own me, you know. I'm the one that owns you."

Paul went cold. "What do you mean by that? What do you mean you 'own' me?"

She tweaked his nose with her fingers. "You

need me to show you the ropes. If you don't have somebody watching you every minute you're going to do something dumb—and then it could be curtains."

"So—so are you going to stay right around here in the neighborhood?" Paul was seized with the fear that he might need her. He had not forgotten how desperately relieved he had been to see her last night.

She shoved the keys into the pocket of her tight jeans. "Nope. I'm driving down to Virginia. So many vampires live in Georgetown, we have to sort of spread out. All those bodies—if we weren't careful, people would start asking questions." She grinned. "Well—later, then!" She waved and closed the door behind her.

When she had gone, Paul leaned against the door and let the tears well up in his eyes. The memory of Verena's empty-headed smile floated in his mind like a reproach. Whatever she thought, she didn't own him. He wasn't going to stay here and wait for Verena to come back. She had forgotten that he had vampires in his own family he could count on. He could go home.

Ari had cried until she felt sick. She was gulping an aspirin at the kitchen sink when she heard the front door open. She ran out to the hall just in time to see Paul step in. He looked terrible. He was pale and unsteady on his feet, as if he had a bad hangover. "Paul!" she cried. "Where have you been? Where have you been all this time? I was so worried I called the police!"

"Leave me alone," he said thickly. He turned toward the stairs.

Aunt Gabrielle came out of her study. Her long hair had been swept up in a bun on her crown, and she looked less like herself than a strict schoolteacher. She regarded Paul steadily, her eyes narrowing.

"You look awful, Paul," cried Ari. "Are you okay? What happened?"

He closed his eyes. "I don't want to talk about it, okay? Give me some space." He opened the door to the stair hall uncertainly and began climbing up the stairs very slowly, like an old man.

Ari turned toward her aunt. "Don't you think he looks terrible? It's not just my imagination, is it?"

Aunt Gabrielle backed away from her. "I have no problems with Paul staying out all night if that's what he wants to do," she said, her voice distant. "It's up to him."

"But he's sick!" cried Ari. "You must be able to see that!"

Aunt Gabrielle raised both her hands. "I can't interfere!" she said, looking alarmed. She stepped back into the study and closed the door.

Ari had the strong impulse to bang on the

door and scream at her. Didn't anybody in this house know what was normal? Something was wrong with Paul—anybody should be able to see that. Even Aunt Gabri.

Ari ran upstairs and charged into Paul's room. She found him lying on the bed staring vacantly at the ceiling. She looked at him a moment, wanting to believe this had all been a false alarm. He looked like himself, and yet . . . She felt fear stirring deep in her stomach.

"Paul," she said, "tell me what happened between you and Verena. Cos told me you two went off together. Why?"

He turned his head toward her and smiled crookedly. He was deathly pale. "Haven't you ever been—parking with somebody?" he asked.

Ari's skin crept. "Paul, Verena didn't *do* anything to you, did she?" She could hear her voice rising shrilly, but she couldn't help it. Hysteria bubbled up in her throat.

"What if she did?" he said in a muffled voice. He turned away from her.

"No!" screamed Ari. "No! It's not true." She sank to the floor sobbing. "No, Paul, it can't be true. I can't stand it. You can't do this to me." She covered her face and sobbed.

Paul pivoted on the bed and sat up suddenly, dangling his legs over the edge. "I'm still the same person, Ari. This doesn't change anything." He gulped. "I mean, not the big things. We still love each other, don't we? I'm going to go on with my life the same as ever." He slid off the bed and began pacing the floor. "I'm not going to end up like Verena, dropping out of school and spending my time watching old movies. I'm going to finish my education, go to college, the whole bit."

Ari watched him through a blur of tears, marveling that the shell of his body could look exactly like the brother she had known.

"This isn't going to change anything!" Paul said fervently. "I'm going to keep running cross-country. I've got a date with Susannah Friday night. I'm going to keep on with school and my social life. Everything's going to be the same as it was!"

"But you can't!" cried Ari. "You're a—" She couldn't bring herself to form the syllables of the word "vampire," but it lay in her throat, choking her.

Paul pushed a lock of dark hair out of his eyes. His pallor was shocking. "Haven't you ever heard of sunblock!" he yelled. "I'm going to live a normal life, I tell you."

Suddenly the phone rang.

Paul shoved his hands in his pockets. "It's for you," he said sourly. "It always is."

Ari fled to her room and picked up the phone.

"Ari? It's Cos." There was a pause. "Ari? Are you there?" he asked.

142

"Yes," she choked out. "I'm here." She was astonished at how normal her voice sounded. She was only a little hoarse, and Cos did not seem to notice.

"Did Paul get home yet?" he asked.

"Yes," she said. "He just came in."

She could hear Cos's laughter. "That Verena's a hot one," he said.

"I hate her," said Ari in a low voice. "I'd kill her if I could."

There was a stunned silence at the other end. "Excuse me?" said Cos.

Ari realized she had gone too far. "I like Paul's girlfriend Susannah," she said frantically. "I like her a whole lot." Funny. Susannah, who used to get on her nerves, seemed like an angel to her now. "I'm worried this might mean that they're going to break up."

"I hear what you're saying," said Cos. "I guess he doesn't want her to find out he went off with Verena."

"No. No, he doesn't. You won't say anything about it, will you, Cos?" asked Ari anxiously.

"Not a word. You and I are the only ones who'll know he just got home today. And *we* won't say a thing." Cos hesitated. "You're sure he doesn't want to break up with Susannah?"

"No," said Ari. "He told me that he didn't."

"Yeah, well, sometimes these little flings

143

don't mean anything. Susannah's a real sweet girl."

Ari glanced at the connecting door. "I think he's having regrets, Cos. He's really worried."

"No problem. You can count on me to keep quiet."

Cos talked a while longer and Ari struggled desperately to make the appropriate responses. But it was impossible. "I guess I'm awfully tired," she said finally. "I've worn myself out worrying about Paul."

"Take it easy, Ari. I told you it would be okay. These things have a way of working out."

"Yes," she managed to say. "I can see that now."

After she hung up she went over to the window and stared out at the darkness. Tears streamed down her cheeks. The trees in the garden were bending under the wind. The night was overcast and too dark for stars. Cos had no idea, she thought wearily. He simply had no idea. She leaned her forehead against the window frame and wept.

CHAPTER
FOURTEEN

WHEN PAUL WAS CERTAIN THAT ARI WAS ASLEEP, HE crept downstairs and knocked on the door of Aunt Gabrielle's study. The door had not been shut all the way, and his knocking made it swing open. He was startled to see that she was gone. His heart felt a jolt of panic. There was so much he needed to ask her. Why didn't she wait for him?

Suddenly, he was overcome with dizziness and he had to grab on to the French doors. He held on to the door frame, resting his forehead against a pane of glass. Staring out at the night, he sensed movement in the flower beds. A strange numbness had come over him. His hands and arms felt warm and heavy. It was as if he were in a trance, he thought, and he felt detached about what was going to happen next.

He quietly opened the door and stepped outside. The night was overcast, and the only light in the garden came from the open French doors of Aunt Gabrielle's study. The trees whispered over his head and he heard a faint rustle among the plants. Deftly he reached into the petunias and grabbed the scurrying bit of fur. The rat was eight or nine inches long. It squirmed desperately, its tiny nails scratching his hand. Its eyes were dark beads of brightness and its small teeth flashed yellow. Its long naked tail thrashed as it fought for its life.

Paul was disgusted by the oily feel of the rat's fur in his hands. He wanted to get this over with as quickly as possible. With a movement quicker than a blink, he bit. Then he gagged painfully and spit out the rat's head. Pressing the limp body to his lips, he sucked as if it were a baby bottle, trying not to think about what he was doing.

The rank smell of rat turned his stomach and its blood tasted stale. Paul flung the limp body into the flower bed. He rubbed his palms vigorously against his jeans, but they still felt oily and smelled like the rat.

Paul dashed inside, closing the doors with shaking hands, and rushed into the kitchen. He squirted soap on his hands and ran the hot water in the sink until clouds of steam enveloped his head. He washed them again and again. Finally he sniffed his palms and this time sensed only the lemon smell of the detergent. His hands might be clean, but his mind was still sick with revulsion.

He gulped and leaned against the sink, glancing at the clock. It was growing late! Ari had taken a long time to fall asleep. He supposed he shouldn't have hung around waiting upstairs, but he had been afraid that she would hear him leave. He had wanted everything to seem as normal to her as possible. But now not much of the night was left. A poker of hot fear shot through his stomach.

Minutes later, Paul heard the front door open and then Aunt Gabrielle glided into the kitchen and placed her bejeweled hands on his cheeks. "Paul, my dear, are you all right?"

"Y-yeah," he stuttered. "I guess."

She glanced at the sink, still foamy with detergent bubbles. "Washing dishes at this hour?"

Paul squirmed and avoided her gaze. He knew Aunt Gabrielle had drunk rat's blood herself. He had once found a discarded rat's corpse in the garden. Why was he ashamed? Was it that Aunt Gabrielle was so lovely, so impeccably groomed, so restrained in her manner that it was impossible for him to imagine her doing anything gross, even when the fact stared him in the face?

"It's a lot to get used to all at once," she said

147

softly. "There's so much you have to learn."

"You knew, didn't you?" he asked. "The minute I walked in the door tonight, you knew."

"Yes, darling, I knew."

"Where's my father?" he cried. "I need him now. I need him!"

Aunt Gabrielle sat down at the desk and held her head in her hands. "I don't know, Paul. I thought when you children came to stay with me—I don't know. Richard's always been this way. He has to be free. We have to accept that."

"Verena did this to me," Paul said in a rush. "She made me. She had her fangs into me before I even knew what she was up to. The pain was awful. She really hurt me."

Aunt Gabrielle looked out the window to the dark garden. For an unnerving moment he wondered if she could see the flattened body of the rat. "You don't have to explain anything to me," she said very quietly.

Paul flushed in shame. "I can't go back there, Aunt Gabrielle. I can't go back to Verena's." He gulped. "You've got to hide me!"

"You can stay in my room for now." She inclined her head graciously.

At the thought of getting into Aunt Gabrielle's coffin with her, his heart sank. "Okay," he said faintly.

But the word echoed in his ears, mocking him.

Nothing was okay.
He had thrown his life away.

When Ari got up the next morning, there was no sign of Paul. He had obviously changed his clothes, because his underwear had been left in a heap in the bathroom. She automatically picked it up and put it in the clothes hamper. He was usually fairly neat, but this was not an ordinary sort of day. Her eyes swam with tears. Where could he be?

A vacuum was roaring, and when Ari went downstairs she saw that Carmel, her heavy dark hair clipped into a tortoiseshell barrette, was cleaning the living room. Her back was to the door and she didn't hear Ari. Feeling oddly invisible, Ari went into the kitchen and found a note taped to the refrigerator.

"Ari—tell everybody at school I've got a bad case of the flu. I've got to get some details worked out.—P."

A bad case of flu, Ari thought bitterly. *Yeah. Right.* She took cold milk out of the fridge, poured a glass, and then drank it, feeling like a robot. She felt cold and dead inside, as if her body belonged to someone else. It was a frightening sensation because she imagined that Paul felt the same way. That was the way vampires felt, wasn't it? Cold and dead?

It was easier once she got to school. Aunt

Gabrielle's house seemed very far away from the everyday world where papers were due and books had to be read and no one knew the truth. Ari took notes in class, laughed at bad jokes, touched Cos's hand under the table in English class, smiled and explained to everyone that Paul had the flu. She acted out the charade so convincingly that there were moments when she almost persuaded herself it was true.

Sybil caught up with her after English class. "Guess what? Rab is staying over until this afternoon so he can meet you." She was glowing with happiness. "He's really anxious to get to know you."

"Good," said Ari, smiling automatically. "That would be nice. I can't wait."

Sybil shot her a concerned look. "Ari, are you okay?"

"Sure," said Ari. "Why do you ask?" Her face felt numb, as if it were full of novocaine.

"I don't know," said Sybil slowly. "You don't seem like yourself. Are you sure nothing's wrong?"

"Everything's fine," Ari lied.

Nadia was coming down the hall toward them, but when she spotted Ari, she turned around and stumbled off in the other direction.

"Jeez," said Sybil. "Nadia gets stranger every day, doesn't she? She and Jesse must be sort of pooling their weirdness. They both used to be just a little weird, but now that they're together they're getting very, very strange."

150

Ari stared blankly at Nadia's back.

"Rab and I will pick you up right after school," said Sybil. "Rab's got to drive back to-night. I wish Paul could go with us, too. It's terrible that he has the flu."

"Yes, awful."

"Just be careful you don't catch it from him," said Sybil.

"Yeah," said Ari colorlessly. "I'll be careful."

After school, when Ari returned to Aunt Gabrielle's dark, silent house, her carefully maintained facade crumbled. Tears streamed down her face as she ran upstairs. She threw open Paul's door and gasped. A very shiny coffin lay on the floor beside his bed. Ari quickly closed the door again.

"This can't be happening," she whispered. She wished she hadn't seen the coffin. She stood in the hall a moment, breathing hard and wondering what to do. At last she gritted her teeth, opened the door again, and forced herself to go back into Paul's room. Whatever was going on, she decided, it was better to face it than to stand out in the hall pretending it hadn't happened.

A note had been firmly taped to the top of the coffin. The script was round and the *i*'s were dotted with little hearts. "Thanks for a *wonderful* evening. Yours forever, and I mean that! Very sincerely, Verena."

Ari gazed at the shiny surface of the coffin,

horrified. Was Paul inside it, she wondered? She dared not open it. Even though the day was overcast, light was coming in the window, which could be dangerous to him. But she had to know whether he was inside. She pressed the heels of her hands up against the side of the coffin and gave it a shove. Slowly it slid on the floor. It was heavy, but not heavy enough. Paul couldn't be inside, she decided.

She stood up, panting. If he wasn't in the coffin, then where was he?

Ari heard the doorbell ring, and she stiffened. That was Sybil and her brother Rab. They had come for her already. She stood up slowly. She couldn't think of anything to do other than to go on as if nothing were wrong. She dashed into her room, hastily pulled on jeans, and ran a comb through her hair. The doorbell rang again. Her heart was pounding.

As she ran to the stairs she heard the front door open. Carmel had let them in. "I'm coming!" Ari yelled, galloping headlong down the stairs. At all costs, she had to maintain the deception. It was crucial that no word of anything strange going on leaked back to Nadia and Jesse. Ari was convinced they were on the brink of discovering the truth about her family—and both were probably capable of hurting Paul if they knew he had become a vampire.

CHAPTER
FIFTEEN

ARI FOUND SYBIL IN THE DOWNSTAIRS HALLWAY looking around curiously. "This is the first time I've been in your house, you know," Sybil said.

Ari was morbidly conscious of the long expanse of black and white marble and the strange bronze gong that gleamed dimly at the end of the hall. She was certain Sybil's eyes were being drawn to peculiar little details—things that now seemed to be a dead giveaway of the truth: the black statuette of a rooster that stood on a table by the door, the gilt clock in the living room with the signs of the zodiac in blue and gold, the odd collection of antiques. Ari darted an anxious glance at the fireplace through the open door of the living room. As far as she was concerned, the sooner they went outside the better. "Is Rab waiting in the car?" she asked.

Sybil seemed to come to her senses with a start. "Yeah, he is. And he's double-parked, so I guess we better go."

Ari saw her friend glance curiously behind her as they left the house.

Rab unfolded his long legs, got out, and opened the door for them. Ari had not expected him to be so tall, and was surprised when he stood up to his full height. Again, she had the nagging feeling that he was familiar.

"We haven't met, have we?" she asked him as she got in the car.

He slid in behind the wheel and smiled. "Believe me, I would have remembered if we had."

Ari blushed. It would be very uncomfortable if he spent the afternoon hitting on her. Already she was holding on to her sanity by only the thinnest thread.

As they drove down Wisconsin Avenue, Sybil suddenly spoke. "I guess your aunt doesn't believe in interior decorators, huh?"

Ari burst out laughing. She realized she was close to hysteria.

"Was it that funny?" Sybil asked, blushing. "I just meant—well, you should see the house, Rab. It looks like nothing's been changed in it for a hundred years."

154

"I guess your aunt has a lot of antiques," Rab said.

Ari shook her head. "Sybil means it's expensive-looking but gloomy," she said, wiping her eyes. "Kind of like the Munsters had suddenly come into a lot of money."

Sybil grinned. "That's it! You've pegged it exactly, Ari. It's elegant, but creepy."

Rab laughed. "In that case, I'm sorry I missed it."

"It's the kind of place," Sybil went on, "where you'd feel funny going downstairs at night for a midnight snack."

"I never go downstairs at night for a midnight snack," said Ari firmly.

"Hey, is the mall okay with you two?" asked Rab. "We could get a bite to eat there."

Sybil and Ari nodded. Normal life, Ari thought to herself, repeating the words in her mind as if they were a magical formula. Above all, she had to behave as if everything were normal.

Georgetown Park had oversized lanterns hanging from its vast ceiling, that lit the elaborate pools, fountains, and palms. Rab led them to a café table on the second floor where they could look both up and down at the different levels of the mall. The floor under their table was like the marble floor of Aunt Gabrielle's hallway: checkerboard black and white. It made Ari feel as if she were a chess piece in a dangerous game, and that she could not afford to make a wrong move. Rab brought a tray of drinks and fries to the table.

"What are you majoring in, Rab?" asked Ari. She knew no question could be more ordinary than that, and she felt mildly pleased with herself.

He smiled. "I'm majoring in history. I've already got applications out to law school."

"Rab skipped two years in school when he was little," said Sybil proudly. "He's very smart. He taught himself calculus."

Rab rolled his eyes. "My sister brags about me a lot. So, how do you like St. Anselm's? You like it better than your old school?"

Ari didn't know what to say. She vaguely remembered that she used• to like St. Anselm's, but that time seemed so long ago that it might have been in another life. She evaded the question. "Did you go to St. Anselm's?" she asked.

"Nah. I went to Exeter. It seems like all my life I've been away at school." His eyes darkened, and Ari knew her question had touched a nerve. She could feel his pain as vividly as if it were a tightly drawn violin string under her fingers.

"I'm sorry," she said. Her gaze met his in a sudden electric charge of sympathy.

"Sorry for what?" Sybil hooted derisively. "Rab's the one who had all the freedom, Ari! I'm the one you should feel sorry for. It was me who had to deal with my parents breathing down my neck twenty-four hours a day. Where are your friends, Sybil?" she said, mimicking her mother's voice. "Can't you get some different friends? Why aren't you homecoming queen? You'll look perfectly okay as soon as your teeth are straight and you get those braces off." She abruptly switched to a low, booming tone. "No, Sybil, it's not that there's anything wrong with a B, but your mother and I know you can do better."

Rab grinned at his sister.

Sybil leapt up suddenly from her chair. "I'm going to wash my hands," she said. "You two can talk."

Ari was embarrassed by Sybil's blatant matchmaking and couldn't think of anything to say. Silently, they watched her mount the steps in the direction of the rest rooms. Suddenly Rab turned to Ari and said, "You can read my mind, can't you?"

Ari's hand jerked and she knocked over her drink. Rab jumped up. "I'm sorry. Hang on, I'll get some napkins."

He brought back handfuls of napkins and began mopping up the spilled drink. Ari grabbed one of the napkins and swabbed at her eyes fiercely. "I cannot read your mind!" she cried. "That was a stupid thing for you to say."

"I'm sorry," he said, giving her a puzzled look. He pushed the sodden napkins into the middle of the table and sat down. His calm eyes met Ari's. "Did I say something wrong?"

"I'm not weird," she whispered, folding her hands tightly and looking down at them. "I'm average and normal." But then her eyes fell on a newspaper lying on the next table, and she realized she saw its headline in many colors. Once she grew close enough to read them, numbers and letters always took on color, even when she knew they were printed in black and white. She could feel herself growing cold inside.

"What's wrong?" Rab said, reaching for her hand.

She quickly put both hands in her lap out of his reach. "Nothing." Her eyes lifted to meet his. "I can't tell you."

He bit his lip. His eyes were troubled. After a minute he said, "You can tell me anything, Ari. Are you afraid I'm going to tell Sybil? I won't. Maybe I can help."

"No," she said. "No one can help me." She blinked back tears. "You don't have any idea what it's like to be completely alone in the world with nobody you can depend on." She choked up suddenly and couldn't speak.

He frowned. "No. I don't. But neither do you. What about your twin brother?"

A tear rolled down Ari's cheek and she angrily dashed it away with her hand.

"Okay, something's wrong but you don't want to tell me about it." Rab paused. "Give me your wallet," he said.

Ari carried a thin wallet in the back pocket of her jeans so she wouldn't have to bother with a purse. She was so startled by his demand that she found herself fishing it out and handing it over without thinking. "What—are you short of cash or something?" she asked.

His mouth twisted in a half smile. "I'm never short of cash. Guilt on my mother's part keeps me loaded." He took out her driver's license and wrote something on the back.

"What are you doing?" she asked.

"That's my phone number at school. If you need help, call me. Anytime."

"Thank you," she said. She supposed this was some very subdued, gentlemanly sort of pass he was making. If only he would dash out of the mall and run away—far away. She felt if she could only be alone for a few minutes, she might be able to pull herself together somehow.

"I'm serious about this," he said, smiling at her crookedly. "Do you hear what I'm saying? If you're in jail, I'm your bail. Are we friends now?" His V-shaped eyebrows rose with his question.

"Okay," she said listlessly. It was easier to agree with him. She was too tired to argue.

Sybil came bouncing down the steps. She put her purse down next to her chair. "What happened?" She eyed the heap of wet napkins.

"I dumped over my soda," said Rab.

As they got up from the table, a familiar voice called Ari's name. Her instinct was to run, but she couldn't make her feet move. She turned around to face the voice. It was Jesse.

"Hey, wait up!" he yelled. Jesse came hurrying down the steps followed by Nadia.

Ari felt as if she were frozen in place. Even Sybil seemed struck dumb.

"Speak of the devil," said Jesse derisively.

Rab shot Sybil and Ari questioning looks. He obviously noticed the nastiness of Jesse's tone.

"Nadia and I have just been talking about you," said Jesse, putting his arm around Nadia's shoulders. She looked scared. "We've been doing a little research," said Jesse, "and we found out when your dad graduated from St. Anselm's. He's the same age as Sybil's mom, but I've met him and he looks like he can't be much more than twenty. I think that's pretty strange, don't you?"

Ari had never felt so vulnerable, so exposed. She was afraid that any minute Jesse was going to proclaim to all the hurrying shoppers around them that her father was a vampire.

Sybil glanced at her and took hold of her arm. "Your life must be really interesting, Jesse," Sybil said sarcastically. "Looking through all those old yearbooks and having fascinating chats about people's parents. We'd love to hear more, wouldn't we, folks? But my brother is in kind of a hurry to get back to school, and we've got to go."

Rab, taking his cue from Sybil, grabbed Ari's other arm. Almost carrying Ari between them, the Barrons squeezed passed Jesse and they all fled up the stairs.

"You think you're so smart," Jesse called after them. "But we're onto you, Nadia and me. We're close on your tail! And Sandy knows what's going on, too."

When they reached the next level, Rab cast a look down over the railing at Jesse and Nadia, who were settling down at the table the three of them had just vacated. "Good grief," he muttered under his breath. "Let's get out of here. What's that guy's problem?"

Ari shook her head. She was trembling by the time they reached the car. Darkness was gathering in the parking lot and the sky was the deep purple of dusk.

"Are you okay?" Sybil asked anxiously. "I'm really starting to think Jesse ought to be locked up. I mean, that was more than weird, wasn't it, Rab?"

"So what is it? Is the guy totally psychotic?" asked Rab.

"He's been strange for years," said Sybil. "Believe me, if Cos knew he talked like that to you, Ari, he'd be furious. I've never seen Jesse this bad. He's delusional. I'll bet he's never even met your dad."

"No, he has," Ari admitted. "Paul said—Paul said that one time when he was with our father at some kind of bar they ran into Jesse and Cos."

Sybil slammed the car door closed. "Well, there you are. Jesse's in some dark bar, probably half drunk, sees your dad, and because your father looks young, suddenly he's off with another of his conspiracy theories. Completely and totally deranged."

Rab drove out of the lot.

"He ought to be on medication or something," said Sybil. "I mean, he was scary, wasn't he, Rab?"

"Not exactly Mr. Charm," agreed Rab.

"He's like one of those nuts you read about in the newspaper, where they go berserk and kill fifteen people in a fast-food restaurant," said Sybil. "I can't believe I used to think he was cute."

"He definitely seems like the ax-murderer type," muttered Rab. "You know what he was

162

doing when I looked down? He was picking up the wet napkins one by one and smelling them!"

"This is serious," said Sybil. "I think the thing to do is for me to go into the counselor at school and tell her that Jesse has gone over the edge."

Ari's voice was faint. "I wish you wouldn't."

Rab shot a glance at Ari. "Better not, Syb."

Sybil was quiet for a moment. "I don't know," she said finally. "I think it might be a good idea."

But Ari knew that Sybil wouldn't do it. She idolized her big brother and she took his suggestions very seriously. Ari exhaled. She hadn't thought Rab could help her, but he already had.

The streetlights were on now and darkness had gathered in alleys and under the trees. Rab turned onto M Street. "I promised Mom I'd pick up a dozen eggs," he said.

"Lately she never seems to go to the grocery store at all," said Sybil. "You'd think she'd been traumatized by the frozen-foods section or something, the way she's been acting. The last couple of weeks she's been getting the store to deliver."

Rab had to park several blocks away from Dean & DeLuca. "This'll just take me a minute," he said.

Slowly it dawned on Ari that Rab had parked the car in front of a neon-lit bar. She could hear the singing of vampires coming from inside. When she covered her ears, she could still hear them clearly, a high flutelike sound that sung shrilly in her mind. She wished Rab had parked somewhere else. She found herself staring at the open door of the bar, sick with apprehension.

Two skinny women came out of the bar arm in arm, looking like a matched pair. One wore skintight jeans and had her hair slicked back so that it looked enameled to her skull. The other was in a wispy shirt with a skirt that tied under her navel. She had a thick fringe of blunt-cut hair that fell over one eye. Ari recognized them at once as friends of Aunt Gabrielle's. To her dismay, they spotted her and came over to the car. The one with the slicked-back hair tapped on the window of the car with a long fingernail and smiled. Her eyebrows were plucked to a thin line over deeply shadowed gray eyes. "Hi, there! I'm Gwendolyn. Friend of your aunt's?" she reminded Ari. "We've met. You remember Tippi?"

Ari gulped and nodded. She remembered them very well. But she hadn't realized when she met them before that they were vampires. Now she wondered how she could have failed to see it. Their stark-white skin was stretched over sharp bones and they stank of blood. The smell of it was on Gwendolyn's breath.

"Isn't this a beautiful night!" shouted Tippi, raising her voice to be heard over the din spilling out of the bar. "Gwenny and I are going to go for a nice long drive to Baltimore." She giggled. "Land of opportunity. *So* many lovely people, huh, Gwen?"

"Nice to see you again." Gwen smiled, and Ari realized that she was being careful not to show her fangs. "Give our best to Gabri!"

"I will," said Ari in a faint voice.

Sybil gazed at them curiously as they sauntered down the street arm in arm. "I wonder if they're lesbians," she said.

"I wish," muttered Ari under her breath.

"What did you say?" Sybil blinked at her.

Ari shook her head. "They're unconventional." She hesitated. "Artists."

"Oh," said Sybil, as if that explained everything.

Ari realized the neon bar must be the vampire hangout Paul had told her about, the very one where her father had attacked Jesse.

A vampire with oily black hair stumbled out of the bar and rocked the car as he leaned against it, looking like an anorexic version of Elvis. The antenna bent under the weight of his white hand. His eyelids drooped and his face was a sickly white.

"I can't believe Rab parked in front of a bar," said Sybil. She glanced over her shoulder. "Here he comes. About time."

The vampire clinging to the antenna showed his fangs to Ari and laughed. She shuddered. It was as if somehow he realized his secret was safe with her. She rolled up the car window hastily. Rab opened the car on the driver's side and leaned on the horn. "Buzz off, buster," he yelled at the vampire. "I've gotta move this car."

Ari began to shake. What if the vampire attacked Rab?

"Are you all right, Ari?" cried Sybil. "She's trembling, Rab."

Rab pulled out of the parking place. He was watching for a break in the traffic. "Are you okay, Ari?" he inquired uneasily. "That looks like kind of a rough bar. I wouldn't have parked there if I'd known."

"I'm all right," insisted Ari.

"How can you say you're all right? You're shaking like a leaf," protested Sybil.

If the vampire ran after them, Ari thought, pressing her head back against the seat cushions, she was going to get hysterical. Her teeth were chattering. "I think I might be coming down with something," she said finally.

Paul was in his room studying when Ari got home. His green-shaded lamp cast a pool of light on the book that lay on his desk. He looked so much like his normal self as he bent over his work that for an instant, Ari wondered if it was all a mistake. Then she saw that the dust ruffle was bulging out a bit. He had shoved something under the bed. She caught a glimmer of the coffin's shiny wood.

"Hi!" Paul smiled. "I've got it all worked out, Ari. I'm going to school tomorrow."

"When I came in this afternoon," Ari said, her mouth suddenly dry, "I saw Verena's note on that coffin you've hidden under your bed."

"Verena thinks she owns me." Paul's glowering dark brows reminded her powerfully of their father. "But she's wrong about that. Don't worry. I've got all the angles covered."

Ari sat down on the bed. Her heel knocked against the wood of the coffin and she winced. "I'm worried, Paul. Sybil's brother took us to the mall and we ran into Jesse and Nadia. It was strange! He acted like he had something on us. He said our dad looked too young!"

"No law against looking young," snapped Paul.

Ari ran her fingers through her hair in agitation. "I got so upset that I can't remember exactly what he said. But he was threatening me! I'm sure of that. Sybil and Rab both thought he was acting really strange. He mentioned Sandy, too."

167

Paul threw his pencil down angrily. "What happened to Sandy wasn't my fault!" he shouted. "I didn't have anything to do with it."

"I know. I know you didn't." Ari looked at him. "But Jesse's so suspicious! And I think Nadia's feeding right into it. I know she's been reading up on vampires, and I have the feeling they're talking about them all the time." Ari looked at him anxiously. "Maybe you'd better not go to school, Paul. I can tell everybody that you're still sick."

"Don't start that, Ari," Paul said. "Pulling this off is going to be hard enough. I don't need to have you undermining me." He scowled down at his open book.

Ari knew he couldn't be concentrating on what he was reading, but she was afraid for several moments to speak.

"I'm going to school tomorrow," he repeated stubbornly. "You just watch me."

Ari stood up, taking a deep, gulping breath. "Will you promise me that you'll stay out of Jesse's way?"

He laughed bitterly. "I'm not afraid of Jesse."

"For me, Paul?" she pleaded with him. "Stay away from him. Nadia, too. Don't push your luck, okay?"

Paul buried his face in his hands. "I'm doing the best I can," he said in a muffled voice.

"I know." She couldn't look at him any

longer. She had begun to be conscious that his flesh was subtly different—hard and smooth looking. She hesitated at the door that connected their rooms. "Are you going out tonight?"

"I might," he said sullenly. "I've already caught up on my work."

"Do you—do you want me to go with you?"

"No!" he shouted.

Ari knew he must be going hunting. What had she expected, after all? She tried not to think about it, but she couldn't stop herself—she wanted to shriek. She went into her room and closed the door.

Ari sat on her bed for a long time, clenching and unclenching her fists. She heard a knocking on the door and jumped. "Come on in," she said. Then her heart leapt up into her throat. It occurred to her that she should lock the door between their rooms. Paul had been so much a part of herself that it hadn't occurred to her to be afraid of him. But she had every reason to be.

He threw open the door and smiled his familiar crooked smile. "You understand that I'm really stressed, don't you, Ari? I didn't mean to yell at you."

"Sure," she gulped. "Of course. I understand."

Paul sat down on the bed next to her and put his arm around her. "Remember when we were little and we used to play together in the back yard? Remember the scuppernong grapevine that was growing back there?"

Ari wiped her eyes. "Mom hated working in the garden. If it were up to her the jungle would have taken over."

"It seemed like we always went barefoot. I can feel that warm dirt under my feet now. All those little metal trucks of mine half-buried out there—forts and moats, roads and hills in the dirt."

"The ants," said Ari, smiling through her tears. "We thought we could train them. We had a school for ants."

"The thing I remember most," said Paul, "is that you were always there. All I had to do was reach out and I could touch you. There's no reason why that ever has to change. Do you hear me? I'm right here. And I'm going to go right on just as if I never even met Verena."

Ari nodded.

Paul squeezed her arm. His touch was cold. "I knew you'd back me up, Ari. You always have."

Later, when Ari got ready for bed, she strained her ears listening for any sound from Paul's room. But all she heard was the running of water in the bathroom and then the sounds of him pottering around in there. Ordinary, everyday sounds. She got dressed for bed and lay down thinking that she would not be able to close her eyes, but she fell instantly asleep and dreamed confusedly of vampires stalking the garden of their old house, their leering faces peering at her through the leaves of the scuppernong grapes.

CHAPTER
SIXTEEN

WHEN ARI WOKE UP THE NEXT MORNING, A LIGHT drizzle was falling. She lay in bed feeling anxious, listening to rain gurgle in the gutters. At first she couldn't remember why she was uneasy, and then it came back to her in a rush. Paul was going to school with her.

She had barely had time to dress when a light knock sounded on the connecting door. Struggling to produce a smile, she opened the door. Paul was tugging fiercely at his tie. She remembered that he used to complain he had never learned to tie it properly because he hadn't had a father to show him how.

"Ready to go?" he asked.

"I guess," she gulped. A faint flush of life gave color to Paul's face, and Ari got chills thinking about what must have given him that lifelike glow.

They went downstairs together. From the beginning they had had a pact that they wouldn't go downstairs in Aunt Gabrielle's creepy old house unless they were together. This morning it seemed a silly and childish sort of agreement. It hadn't protected them, had it? And now the oddities of Aunt Gabrielle's house seemed like comical stage props compared to the frightening reality of the changes in her twin. Ari realized she was avoiding looking directly at him. She looked at his tie, his shirt, his buttons—anything but his changed flesh. Still, her skin crawled if she brushed up against him. She sensed something odd about his fingernails. His skin was taut, and she was terrified of looking into his eyes. It was as if she were afraid that when she met his gaze he would somehow pull her into the darkness with him.

In the kitchen, Ari turned her back to Paul and poured herself a glass of orange juice. "Do you want anything?" she asked, glancing at him uncertainly.

He ran a finger around the inside of his shirt collar. "Not now," he said. "No, thanks."

Aunt Gabrielle never ate food either. Ari gulped down the orange juice and wiped her mouth hastily with the back of her hand. "Paul," she said suddenly. "Are you sure this is a good idea?"

His Adam's apple bobbed. Ari couldn't look at his eyes. "I'm wearing number fifteen flesh-colored sunblock, Ari," he said. "I'm covered in it. Even my hands. I've got sunglasses in my pocket. It's going to be fine."

If it was that easy, she wondered, why didn't the other vampires go skiing at Vail? Why didn't they get jobs in the summer as lifeguards? She felt certain it was a bad idea, but fatalism fell over her like a chilling frost.

On the drive to school, Ari stared out the windows as if she were trying to memorize the wet landscape. On street corners, flower vendors and magazine vendors had swathed their booths in plastic. Umbrellas had mushroomed on the sidewalks. The rain had picked up. She supposed that was good. If the sun was really hidden on a dark and gloomy day, vampires could go out. She had known Aunt Gabrielle to do it. Ari supposed Paul was going to pull it off, after all. At least for today. Her stomach quivered with nervousness.

Cos was watching for her and came to meet her as soon as he spotted her. To her relief, Paul struck off in the opposite direction. "Jeez," Cos said, glancing at Paul's back. "Paul looks terrible. Are you sure he didn't come back to school too soon? Looks to me like he's still got the flu."

"He does what he wants." Ari pushed her damp hair out of her eyes. "I can't tell him anything." Rain falling softly on her face and beading in her hair felt good somehow.

Cos opened an umbrella and grinned at her. "We met on a rainy day just like this, remember?"

Ari looked at him blankly. Her mind was so full of Paul that there was scarcely room for anything else.

"I ran right into you, remember?" said Cos. "And I thought—wow!" He put his arm around her and squeezed. "I still think that." He nuzzled her ear.

Ari could feel water seeping into her shoes. She loved the warm roughness of Cos's face against hers and the cold touch of his fingers where they crept under her blouse at the waist. After a moment she realized why. All these things reminded her that she was alive.

"Don't you love rainy weather," Cos said. "It's like we're in our own private world."

"I wish we were," said Ari wistfully. Rain streamed off the umbrella and onto her shoes. She closed her eyes and breathed in the damp air. "It's so good to be alive," she said.

Cos laughed. "It's way ahead of whatever's in second place," he said.

"I want to have eight children," said Ari passionately. "I'll take them to the beach and we'll play with blocks in the sunshine and raise tomatoes and roses and bake all our own bread."

Cos lifted her hand to his lips and gently kissed her fingertips. His eyes were laughing at her. "Hey, there's plenty of time for that stuff later."

"I hope so," said Ari.

"Right now," he said, "all we've got to do is get our homework done and kiss." He kissed her, and Ari clung to him with desperation. When they were clinging together she felt herself drifting happily without thoughts, without worries, conscious only of Cos's warmth.

Suddenly she was jolted by the sound of Jesse's voice. "Hey, Cos!" he called. When she looked around, alarmed, Jesse was sneering at them.

"Watch out for those public displays of affection," called Jesse. "You don't know what it's going to lead to." He paused meaningfully. "Especially in this case."

Ari shivered. She felt frozen by Jesse's suspicious glare.

"Get lost, Jess," shouted Cos good-naturedly.

"How can you stand him?" whimpered Ari after Jesse had turned away. "He scares me." She looked appealingly into Cos's eyes. She didn't know what she expected from him. How could he protect her?

"You have to know how to take him," said Cos.

Ari shivered. "He gives me the creeps."

176

Cos looked uncomfortable. "Okay, he's a little strange. I admit it. But who isn't? He's had kind of a tough time, Ari. And you know when you've known somebody practically since you've been kids. . . . Well, Jess doesn't have a lot of other friends. I can't just drop him."

Ari closed her eyes. "I know you can't," she said. Who should know better than she what it was like to share a whole lifetime with someone? She and Paul were so close, nothing could tear them apart. She would never give up on him, she thought fiercely. Never!

As the day went on Ari went from class to class in a daze, so worried and preoccupied she felt half-crazy. She wished Cos could have held her hand every minute, every hour, because it seemed as if he was her only anchor to ordinary life. She had felt uneasy even with Sybil since that disturbing time at the mall. That thing Rab had said about her reading his mind—it was as if he knew something about her that she didn't know herself. She didn't like the way he assumed they already had some kind of special relationship. Why did people have to act so oddly? Why couldn't they be normal, like Cos?

Ari caught sight of Paul only once that day. He was talking to Susannah near a dark stairwell. The scene looked unremarkable, and they seemed to be talking so happily together that she almost wondered if she had imagined that Paul had turned into a vampire. Could that be? Then she remembered the coffin shoved under his bed and turned away hastily, her pulse racing with fear.

"I think you may have gotten out of bed too soon," Susannah said, looking into Paul's eyes. "You're pale. And you look too thin, Paul. Are you sure it isn't mono?"

"Oh, I'm sure it's not mono," said Paul, smiling carefully so that his fangs wouldn't show.

"Maybe not, but I think we better not kiss until we're sure you're really, really well," said Susannah. "I can't afford to get sick right now. I'm already way behind in history."

"Okay," said Paul. "Have I ever told you how much I like you, Susannah? I mean, as a person." He remembered Verena and quelled a shudder. "You're interesting to talk to, and the way you know so much about art—that really impresses me."

"Oh, Paul!" Susannah's finger touched his lips. "I think it's wonderful the way our relationship is getting deeper. I didn't tell you this, but when I first went out with you, my friends said you were only interested in making out."

"It's not like that at all," he protested. And it wasn't. He didn't care anymore whether or not they made out. "I really like you." His eyes softened as he stroked her arm. Her soft, warm flesh gave him a strange quivering feeling inside that he scarcely understood. He loved the way she glowed with life. Lifting her hand to his lips, he kissed the inside of her wrist. He held her, fascinated by the way the blue of the blood vessels showed under the skin.

"You're so romantic." She sighed happily. "I like you, too, Paul. I really like you a lot." She looked into his eyes a long time, then frowned. "Did you get contacts?"

"Wh-why do you ask?" he stuttered.

"Your eyes look so different. Maybe it's the lighting here."

"Yeah," he said, "it's a new kind of contact lens. Special new plastic. Repels dust, retards drying. I thought it was a fair trade-off, even if they do look a little weird."

It was ironic, Paul thought later as he rushed to class, that suddenly he wasn't a bit nervous or shy around Susannah. He seemed to know just what to say, as if his shyness and uncertainty had dropped from him like a worn-out garment.

By afternoon the rain had turned to a cold mist. Condensation gathered in the trees and dripped with slow monotony. Paul jogged easily around the wet track. He wasn't even winded and he'd already run over a mile. He could hear grumbling and swearing as he passed other guys. Their shoes made wet sucking sounds on the sodden track. The others were tiring fast in the mud, but Paul felt as fresh as if he were only warming up. A slow smile grew on his face. Suddenly he drew a deep breath and took off.

He saw Coach look up at him, startled as he passed him. He loved the feel of the wind in his hair. His leg muscles were like steel bands, yet he was so light he could almost float. It was more like being launched from a slingshot than like running. The next time he went around the track, Coach shook his stopwatch and stared down at it in amazement. A cold realization sobered Paul. Going too fast might look suspicious. He remembered he had caught the rat with his bare hands. Too fast to be human—that was his problem. He slowed to a deliberate pace.

"Show-off!" snarled Bryan as Paul passed him.

Paul was grinning now. He had always been a good runner, but now he was the best.

Coach blew his whistle and called them all in. Paul passed a hand quickly over his wet face, feeling the slickness of the sunblock on his fingertips. He wasn't sweating, he realized, coming to a dead halt. That could be a problem. He was grateful now for the cold mist; his clothes were almost as damp as everyone else's.

Coach thrust his stopwatch into his pocket

and walked over to him. "Paul, have you ever done any sprinting? Something's wrong with my stop-watch. I couldn't tell exactly how fast you were going, but you looked pretty fast out there to me. Did you sprint at your old school?"

Paul shook his head.

"Maybe you ought to give it a try."

Paul grinned. Why not? He was fast, that was for sure.

All that week Ari found herself scanning the newspaper weather reports with morbid interest. A front stretching from Texas to the Maryland coast had stalled in place. Across half the nation the skies were overcast. Everyone at school was preoccupied with the rain. The hallways were muddy and gritty, and brown leaf fragments stuck to people's shoes. Limp folded umbrellas stood in puddles near the entrances of the buildings.

"I've got major frizz," Sybil announced at lunch. Her hair stood out around her head like a copper halo. She shook her head and some glitter fell to the table. "I give up on fighting it," she explained to Ari. "I've poured glitter on it and squirted it with hair spray. I thought it would cheer me up." She looked dubiously at the shower of glitter that had fallen on her plate and on the table. "Now I'm kind of thinking that I overdid it."

"You look great, Sybil," said Ari. "You always look great to me. You look just like yourself." She wanted to throw her arms around Sybil and beg her not to change anything about herself, but she knew she had to concentrate on behaving normally. Was it normal to ride back and forth from school with your brother and never once to look at his face? she wondered.

"I'm allergic to mold," said Cos. He promptly sneezed and reached for a paper napkin. "Jeez, when are we going to get some sunshine? I may die if we don't!"

After lunch, Ari stepped outside and looked up anxiously at the luminous gray sky. It was so dark that the trees and buildings cast no shadows. It seemed that a permanent damp lid had been slapped over the world, but Ari knew it couldn't go on this way. Weather always changed. Some fine day soon the sun would peek out from behind the gray, cottony clouds that blanketed the sky.

Every day that week, Paul went to school, and every afternoon, he came in, drew the curtains on his windows, and did his homework. His bed was invariably neatly made in the morning, but Ari couldn't muster the courage to ask whether he had slept in it.

Dinner became a strained affair. Ari picked at her food and Paul and Gabrielle pushed theirs around on their plate. But always, afterward, the plates were carefully scraped into the garbage disposal to give Carmel the impression that they had all eaten.

Sunday night Paul listlessly prodded the slice of roast beef on his plate. "I should have studied harder for that chemistry test this weekend. My teacher said it's going to cover five chapters."

Aunt Gabrielle blinked. "Paul, you aren't going to school still!"

"Why not?" he challenged her.

Ari's eyes went from Paul to Aunt Gabrielle swiftly. She hadn't realized that Aunt Gabrielle didn't know about Paul's plan to stay in school. But how could she know? She was in her room from sunrise to sunset.

"Of course, it's been a very dreary week," said Aunt Gabrielle doubtfully. "I've been out some myself once or twice on days like this. But you can't keep it up."

"I don't see why not!" said Paul defiantly. "I'm wearing sunblock. I'd think you'd want me to keep up with my education."

Aunt Gabrielle twisted her ring in some agitation. "I do. I do. But we can arrange for tutors. Really, Paul. It's so dangerous. All it would take is one bright interval! Especially when spring comes and the rays of the sun are more direct." Her eyes widened with fear. "No, you really mustn't! You're taking a dreadful risk."

"May I be excused?" asked Paul sullenly. He

stood up. "I've got a date with Susannah. I don't want to be late."

They watched in silence as he left the dining room. Aunt Gabrielle sighed heavily. "Paul is so much like his father."

Ari leapt up suddenly and fled the table in tears. Paul was a vampire, but he was different from the others. She ran upstairs and stood at the door of Paul's room. From his bathroom, she could hear the sound of running water. A moment later, he strode out, pulling a comb through his abundant dark curls. He had not bothered to turn on the light in his room, and Ari could see him only dimly, a shadowy figure standing at the foot of the bed.

"Aunt Gabrielle gets on my nerves," Paul complained. "Did you hear the way she was nagging me? She thinks the only way to do things is the way she does them. I've got an idea or two of my own. You've seen me at school, Ari. I'm doing fine, right? Coach wants me to try sprinting. Susannah says our relationship is deeper and purer." He gave a short laugh. "I'm getting along great."

"Paul," asked Ari hesitantly, "when you go out tonight you aren't going to—hurt Susannah, are you?"

She saw his teeth flash white in the darkness. He was laughing at her. "Heck no, Ari. I *like* Susannah." His eyes glowed in the dark, and Ari felt sick.

Paul came over to her and put a cool hand on her shoulder. His fingers were white and thin and his fingernails were glassy. It took all her self-control not to pull away from him. She darted an anxious glance up at his face. The pale skin was stretched tightly over the bones of his skull, and his eyes were luminous. "Don't worry," he said huskily. "All I'm trying to do here is to have a normal social life. Okay?"

"Okay," she gulped.

He ran his fingers through his damp curls and laughed. "Funny. I used to be so nervous before I went out with Susannah. I was always worried that I would say the wrong thing. Lots of times afterwards I felt stupid and could have kicked myself a hundred times for the things I said and the things I didn't say. Know what I mean?"

Ari nodded. It sounded very human, she thought sadly.

"I guess I'm a lot more comfortable with myself now," said Paul. "More mature, you know?"

"Be careful," said Ari anxiously. "You will be careful, won't you?"

"Sure. Sure." He smiled, and for an instant as he stood in her doorway, his radiant good looks reminded her of how happy they had once been. She turned away quickly to hide her tears.

CHAPTER
SEVENTEEN

AUNT GABRIELLE CAME OUT OF HER ROOM DRESSED in jogging clothes and began stretching. "I've left messages everywhere for Richard, Ari," she said. "Paul needs his father's guidance. I feel certain Richard could talk frankly to him in a way I can't."

"You think he could make Paul stay home from school," said Ari.

Aunt Gabrielle nodded. "It's so dangerous. Even apart from the risk of sunlight." She lowered her voice suddenly. "He's simply asking for someone to notice that he's changed." Her eyes were anguished. "I mean, no one can say that we actually look like other people. It's so difficult—"

Ari gulped. Aunt Gabrielle was frightening her. She remembered Jesse's taunts. How many other people had noticed that something was wrong?

Once Aunt Gabrielle was gone, the house seemed even more ominously silent than usual, as if it were holding its breath waiting for something terrible to happen. Ari couldn't bear to be alone any longer. She put on her jacket and walked toward Dunbarton Street. Dark shadows were thick around her, and she shivered as she walked, her hands thrust deep in her jacket pockets.

On the corner of Dunbarton Street stood a house with a picket fence and a front yard—an unusual feature in Georgetown, where most houses were built up to the street and jammed against their neighbors. Ari peered uneasily at the house's broad front porch, now cast into shadows and only partly visible through the skeletal branches of the huge, low-growing tree before it. Ari had had an eerie experience on this corner once before—she knew the house was haunted. She wished Sybil lived on some other street, any other street.

Suddenly she made out a gray shape in the shadows of the old-fashioned front porch. The flesh at the back of her neck prickled. A small woman wearing a stiff, old-fashioned skirt glided swiftly down the steps toward Ari, and in a moment she was at the gate, resting her small hands on the white pickets. The gate creaked noisily. The woman had a tiny waist and plump arms bare to the cold night air. Her black glossy hair, done in sausage curls, gleamed in the lamplight. Her full skirt shifted and moved like mist. The contours of her plump cheeks moved, and Ari's heart fluttered. "Good evening!" said the ghost.

Ari stared horrified at the insubstantial image.

"What's the matter?" asked the tiny woman. "Cat got your tongue?" She tittered and covered her mouth with one plump hand. Ari could see little dimples at the base of each finger.

"Go away," whispered Ari.

"You think I'm different from you." The small woman cocked her head coyly. Her flesh was white and translucent with a faint sheen. "But I'm not so different," said the woman. "The living and the dead are as alike as two fingers." The woman held up her hand. Ari could see the house through it. She wondered what would happen if she grabbed at it, but she couldn't bring herself to try.

"Come with me." The woman began moving away, beckoning. "Can you hear the music?"

Lights came on in the big old house, and Ari became aware that music had started. The sound was thin and mechanical—like the music from a player piano.

"Come on!" said the ghost. "It's what you want to do, isn't it? Join the dance!"

"No!" cried Ari.

The woman's image grew thin and vanished

then, as if she were smoke. Yet her mocking laughter continued to ring in Ari's ears. Ari blinked, and she realized the big old house was silent and dark.

She stumbled on the uneven brick of the sidewalk as she hurried on to Sybil's house. She knocked on the door until her knuckles rang with pain.

Mrs. Barron answered the door and blanched at the sight of Ari. "Why, h-hello," she stuttered. "What a surprise."

Ari took a deep breath. She hoped she didn't look as upset as she felt. "Is Sybil home?" she whispered.

A balding, gray-haired man about Ari's height walked into the foyer. He had mild gray eyes and looked dry and dignified. Ari recalled that Mr. Barron was a corporation lawyer.

"George, this is Sybil's friend, Anne-Marie Montclair," said Mrs. Barron, slightly stressing Ari's last name.

Mr. Barron shook Ari's hand, and she was reassured by the warmth of his clasp. She knew that no spirits lived here. "Nice to meet you at last, Ari," Mr. Barron said. "Sybil's upstairs. You can run on up. Are you parked outside?"

"No, I walked," said Ari.

He looked at her sharply as if there were something odd about walking at night. Ari supposed there was. She, of all people, should know

189

that the night was thick with danger. But when she had left the house she had been too upset to think of that.

She turned away from them, but as she mounted the stairs she could feel Mrs. Barron's gaze on her back. Mrs. Barron always looked at her strangely. Already too many people had clues about what was going on. Sandy. Nadia. Jesse. Mrs. Barron. She felt as if a noose were tightening around her neck.

When Ari reached the top of the stairs she could see Sybil through the open door of the bedroom. She had her books spread out around her on the bed.

"Ari!" Sybil exclaimed. "You came just in time. I was just about to study history. Can you think of anything more gruesome?"

Ari couldn't answer. She could easily think of things that were more gruesome.

"I thought you and Cos would be out partying," Sybil went on. "Or I would have called you up."

"Cos has taken a bunch of antihistamines for his allergies, and his mother won't let him drive." Ari closed the door behind her. She gulped. "Syb, I need to talk."

"Shoot," said Sybil. "What is it?"

Ari sat down on the bed. There was so much she couldn't tell Sybil. But she had to talk, because she felt she was about to burst with the weight of her secrets. "It's about Paul," she said finally. "I'm really worried about him."

"He looks sick," said Sybil sympathetically. "Are you afraid it's something really serious?"

"Sort of," said Ari, looking down and pleating the bedspread between her fingers. "He's changed, Syb."

"It's that girl he went off with at Cos's party, isn't it?"

Ari choked uncomfortably. Sybil was closer to the truth than she realized. "I guess you could say that. How—how did you hear about that?" She glanced up at her friend.

"Nobody has any secrets around here. Three different people told me about Paul's going off with her."

Sybil was right. It was hard to keep a secret. Ari realized she would have to be very careful what she said so that she didn't give anything away. Maybe she had made a mistake coming here tonight.

"You're worried that he's started running in a fast crowd, huh?" suggested Sybil.

Ari nodded. That was one way of putting it. Her eyes lit on Rab's picture. She was glad he wasn't here. She had the uncomfortable feeling he would have seen right through her evasive answers. "Paul's in over his head, Sybil," said Ari in an anguished voice. "I feel as if I hardly know him anymore."

"He's drinking a lot, I suppose," said Sybil.

"I don't know." Ari made a helpless gesture. "He's not himself. I guess I don't know how to handle it."

Sybil looked at her soberly. "You've got to be there for him, Ari. If he can't count on you, who can he count on? From what you're saying, it sounds like he's going off the rails, completely out of control."

"Yes," said Ari gratefully. "That's it exactly."

"This is when a guy needs his family to stand by him. You've got to hang in there."

"I know," said Ari miserably. "I'm really all he's got." She clutched her hands. "We always said we would stick together no matter what. I want to help him. I really do."

"I know," said Sybil. "It's hard."

Sybil had no idea how hard, thought Ari.

Paul could feel Susannah's hand resting lightly on the back of his neck. She was playing with his hair where it curled there. Her loose-woven, fuzzy sweater tickled his skin.

"You didn't touch your pizza, Paul," she said. "Are you feeling okay?"

"I ate before I left," he said. "I forgot I'd said we'd go out for pizza."

"But you didn't even take one bite!"

He was going to have to be careful. He used to eat a ton of food. "I'm fine," he said shortly. "Want to go to a movie?"

"Well, we *could*." Susannah touched a finger to his nose. "But I thought we'd go look at the monuments." She giggled. "We could park by the Reflecting Pool and then we wouldn't have to get out of the car."

Paul shivered. He wasn't exactly anxious to revisit the scene where he had become a vampire. A chill fell on his heart.

"We can leave the car heater running and see how long it takes the windows to fog up," Susannah whispered in his ear.

Paul knew if he didn't sound enthusiastic, she was going to wonder what was wrong with him. "Terrific," he said. His tone was all wrong, but Susannah didn't seem to notice.

"I thought you'd go for that idea," she said, snuggling close to him.

Paul drove to the Reflecting Pool and parked. He reminded himself that Verena couldn't hurt him now so there was no reason to dread returning to this spot. Still, he felt uncomfortable.

"You're shivering," said Susannah. "You aren't coming down with the flu again, are you?"

"I'm fine." Paul took her hand and brushed his lips against her fingers. "I love to look at you, Susannah." He was fascinated by the way tendrils of her silky hair clung wispily to her soft white throat. He could see where a long vein ran under the flesh from her jaw to her collarbone, and his heart fluttered in excitement.

Susannah sighed. "When I saw you, I took to you right away. I don't know why. You were just special."

They kissed, and he pressed his lips tightly together, terrified she would accidentally feel his fangs. Nervous that she would sense something was wrong, he ran his hands up under her sweater and tickled her ribs. She giggled and squirmed frantically. "Stop it, Paul! Stop it!" she shrieked. "Ouch! Look what you've made me do! I've torn a nail."

"I'm sorry," he said, looking down at her hands. Her long nails were enameled pink, perfect ovals. But he saw that one had torn close to the cuticle and a dark and glistening bead of blood had formed on the skin. Staring at it, Paul felt a quiver of excitement deep in his stomach.

Tenderly, he lifted her hand to his lips and licked the blood. He felt himself shudder with pleasure. His heart began to pound so hard that he grew dizzy. He bent his head and pressed his mouth against the soft white flesh of her neck, feeling with his tongue the heat of the blood pulsing just under the thin skin. He trembled. Then in a sudden movement he bit the flesh. With the hot blood of excitement pounding in his ears, he was only half-conscious of Susannah's sharp cry of pain and her sudden frantic struggle. He held his hand tightly over her mouth until he felt the tension in her body slacken. Then he bit deeply until the blood jetted against the back of his throat.

His toes and fingers tingled and he sucked greedily, pressing his nose against her flesh. His vision misted over with red, and he heard a loud drum pounding in his ears with a smaller drum echoing its beat. Its steady intoxicating rhythm was as satisfying as the ebb and flow of the ocean waves, and he felt himself swept into it, shuddering with pleasure. He seemed to be drifting on a still sea with no yesterday or tomorrow.

Paul wasn't sure when he became aware that the warm blood had quit jetting and that only one drum was beating. Confused and woozy with an unaccustomed warmth, he shook his head. Slowly, he loosened his grasp and pulled away.

"Susannah?" he whispered.

Her open eyes stared blankly at him. Her face was waxen and empty of expression. She was dead!

"No!" He shook her and her head flopped loosely. In a panic, Paul pressed his mouth to hers and breathed into it. "Don't die!" he whispered. He felt her rib cage expand, but slowly he realized that her lips and tongue were cool.

He choked on a sob and pulled away from her. What good was it, trying to resuscitate a corpse? She was gone. Forever. He wasn't even sure how long she had been dead. Certainly there were no faint embers left that could be stirred back to life. It was too late to try to make her into a vampire. Staring into her lusterless eyes, he knew that even if it had been possible to do that, he wouldn't have. How could he bear to face her afterward?

He fell limply against the seat, closing his eyes, unable to endure looking at the pathetically slumped body so still and white beside him. "Susannah," he whispered. "I'm so sorry!"

Paul sat there some time in a stupor of grief, until suddenly a coldly rational thought shook him. He had a dead body in his car. A police officer had been walking around here the night he was with Verena. What if this was the cop's regular beat? Any minute he might stroll by and see Susannah's lifeless body.

Paul stiffened. What was he going to do?

CHAPTER
EIGHTEEN

WHEN PAUL BURST INTO ARI'S ROOM, SHE LOOKED up fearfully from her book. The look on her twin's face frightened her so much that she couldn't speak.

"Susannah's dead!" he cried.

A horrible sick feeling swelled in Ari's throat when she realized that Paul's face was flushed. He had drunk Susannah's blood—that was why he looked so much like his old self.

"It was an accident!" he cried. "I didn't mean to do it." Paul began pacing the floor in tight little arcs. "I must have been out of my mind. I don't know." He glanced at her. "What are we going to do? It's only a matter of time until the cops come for me!"

"Where is she?" whispered Ari. "Where did you put her?"

"In the trunk of the car," said Paul. "I couldn't risk anybody's seeing her, so I stopped at the first dark place I could find and carried her back to the trunk." He hesitated. "I was right near a Dumpster when I moved her, and at first I thought of putting her in there—but I just couldn't."

"Don't worry, Paul." Ari gulped. "We'll think of something."

As they drove past Sybil's house on Dunbarton Street, Ari was appalled to remember that she had once longed for Paul to go out with her friend. She had envisioned happy double dates. Paul's having Sybil for his girlfriend had seemed like a wonderful idea. Ari shuddered, thankful she had been unable to persuade him. It could have been Sybil whose cold body lay in the trunk of the car!

"Are you all right?" Paul glanced at her.

Ari nodded.

"I hope her parents aren't home." Paul had a tight grip on the steering wheel. "Susannah said they had to go to a party, something to do with her dad's business."

They pulled up in front of Susannah's house. The house was dark except for two narrow windows on either side of the front door, but a streetlamp illuminated the front yard. "That light's got to go," said Paul. He got out, and Ari saw him stoop to pick up a rock. He drew his arm back and threw. Ari heard the tinkle of thin glass, and suddenly that entire end of the street was dark. All around stood lighted houses. Anyone leaving or even looking out their windows carefully would probably see them. But they had to take the chance. Ari got out of the car and handed Paul the key she had found in Susannah's purse.

"You'd better take the key yourself and go in the back way," Paul said in a low voice. "Unlock the front door. Then I'll bring her in."

Ari tried not to think about what could go wrong for fear she would lose her nerve. The grass felt soft and plushy under her feet as she crept along the hedge, letting her fingers brush against the leaves of the holly bushes. She hadn't realized how much light came from the night sky of the city until she lost its glow by stepping into the house's shadow. Walking in total darkness was unnerving. Her foot struck something light that rattled out of her way. Next she tripped on something soft and tangled. A garden hose? Breathing heavily and verging on panic, she turned the corner of the house. The back yard was not as dark as the side of the house. The glass of a sliding glass door gleamed, and she could make out the shapes of what looked like patio furniture.

Ari found the back door at once and slipped

Susannah's key into its lock. She put on gloves then and pushed the door open. She knew she couldn't leave any fingerprints. Her ears strained to hear any noise. She hoped Susannah's folks didn't have a dog. She heard nothing, but her imagination filled the darkness with dogs and burglar alarms. A faint glow of light loomed ahead, and she forced herself to move in that direction.

When she reached the brightly lit foyer at the front of the house she became aware that she was probably clearly visible from the street through the slender windows on either side of the door. She quickly unlocked the front door and turned off the lights. A moment later, the door swung wide and Paul entered, carrying Susannah's body.

"I'm standing by the staircase," she whispered in the darkness. "Over here."

She heard the door close. Now that her eyes were growing accustomed to the dark, she could see a suggestion of light coming through the windows and she could make out Paul's tall shape on the stairs. She heard his footsteps, slow and heavy. After hesitating for a few seconds, she followed him.

When she got upstairs, she found Paul standing at the foot of the bed in Susannah's room, all the lights on. Susannah was on the bed, looking as pale and lifeless as a wax doll. Her pale flesh seemed to have shrunk. Only her golden hair, spilling around her head on the pillow, was unchanged. It gleamed and shimmered just the way it always had. Ari had never realized before how very different the dead were from the living.

Susannah's drawings were pinned up on the walls. She had had a gift with pen and paper, and her drawings were as eerily full of life as she was empty of it. Paul reached out and gently touched a charcoal sketch of a dark boy sprawled in a chair with a sketchbook.

"That's you, Paul!" Ari whispered.

"I know. Susannah drew it on the first day we met." He closed his eyes. "We've got to get out of here, Ari. I can't stand looking at her and at all these things she drew. Much more of this and I'm going to freak out."

Ari glanced at the silent body lying on the bed. "We've got to make her look natural," she said. "We can't let them find her like this." Abruptly, she knocked a lamp over.

Paul gaped at her. "What'd you do that for?"

"It ought to look as if there was some kind of struggle," said Ari, "or they're going to be sure she was killed by someone she trusted."

Paul winced. "You didn't have to say that."

"It's got to look like burglars broke in," Ari insisted.

The next fifteen minutes felt like a nightmare. Ari led Paul downstairs. Paul pried a paving brick from the patio outside and broke the sliding glass door with it. The crash of the breaking glass was deafening, and Ari was in an agony of apprehension, certain that the neighbors could hear.

She thought she heard a noise and glanced toward the front door. It was dark, but her flesh crawled with anxiety. "Be careful," she warned Paul as he came in the back door. "Don't get any of the broken glass on your shoes. That's the kind of thing the police are going to be looking for."

"Let's get out of here," pleaded Paul.

Ari was surprised at how her mind continued to work, even though a cold sweat beaded her face and her hands trembled. "No!" she cried. "You'd better—cut her throat or something so it will look like she bled to death."

"It won't work, Ari," cried Paul. "Even if I cut her throat, there won't be any blood."

Ari's gloved hand took a knife from the kitchen drawer and handed it to him. "You've got to try. Anything's better than having her found bled to death without a mark on her."

Paul's eyes were wide as he took the knife. "I can't do it," he said.

"Yes, you can," said Ari.

He turned without another word and went upstairs. Ari stood at the back door waiting for him, trying not to think of what was happening in Susannah's room.

A few minutes later, Paul came back. "Let's go," he said abruptly.

The twins drove home in silence. Ari kept imagining how awful it would be for Susannah's parents to come home and find her dead. It was horrible! Cruel! Yet she had helped Paul conceal her murder. What else could she do? She loved him. How could she abandon him now? It wasn't as if punishing him would bring Susannah back to life, she told herself miserably.

Maybe she should let Paul kill her, too, she thought. It would be easy to be a vampire, much easier than living torn between her loyalties to the living and the dead. The music of the haunted house echoed in her mind. Unconsciously, she put her thumb in her mouth and began to suck, rocking back and forth.

"Ari?" Paul said sharply. "Are you okay?"

She blinked. "Yes. Sure," she said. But her voice sounded empty, even to her own ears. She was the only real human being in her family now, she thought. Despair swept blackly over her.

When they got back to Ari's room, Paul began to talk quickly. "What happened wasn't my fault, Ari. I just didn't know when to stop. You know that I didn't mean to kill her, don't you? It's not my fault that I'm a vampire. It's something Verena did to me. It's no different from being hit by a truck! It just happened."

Paul remembered with shame that he had told Verena he wanted to live forever. It had seemed too hard to be human back then. Maybe he had wanted to escape from life. But he hadn't meant it! Not really. "You aren't going to give up on me, are you?" he cried. "Remember how we promised we would stick together no matter what?"

"I have stuck with you," said Ari sharply. "You don't see me calling the police, do you?"

A strained silence came between them as Paul pushed open the door to his room. "This is the worst part," he said. "We have to wait and see what happens when they find her body. I think I'd better not try to go to school tomorrow."

Ari nodded. She was very pale. "Okay," she said. "Maybe that would be for the best."

Paul closed his bedroom door and pulled out the shiny coffin Verena had given him. He felt tired and longed to lie in it, safe from the strident danger of the dawn. He lay down and let the top fall closed over him. A feeling of intense well-being permeated his entire body, and he sighed contentedly. He was sorry that Susannah was dead, but it was hard to keep his mind on her when he felt so warm and tingly and sleepy. He felt himself drifting into oblivion. All of a sudden his supernaturally sharp hearing heard the click of the lock in the connecting doors. Ari had locked the door. Suddenly he was wide awake and sick with shock. Ari was afraid of him!

CHAPTER
NINETEEN

ARI WAS WAKENED BY HER ALARM CLOCK AT SEVEN.
The sky was light outside and she felt sick with
dread. The police must be at Susannah's house
this very moment dusting the place for fingerprints. Could she have possibly left any fingerprints? She had been wearing gloves. But
perhaps she had left some other trace of her
presence—a hair, perhaps, or a tissue. Could she
have somehow picked up a shard of glass on her
shoes without realizing it? She picked up her
shoes and stared at the soles, shuddering. Guilt
was what was unnerving her, she realized. She
knew she had done something wrong and that
was why she was so afraid of being found out.

She dressed quickly and went downstairs. In
the kitchen, she poured a cold glass of milk. Then
she pinched her arm, reassured by the pain and

the angry pinkness of her skin where she had hurt herself.

Ari took a bowl of fresh cherries out of the refrigerator and walked into the dining room. She ate them as she gazed out the window. Long shadows made patterns on the paving stones of the garden. A brown wren hopped onto the planter and tossed a bit of pine straw aside. Ari could see the shiny bead of its eye, surrounded by a patch of white feathers. She gazed at it steadily, as if she were in a trance. *Ordinary life.* She hadn't realized before quite how much she loved it.

"Where's Paul?" Sybil asked at lunch. She leaned close to Ari and lowered her voice. "He isn't hung over, is he?"

Ari shook her head. "He's sick, Sybil. I'm beginning to think it's mono." She gulped. "He looks terrible."

"I knew somebody who missed a whole year of school from mono," said Sybil. "It's the worst. You get so run down. Has Paul gone to the doctor for a blood test yet?"

Ari's hand jerked involuntarily. She took a deep breath. "I think he's going to go to the doctor today, but I'm positive it's mono. I'm sure he's going to have to miss a whole bunch of school."

Cos pulled up a chair next to Ari. "Maybe Susannah caught it from him. She's not here today either. You know, they call mono the kissing disease."

Ari closed her eyes and tried to catch her breath. The image of Susannah's still, pale body and the golden hair pressing against the white pillowcase swept over her.

"At least the rain has let up," Cos went on. "And about time. Toadstools and creeping fungus aren't my idea of beautiful."

"Speaking of beautiful," Sybil beamed at them, "notice anything different about me?"

Cos looked at Ari and shrugged.

"My braces!" cried Sybil indignantly. "I got them off this morning! No more tin smile. My orthodontist, Dr. De Sade, who has been truly *torturing* me for years with wires and rubber bands, was at last forced to admit that my teeth are perfect. Admire them, please." She bared her teeth.

"Perfect," said Ari. Sybil had looked beautiful to her even before her braces were off. Warm and loving and human. She wanted to hug Cos and Sybil close to her and tell them how much she loved them just the way they were, freckles and crooked teeth and allergies and all. But she knew that above all she had to behave as if nothing were wrong. She looked down at her plate. "I can't believe we're having meat loaf again," she said.

"We ought to refuse to eat it," said Cos,

stuffing a forkful of it greedily into his mouth. "It is so dull around here. The same food, the same old books. You know, we ought to do something really different today." His eyes rolled speculatively.

"Ari can't go along on any of your crazy schemes," said Sybil at once. "She has to come home with me. I'm having a getting-rid-of-braces celebration." She looked smug. "My brother is coming home from college specially to celebrate this great day."

Cos shot her a suspicious look. "You used to complain that your brother never came home, Sybil. Wasn't he just here?"

"Yes, but he's coming again." Sybil smiled broadly. "It's not every day a girl gets her braces off."

"Just as long as he isn't trying to put the moves on Ari," said Cos.

Sybil raised her eyebrows in a look of innocence. "You are so suspicious. You've been hanging around with Jesse too much, you know that? Paranoia can be contagious."

"Don't even mention it," groaned Cos. "I hate to admit it, but since Jesse has started going out with Nadia he's gotten really strange."

"He's always been strange," said Sybil, dicing her meat loaf and mixing it with the mashed potatoes.

"But this is different. I was over at his house

yesterday and he had a bunch of two-by-fours cut into short pieces and he was whittling their tips into points."

"Okay," said Sybil, looking at him expectantly. "I'm waiting for the punch line."

"So I said, 'Whatcha doing, Jess?' and he said, 'Sharpening stakes. For vampires.'"

Cos insisted on going with Ari to Sybil's after school, and Ari was glad to have him. She hoped his presence would help put a lid on Sybil's matchmaking efforts. She liked Rab—he reminded her of Sybil. But she still felt that there was something about him, something familiar, that made her uneasy.

Sybil went upstairs to get Rab, leaving Cos and Ari together in Mrs. Barron's elegant living room. Cos scowled at the Barrons' wedding picture—Mr. Barron had all his hair, and Mrs. Barron, with a handful of white flowers pinned to her hair, looked twenty years younger. "It's hard to imagine getting middle-aged, isn't it?" said Cos.

"I think getting older sounds nice," said Ari wistfully. "It's such a human thing to do."

He grinned. "That's a weird thing to say, Ari. Has anybody ever told you that you're a little bit weird?"

She felt her face getting hot. It was as if her secrets were written on her forehead and Cos had figured out that she could see ghosts and that she came from a family of vampires. "I guess everybody's a little bit weird," she said, turning away from him.

"But in a good way!" he added hastily, throwing his arms around her. "I guess you think I'm weird to be jealous of Sybil's brother."

She smiled. "No. I don't think that. I can tell that Sybil's hoping that Rab will fall for me so he'll come home more often."

"Jeez! And she had the nerve to say I was paranoid!" cried Cos indignantly. "I can't believe Sybil is working against me like that." He frowned. "Why didn't you tell her he's too old for you?"

"He's skipped a lot of grades," said Ari mischievously. "He's not really that old."

"Cut it out, Ari," pleaded Cos. "It's not funny." He glanced at the Barrons' wedding picture. "Maybe Rab's adopted."

Ari glanced at the Barrons' wedding picture and stiffened. She saw at once why Cos had made that remark. Rab was so much taller than either of his parents. It was odd. And it wasn't the only odd thing about him. Ari could feel something tugging at her memory, just beyond her power to recall it. What was it about him that made him so uncomfortably familiar?

"Look," said Cos, "a bunch of guys I know are talking about getting together with our girlfriends and going to some fun place together this weekend. Maybe we'll rent a cabin in the woods or something. How does that sound?"

"I can't," Ari said promptly. "I can't leave Paul alone when he's sick."

Cos frowned. "I don't know why not. He's not dying. And your aunt'll be here with him."

"I can't, Cos. I just can't."

"You can't? Or you don't want to."

Ari shook her head. "I can't."

"Maybe I can get somebody else to go with me," Cos said. He looked hurt.

Ari swallowed. "I'm sorry." She could feel Cos slipping away from her, but she was powerless to do anything about it. She couldn't go out of town with him. It would be much too dangerous to leave town now. She had become an accessory to murder.

Sybil and her brother came downstairs and strolled into the living room.

"So, when am I going to get to meet your brother, Ari?" Rab asked, tugging at his collar to straighten it. "Seems like he's never around. Sybil tells me you two are an awful lot alike."

Ari gazed at him, unable to speak.

"Did I say something wrong?" asked Rab, glancing at Sybil.

"Paul's sick again," said Sybil. "Ari thinks it's mono. Isn't that grim?"

"Gee, that's too bad," said Rab.

On the way to the mall Sybil was full of chatter, but the others didn't have much to say. When they got out of the car, Ari watched Cos make a conscious effort to be pleasant. She gave him credit for that. He wasn't happy, but he was trying not to ruin Sybil's celebration. "Okay, Syb," he said lightly. "What's it going to be? Caramel corn, candy applies, chewing gum?"

Sybil threw her arms in the air. "All of the above!" she cried.

Inside the mall, they linked arms as they went looking for formerly forbidden goodies that Sybil could finally sink her teeth into. They bought popcorn and then a bag of caramels. "I'm not hungry," Sybil explained. "But I just feel as if I ought to eat all this stuff."

"Not to worry," said Cos. "Rab and I will help you with it." He stuffed a handful of popcorn into his mouth and grinned at Ari. For now it seemed the cloud that had come between them had passed.

"Look!" cried Sybil. "It's a purple hippopotamus!" She was pointing to the window of a toy store.

"Consider it yours," said Rab. "My treat in honor of your special day."

Sybil beamed. "Cool! But maybe they have a little one. One that would be easier to feed and clothe."

"I don't think they eat much," said Rab.

"Once in a while you throw it a cheeseburger."

In the toy store, Rab and Sybil settled on a medium-sized purple hippopotamus and Cos bought himself a mask with a large hooked nose.

"You're going to wear that?" asked Sybil.

"Why not?" asked Cos.

Ari was conscious that they made a funny-looking bunch—Sybil embracing her purple hippopotamus, Cos with a hook-nosed plastic mask, and Rab, tall and loose-jointed, shepherding them along. *Only, I'm the oddest of all*, Ari thought sadly.

"I'm ready for real food," said Sybil. "Maybe corn on the cob."

"Well," said Cos, "it is almost suppertime."

Ari glanced at her watch and was astonished. Where had the time gone?

"I think I'll have a bag of caramels for dessert," said Sybil. "It is so great not to have a mouthful of rubber bands. You can't imagine."

Suddenly they saw Amanda coming out of a store. "Sybil!" she cried. "Have you heard? Susannah's been murdered!"

They all stared at her in numb shock.

"It's true!" cried Amanda. "Somebody broke into her house last night while her parents were out, and they killed her!" She shivered. "It's unbelievable. I thought she lived in such a safe neighborhood. I'm going to sleep in a sleeping bag in my parents' room tonight. They said I could." She dashed a tear from her eyes. "My dad says he's going to buy a gun. Isn't it awful? I can hardly believe it. To think she was all alone when they broke in." Amanda shivered. "I can just picture it. She must have been terrified. And then to die like that!" She choked on a sob. "Murdered!"

"But Susannah wasn't home alone last night," said Cos, puzzled. "She was out with Paul, wasn't she?"

"Paul took her home early," Ari put in quickly. "Because he was feeling so sick. Remember? He's been really sick."

"So because Paul got sick, she was home alone—" whispered Amanda. "And they came in and cut her throat. It's too horrible."

Sybil squeezed her plush hippopotamus and whimpered. "Oh, no!" Very pale now, she gazed at Ari in horror. "Ari, you're going to have to tell Paul!"

"I'd better go home," said Ari.

"Do you want me to go with you?" asked Cos. His silly mask hung loosely around his neck, forgotten.

"No," Ari said. "It'd be better if we're alone."

Cos nodded.

But when Ari got home and stepped in the front door, she knew at once that Paul wasn't there. No one was home. The house was dark and silent.

* * *

214

Paul strode toward Verena's place. He had some confused idea that it would be pleasant to hurt her, but that was all. The feel of wind on his cool cheeks was intoxicating. He sped through the streets and laughed at the lightness of his step. After the long sleep in his cramped coffin, he reveled in his strength. Around him the low hum of the car engines, the sound of running water, the quiet click of the traffic lights made a symphony of sound. Streetlamps pulsed and glowed along with his heightened senses.

When he arrived at Verena's place loud music was blaring through the closed door. A skinny woman slithered out Verena's front door, letting a blast of music escape into the hall. She was so thin that at first Paul wondered if she was ill, but then she smiled vaguely at him and her eyes glowed. A vampire. Paul instinctively backed away from her. He pushed Verena's door open and stepped inside. The light was dim and at first he couldn't recognize anyone, but then he spotted Verena waving at him and he stiffened. A second later, her long white arms were wrapped around his neck. "Paul!" she cooed. "It's so great to see you."

He was rigid with hatred, but Verena didn't seem to notice. "Did you like your present?" She smiled.

"Present?" He blinked at her, momentarily bewildered.

"Your coffin, silly. It wasn't too flashy for you, was it? Gabrielle's such a snob, I was afraid she might want you to have an antique. I would have called you about the party," she smiled sweetly, "but I didn't want to tempt you away from your school work."

Paul reflected bitterly that she hadn't hesitated to tempt him into being a vampire. He would have loved to squeeze her lily-white throat until he choked the life out of her. But it was too late for that. Verena had been dead for years.

"Make yourself at home!" she said, and then disappeared into the crowd.

Eyes glowed at Paul in the darkness, and the dimly lit faces looked like ovals of white. He had the impression of many tightly packed, skinny bodies squeezed into silk dresses and cashmere. Paul noticed that unlike Aunt Gabrielle, Verena did not bother to pretend this was a party for human beings. No food or drink was in sight. He glanced around the room distastefully, suddenly sickened by the slithering partygoers.

Fresh air, he thought. *Space*. That was what he needed. He pushed open the door that led out onto Verena's little rooftop terrace. He almost tripped over two vampires who were writhing on the pavement. His confused impression was that a highly muscular vampire had buried his fangs in the neck of a thin blond vampire

216

whose hair was streaming down her back, stringy and damp with blood.

"Excuse me," said Paul, backing off hastily. He stepped back inside, feeling sick to his stomach. The tangled white bodies on the terrace had looked so bizarre that it was almost like a hallucination. Had he only imagined what he had seen? But he shrank from pushing the door open again for another look. "Jeez," he whispered, shaken.

"Hi, there." The voice sounded close to his ear.

Paul wheeled around to face a vampire whose eyes were a glittering ice blue. Her dark hair was short and wispy, and she was pretty with high cheekbones, slightly flared nostrils, and sensitive pale lips. "I'm Sophie," she said.

"Paul," he said shortly.

"You look like you're in shock," she said. "I guess you've never been to one of Verena's parties before."

"No," he admitted. "This is my first."

Sophie smiled. "I'm surprised. Verena is usually pretty quick to rake in the guys that look good. She collects them."

Paul didn't want Sophie to find out that Verena had collected him. Now that he thought of it, he realized she had turned him into a vampire as casually as she would have acquired a new bracelet—and with as little regard. He hated her, and he hated himself as much. He had been a fool. Burning in his soul was the desire to make Verena pay for what she had done to him, but instead he stood here like an idiot making chitchat with Sophie.

"Did I say something wrong?" Sophie looked at him from under thick black lashes.

"No," lied Paul. "No, I was admiring your eyes. They really are beautiful."

"Thanks." Sophie looked gratified. "You're nice, you know that? You're not—you know—self-centered the way a lot of guys are."

Paul leaned against the kitchen counter and stared at her. "Thanks." He smiled.

"Hey—you wouldn't happen to like poetry, would you?" she asked suddenly. She took a small bit of paper out of her pocket. "I'm working on a poem right now, and I'd be very interested to hear what you think."

Sophie's poem was about smoke and the shadow of smoke. Paul thought it was lovely and said so. She seemed a world away from Verena and from the disgusting vampires he had glimpsed on the terrace. *Delicate and flowerlike*, he thought when he looked at her.

He touched her hand. "You are something special, you know that? As soon as we met I could almost hear a 'click.' I think we could really have something good together."

She looked up at him with a smile.

218

"Sometimes it's so hard to find someone at these parties that you can talk to. I mean *really* talk. A lot of these guys, all they want to do is get you out on the terrace and suck your blood." She grimaced.

So that's what they had been doing out on the terrace. Paul found himself looking with fascination at the slender white stem of Sophie's neck. He had only tasted vampire blood once—and that first night with Verena was pretty much a blur. He had the vague impression that it had been intoxicating, like brandy. He remembered that his heart had pounded wildly and then afterward he had felt sick and shaken. "You don't like to—?" He made a helpless gesture toward the terrace door.

"Oh, sometimes," she said quickly. "But only if I feel really, really close to a person."

Paul discovered to his surprise that he was enjoying himself. He felt comfortable with Sophie. He glanced around the room. "I'm kind of new at this," he said.

She gave a quick smile. "I know. A girl can always tell."

"I feel like I can tell you that I'm a klutz and you won't make fun of me." He looked at her curiously. "Why is that, I wonder?"

"I dunno." She shrugged. "But I like you, too."

"Do you come to a lot of Verena's parties? You seem so different from her."

"Well, I would never meet anybody sitting at home, would I?" Sophie shrugged. "And it's so easy here. We've all got a lot in common."

"Yeah," said Paul with sudden understanding. "You don't have to pretend to be what you're not." He wondered now why he had ever bothered to go back to school. Why had he tried to pass as human? The sunblock, the careful smiles, the homework. And all the while he knew that if any of his classmates found out what he really was they would despise him and fear him. Who needed that?

"Haven't you noticed that musicians hang out with other musicians and that jocks hang out with other jocks?" asked Sophie.

Paul nodded. "That's why the vampire bar on M Street does such big business, I guess."

Sophie nodded. "Right. And all they're selling is outdated blood-bank plasma. I mean, it doesn't even taste good. Who wants pasteurized blood? But guys come from all over the world to party at that bar."

Paul noticed that Sophie avoided using the word "vampire." She kept saying "guys" instead. She was obviously sensitive.

"It would be nice if we could all live in the same neighborhood," she went on, "but there's sort of a problem with that."

"It's like lions," said Paul suddenly. "The ecosystem can only support so many."

Sophie nodded. "We have to spread out. We can only come together for parties and stuff."

Paul was amazed that he hadn't realized it before. Vampires were like lions. Strong, noble, and predatory. Nobody criticized a lion for bringing down a gazelle. Why should it be any different with vampires? Ari was trying to make him feel guilty for drinking Susannah's blood. She was making him feel like dirt. Sure, he was sorry he had killed Susannah, but that was because he knew her and liked her. It was sort of like he wouldn't eat his own dog but that didn't stop him from eating a cow or pig.

It all seemed crystal clear now. He threw his arms around Sophie and beamed at her. He was amazed to remember that he used to be kind of shy. "You're beautiful, you know that?" he said. "When I talk to you, everything seems clear and things just fall into place somehow."

Her eyes gleamed when Paul touched her smooth cheek. It was white like ivory, and the cheekbones were sharp under her translucent skin. "I want to see you again," he said huskily. "How about your phone number?"

"You don't think Verena would mind?" she asked.

Hot shame burned behind Paul's eyes. Verena had told Sophie what she had done to him. He wanted to smash Verena's face into the dirt for that. He wanted to fling her into the sunshine and watch her smooth skin wither. He jerked Sophie's arm. "Shut up," he said, his eyes burning. "Don't mention Verena to me."

She cringed. "I'm sorry," she whimpered. "I thought you two were—"

He pushed her against the wall with one hand. "Don't mention her to me," he said between clenched teeth. "Do you understand?"

"I won't!" she whispered, wide-eyed.

Sophie looked terrified, and suddenly Paul felt disgusted with himself. What was he doing? He let go of her suddenly. "I'm sorry," he said shortly. "I got carried away."

Sophie rubbed her white arms with her hands. "I don't think I'll give you my phone number," she said.

"Oh, come on, Sophie." He smiled. "So I lost it for a minute. That wasn't really me."

Sophie drew back her hand and slapped his face so hard that several vampires nearby turned around to look at them. Paul's cheek rang with the blow.

"Oh, that's you, all right." Sophie laughed bitterly. "You're no different from the rest." Tears glittered in her eyes.

He held her wrists tightly in his hands to keep her from slapping him again. "Look, it's going to be all right. We're right for each other. I know it!"

She twisted free of his grasp. "I have to go now," she said. With a swiftness that surprised him, she slipped away and out the front door. It closed behind her with finality.

But Paul knew she wouldn't be walking out of his life forever. He had all eternity to find her. He could feel his future stretching out blackly before him like an infinite starry universe filled with infinite possibilities.

CHAPTER
TWENTY

PAUL SWUNG AROUND A LAMPPOST, GIDDY WITH happiness. His hand left a phosphorescent circle on the metal, but he scarcely noticed. The dark streets seemed new, as if he had only just become a vampire. The night was satiny black and sparkled with mysterious delights. Just ahead of him was a Cadillac with a diplomatic license plate. Paul peered in its heavily tinted windows and smiled. When he stood up again he saw that his fingers had left glowing prints on the smoky glass. He wanted to sing with joy.

A town house door opened and a woman in a satin evening dress tottered down the steps. Paul could hear the click of her heels on the steps and the swish of her skirt. "Lovely party." She laughed. "I feel positively tipsy. And on good wine, too." The man who was with her gave her his arm. A sash was drawn diagonally over his black coat and it was stiff with military medals. In the dim light, Paul's sharp eyes could make out rosettes of ribbon, odd-shaped crosses, and bars of different colors, as if the old man had been decorated by many governments and had fought in countless military campaigns.

Paul stood still as the couple moved in front of him; he was dazzled by the gleam of the woman's dress. She was a middle-aged woman whose flesh was no longer firm, but her dress was beautiful, overlapping petals of smooth satin at the bust with a single maroon satin rose where the petals overlapped. She fussed with her petticoats as the old man opened the car door for her. Paul was fascinated by the elderly warrior and his array of military medals. An old lion, Paul thought—once splendid, but now weak, slightly tipsy, and ripe for the kill. The soldier had a handlebar mustache and his carefully groomed silver hair gleamed in the lamplight. Paul thought of blood spilling on the satin and the golden medals and his stomach stirred with pleasurable excitement. The woman lifted her skirt, smiled and said something to the man, then slid in awkwardly and the door slammed shut with a solid sound.

"Do you, by any chance, have the time?" Paul asked the man politely. His gaze fixed on the bare flesh just above the man's stiff white collar.

It was pink there, as if it had been scraped with a razor, and Paul could sense the pulsing of the warm blood that lay under the skin. It seemed to call to him, a surging sound like a great river, and he trembled in joyful anticipation.

"Uh, yes. Just a moment." The man fumbled with a pocket watch.

Paul leapt on him at once and sank his teeth into the soft flesh. Heedless now of the sprawling body beneath him, he pressed his lips to the torn flesh so as not to spill a drop. The sharp edges of the man's medals caught at Paul's clothes, but with a delicious slurp, Paul sucked, shivering in pleasure. Suddenly he heard the door open behind him and light spilled out onto the street. Paul looked around, startled at the sight of six or eight people in evening dress coming down the stairs. He realized he would soon be surrounded by people leaving the dinner party. He pressed his hand against the torn flesh. Feeling the heat of the electric force surging from his hand, he smiled. Some of the partygoers might have already seen him bending over the old soldier, he realized. "Somebody dial 911," Paul shouted. "I think he's had a heart attack."

Paul heard a cry of distress and hurrying steps. Frightened voices filled the night air as the man's friends crowded around. Paul slipped away.

What he had said was true—the old man's

226

heart had given out. He must have had a pace-maker. Something had been wrong there. Paul had sensed no answering heartbeat.

But soon Paul had forgotten the confusion he had left behind. He sauntered down the street. Warmth and contentment suffused his hands and feet, and he stretched luxuriously. He had enjoyed the taste of the blood, and most especially, the spice of danger. He had seized the moment impulsively, a bird of prey spotting a likely sparrow. It hadn't worked out the way he had hoped. He hadn't drunk his fill this time, but better prey would come his way.

Suddenly, he remembered his sister. Ari. Dark and beautiful. Thinking of her, he was over-come with pity. She was weak, soft and human. Pathetic. He wanted to share his strength and happiness with her. He was the eagle, warm and happy, triumphant in his strength and immortal-ity. He would be able to give that all to her.

Paul knew that if he held Ari in his arms, he could make her see it his way. He had the power of persuasion. He leapt up, his heart pounding in excitement. Ari! She was waiting for him!

Ari stood in the kitchen absently cradling a cup of tea in her hands. She caught a glimpse of her face in the glass front of the microwave oven, put down the cup, and blotted her lips with a paper napkin. The quiet in the house was eerie. Even the refrigerator's motor had fallen silent. Where was Paul? Where had he gone? She urgently needed to tell him the news.

Suddenly she heard the front door open. She rushed out of the kitchen and when she reached the gong that stood at the far end of the hall, she saw Paul striding toward her. At first she scarcely knew why her heart leapt in alarm, but a moment later, backing away, she decided that it was because he seemed too sure of himself somehow. As he drew closer, she saw that his dark eyes glowed with a strange beauty. She could scarcely look away. His gaze was like a magnet. A smile played on his lips.

"Wh-where have you been?" she stuttered. "They've found Susannah's body. We saw Amanda at the mall and she told us burglars broke into the house and killed her." Ari's hands worked nervously. "That's good, isn't it? Maybe they don't suspect you. Maybe we pulled it off, after all." She stared at him, puzzled. How could he be smiling when she was telling him about the police investigation?

Paul made a gesture so quick that his hand was a blur. "It doesn't matter. Forget that. Don't worry about it, Ari." He spoke urgently. "Listen to me—I've been having the most incredible time. I went to a party at Verena's and I met this amazing girl. Sophie."

He paused a moment. Ari felt herself growing

228

breathless with anxiety. It was terribly wrong for him to be so happy.

"Don't you love that name?" Paul smiled. "It's soft like a breeze—Sophie. We talked, you know, the way you do when you're on the same wavelength—and suddenly it was all crystal clear to me." He threw his head back, showing an arched expanse of throat, and laughed.

"Paul," Ari demanded, "are you drunk?"

He gazed at her, cocked his head, and then smiled slowly. "I don't touch the stuff anymore, Ari. I don't need it. I only want to share my happiness with you. That's all I've been able to think about on the way home."

Ari gazed at his outstretched hands in alarm. His fingers were smeared with blood! He reached for her and she leapt backward suddenly. A candelabra fell to the floor, its thin bulbs shattering. She pushed a dining room chair in front of her to block his way.

"What's the matter?" asked Paul, looking hurt. "Why are you doing that?"

"Don't touch me!" she warned. When she looked at him, seeing that smile so much like his old self and yet so different, she could have burst into tears.

"We slept in the same crib, remember?" he said softly. "We took baths together when we were little and chewed on each other's toys." He moved closer to her. "What are you afraid of? It's

229

only me—Paul. Your twin. We belong together. We're as close as two people can be." His dark eyes were like embers, flickering with a strange light, and Ari trembled under his gaze. She felt as if her soul were pierced by the glare. Her knees were weak.

"Paul," she whispered. "I don't want to be a vampire. I'm begging you, please don't do this."

"We swore we'd stick together no matter what, Ari," he said softly. "You promised me. You gave me your faithful promise that you'd never leave me."

Her heart squeezed painfully at the appeal from her old playmate, her first love. The two of them were so alike, always. How could she ever leave him? He was her twin—a mirror of her own soul.

"Do you want to grow old and die all by yourself?" He moved the chair out of the way. "I'm offering you a love that will cut through your soul like a knife, a love that lasts as long as death. What could be better? We'll be close, so close that you'll never be alone," he murmured.

Tears blurred Ari's vision. Like a premonition of death, she felt Paul's cold hand on her neck. Was it all over, then? she thought, suddenly chilled at the darkness she felt swelling inside her like a cloud of ink. An electric shock surged through her brain. *No!* she thought, cold sweat beading on her face.

"Get away from me!" Tears streamed down her cheeks, and she jerked away. She knocked over the chair and backed off, breathless. At least she had pulled away from the cold touch of his hand. She groped behind her back for the doorknob, but when she met his gaze her knees felt weak. Paul's eyes glowed brightly enough to illuminate the hard flesh of his face.

"Stop!" she cried. "Or I'll kick you—I'll hurt you. I will!"

He smiled. "You can't hurt me, Ari. I'm already dead." He drew closer. "You want me, and you know you do. Deep inside, you want for the two of us to be together like always—forever."

The doorbell rang, and Paul's head turned in alarm. Ari pushed the French door open then and half fell onto the patio, choking with her fear. The cold night air was like a slap in the face. She had to get away. Her one thought was to get out of reach of light that spilled from the dining room into the garden. She scrambled up on a brick planter and stood there shivering. At least Paul had not come after her. He must have gone to answer the door.

Ari looked around frantically. A row of houses blocked her in back and both sides of the garden were hemmed in by tall bamboo fences. Ari heard a scuttering sound and determinedly averted her eyes from the rustling leaves at her feet.

The only way out was through the narrow path that ran between the house and the garage to the street. She would have to slip off in that direction and run for her life.

Teetering, she made her way around the garden, keeping out of the light until she reached the gate. Her heart pounding, she pulled the gate open. A dark, narrow pathway stretched ahead of her, the garage looming high on one side and the house on the other. At the end of the path flashed a blue light. A police car!

Ari glanced over her shoulder. She could see by the moving shadows that people were walking around inside. The police! There was no way out for her now. She was trapped.